NEXUS POINT

K. PIMPINELLA

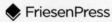 FriesenPress

Suite 300 - 990 Fort St
Victoria, BC, V8V 3K2
Canada

www.friesenpress.com

Copyright © 2021 by K. Pimpinella
First Edition — 2021

Editing by Randy Surles (www.randysurles.com)

Author Photograph by Yvette Walpert Photography

ISBN
978-1-5255-9548-6 (Hardcover)
978-1-5255-9547-9 (Paperback)
978-1-5255-9549-3 (eBook)

1. FICTION, ACTION & ADVENTURE

Distributed to the trade by The Ingram Book Company

PROLOGUE
1634, FRANCE

NAKED cadavers lay across crude examining tables, waiting to be exploited. Dr. Arnault closed the double doors of his classroom and walked toward the crowd of students and barber-surgeons who were surrounding the tables and waiting for him. Sweat threatened to glisten his forehead, which he dabbed lightly with a handkerchief. Arnault had given up a posh life working in an air-conditioned lab amongst other educated and sophisticated scholars to come to this disease-ridden, archaic time. And the faster Arnault initiated his mission, the sooner he could retire to the countryside and live out the rest of his life as he saw fit.

"The future will appreciate my sacrifice," he sighed to himself. "After all, it's doomed without it."

He took a deep breath and turned to his students. "It's time for medicine to take a giant leap forward. Your church, your King Louis XIII, are holding back the medical world with their pomp, piety, and youthful indecisiveness. We must take matters into our own hands. Here, we will break their rules and you will learn the intricacies of the human body by seeing it firsthand. You must know how the body ticks in order to stall mortality." He glanced at the tall gentleman in a black robe standing beside him. "My assistant will take it from here."

Chest broad and shoulders back, the robed man stepped forward and spoke in an elegant voice. "Like myself, you are here because you have a desire to learn, to better yourself, and to help the citizens of France. Dr. Arnault will demonstrate how the body truly works, introduce us to medicines beyond our understanding, and you … I … will take this knowledge and spread it throughout France. No longer will the universities hold themselves above those not lucky enough to be born of wealth. No longer will we be subjugated to the mere slave work of the physicians they produce. We will call ourselves surgeons and physicians!"

A student raised a tentative hand. "Uh, sir, where did all these bodies come from?"

"You need not worry about such details. Dr. Arnault has arranged an endless supply for our educational needs. It is your job to practice and learn."

Dr. Arnault studied the worried faces of his students, confident that with his twenty-second century knowledge he could revolutionize the medicine of this century within the year, as long as these students absorbed his teachings.

With his hands clasped behind his back, he turned to the nearest window and glanced up at the sky. The twenty-second century seemed a long time ago, yet it was only recently he'd sat amongst a group of eager vacationers in the ThirdEye Corporation vacation shuttle. He recalled the tiny vibrations that ran through his bones when the space vessel's faster-than-light omni-drive had throttled up for its launch through the Nexus Point, a fabricated star-like construct located several light seconds away from Nexus Station, and which made time travel possible.

It was a thrilling ride Arnault would never forget but would also never take again. His mission both started and ended in the seventeenth century. But unlike the barber-surgeons and students before him wanting to change and better their own lives, Dr. Arnault needed to change the future.

1.

DECEMBER 15, 2195

CADET Kai Sawyer shoved his best friend against the wall and pointed a finger in his face. "Hawk, I swear if this goes sideways, I'm blaming it all on you!"

"Relax. I know what I'm doing. Besides, this was your idea."

Sawyer shook his head. "No. I changed my mind. There's too much to lose. You'll only get expelled from the Academy, but my father will jettison my dead body into space if I tarnish the family name."

"Your dad scares the bejesus out of me too, but guess what? He's not here."

Hawk pulled Sawyer across the dark lawn between their guest dorm at the Marshall Space Flight Center in Huntsville, Alabama, and the museum's back door. The concrete paths that wove between the buildings were well lit and too conspicuous, so the cadets darted between the scattered rocket and thruster monuments until they arrived at the Pathfinder orbiter. The shuttle stack loomed over the other monuments at the centre of the museum grounds. Perched high on a pedestal, it cast a shadow they could use to their advantage.

A security guard came around Miss Baker's grave at the front entrance of the museum. Sawyer bolted behind a nearby thruster assembly, yanking Hawk along with him. "We're cutting it too close."

Hawk's laugh cut through the night.

Sawyer clapped his hand over his friend's mouth. "You're a dick. You want us to get caught, don't you? You think this is funny?"

Hawk lowered Sawyer's hand and produced a small mechanical box into which he entered a sequence of numbers Sawyer recognized.

"That's a skeleton security code box. How the hell did you get that?" asked Sawyer. "Shit. You stole it, didn't you?"

"How else are we supposed to get in? I'm good, but even I can't pick the triple sequential numeric-hybrid lock code keeping us from that solar panel. You remember why you wanted to do this, don't you? I mean, if you want to back down, I'll tuck tail and run back to the dorm with you, but I'll forever consider you a pussy."

Sawyer could almost feel the cool metal of the old Hubble Telescope laying beyond the museum wall and see his morphed reflection in its shiny solar cells. It wasn't the entire telescope, only a section of one of its solar panels. Earlier, during their Time Ranger Academy's class tour of the museum, Sawyer had nearly jumped the barrier to touch the artifact. It wasn't just a part of history, but a part of space history, from back when humans had barely explored their own backyard.

"Come on, let's go. We don't have all night, time's ticking," urged Hawk.

Thanks to Hawk's ingenuity, the emergency lights of the Space Flight Museum were disabled, which meant more security at any moment if they detected the problem. If Sawyer and Hawk were going to do this, they needed to move now. *My career as a Time Ranger could end tonight,* Sawyer thought. *I could end up a freaking Space Fleet Regular. Is it worth the risk to touch a damn solar panel?*

Sawyer drummed his fingers on the monument. *A panel that's seen further into the galaxy than any ship or probe known to man and survived to tell the tale? Hell yeah, I want to touch it.* "All right. Let's do this."

They slipped out from behind the giant thruster into the cool December night and raced across the expansive lawn until they reached the museum's back door. As a Spawn, a genetically enhanced human with exceptional stamina, speed, strength, and chosen genetics, Sawyer had expended little energy running across the lawn, and he leaned, calm and smug, against the wall as Hawk panted beside him. "Took that much out of ya, did it?" mocked Sawyer. "I thought you were in great shape?"

Hawk frowned. "Spawn-ass. Just because you're a super freak, it doesn't mean you get to belittle us regular humans."

"Yeah, it does." Sawyer pushed off the wall and crouched at the back door. "Here, let me do it." His excitement got the better of him now that they were within range of their target, so when Hawk passed him the decoder, Sawyer nearly dropped it on the ground.

"Your damn hands are shaking so much you'll probably set off the alarms instead of disabling them." Hawk snatched the decoder back and pushed Sawyer aside. Moments later, the door popped open and they stood inside the dark, quiet museum. "Now get moving before security shows up."

Sawyer led them down the back corridor into the main body of the museum, where they entered a room as large as a football field. Sawyer looked up at the rafted ceiling twenty feet above them, then surveyed the Apollo capsules on his left with their archaic push-button controls and cramped quarters. Scattered on almost every nanometre of wall hung images of Earth's early astronauts with their tiny heads atop their bulky space suits. Moon landers and Saturn probes, the first faster-than-light engine, and a replica of the ship Dr. Langdon Jackson used to explore Earth's main asteroid belt filled the room with not only steel, ceramics, and fibreglass, but history. "One day, we might actually get to see all this firsthand."

"Not if we get caught."

Sawyer crept deeper into the centre of the museum until Hawk grabbed his arm. "Hey, did you hear that?" whispered Hawk.

Sawyer shook his head, barely listening as he stared up at the seven-foot-tall panel display. Any light shone upon its silicon solar cells, whether moonlight breaking through an upper window or the glowing interface of a decoder, reflected back at him like a lighthouse guiding astronauts to safety.

"I swear I heard something. Maybe this was a bad idea."

"No, this was a fucking fantastic idea." Sawyer shrugged him off and stepped closer to the barrier poles protecting the historical artifact, their alarm system now turned off thanks to Hawk's stolen security code.

Sawyer drew closer to the panel, his attention scope-locked. The Academy's commandant, with them during the earlier tour, had warned them all not to touch anything. Sawyer had obeyed like he always did, but he didn't care about rules when he was this close to touching a piece of space history.

His fingers grazed the cool, smooth panel, and for the first time in his life he felt connected to something bigger than himself. Even bigger than his family name. When he closed his eyes, he no longer stood in the closed museum but was floating in space looking out into the cosmos. He was looking deep into the history of the universe like Hubble had done over a century ago. Sawyer felt alive. Free.

Space and time; that's what this panel represented. The ultimate mysteries of humankind. He turned to Hawk to share his epiphany and found him several feet away peering around Sputnik into the dark recesses of the museum display floor. "Hey, Hawk."

Hawk crouched and pushed his back against the Russian satellite. He held a finger to his mouth then made a fist.

Squeak. Squeak. Squeak. Sounds of boots walking across a polished floor grew louder.

Sawyer dropped prone, crawled to Hawk's position, and pulled himself up beside him. Sawyer risked a glance around the corner, where he saw a security guard now standing between them and the back door. Sawyer estimated the guard stood an easy six-foot-four-inches tall to his own six-one. He weighed two hundred and seventy pounds to his own lean one-ninety. And evidently the guard had eaten too many donuts working the graveyard shift. "No problem," Sawyer said with a shrug.

"Maybe no problem for you, Spawn-Ass, but for me he's more than enough." Hawk leaned his head back and closed his eyes. "Shit, dude. I can't handle getting expelled. I'll end up here on Earth working at my uncle's crappy wind farm. And that's after I get released from prison."

Sawyer scanned the room for an egress, knowing he could outrun both Hawk and the guard, then noticed his friend's dour expression. Hawk's confidence had shattered in an unprecedented moment, which bothered Sawyer more than he thought it could.

"Fuck it." Sawyer sprang up and ran for the door on the far side of the room, sending a barrier pole crashing to the ground to create a distraction for Hawk to escape. But as the distance between Sawyer and the security guard widened, it dawned on Sawyer that he might actually be able to save himself as well.

Sawyer picked up his speed, turned a corner too fast, and stumbled over a display stand. Before he got his feet back under him, the hulking mass of the security guard landed on his back, propelling Sawyer to the ground where he smacked his face against the marble floor. The taste of blood on his lip ignited his anger, but his father's number-one rule screamed in his head: *keep calm and control yourself.* Sawyer swallowed down his urge to retaliate, rolled over, and shoved the security guard off him. When Sawyer was on his feet and ready to sprint for the door again, the guard grabbed his ankle, toppling Sawyer back down to the hard floor.

Sawyer kicked and wrenched his ankle free from the guard's grasp. "I will end you right now if you touch me again!"

The guard stood and hauled Sawyer to his feet by the lapels of his uniform. "Get your ass ..."

An image of his father flashed in his head. He stood in front of Sawyer like the guard was now, angry and ready to swing. Sawyer couldn't shake the image, couldn't stop his instincts from protecting himself, and his fist landed in the middle of the guard's face. As blood poured from the guard's now crooked nose, he reached again for Sawyer, who punched him, again and again, and didn't stop until Hawk's arms wrapped around his chest and yanked him back.

"Whoa, Sawyer ... you're gonna kill him."

Chest heaving, Sawyer looked down at the guard's bloody face where he lay unconscious on the floor. Sawyer's eyes ticked away for a moment then settled back on the carnage he'd created as guilt and fear battled for control of his nerves. "He touched me, Hawk. He fucking touched me. It was like my father was standing there ... he was going to ... I couldn't stop myself."

"I know." Hawk held out his hands as if Sawyer were about to fall over. "It's okay. It's over. Let's just get out of here. It wasn't your dad, so let's get him some help ..."

Eye-searing pain forced Sawyer's eyelids shut as the museum's overhead lights bathed the room in a harsh white glow. Security guards surrounded him and Hawk from all directions. Sawyer hung his head and slowly raised his arms in the air, unsure what scared him more—what he'd just done to the security guard, or the beating he would receive from his father.

2.

SPECIALIST Greg Perry rushed through the back doors of the Time Ranger Academy's auditorium in time to catch the final words of the commandant's commencement speech.

"*Pristinae Virtutis Memor*: remembering their gallantry of former days," bellowed the commandant, his voice echoing in the vast glass and fuselage hall.

Perry remained at the back door where he enjoyed a full view of the graduating class up on the stage. Graduating as an officer, Sawyer looked the spitting image of his father standing up there centre stage in his unit's grey dress tunic, just like Sawyer's father had at the Time Ranger's inauguration ceremony just over twenty years ago. Pride welled in Perry's chest. He almost hadn't made it here on time. Hurried arrangements had been made, a temporary switch with a historical specialist on another Time Ranger team in order to get here, but it was worth the hassle.

"I say with utmost conviction," continued the commandant. "These soldiers behind me, these Time Rangers of the Academy's graduating class of May 2196, are passionate about safeguarding our history despite the many challenges of both time travel and the Time Runners they are trained to capture. Their job is not for the weak or fainthearted, and I wish them luck on their future endeavours. Without further adieu, it's time to introduce our class valedictorian. Not only is he the first Spawn to graduate from our Academy, but he is also the grandson of Staff Sergeant Luca Sawyer, one of the first Space Fleet Regulars to travel through the Nexus Point, and he is also the son of the Time Ranger's current commanding officer, Rear Admiral John Sawyer. Please stand for Lieutenant Kai Sawyer."

Sawyer shook the commandant's hand before he turned to address the audience. "Recognizing that we volunteered as a Ranger, fully knowing the hazards of our chosen profession," he said in a voice barely heard at the back of the auditorium.

"Just recite the Creed," whispered Perry.

Sawyer cleared his throat. "We will always endeavour to uphold the prestige, honour, and high esprit de corps of the Time Rangers."

Perry noted the tremor in Sawyer's voice and realized this young man did not like giving speeches. An oddity, since Sawyer's father loved the sound of his own voice and never shied away from any opportunity to self-grandize.

After a notable swallow, Sawyer continued. "Gallantly will I, and my fellow graduates, show the world that we are specially selected and well-trained soldiers. Readily will we display the intestinal fortitude required to fight on to the Ranger objective and complete the mission, though we may be the lone survivor. It is our duty to preserve, maintain, and reinstate our past in order to continue our present into its natural future, no matter the danger to our well-being. We acknowledge the fact that we are a more elite soldier. And as Time Rangers, we accept the fact that the United Utopian Government of Earth, and all its citizens, planet-side, station-dwellers and colonists alike, expect us to move further, faster, and fight harder than any other soldier in order to preserve our present way of life."

A pause drew out. Perry wondered if Sawyer had grown nervous again. *You can do this, Kai. Just remember the Time Ranger Creed.*

Sawyer looked over his shoulder as if searching for someone amongst his classmates. When he again addressed the crowd of dignitaries and family members in attendance, Perry was convinced he saw a smile on the young lieutenant's face.

"It is our job to prevent the destruction of history," stated Sawyer. "*Celer et Audax*: swift and bold. We do not take our responsibility lightly. Thank you."

The clapping was thunderous, the music from the Regimental Pipes and Drums heart-stopping in its sudden start. Perry watched as the graduates filtered in a straight line down the centre of the auditorium, Lieutenant Sawyer in front, leading the way.

The class turned at the end of the aisle, steps from where Perry stood, and formed rank along the back wall of the auditorium. A class photo was taken in front of the unit's cobalt-blue circle surrounding three five-point stars, before the unit's rear admiral addressed them. After a brief speech, the rear admiral dismissed the class, but to Perry's surprise, Sawyer did not approach his father. Instead, Sawyer moved to the side of the room where he stood looking over the crowd.

It had been years since Perry had last seen Sawyer, and he knew this estrangement was his own fault. He considered maybe now was the right time to remedy his mistake. He moved through the crowd, pushing aside those who stepped in his way, but he came to a stop when he noticed he wasn't the only attendee craving the valedictorian's attention. When the music and cheering had died down, the invited officers from both the Time Ranger Unit and their parent regiment, Space Fleet, meandered through the auditorium with more ambitious pageantry than Perry could handle. And it seemed they, along with every student from the graduating class, also wanted to shake Sawyer's hand.

But Perry knew he'd regret it later if he didn't go re-introduce himself.

3.

AFTER the class photo was taken, with every graduate dressed in their new grey Time Ranger fatigues except the graduating officers, who wore their dress tunic with the crisp gold lines of their lieutenant bars displayed on their epaulettes, Sawyer moved to the side of the auditorium.

The other graduates busied themselves grandstanding their uniforms for friends and families and giving tours of the Academy's elaborate auditorium, particularly the impressive view out the space station's window revealing the galaxy outside. Sawyer watched quietly, but his solitude didn't last long. Along with the officers in attendance, many of his classmates came by to shake his hand and introduce whoever they were with because, as Sawyer learned from an early age, his family name would be the cross he bore.

"I sat behind you in second-year history, " one graduate said as he passed by. Sawyer waved but didn't actually remember him.

"We were in first-year space sciences," another said. Sawyer feigned a smile. *Don't care.*

"We did drill class …" *Yeah, whatever.*

"Excuse me, Lieutenant. I just wanted to congratulate you."

Before Sawyer could roll his eyes at another glory-seeking graduate, he spotted the laurels on the soldier's epaulettes. "Specialist."

"My name is Perry. I wanted to congratulate you."

Time Ranger Specialist or not, Sawyer was tired of shaking hands and forcing smiles. "I'm sorry, there's someone I need to speak with," he said, brushing the older man off when he saw Hawk approaching with his parents. He focussed his attention on them as the specialist walked away. "Sir. Ma'am."

"Never thought this could happen," said Hawk, craning his neck to admire the stripes on his shoulder.

Mr. Hawk put an arm around his son. "We're very proud. First officer, and first Time Ranger in the family."

Sawyer hid his shame behind a weak smile. *Almost didn't happen.* It had been his idea to break into the museum. He remembered the bloody mess he'd left on the floor and forced down a guilty swallow. He remembered the commandant later scolding them, threatening their expulsion … He shook his head to dispel the nightmare. "He's a fine officer. I'm sure he'll make an excellent commander one day."

"Probably no thanks to you keeping him in line," said Mrs. Hawk with a soft chuckle. "We know our son. His father and I had a bet he wouldn't make it past second year without expulsion. Guess I won."

Sawyer smiled politely. "I for one never doubted him. But thank you for the compliment, ma'am."

"So formal," she remarked. "And so skinny." She *tsked* at him as she looked him up and down. "Next time you and Maxim are on Earth I need to fatten you up with some good old-fashioned root-veg stew. Our home isn't as fancy as the space stations you're probably used to, but it's a proper home on solid ground."

Sawyer remembered the last time he'd visited Hawk's home. Hawk had grown up outside Earth's capital and seat of the Utopian Government, Nunavut, located in the Republic of Canada's most splendid and undisturbed land. During the asteroid war of 2082, climate changes on Earth had been immense, leaving Mother Nature devoid, like a sick child trying to breathe. But in and around Nunavut, trees still existed, tall and old, with histories dating back farther than most people had ever time travelled.

The Hawk's home was rural, small, and lacked much of the modern technology most space-station homes possessed, but it was warm and inviting, and Sawyer had never slept so well. "I would like that, ma'am."

"Speaking of space stations," said Mrs. Hawk, nodding toward the massive window. "I've never seen such a view. It's our first time off Earth. I prefer roots, soil … terra firma under my feet, but this is something everyone should see at least once in their lifetime." She looked at Sawyer, eyebrows furrowed. "I'm educated, but not in any way to which you two are up here. I've always wondered … how do you Rangers speak with each other when you're in different time zones?"

Hawk rolled his eyes. "Mom, I've explained this a hundred times."

"I want to hear it from Kai," she replied, hushing her son with a swat of his arm. "It might make sense coming from him."

Her eyes shone with a brightness Sawyer imagined only a proud mother could possess. As a Spawn, manufactured from a genetically enhanced egg and his father's natural sperm, Sawyer never had a mother, only a father. Maybe he'd have two fathers one day if his own ever settled down.

"Although now illegal for civilians to travel through the Nexus Point," he started. "The Time Rangers and certain trained members of Space Fleet can still do so, but there are strict rules. Since we can open and close the Point at our specific choosing, when a team is in the past containing an HCA, the Point is sometimes re-opened for communications only since the connection is already established …"

"HCA?"

"Historical Contamination Act," explained Hawk. "Mom, I've told you all this. It's what the Nexus Point calls a detected change in history."

"We, the Rangers, don't actually detect the changes in history, ma'am," added Sawyer. "The Point tells us something has happened in the past. And it sends the Nexus Station a time when it will open and when boomerang will occur so we can stop it before it reaches our present. The boomerang is the automatic retrieval of the ship sent back in time. But we have to be in the exact coordinates for boomerang capture or the ship will get stuck in the past … I'm sorry," he finished in a rush. "If you'll excuse me, I see my father coming."

Mr. Hawk spun around and raised himself onto his toes to search the crowd. "I would love to meet the admiral. Where is he?"

Hawk directed his parents toward the refreshment table. "Sorry, guys, but he's not the kind of man you want to meet. And he's only a *rear* admiral." When Hawk's parents walked away, Hawk glanced back at Sawyer. "Uh, thanks again for getting my parents up here. I told them I worked a few shifts in our mess to pay for their trip."

Sawyer nudged him with his shoulder. "No problem. It was my graduation gift to you."

Surviving the Academy was no easy task with a ten-percent fail rate and a thirty-percent drop-out rate in first year alone, especially when only a handful of cadets enrolled each year. So, for anyone to qualify for officer track in the third year was quite the accomplishment. Sawyer was proud of Hawk, but as for himself, it was never on his agenda to fail. Nor his father's. He wasn't surprised when his father greeted him with nothing more than a curt nod.

"Lieutenant."

"Rear Admiral."

"I have a team in line for you."

"Already, sir?"

Rear Admiral Sawyer's brows pulled together. "Your assigned team is waiting for you at Nexus Station. I expect you there for changeover on time and ready."

"I've fulfilled my promise to you and graduated from the Academy, sir, top of the class. I was hoping I could take a look at the specialist track now. I've been wanting to take further medic classes, and I've already spoken with Professor Murello …"

"You will be there tonight."

Sawyer knew if he didn't take this chance to say what he wanted, he might never get another. Unfortunately, his father was not an easy man to reason with. "Did you hear what I said?"

"Being a specialist, a medic, was a silly childhood dream. You're a soldier. I've arranged for you to work with the best commander in the unit, AJ Beaumont. You know the plan. In two years you will attend Command School. Three years from now you will be the youngest commander to take his own unit."

"No."

"What did you say?"

Sawyer knew speaking against his father would create more trouble than it was worth, but he'd already started down the path, so there was no use stopping. He crossed his arms and stared into his father's eyes. "Sir, I'm twenty-two years old, a grown man, you don't get to have this much control over my life anymore. I've done everything you've asked, and not only succeeded but excelled at every challenge you've thrown at me. This is bullshit!"

"Are you done?" His father was a statue before him, lips thin, pale-blue eyes as cold as the arctic ice they resembled. His voice was low and calculating, sending a shiver up Sawyer's spine. "If you raise your voice at me again, I'll have Lieutenant Hawk's record of that fiasco at the museum released. I saved both your asses that night! Both of you fools would have been thrown out of the Academy if I hadn't intervened. And the only reason I protected Hawk was for you. You two have grown close, and I knew you'd slip in your studies if he'd been expelled. You would have lost your standing at the top of your class. And Sawyers do not take back seats to anyone."

Sawyer flinched. "I didn't know, sir. I thought …"

"You thought your previous good grades and behaviour kept you in the Academy? I've warned you about your temper. You need to keep it in check. That security guard is still in a damn coma!"

Sawyer paled. His stomach tied in knots. *Oh shit. I didn't know the guard was still in the hospital . . .*

"Now, smarten up, son. I was the only thing keeping you and Hawk in the Academy that night, so you show some respect when you speak to me, and don't you *ever* forget what I'm capable of." He leaned close, his mouth an inch from Sawyer's ear. "Do I make myself clear?"

With the security guard's predicament weighing heavily on his mind, Sawyer's voice cracked when he responded, "Yes, sir."

"Now listen to me, and do as you're told, and I'll make sure no one finds out about Lieutenant Hawk's involvement that night. But you question me again and I'll not only remind you how I earn respect, I'll make sure your little friend Hawk never sees the inside of Command School."

Sawyer nodded.

"You will be present for the team changeover tonight at twenty-two hundred hours. No excuses. If I hear you were one minute late, I'll make sure Hawk sees nothing more than an office in the Time Ranger Archives. Understood?"

"Yes, sir."

"Commander Beaumont's ship, the USV *Spectre*, is currently docked at Nexus Station. You will have to arrange for your own flight there, as I have business on Earth to attend. The commander is aware of this substitution, and he is neither pleased nor in any position to argue with me."

"Sir? I'm fresh out of the Academy. Are you sure his team is appropriate?"

"That was a close-ended statement, not open for debate, Lieutenant."

"Yes, sir."

As much as Sawyer was battling his nerves to remain calm amidst his father's anger, he couldn't ignore the reverence he felt toward working with the Time Ranger's most elite commander. Like touching the Hubble Telescope, now that this incredible opportunity was close at hand, Sawyer's excitement overpowered his reservations. It was finally time for him to make a name for himself. Prove his worth without his father standing over his shoulder pulling the strings.

4.

THE Time Ranger Academy was a self-contained space station located close to Earth and several hours away from Nexus Station, the station that headquartered both Space Fleet and its Time Ranger Unit. A quick flight on a shuttle with faster-than-light capabilities landed Sawyer at HQ shortly before he was to meet his assigned team. Carrying his own gear, he traversed the station to docking ring-A where the Utopian Space Fleet Vessel the USV *Spectre* and his team were waiting.

Sawyer's smile quickly formed into a frown when Commander Beaumont stepped off the *Spectre* with his team onto Nexus Station. The commander's tight jaw and narrowed eyes let Sawyer know his father was putting him in a position where he wasn't welcome. Top marks at the Academy granted new Rangers some privileges but being placed with AJ Beaumont was something a soldier needed to earn. Based on his excessive lifelong training, Sawyer knew he was capable of working with such a prestigious team and commander, but he didn't feel he'd earned it yet, and it appeared he wasn't the only one who felt that way.

The Ranger he was there to replace knocked Sawyer in the shoulder when he passed by. "Must be nice being a Sawyer," he whispered. "The rear admiral's little toy soldier."

Sawyer smiled stiffly. *Suck it up and act like a soldier. Following orders is what we do ... whether we agree with them or not.*

The historian of his new team extended his hand. "Specialist Sokolov. Our room is where it always is on these ships—deck two, across from med-bay. Put your shit under the bunk and don't even think about touching my books. They're old-school paper texts and worth a fortune. They're also everywhere. That's how I like it and that's how it stays. Got it?"

Sawyer frowned. "Yeah, got it," he replied, then looked at the commander in anticipation of their inaugural introduction.

"Do as I say and don't fuck up," said Beaumont. "Because we have a mission briefing in one hour in the operational control centre on the station. Don't be late." He walked away, leaving Sawyer standing there with his hand extended.

When Sawyer realized everyone had left, he slung his kit bag over his shoulder and grabbed his barrack box. "Some fucking courtesy would've been nice," he said under his breath as he crossed through the boarding hatch into the *Spectre's* debarkation room. "But what did I expect being the son of a fucking rear admiral? I swear that's going to haunt me my entire career."

He stowed his gear in the unit's crew cabin, changed into his battle uniform, which consisted of grey fatigues and a form-fitting skinsuit underneath, and then left for the OCC. Overwatch, the team responsible for deciphering the information spat out by the Nexus Point, stood around a large table raised on a podium at the back of the cavernous, nearly all glass room that looked out over the Nexus Point Actual. Commander Beaumont and Specialist Sokolov both glared at Sawyer as he took his place beside them.

You may not be happy about being stuck with me, but you don't have a choice, and neither do I, he thought as he glanced across the table at his father, Overwatch Actual.

"Adrianne Howard," began his father. "A journalist from the *Utopian Star,* based out of Lunar City, is your target. Back when it was legal, she bought a ticket for a ThirdEye time-travel vacation to visit London and purposely missed her ship's scheduled boomerang event. And since we recently found alterations in London, and the Deviation Point is located outside a specific flat in Camden Town, we suspect she's after the footage of the bogus Roswell alien autopsy that rattled the world in 1995. And if you've ever read her work, you'd know she has a penchant for alien conspiracies. You are to make sure she doesn't find the truth and bring her back to 2196 for trial and subsequent sentencing."

Beaumont nodded. "Yes, sir."

Overwatch Actual nodded in return. "The consequences of the HCA perpetrated by this Time Runner could be dire if this Runner finds and reveals the truth. We all know the Roswell alien autopsy was a ruse, but if the Runner verifies this truth too early ... before the actual filmmakers admitted it was a fake, our Consequence Report shows a large-scale change in America's late-twentieth-century government, and research and development into stealth technology will be slowed. And that will have devastating effects to our present. Particularly our military. Therefore, she must be stopped."

"Attire?" asked Sokolov.

Lieutenant Coy of the Acclimation Department cleared her throat and responded. "You will wear business suits customized for the time and will be disguised as British MI-5 agents to give you authority to make a public arrest without involving the London Police Department. No skinsuits, for there is a high likelihood you will have to interact with citizens."

"British accents will be required," said Specialist Anwar from the Historical Department. "Ear-pin translators do not accommodate for this, so try and remember your linguistics classes from the Academy and you should do fine."

The rest of the briefing included landing coordinates, and the use of their Earth-Lander's mask, to which Sawyer tuned out. It was the basic stuff re-iterated in each briefing, and it was directed more to the team commander. All Sawyer needed to know was that the Nexus Point would open in seven hours for their launch-through, and that he was not to be late meeting his team on their Earth-Lander currently docked in the debarkation room of the *Spectre*.

He'd been on many space stations and Utopian Space Fleet Vessels through-out his life, so finding his way back to the Time Ranger crew room wasn't dif-ficult. He checked his gear under the single bunk bed in the cramped room, took the history books off the lower rack, placed them on the small desk, then lay down. As commander of the team, Beaumont had his own cabin. Only a select few ever saw inside a commander's quarters, as it was reserved for personal space and the occasional secure communication.

On the underside of the upper rack, Sawyer noticed the ThirdEye Corporation logo. "Man, you guys have your hand in everything. Land cruisers, toothbrushes, military-grade weapons, and once upon a time, time-travel vacations."

He shook his head and closed his eyes as he tried to remember the company's old vid-ads of ancient castles and untouched beaches of Earth's yesteryears, but Commander Beaumont's grim face popped into his mind and washed it all away like bitter acid. Sawyer knew he had to impress this guy, show him what he was made of, what he was capable of achieving. Not just as a Spawn or Sawyer, but how his father had trained him for this his whole life.

Sawyer decided the best thing he could do was take his own earlier advice and act like a soldier. It didn't matter that his team showed nothing but contempt toward him—they'd learn his worth soon enough. Until then, he'd shove every fear, every single self-doubt he had, down into the pit of his stomach. Show Commander Beaumont and Specialist Sokolov who he really was, what he was trained to be ...

A professional, hard-working soldier.

With the accumulating anxiety of already being assigned his first mission, Sawyer couldn't sleep. He got up and sat on the edge of his rack where he stripped his standard-issue Stormguard pistol over and over again.

The Stormguard, issued on day of graduation to all officers along with the skinsuit, was a bastard of a weapon with dual-action settings; debilitator pulse for knocking people out, and a fixed-mass setting that fired high-impact projectiles used for killing. Sawyer thought debilitating someone was for pussies. If you're going to point a gun at someone, you should mean what you say. He preferred the semi-automatic fixed-mass setting with its hundred-round clip and single or short-fire bursts. Made of metalloid ceramics, it was the type of weapon that meant business. When facing down the barrel set on fixed-mass, one typically knew things were going to go very badly for them. On debilitator setting, it could drop a person in their tracks, even make them unconscious, if the setting were high enough.

Sawyer scrubbed at his face with both hands. His eyes were burning, his back aching. Locking his pistol away, he took to his bed and fell asleep, only to wake several hours later to his alarm. Sawyer dressed and left the crewroom, still holding tight to the belief that if he stayed true to his training, behaved professionally, and followed his father's lifelong advice, he'd be all right. In time he hoped his team would treat him with the respect a Sawyer deserved, but in the meantime, he'd take their glares and jibes as nothing more than the good-natured ribbing of an FNG. The fucking new guy.

He lengthened his steps to bolster his conviction as he strode toward the station's Time Acclimation Unit where he would be appropriately costumed for the coming mission. Each step he took proudly brought him closer to the first mission of his Time Ranger career.

5.

HEY. Hey, wake up." Sawyer shook Specialist Sokolov, who was sleeping on the team's Earth-Lander bench. The small space craft used to shuttle Rangers planetside was still docked in the *Spectre's* debarkation room. "Wake up. What are you doing? The commander will be here any second. We have a mission, remember?"

Sokolov crossed his ankles, rubbed his back against the wall, and snorted.

"Good morning, Lieutenant Sawyer. Why aren't you sleeping?" said Commander AJ Beaumont when he stepped through the Earth-Lander's back hatch.

Sawyer flinched then quickly squared his shoulders. He would have saluted if they'd been wearing head dress. "Didn't think it was appropriate, sir."

Commander Beaumont frowned. "You Sawyers really are rigid, aren't you?"

"Are you referencing my father, sir?"

"Yes. And I don't want *him* on my team, so stand down. It's my job to shape you into a great Time Ranger, but I'm not willing to break down that pompous Sawyer reputation—too much work. So you better learn to be more like Specialist Sokolov napping over there." He hooked a thumb over his shoulder at the man sleeping on the bench. "He's got years of experience. And I only want ten-year Ranger attitude, not FNG attitude. Or there's no place for you on this team."

Sawyer's cheek stung from the imaginary slap. "Sir, I don't need hand holding. I'm trained ..."

"Stop talking, Lieutenant. Now sit. The *Spectre* is prepped for launch-through to the Nexus Point into 1995 where it's oh-two-thirty in the fucking morning.

21

We'll be departing for Earth soon after we go through, so take a nap. You never know if you'll get a moment's rest on a mission, so take it when ya can."

"I know I'm new, and you and Specialist Sokolov have been working together a long time ..."

"Yes, Soko and I have, Lieutenant. But you and I haven't, so I expect a sir at the end of that question."

"Yes, sir."

"You *are* new, so let me explain something to you. I'm sure you know the difference between specialist and officer ..."

"Treated as the same, but specialist falls outside of rank even though they're given officer status. They hold authority, attend the Academy, but take a separate track after first-year basic. Sir."

Beaumont stared at him with a deadpan expression. "Thank you. May I continue? Before a team commander gets familiar with their teammates, specialist or not, they better have their respect and undivided obedience first. You'll lose control of your team without that."

"Sir, I wasn't meaning to be disrespectful ..."

His commander crossed his arms. "Stop. You're a Sawyer. So I know you'll be professional. Too professional. But sometimes professionalism gets you nowhere. After you've achieved your team's respect, you need to gain their trust. Then you'll know you have a team worth keeping. Your father's the only reason you're even on my team. He pulled some mighty big maneuvers to get you placed with me. Usually I don't take anyone this fresh out of the Academy, but when a rear admiral demands it, you can't say no."

Sawyer's neck tensed, and his hands balled into fists before he caught himself and released a long breath. "Sir, there are consequences when I don't obey ... I'm sorry. Forget it. Ten-year Ranger, not an FNG with daddy issues."

"Good." As the commander crossed through the hatchway into the cockpit he mumbled over his shoulder, "Morning, Soko."

Sokolov grunted in return then cracked open an eye and stared at Sawyer with a lopsided grin. "Are you really Rear Admiral Sawyer's son? I see the resemblance with the black hair and crazy blue eyes, but I didn't make the connection."

"Yes."

Sokolov whistled. "Wow, what's that like?"

"It's the bane of my existence. Can we talk about something else?"

"Hm." Sokolov closed his eye and retook his nap position.

"Prep for L-T," called Commander Beaumont.

Sawyer sat across from Sokolov on the opposite bench and considered strapping into the safety harness, but since Sokolov wasn't moving to do so, he decided to play it cool and leave his off. *Ten-year Ranger, not a Fucking New Guy.*

Through the frame of the Earth-Lander's cockpit window, and through the incandescent webbing of the *Spectre's* shield, which held back the universe from entering its debarkation room, Sawyer saw the Nexus Point Actual. Sequin-blue and white, and smaller than the smallest star in their known galaxy, the Point shimmered and pulsed against the inky black backdrop of space. The Point was neither round nor oval, but somewhere in between, with jagged, stiletto-shaped spikes randomly striking out from its near-white core like Tesla coils.

The Academy trained their soldiers and officers to go through the Point with simulators. *Close, but not nearly as thrilling,* thought Sawyer.

Over the Earth-Lander's comm, the *Spectre's* captain counted down the remaining seconds before actual launch-through. Sawyer pressed his back against the wall, held his breath, and white-knuckled the bench on either side of his knees as the *Spectre's* FTL omni-drive jolted and drove them forward into the Point's core.

Everything went white.

Travel through the Nexus Point was cold. Damn cold. On the other side, Sawyer rubbed his arms to help dissipate the chill running through him and smiled. *Yeah, that was cool.*

After the Earth-Lander exited the *Spectre's* debarkation room and had been travelling for awhile, Sawyer leaned forward to look out the front window again where he could see Earth in the distance. The coordinates for the Nexus Point Actual were now behind them. Exactly 0.2 Astronomical Units beyond their solar system's main asteroid belt, awaiting their return to boomerang them back to 2196.

Other than the quiet hum of the engine and air cycling through vents, the Earth-Lander was still. Quiet. Until entry into Earth's atmosphere lit up the small vessel. Sawyer watched while blurry streaks of orange and red blanketed the front window, mesmerized by the kaleidoscope effect.

Still cool.

When the vessel broke through the upper atmosphere, the Earth-Lander's

flare kicked in, dropping the Earth-Lander's back end. Its speed decreased significantly for final approach. Sawyer knew the Earth-Lander's mask, used for
cloaking the ship, was engaged, so the people below in 1995 Camden Town,
London, wouldn't see them flying over their city.

When the Earth-Lander touched smoothly on the ground in Castlehaven
Park, and its engine turned off, Commander Beaumont entered the rear compartment. "Scan-tact check. Soko, I want you on historical relevance, as always."

"Check," reported Sokolov. "If an aura is green, you can't be mean. We don't
want to kill anyone the future may need."

"Lieutenant Sawyer, I want you on radiation aura. I'll be on radiation as well."

Sawyer blinked twice to activate his contacts, then once more. His commander and specialist glowed red, indicating a specific radiation level attuned
with time in space, hence from the future. Sawyer winked his right eye to turn
them off. "Check."

"Get your game faces on, I'm opening the hatch," said Beaumont. "Cassie?"
he asked his implanted AI. "Is it all clear?"

"All clear, Commander. It is safe to proceed," the AI's voice replied over the
Earth-Lander's communication system in a distinctly feminie voice.

Beaumont paused before opening the hatch and glanced at Sawyer. "Unless
you'd like to do the honours and kick it open, Lieutenant?"

Sawyer fought the roll of his eyes. "I'm a Spawn, Commander. Not a superhero. Even that's too much for me."

The rear hatch lowered with a hiss onto the damp grass. The clock above the
helm hatchway read three times: SGT actual, which denoted standard galactic
time back in 2196, time actual in 1995 London, and the time remaining until the
Nexus Point's pre-determined boomerang event that would return them back to
their time. Sawyer noted the middle time with unease, as there wasn't a lot, then
followed his team down the ramp out the back of the Earth-Lander.

"Stormguard?" asked Sokolov.

Beaumont patted his hip where his suit jacket bulged. "Only in case of emergency. And I have a feeling, based on her being a journalist, I'm gonna need it."

They walked across the damp grass of the park until they reached pavement.
Across the empty four-lane street a well-lit coffee shop with a large front window
flashing an open sign caught Sokolov's attention, and he darted across the road.

Sawyer watched as Sokolov flirted with a female patron in the shop then turned to Beaumont. "Coffee? Really, sir?"

"Yes, really. Now shut up."

When Sawyer turned back to the shop, only the woman stood at the counter, a Stormguard in her hand pointed at where Sokolov stood moments ago. Sawyer blinked twice to activate his scan-tacts, then again to activate the radiation aura. The woman glowed red.

Beaumont also noticed. "That's our Runner! Go!"

Sawyer chased after Beaumont into the coffee shop, arriving as their Runner bolted out the back door. Sawyer stopped beside Sokolov, where Beaumont was helping the specialist to his feet. "Is he okay?"

"Hit with a debilitator pulse. The damn Time Runner has a Stormguard."

"Obviously on low setting; he's up now, so he'll be fine." Sawyer edged toward the back door. "Sir? Shouldn't one of us be going after the Runner?"

"Let's get Sokolov outside first. There's a bench out front. The night air might revive him quicker."

"What about the Runner, sir? The mission? We should be going after her."

Commander Beaumont stared harshly at him. "Listen here, dipshit. The mission is to secure the future, and Sokolov is part of that future. All your team members are. Don't you ever forget that! We wait until Soko's back to ..."

"This is bullshit!" Sawyer hadn't meant to be so blunt, but all he heard yelling in his ear was his father's voice demanding perfection. To succeed in every mission. "The Runner has to come first! You're going to bag this mission!" Sawyer couldn't stop himself; he turned and ran for the back door.

Outside, the smell of wet pavement mixed with the sweet stench of dust and vinegar filled Sawyer's nose as he ran down the dark alley behind the coffee shop then back out into one of Camden Town's main streets. He spotted Adrianne Howard pacing in front of the grand red- brick building of a train terminal, her head pivoting back and forth like a caged animal's. He'd have to consider the Stormguard—she obviously wasn't afraid to use it, and who knew if she'd changed the setting. Did she know it only took ten seconds to charge the debilitator pulse?

"I have a good mind to drag your sorry ass back to the Earth-Lander and lock you in."

Startled by his commander's voice, Sawyer turned to see Beaumont and

Sokolov coming out of the alley behind him, the latter still unsteady on his feet. "Our Time Runner is right there, sir," he replied. He looked back at Adrianne Howard and saw her move toward the station's front doors. "She's going in!"

Sawyer bolted across the street. Inside the Underground, people moved around him in chaos. Several subway lines diverged from this station, and it was easy to get lost. Sawyer focused on his scan-tact reading and saw the red glow of their Runner moving through a turnstile, heading toward the downtown London tube. He shoved his way through the crowd and jumped the turnstile, setting off alarms. Any moment, transit police would be after them.

"Keep going!" ordered Beaumont, from somewhere close behind him. "She can't get on a train!"

Sawyer shoved people out of his way as he ran down the crowded stairs leading to the southbound platform.

"MI-5! MI-5! Get out of the way!" came Sokolov's voice from halfway back up the stairs.

Up ahead, the bobbing and weaving red glow of the Time Runner made its way toward the front of the tube platform where the train was entering.

"MI-5! Everybody down!" Beaumont screamed.

People cursed, dropping their bags and briefcases. The rumble of the coming train echoed in the long chamber. The Runner stopped and pointed her Stormguard at Beaumont. The thwump sound of a debilitator pulse filled the platform and the commander went down, sending the Stormguard hidden under his suit jacket skittering across the floor. To Sawyer's right, the train had stopped, and the doors started opening. He ran forward, scooped up his commander's Stormguard, and fired.

Nothing. It wasn't charged.

"You don't know what you're doing!" cried Adrianne, her Stormguard now levelled at Sawyer's chest. "You shouldn't be stopping me! The world needs to know the truth!" When the train doors fully opened, she turned to enter.

Sawyer flipped the switch near his thumb to the fixed-mass setting and aimed for her thigh. *No, she'll fall into the train alive. Doors will close. She'll get away.* He aimed for the base of her skull and fired.

The train doors shut, and it pulled out of the station, whisking away the dead Time Runner along with it.

"That was a hell of a shot, but we've gotta get out of here," said Sokolov. His face was red and sweaty and he was panting. "The transit cops will be coming for blood after this. Let's go."

Sawyer tucked the Stormguard into the back of his pants and helped Sokolov retrieve their commander. It had only been a glancing shot, so although unsteady on his feet, Beaumont could move.

With the threat of the transit police hot on their heels, and working backward through a panicked crowd, they finally made it back to the Earth-Lander. Adrenaline must have counteracted the debilitator's effect, for Sawyer was amazed at how functional his commander was when they deposited him on one of the aft benches.

Beaumont stood immediately and slid into the pilot's seat, where he ran his hands over the console. "Cassie, how close are those cops?"

"The transit police have now entered the park. I suggest you move quickly before they converge on our location," replied the AI's calm voice over the Earth-Lander's comm speakers.

Beaumont closed the hatch and called over his shoulder, "Engaging omni-drive! Strap in!"

Sawyer did as instructed and noted Sokolov doing the same. It wasn't common to engage the faster-than-light omni-drive so close to Earth, but time was of the essence. They needed to leave before the transit cops accidentally ran into the side of their invisible ship.

The Earth-Lander lifted smoothly from the grass then shot forward and upward, the sudden momentum pushing Sawyer and Sokolov sideways in their seats until the Earth-Lander's internal gravimetrics settled. Sawyer released a long breath as he rested his head on the Earth-Lander wall. Immediately his heart rate decreased, his breathing regulated. *Benefit of being a Spawn*, he thought, as he noticed Sokolov still panting and sweating across from him. *And … saving a mission*, he added with a smile.

Sawyer wasn't expecting a congratulations for a job well done, but he hadn't expected his team to completely ignore him. It took approximately twenty-minutes for the Earth-Lander to reach the Point's coordinates at FTL, wherein Beaumont kept the vessel at bay outside the *Spectre's* debarkation room. He'd closed the door to the helm, and remained there for several hours. Sawyer didn't know why, and it wasn't until after docking in the *Spectre's* debarkation room, and the launch-bay doors slid closed, that anyone said anything. And it was the commander's AI who spoke, not either of his teammates.

Cassie's simulated voice came over the Earth-Lander's communication system. "The *Spectre's* captain has announced preparations for boomerang capture through the Nexus Point."

Sawyer closed his eyes and braced for molecular disintegration.

The USV *Spectre* bucked once then everything went white as the ship entered the Nexus Point core on its scheduled trip back to 2196. A shiver racked Sawyer from the inside out, letting him know all his molecules had just dissolved and re-established in another timeline.

"Docking with Nexus Station will begin in thirty minutes," stated Cassie. "Prepare for station capture. Docking ring A-1 is ready for hard berth. Prepare for station orientation."

"Thank you, Cassie," said Beaumont when the helm door finally opened and he stepped into the aft cabin. "Let the captain know I'll be there to give my report shortly. I have something I need to take care of first." He strode up to Sawyer and stared at him. "What the fuck was that?"

"Sir?"

"Who at the Academy taught you it was okay to disobey your commander's orders?".

"You gave the wrong order ... my father always says ... Sir, you were going to blow the whole ..."

Sokolov whistled low. "Oh, Lieutenant, I wouldn't finish that sentence if I were you."

Sawyer undid his harness and stood. "The future is secure. Adrianne Howard can't contaminate the future now. The Stormguard uses case-less dissolving rounds, so her death will go down as another unsolved murder on the London Underground. I thought I did what was right."

Beaumont stood an inch away from Sawyer, his jawline defined by the extraneous clenching of his teeth. "Aw, another Sawyer saves the day. Do you want a medal?"

"I put the mission first, sir. As a loyal Ranger does. Stop treating me like a child!"

"Then stop acting like a child! Because you just proved to me you're nothing *but* a spoiled child of a rear admiral!"

"Training is learning the rules, experience is knowing the exceptions," stated Sokolov.

"And you don't have the experience to be making command decisions, or to go against your commander's orders. In the end, that was an impressive save, Lieutenant, but if you had followed the established plan, we would have caught the Runner outside the London flat! A quiet snatch and grab. She would have been too preoccupied with the filming to see us coming! Save the future, yes, but don't forget rule two: don't contaminate the past! Because of you we just fired a Stormguard in a crowded station! And we let one get away when our Runner fell into the train! If there are repercussions from that, I'll rip you more than a new one!"

I followed all my training. How did this happen? But Sawyer knew the consequences of screwing up, so he decided to take it like a man. He stood straight and looked his commander in the eyes. "Then with your permission, I'll request another team."

"That's your first reaction? Son, Rangers don't quit. They learn from their mistakes, get better, and be better. That's some aim you've got, and I'm not willing to give *that* up so easily. You killed the Time Runner, and that wasn't an easy choice either. Not when it's supposed to be our last resort. And you did it without hesitation. I want that quick thinking on my team. But if you ever disobey me or talk back again, I'll have you cleaning out this Earth-Lander with your tongue."

I can stay? Sawyer stood aghast. "Uh, got it, sir."

"Good. Now, after we dock, shower, change, eat, and meet me on the *Spectre's* bridge in two hours. This was your first mission, so I want you there when I give the report to the ship's captain."

Sawyer did as instructed and after downing two bottles of his cyto-juice, along with a protein bar in lieu of a meal, he made it to the bridge in a fresh uniform with three minutes to spare.

"Lieutenant Sawyer, I presume," greeted the *Spectre's* captain. "Commander Beaumont tells me you did good work out there. Wish I could have seen it, but you know how it goes, no glory for the Regulars."

Beaumont stood next to the captain outside the secure communications room on the bridge, Beaumont's eyes crinkling in the corners as he laughed at the captain's self-deprecation. "You wouldn't last a day as a Ranger, ma'am."

"You're probably right, Commander. I'm too old to be out there chasing Runners now anyway. I've earned the right to captain this ship, shuttle your

Ranger asses through the Point, and then sit back and watch. I'd like a little less paperwork to send up to Admiral Shenouda, but that's the life of a Space Fleet Regular. That is, when we're not busy with our daily duties of protecting the colonies from their own self-interests or keeping the spacers on the geo-dome stations from blowing themselves up with their petty differences. You know, the boring shit."

"Hey, don't be so hard on yourself, Captain. There are only ten Ranger units active at one time, so they only had to scrape a bit off the bottom of the barrel to find enough ship captains capable of keeping up with us."

Sawyer studied the strange dynamic between the captain and his commander. They spoke with calmness and familiarity, not as superior and subordinate. He found it refreshing and wondered if he'd ever have that closeness with anyone again. Hawk was gone, probably placed with his own team where, most likely, he was already causing shit. Sawyer chuckled and wondered if he'd see him again. He made a mental note to contact him if he had the chance.

"Oh, by the way, Lieutenant Sawyer," said the captain, turning to him. "The damn minute we cleared the Point I received a message from your unit's rear admiral. He wants you in his office immediately after we dock. And he expects my report, and yours, Commander, before we get there, so we better get this debrief under way."

6.

AT the back of the operational control centre, beside the admiral of Space Fleet's office, Sawyer entered his father's smaller office. He'd spent half his childhood in this cold, sparsely decorated room, sitting on the floor in the corner reading Time Ranger manuals when his father wasn't making him blindly strip down pistols and put them back together. The wall behind the glass-and-steel desk held pics of all the Space Fleet ships appointed with Time Ranger teams. The Utopian Space Fleet Vessel USV *Spectre* was in the middle of the line as the most prominent.

His father was finishing a communication over his personal Quantum Entanglement Comms Suite when he entered. "I told you everything will be in order. He will be ready. Are you questioning me?" There was a pause before he spoke again. "I will notify you when it's done."

The rear admiral closed down the QECS and swiped his hand across his desk, scattering data-pads across the floor. "Sit down, Lieutenant."

Sawyer sat.

"You fired a twenty-second-century weapon in a public place. The Time Runner is dead because of you, her body now unretrievable. And don't get me started on the fact that you left a fucking Stormguard in the twentieth century! You're lucky nothing came of it. So, what say you?"

"Sir, the Historical Contamination Act was stopped. The Time Runner would have escaped if I hadn't fired the weapon."

"Don't give me excuses!"

Sawyer stood. "They're not excuses, sir. They're facts."

"I expect better from you. And how did Specialist Sokolov even get hit by a Stormguard in the first place? We can't have these mistakes on your record. I can't have these mistakes reflected on you or me."

Sawyer felt like his five-year-old self, wanting to crawl under his father's desk and hide. He would have apologized, but weakness was something one didn't show in front of his father. Not unless you wanted a black eye. Instead, he absently rubbed the keloid scar under his chin.

"Stop that. And get that scar fixed. It's a blight on your appearance. Proof of a mistake, and it shows sentimentality."

At seven years old, his father had left him in a cave on Earth. San Fernando Valley, to be accurate.

"Find your way home," was all his father said when he left him one cold February night with nothing more than the clothes on his back and a single bottle of cyto-juice he was required to drink due to his faster than normal metabolism.

His fingers nearly frozen blue, and working on energy reserves, Sawyer had fallen more than once trying to claw his way out from that cave onto higher ground. On one attempt, he'd managed to crawl further than he had on previous attempts, only to slip on loose rocks at the top and tumble down the cliff outside the cave. His torso scratched, clothes torn, his body shivering, he'd cut the soft flesh under his chin on a sharp rock, which left a blood trail down his tattered shirt and chest.

Sawyer thought maybe his father wanted him to fail, so as a big 'fuck-you,' he'd crawled over the cliff and made it home just after sunup. Reward for returning home later than his father had hoped was a scolding over breakfast for taking too long and a promise that he'd do it again that night.

"Now get out of my office," said his father, breaking Sawyer from his memories.

With his head low, Sawyer moved toward the door, trying to hold on to what self-esteem he could. "You know, sir, Commander Beaumont thinks ..."

His father tossed the data-pads he'd thrown on the floor back onto his desk. "I don't care."

Sawyer opened the door with a swipe of his hand, stepped one foot into the OCC, then looked back again at his father. "I'm ..."

"If that's an apology about to come out of your mouth, I don't want to hear it!"

***

SPECIALIST Perry looked up at the last second and stopped suddenly to avoid walking into someone coming out of the rear admiral's office. "S … sorry," he stuttered when he realized it was Lieutenant Sawyer.

As the lieutenant stalked away, he didn't register Perry's apology or his presence. Perry shook his head, bit his lip, and looked in through the office door to see the rear admiral bent over his desk holding his head. The last time he saw the rear admiral was at Sawyer's graduation, but it had been a long time since they'd last spoken. Perry wasn't sure if he'd be welcome as he stuck his head hesitantly into the office. "Sir?"

"What is it!" The rear admiral froze the moment he caught Perry's gaze. "Greg … uh, Specialist. I didn't know it was you."

The look of surprise on the rear admiral's face made Perry reconsider his agenda, but when he saw Kai's graduation picture on the desk, he firmed his resolve. "You're still too hard on that boy."

Rear Admiral Sawyer came around his desk. "That is none of your concern, Greg. You gave up the right to intervene long ago."

"He's a good boy, a good soldier. Ease up before you break him."

"He needs to be better!" The rear admiral pointed a finger in Perry's face, his own face red like he'd just embarrassed himself in front of the other admirals. "There's too much at stake for him to be less than perfect, less than the Spawn I created."

"Yes, he's a Spawn, but he's still human."

"A human with more importance than anyone alive …"

"What are you talking about?"

Rear Admiral Sawyer forced out a breath. "He has a legacy to fulfill or we're all in more danger than you can imagine."

"You and that damn legacy! I don't even know what that means! And if you keep on about that he's going to crumble. He'll fall apart, and you won't be able to put the pieces back together. And I won't be there to help." Perry spun around and marched out of the office.

7.

OUTSIDE the secure communications room on the bridge of the USV *Spectre*, Lieutenant Sawyer paced. Commander Beaumont was receiving last-minute details concerning their newest mission over the Quantum Entanglement Comms Suite and had wanted Sawyer there to discuss something with him afterward. Sawyer knew nothing about what was going on. *Am I about to be benched? Did I do something wrong?* His heart nearly stopped when the commander exited the small room and stepped onto the bridge.

"Sir, you wanted to see me?"

Beaumont put a hand on Sawyer's shoulder. "It's been a crazy year since you joined my team. Remember the Cook Islands? Running from those cannibals?"

"Yes. Soko nearly got beheaded. I took a blow dart to the leg."

"But yet your speed and quick thinking still got us out of that situation. And then in Ancient Egypt your freakish strength saved me from being crushed by that boulder."

Sawyer nodded. "I remember, sir."

"Well, it's time to put your special skills back to work. This mission is a bit complicated, so the decision will be yours if you want to follow through."

Several hours later, Sawyer stood in the aft compartment of their Earth-Lander listening to Commander Beaumont recite the details of their mission, which had them currently hovering over a cruise ship crossing the Atlantic in 1912. Sawyer wasn't happy about the circumstances, but he thought maybe this would give him an opportunity to really prove himself, show the Rangers his real capabilities and make a name for himself. If there was any time his unique capabilities would shine, it would be now, because contrary to Ranger training, he'd be doing this mission solo.

"There's a high likelihood this cruise ship has been exposed to a twenty-second-century virus with no known cure," stated Beaumont. "When passengers of a ThirdEye vacation trip returned home to our time and started getting sick, catching this vacationer who'd purposely missed his trip back became a priority. Overwatch was ecstatic when the Point finally noticed him and opened for retrieval."

Commander Beaumont crossed his arms, looked Sawyer directly in the eyes. "You're the only one who can do this, Lieutenant. The *Spectre's* doctor informed me that because of your enhanced genetics, your chances of contracting or carrying the virus is less than zero-point-two percent. But for Soko and I, it would be almost ninety percent if this Runner is infected. There's still a risk for you, so I'll understand if you don't want to do this."

"Life or limb," recited Sawyer from the Time Ranger Creed. "I fully recognize the hazards of my profession."

"I knew you'd say that, but I had to double check. Cassie, I'm opening the hatch. One for debarkation." He turned back to Sawyer. "Keep your mask up and we'll stay in contact through the ear-pins. Land safely, move swiftly, and good luck."

Since space was a premium on cruise-ship decks, the Earth-Lander hovered above its poop deck. Sawyer looked out to the four smokestacks, his lungs sucking in the grey smoke pouring from their tops, his face already wet with cold, salty sea spray. He jumped out the Earth-Lander fully masked and landed on the slippery deck. Once acclimated to the sway of the ship, Sawyer pressed the button on the right cuff of his fatigues, which linked with the skinsuit he wore underneath. A three-inch transparent computer screen appeared above his left forearm, visible only to him under his personal mask. "Find the Runner, verify if he's infected, clean up the mess."

He touched the ear-pin, a small opaque sticker behind his right ear, to open a communication channel with the Earth-Lander. "Radio check."

"Five by five," replied both Beaumont and Sokolov.

"Deviation Point coordinates?"

"Overwatch determined it occurred in parlour suite fifteen, amidship. That's our Runner's cabin," replied Sokolov. "Head forward and below. I'll send you the coordinates."

Sawyer found a hatch and dropped down. As he made his way through the wide hallways with their brass rails and thick, carpeted floor, he heard soft music and quiet conversations coming from some of the passenger's rooms. Occasionally a first-class steward dressed in a white shirt, short dark jacket, and visor cap passed by.

"It smells like dust and vinegar here," Sawyer said, wrinkling his nose.

"The smell of history," sighed Sokolov over the ear-pin. "I wish I was there with you. This ship was the finest of its class. Decorated in Queen Anne. Man, I bet there's brass. Lots of brass. We don't see a lot of that in our time."

"Yeah, yeah, it's a wonderful sight," deadpanned Sawyer. He verified the location of the parlour suite on his computer, and a short while later he arrived at the correct cabin. After an easy pick of the archaic lock, the door opened. Sawyer listened carefully, noted the room was quiet, and peered in to see the Runner asleep on his bed. Sawyer slipped into the room and closed the door behind him.

From a cargo pocket on his fatigues he produced a medical field-testing kit, approached the sleeping Runner, and disengaged his mask. He placed the kit on the bedside table then pulled out his Stormguard. It was set on debilitator, and he fired it at the Runner to render him incapable of waking. "Why can't I just haul his ass back to the Earth-Lander? Why go to the trouble of testing him for the virus?"

"Because Soko and I aren't immune like you, dipshit," replied Beaumont. "If he's not infected, then yeah, haul his ass back here. But if he is, well … we'll have a completely different problem on our hands."

Sawyer figured it would be easier to dump the Runner overboard regardless, but there were rules in place that prohibited the random killing of Time Runners. "Fine," he said with a sigh.

He drew blood onto a test strip, slid it into the field tester, and waited for the results. "Hey, Soko …" he said, looking around the large suite. "The White Star Cruise Line really did an amazing job with these rooms. It even has its own washroom with a claw-foot bathtub. And you should see the wallpaper …"

"Quit mocking me."

Sawyer laughed, but he really was impressed by the opulence of the suite. "No wonder this ship was considered the most impressive of its time. ThirdEye chose this vacation well. Too bad it sunk." He paused for a moment. "I'm assuming ThirdEye had a contingency plan for that? A way to save its own vacationers before everything went to shit?"

"Probably. Some of the richest people in the world are on board right now and they didn't all make it," replied Soko. "Part owner of the Waldorf-Astoria ..."

"The what?" interrupted Beaumont.

"Famous Earth hotel. Do you guys know anything about history? You're Time Rangers, for Christ's sake."

Sawyer imagined Soko shaking his head in despair and laughed harder. A moment later the field tester pinged that the results were ready. "Damn, he's positive."

"Then there's no chance others on the ship aren't infected. The virus is highly virulent," said Beaumont. "This Runner and now the whole ship is a ticking time bomb for the citizens of New York if it docks."

The implications swept through Sawyer, casting goosebumps on his skin. "There's nearly twenty-five hundred passengers and crew onboard, sir."

"And they all could be infected by now," said Soko. "And the repercussions of infecting New York are catastrophically worse than losing a few influential passengers who actually survived, so I'm with the commander on this, we can't let it touch shore. It's due to dock in three days, and we have less than a day before boomerang."

Sawyer hung his head. He didn't know a single living soul on this ship, and he wasn't against killing for the sake of history, but mass murder was on a completely different level. His hands shook as he put the testing kit back in his pocket. "We have to make sure no one survives, don't we, sir?"

"Yes," came Beaumont's strained voice.

Sawyer swallowed down the uncomfortable lump in his throat. "Then let's get on with it. Soko, send the coordinates of the bridge to my computer and find me that damn iceberg."

There was a moment's pause before Sokolov answered. "Done. Just follow the map." Another pause. "It's a lot easier to digest what we're ... you're, about to do from up here. So, yeah, I'm sorry you have to do this alone."

Sawyer started moving, his legs heavy like they were weighed down by cement. Each step he took was slower than the last, and reaching the stairwell took longer than it should. His skin felt cold, a sheen of sweat had encompassed him, and somewhere deep in his stomach a knot formed. *I do not feel very good*, he thought.

"You can do this, Lieutenant," said Beaumont. "Think about each step you take, not the faces around you. Breathe."

"Of course I can I do this, I'm a soldier." But the stairs felt like a mountain for Sawyer. At the landing, he had to stop to gather his sapping energy, and two of the ship's passengers passed him by, their faces red from probably too much wine, their laughter echoing in the enclosed space. It made him feel sicker.

In the wheelhouse at the back of the navigation bridge, Sawyer slowly maneuvered his invisible form around the crew until he stood behind the main ship's wheel. Although the personal mask of his skinsuit hid him from sight, it didn't mask the sound of his heavy breathing or softly spoken voice, nor his mass. He'd have to move slow and quiet, which he found difficult as his heart seemed to want to beat at an exorbitant pace. "How do you want to do this, sir?" he asked in a hushed voice.

"Wait out," came Beaumont's voice.

"Hey, Sawyer," said Soko. "You okay?"

"Can we just get on with this?"

"The commander's coming up with a plan, hold tight."

Sawyer couldn't wait. "Sir? I did my research prior to the mission. I'm pretty familiar with helm control. It's not much more than a giant steering wheel and tiller. Maybe I can run the ship ashore?"

"I think the crew might notice a course change that big. And it wouldn't solve the problem," replied Beaumont. "All you need to do is steer the ship off course by a fraction. Make sure this ship really hits that iceberg. I'll send you the exact coordinates, then get your ass out on deck for egress."

Sawyer read the details on his computer, then with careful movements, he moved the giant, wood-notched wheel several points starboard and held it steady until he was sure no one had noticed the slight change. When satisfied, he immediately made for the door. Outside on the port bridge wing, he breathed in the cool night air. "What have I just done, sir?"

"What you had to do, son. We'll pick you up where we dropped you off. Soko will drop the cable ladder for you to climb. Go now."

Resistance fought Sawyer each step he took. Slow and methodical, he walked lost in a daze down the stairs and across the deck as he watched happy people strolling and lounging and enjoying the magnificent night sky. His father told him people would have to die on missions, sometimes they even needed to die. End of story. Death and killing wasn't foreign to Sawyer, but he couldn't stop a deep hollowness from encompassing him.

"Keep going, Sawyer," came Beaumont's voice, loud and jarring in Sawyer's ear. "But you're going to have to pick up your pace if you're gonna make it to us in time. We can't come any closer."

"I can physically see you," said Soko. "You're almost here. Hurry."

Sawyer kept walking, head down, and nearly bumped into a passenger making his way along the upper deck. *Don't look at him. Just keep walking.*

Before he reached the poop deck, Sawyer stopped to look out over the dark, cold ocean. "Maybe I can save some of these people?" He watched as an elderly couple strode up to the rail beside him, so he moved further down the ship to avoid being heard. "I have a few more test strips … maybe if they're not infected …"

"Lieutenant, stop," ordered Beaumont. "There's no time, and what would we do with them? We can't expose our technology …"

"I'll knock 'em out. Debilitate them. We can drop them on shore …"

"Lieutenant. There isn't enough time."

His commander's voice brooked no argument, and Sawyer knew he was grasping at straws anyway. "Yes, Commander. I'm good. I'm on my way."

"The ship will hit the target in less than a minute. And a lot harder than history remembers, so double time it. Now, Sawyer."

Sawyer ran for the stairs leading to the poop deck, where he knew the Earth-Lander and his team were waiting. But as he reached the bottom step, somewhere from above he heard someone scream, "Iceberg, dead ahead!"

The ship jolted, tipped sideways. Sawyer's ears filled with screeching metal and two passengers beside him screaming for help as they slid across the deck toward the edge. The ship rocked again, throwing Sawyer sideways. The wet deck made it impossible for him to regain his footing as he slipped toward the railing. Waves crashed over the deck, washing away lounge chairs and tables. Other passengers he hadn't noticed were now careening toward the ship's edge, him along with them.

Sawyer grasped for anything he could find as his body slid toward the ever-rising ocean. "Ex-fil now!" he screamed, frantically grabbing for the right cuff of his fatigues.

"Lieutenant!" screamed a voice in his ear. "Find something to hold onto!"

Sawyer missed the railing and dropped over the ship's deck into the freezing water below. On splash down, his heart nearly stopped. His fingers froze.

His breath caught in his throat. His internal dive reflex kicked in as water tossed and turned his body with the turbulence, pulling him down along with the ship. Sawyer lost his orientation; he didn't know what was up or down. Fear washed through him as memories of his father holding him under water as a child, testing his static apnea, flashed into his mind. *Seven minutes*, he thought, as his muscles cramped from the cold. His father always stopped him at seven minutes.

He tried to curl into the fetal position to conserve heat as his body continued to tumble with the inertia of the churning water, but his arms and legs were nearly frozen. Time Rangers trained in cold-water exercises, but his father had been submerging him in near-frozen water since he was a child. But none of that training seemed to be working. The only thought in his head was that carbon dioxide was building in his system, and that he really wanted to breathe.

Seven minutes ... this was his last thought before he smashed into the great wall of steel comprising the ship's hull.

He came back to consciousness shivering, splayed out on the Earth-Lander's floor with a warm survival blanket tight around him. "What ..." Sawyer croaked. "I'm ... freezing."

"But you're alive," said Beaumont. "Almost missed you. Thank god you turned off your mask."

"How ... how ... long was I under? That water was freezing."

"Below freezing," replied Soko. "And you were under for almost eleven minutes. Damn, I wish I was a Spawn."

Beaumont shook his head. "I don't know how you survived."

Eleven minutes! That's impossible! Without pre-oxygenation that was unheard of, even for a Spawn. *How ...? Oh god, I'm cold.* He shivered, swallowed, and remembered it wasn't him that was important, but the mission. "Did it work?" he asked through chattering teeth. "Did the ship sink?"

Beaumont blew out a breath and rubbed a hand down his face. "Snapped in two like a twig, just like in the history vids. It's still going down as we speak. We had to divert the *Carpathia*, another ship in the area making its way over to search for survivors. We couldn't afford anyone from this ship making it to shore. If only one survivor had been infected, that could have meant the end of ... well, you get the picture. And whatever was left of the virus was killed in the below-freezing waters. Along with the Runner. And you, my friend, have been out for almost four hours since we fished you out of the ocean. We're almost back to the *Spectre*."

Sawyer looked into his commander's face and saw tired, drawn eyes. "Are you all right, Commander?"

"Me? It's your ass we almost lost. Forget about me." Beaumont sat on a side bench of the Earth-Lander and closed his eyes. "We almost lost you, kid. That was too fucking close."

Sawyer didn't know how to process that information. He didn't know how to respond.

"On a good note," said Soko, kneeling next to Sawyer on the Earth-Lander floor. "We stopped the spread of the virus and saved possibly millions of lives. But no movies were made about this night. Well, a few, but the reviews say they sucked. Too depressing to watch everyone die, I guess."

Sawyer frowned, but nevertheless appreciated Soko's attempt at lightening the mood. "Already have a consequence report?"

"Came almost immediately after we cleared Earth's atmo," replied Soko. "I had to check. Killing everyone on the world's most luxurious ship of its time had to have consequences. But not as many as I would have thought. Like I said, a couple of sad movies, some rather inept searches for the wreckage and a hell of a lot of folklore came out of the disaster ... some even think aliens had something to do with the sinking ... but not so much any consequences to the actual time-line. Guess those hoity-toity who survived the *Titanic* didn't mean as much to history as they may have thought. Oh, well, so be history."

Realizing his arms and legs still felt like frozen blocks of ice, Sawyer curled deeper under the warming blanket. "Then we did good."

"No, Lieutenant," said Beaumont. "You did good."

8.

SAWYER next awoke to a pristine white ceiling above him, surrounded by the smell of antiseptic. He jolted upright and quickly scanned the Nexus Station's med-bay for his father.

"Hey, lay down, Lieutenant," said a calming feminine voice. "You can leave when the doctor clears you."

"I'm fine. Just a little hypothermia. Does anyone know I'm here?" Sawyer yanked out the IV catheter piercing into the back of his hand. If his father knew he'd hesitated on the mission, almost gotten himself killed, he'd give him a real reason to be in the med-bay.

"Your team visited. Very protective. Oh, another Specialist came to see you as well. Didn't leave his name. Kind of rude. As for anyone else, I wouldn't know. I'm a nurse trainee. I'm not privy to visitor lists. Let me get the doctor."

Sawyer noticed the red T on the nurse's epaulettes and knew she couldn't stop him, so he threw his legs over the bed. "No. Please. I'm fine. I just need to leave before ... I just need to leave."

"I'm not authorized to release you ...?"

Sawyer smiled. She didn't know who he was. "Kai. And you?"

"Aurora."

They shook hands, and Sawyer liked the way her smooth skin felt pressed against his own calloused palm. He also liked her slight accent. Possibly Norse, from back when that mattered. "Aurora, it's a pleasure to meet you, but ... where are my clothes?"

She pointed to the chair beside the bed. His battle fatigues and skinsuit hung over the back, both reeking of salt and brine. As he dressed back into his smelly uniform he said, "Trainee, you can either help me or have a superior officer put in a complaint concerning your unhelpful bedside manner. You choose."

"Well, I wouldn't want that on my record. It might hinder my chances of being posted on a prestigious ship or station when I graduate."

Sawyer recognized the tease in her voice and smiled. "You're very right." He closed the Velcro tabs of his shirt, slid his feet into his combat boots and didn't bother tying them in his rush. "Look, I'm a Spawn. I'll be fine. Now, are you going to let me leave or not?"

She stepped close to him and whispered in his ear. "I'll help you, but what's in it for me? I'm thinking at least a date." She slid her arm through his and led him toward the door. "Perhaps coffee? Later?"

She was bold. Sawyer liked that. "That would be nice. Twenty-hundred hours in the station mess?"

"Sounds good. See you then, Kai."

After returning to his rack on the *Spectre*, Sawyer undressed and tossed his dirty uniform into the laundry bin under the closet where it would come back to him clean when next he punched in his IDENT code. He took a hot shower then dressed back in clean fatigues. His skinsuit required special care, and he dropped it off at the ship's armoury for cleaning on his way to meet Aurora in the station's mess.

He saw her immediately when he entered, her pale blonde hair like a beacon of beauty. "I was thinking we could take our date over to the OCC. There's a ship launching through for a mission," he said on his approach.

"Oh, okay. That sounds … nice."

She was expecting something romantic and here Sawyer was wanting to take her to watch a ship launch through the Point. "We could stay here …" he rushed to say.

Aurora nudged him toward the mess hall door. "I've only been on the OCC once, as part of our class tour. Maybe it'll be more interesting this time with you there with me."

When they entered the OCC, Sawyer pulled them up to the railing protecting the floor-to-ceiling viewing window. Outside, a Utopian Space Fleet frigate sat ready to enter the Nexus Point Actual. The ship was majestic. Short yet sleek, two powerful nacelles protruded from its narrow body sporting the Utopian Space Fleet colours of blue-and-black stripes along its white hull- an indication the ship carried a Time Ranger team. At its convex nose was the bridge, the cobalt-blue circle and stars of the Time Ranger's insignia painted under its window. Sawyer marvelled at the ship's efficient layout and design as the nacelles glowed red in preparation for launch-through.

Aurora leaned over Sawyer's shoulder as she stared gaping out the window. "This is amazing. But the science behind all this ... I ... I just can't get my head around all of it."

Sawyer laughed. "Why the Nexus Point works, we don't exactly know. Remember, Doctor Langdon Jackson discovered it here on one of his exploratory missions to see past our solar system's main asteroid belt. The Nexus Station was here as well, abandoned, no one on board. ThirdEye and Space Fleet sent scientists and engineers to investigate, and it took them months to figure out what little they could. Thankfully, everything was all in English. But we still don't understand everything."

"Which is why we suspect the station and the Point were left or sent here for us by our future selves. The history I'm clear on. But how does everyone figure everything out? Why doesn't the Point allow for forward time travel?"

Sawyer laughed again. "This was all covered in Professor Hatchet's class in Basics at the Time Ranger Academy. I guess Space Fleet Medical doesn't go into it as much."

Aurora winked at him. "But I'm sure you can explain."

Sawyer cleared his throat. "Uh ... yeah, so, the Point notifies us of the HCA then Overwatch takes it from there, trying to pinpoint where the deviation point occurred. They do their projections and whatnot. It's a lot of research. Not really my forte. When Space Fleet took over control of the station and Point, they immediately halted all arbitrary openings. People were missing their flights back, some tried to take their own ships through, and these people started messing with history. As for future time travel, well, technically the Nexus Point allows us to travel back, which is to say forward to our own present from the past, by way of the boomerang event. But that's the only forward travel we've been able to figure out. And if an HCA occurred, the Point won't ever open again in that time. That we don't have control over at all. Maybe one day it will, or we'll be able to control it better, but we're still relatively new at all this, and so far it hasn't happened yet."

Aurora smiled, albeit placatingly, and Sawyer considered she was playing dumb for his amusement. But he was enjoying himself, so he didn't much care. "So, do you want to know how everything happens?"

Aurora nodded eagerly.

"The console in front of the crewman over there shows four time displays when an HCA occurs. The red time indicates the infraction date. The green time indicates the present date, the yellow indicates time till the HCA affects the present date. And the blue indicates time of boomerang capture. That part is simple. And that part we have no control over. The Nexus Point Actual sends us this data, and then the alarms go off and we take it from there."

Sawyer paused to see if Aurora was bored yet and found her staring at him with a broad grin. *Hm, cute and a curious mind.* "After the discovery of time travel, we quickly learned time works in a straight line, not three-dimensionally, which was the common theory before the Nexus Point was found. If time were three dimensional, it would mean the past, present, and future were happening at the same time. The Point proved this wrong, because as changes are made in the past, it takes time for the repercussions to appear in the future ... our present. So they can be stopped. And if the Nexus Point has taught us anything, it's that time is resilient. Except to really big changes which can cause catastrophic ripples throughout history, culminating in even bigger changes in the future, maybe even irreversible changes."

"It's not quite that simple," interrupted a brusque voice behind them.

Sawyer and Aurora stood straight when they saw the rear admiral standing behind them.

"At ease," said Rear Admiral Sawyer.

Aurora, who'd been standing as close to Sawyer as one could, slid her arm through his. "Rear Admiral, it's a pleasure to meet you. Your son and I have been getting to know each other. Perhaps you'd like to join us for dinner later?"

You did know who I was! You're using me! Sawyer's face flushed. *Not here,* he thought, with a deep breath. *Not in front of my father.*

"That will not happen," said the rear admiral. "Lieutenant, please escort this trainee off the OCC. Now."

Not only was it an inappropriate way to act in the OCC, but Sawyer realized Aurora hadn't been interested in him at all, only his name. *Story of my life.* He was glad to end their date.

After he ushered Aurora to the closest exit, Sawyer wandered the station's main hub dejected and wondering if he would ever meet someone who liked him for him, and not what his family could do for her and her career. But then, did the fairytale really exist? Not as far as he knew. Relationships were based on what people could get out of each other, so maybe Aurora wasn't such a bad choice after all? As he headed for the *Spectre's* docking port lost in thought, he bumped into Sokolov.

"Just who I was looking for," said the specialist. "Since you're feeling better, I think it's about time you partake in a little post-mission tradition. After all, it is our one-year anniversary as a team."

Guided by Sokolov's hand on his shoulder, Sawyer was led onto the *Spectre* and into its mess, where he sat across from Beaumont. Dinner had ended, but many of the ship's crew stayed behind since the room provided the only place large enough for social gatherings on the small ship.

Commander Beaumont pushed two glasses across the table toward him and Soko. "Guess I'll just drink from the bottle," he said, and took a swig before filling the glasses.

Sawyer lifted his glass to his nose and sniffed. "Whiskey?"

Sokolov gulped his down and motioned for Beaumont to pour another. "Tradition. Bottle for mission. You'd know that if you ever joined us."

Sawyer took a sip and put the glass back on the table with a grimace. "That's strong."

Beaumont raised a brow. "This isn't your first ..."

"No, sir." He swallowed, face flushed. "No, it's ..."

"I get it," said Beaumont with a raised hand. "Your father isn't someone I'd readily piss off either. Speaking of him, though, any news on the Ranger front you can share?"

Sawyer cleared his throat and sat up straight in his chair. "Uh, there's a new ship being built."

"Ah, yes. A new Intrepid class frigate," said Soko. "Smaller, faster ... and aren't they doing something different with the command?"

Sawyer wrapped his hands around his glass of whisky. "Space Fleet wants to keep a hand in the mix, but they're spread thin with the colonies and space stations, so the Rangers are going to be commanding the new ship. No more Regulars as captains. It'll still fall under Space Fleet jurisdiction, but ultimate control will be with the Time Rangers. It's the new prototype structure for the future."

"Have they named her yet?"

Sawyer shook his head. The whiskey sloshed as he traced circles on the table with his glass. *Maybe it might help loosen me up?* He raised the glass, paused at his lips then drank its entirety. When he slammed the glass back on the table coughing, his throat burned and his teammates were laughing at him.

"There you go, Sawyer," said Soko, patting him on the back. "You need to loosen up."

Beaumont filled Sawyer's glass then nodded toward the food dispensing units along the far wall. "Hey, Soko, why don't you get Sawyer something to eat. It might help make his tomorrow morning feel a little better."

Soko rose from his chair. "Something with lots of carbs. It's carbs you Spawns need, isn't it?"

"Actually, it's protein and cyto-greens," replied Sawyer. He hated talking about being a Spawn, particularly its drawbacks. "I expend energy fast."

"Worth it," mumbled Soko as he left the table.

"I agree," said Beaumont. "To have your agility, your strength …"

Sawyer shifted in his chair. "They are only enhancements, sir. I'm not a superhuman. And trust me, being a Spawn doesn't really make life easier for you. There aren't many of us. We're kind of considered outcasts."

"I haven't met many Spawns. You're a rare breed, my friend. If I'm right, Spawn are children missing one side of the procreation equation? But it's not the same as artificial insemination? It's still a new science …"

"It's not *new* science," said Sawyer. "CRISPR-Cas9 gene editing has been around a long time. It's just legal now. Or at least, recently legal. That's why it's still expensive. But scientists have been able to enhance and alter genetics for centuries."

"Using a vat-produced egg?" Beaumont shook his head. "That seems unreal."

Sawyer smiled. Beaumont had no trouble understanding time travel, but enhanced humans seemed like a pipe dream to him. "Depending on your sex," said Sawyer. "It's either the egg or sperm that's vat produced, which they merge with the purchaser's genuine egg or sperm. In fact, I was vat produced. Spawn aren't born like Mother Nature intended humans to be. And since Rear Admiral Sawyer wanted a little toy soldier, he purchased an egg and created me in his own image. I have one purpose in life. To sustain the Sawyer legacy ... whatever that is." Sawyer took another sip of his drink. It burned, but not as much as before, so he took another larger gulp.

A moment later Soko arrived without food, but with two young female Space Fleet trainees on his arms. "I'd like to introduce you to my new friends," he said with a broad grin. "They boarded the Nexus Station a couple of days ago and heard about our kick-ass team so they came by to say hello."

"Word spreads quickly," said Beaumont, offering a chair next to him for one of the girls to sit.

Sawyer also pulled out a chair beside him, then noticed it was Aurora standing beside the table.

She smiled as she sat next to him. To Beaumont and Soko she said, "Hi, I'm Trainee Heikkinen. Nice to meet you." Then, directly to Sawyer, she said, "Hello, Kai."

Sawyer glanced at his teammates. "We've met."

"Yes," replied Aurora. She sat forward, elbows on the table, back straight like she was the most important person there.

At first Sawyer found her bold, but now she just seemed small and begging for attention. But either way, she was still very attractive.

Aurora's friend leaned over the table. "Aurora told me about your date. Wish I had been there to meet the Rangers' rear admiral. What an honour."

"Did you know his grandfather also represents one of the stars in our insignia?" boasted Soko.

Sawyer blew out a breath. Soko wasn't helping. "Yeah, I come from a long line of ..." he wanted to say assholes, but said, "heroes."

The door to the mess was only metres behind him. Sawyer considered dashing, but Aurora had him trapped with her arm now entwined with his just like on the OCC. Somehow, she felt as if she knew him. He slowly pulled his arm out and reached for his whiskey as an excuse to get away from her.

Aurora quickly retook his arm. "You two must get a lot of special consideration being on his team."

Beaumont spit out his whiskey. "*His* team?"

Sawyer took a deep breath. He had to stop this fiasco from continuing. "Your ploy to meet me worked," he said to Aurora, "but that's as far as your game will go. You don't know me. Now, you've just insulted my commander, you are excused. You and your friend can leave."

Before Aurora and her friend left the table to find seats with other new recruits sitting in the mess, she winked at Sawyer with a coy smile.

Yeah, keep trying, Sawyer mused with a frown. He assumed that when Aurora moved to the other table, she had quickly busied herself telling tales of how she was good friends with him and *his* team. Sawyer didn't care as long as he didn't have to listen to it anymore.

"That was harsh," said Sokolov.

"It was needed," Sawyer replied, refraining from also saying that he enjoyed it. "So, how about another drink? And Soko, didn't you mention food earlier?"

9.

THE next morning, a little hung over from the night before, Sawyer was summoned to his father's office on Nexus Station.

"I know what happened on the last mission in 1912, and I don't want to hear a word out of your mouth. That was a disgrace ... almost getting yourself killed. Why did you hesitate returning to the Earth-Lander? You know what, forget it." His father paced behind his desk. "I summoned you here because I have good news. I want you to take a more authoritative role with this team, to prepare you for your own command. And you're now a Lieutenant Commander. Get your new epaulettes from the *Spectre's* captain. There won't be a ceremony, which is unfortunate, but the promotion is deserving and I was barely contested when I put it forth."

Barely contested? You mean you forced this on them, on me. But the headache pounding a tattoo in his head was already making him irritable and pissing off his father right now wasn't something he needed. "Thank you, sir. Appreciate it, sir."

There was something still bothering him since the *Titanic* mission, and he felt now was a good time to address his concern. "I was wondering, sir, Commander Beaumont and Sokolov said I was under for eleven minutes. In below-freezing water ..." He stopped when his father's expression turned deadpan.

"Eleven minutes? It must have triggered early ..."

"Triggered what?"

"Your ... your enhanced mammalian dive reflex."

His father's voice was shaky, which wasn't just rare, it was unheard of. And he wasn't making sense. "What does that have ..." started Sawyer.

His father cleared his throat, his perm-a-scowl returning to his face in the blink of an eye. "After your next mission I'm seeing to it that your name is put in for Command School."

Sawyer's eyes grew wide. "I can't take command! I don't have the experience! It's enough I've already been made a lieutenant commander before my time. I can't possibly take my own command, sir."

"It's not your decision! From the moment you were born, you were made to command. The day I brought you home from the lab was the day I knew I'd created someone special. And from that day, I owned you. I owned your future. You are not simply taking command, son. Command is waiting for you. And as your father, and as your commanding officer, I am giving you an order and you will not shy from your responsibilities."

Sawyer flushed. He could barely speak as anger took over his body. "This is ridiculous! I won't do it! I won't accept command! You can't force my career like this! When do I get to stand on my own two feet? Be my own man and make my own decisions?"

"When I'm dead. Now, you're dismissed."

Sawyer turned and slammed his open palm on the control pad of his father's office door, revelling in the satisfying pain that shot through his arm. "I can't take command," he said, lashing out to punch the nearest wall as he walked down the hall.

When he arrived at the station lift, he entered and fell against the back wall. He felt the need for release before he did something stupid. *I'll re-enrol in the Academy under the specialist track. That'll show my father I can be my own man!*

But he knew there was no point. People saw the Sawyer name and couldn't see past the history, the statue of his grandfather outside study hall at the Academy, the shiny rank on his father's shoulders. The people wanted another Sawyer, chest full of medals and brimming with heroism. But they didn't care what it took to be that man. People didn't care what he went through to be that man. Most importantly, they'd never listen to him, only to his father. And his father would never let him give up being a commander.

When the doors opened, his anger carried him down the corridor until he reached the firing range.

"I'm off duty in five minutes," said the master warrant officer when Sawyer entered. "We're closed ... oh, sorry, sir. I didn't know it was you."

The room was large, utilitarian, with ten ranges stretching away from where

Sawyer stood. A locked box hung on a wall protecting Space Fleet regulation weapons and ammunition, and a small desk behind a plexiglass screen took up the space to Sawyer's left. But it was the lock box to his right that he wanted. He walked over to it as he waved to the master warrant. "Take off early. I'll close up after myself."

"Thank you, sir, but … uh … sir, those weapons in there aren't available unless your designated to a mission. I'm sure you knew that, but it's just there's no team registered on my manifest right now." He waited a moment before continuing. "Maybe I'll just stay awhile longer until you're done, sir. You know, safety regulations and all that."

Sawyer shrugged as he swiped a hand over the panel beside the box and a control pad opened. He keyed in his father's code, knowing his father wouldn't much care that he was using it for weapons training, and the locker opened.

The master warrant stepped back to his desk. "I'll open range five for you, sir."

Sawyer scanned the antique pistols, searching for one that would give him the most satisfaction. He chose the Smith and Wesson Model 3 Revolver and grabbed a canister of .44 calibre ammunition—an American "Old West" classic. Set up at one of the centre ranges, he turned back to the master warrant. "Open all the ranges."

"I can't do that. Regulations …"

Sawyer walked over to the desk, entered his father's code again, and opened all the ranges. "You can still leave if you want, Master Warrant. No use in us both getting in trouble."

The master warrant shook his head as he took his seat behind his desk. "As long as you sign for my overtime, sir, I'll stay as long as you want."

"Done," Sawyer said with a nod, then he returned to his station where he loaded the six-shot pistol. He fired four shots downrange. The discharge of each round thumped in every hollow cavity of his body, and combined with the stench of sulphur it invigorated him to keep shooting. This is what he needed, to feel the anger of a bullet leaving its chamber. To smell it, taste bitter sulphur on his lips, to hear the crack and feel violence explode in every bone of his body. It was this or he'd beat the shit out of somebody.

"Born to be your legacy! Fuck you!" Sawyer fired the last two rounds then dumped the contents of the ammo canister across the ledge in front of him and reloaded. He felt strong, powerful, as he decimated each humanoid target screen. "Why'd you even create me when you can do everything yourself! Better than me! I'm just a fucking tool!"

After he fired the last shot, the room reeked of acrid smoke and the master warrant was covering his ears. "Jesus Christ, sir! Those screens weren't set for fixed-mass! Do you have any idea how much those things cost! It's not coming out of my overtime pay, sir! And I've reported this, so you know. I'll take some heat, but not this much, sir."

Sawyer leaned forward, hands braced on the ledge, and he took deep breaths to control his still unsatiated anger. He hadn't meant for the master warrant to get in trouble, but sometimes he couldn't control his own anger.

"Lieutenant!"

Sawyer stood and turned when he realized it wasn't the master warrant's voice. "Commander Beaumont."

"Thank you, Master Warrant, I'll take it from here." The master warrant left the room.

Commander Beaumont gave him the same look he did after their London mission. Sawyer glanced over his shoulder at the smashed targets, now realizing what he'd done. "Sir, I can explain."

"I don't need an explanation. It's evident what happened here."

Sawyer's head fell forward, his hands rested on his hips. Could he talk to Beaumont? Would he understand? "My father called me into his office and told me I had to get ready to command."

"Is that what you want?"

Want? Sawyer had rendered decisions before, but being asked what he wanted, this was new. Unexpected. He thought about it a moment then replied, "Yes. Yes, sir."

Beaumont moved closer to Sawyer. "I've known the rear admiral long enough to recognize his disposition. That first day on the Earth-Lander I purposely mentioned his name to gauge your reaction, and the look on your face told me everything I needed to know. But you've come a long way since that day, Sawyer. I don't want you backsliding."

Sawyer looked into his commander's eyes and suddenly felt the need to tell this man the truth. "I hear his name and every childhood nightmare screams through my mind. Did you know I've only ever had one friend before you and Soko? He left after the Academy; the Rangers sent him off on another ship.

Probably my father's doing. Before that, my whole life was spent on Ranger bases around the system. I started training when I was three! I was running kilometres every morning since I was four! I knew the Ranger Creed and handbook inside and out since I was five! I graduated the Academy younger than any other cadet! I've never been part of a team before. I've always had to look out for myself. And if I ever complain, slow down … there's penalties."

"Stop thinking about your damn father! He's not here, only you and I are. Besides, your father only wants you to be the best."

"He doesn't want me to be the best! He needs me to be the best! He has some convoluted agenda that I have to follow in his footsteps, be more, better, than everyone else! Why do you think I'm a Spawn? To give me that extra advantage! To make me look better so he can look better! Every time I achieve something, it's a medal on his chest, not mine."

Beaumont put a hand on his shoulder, but Sawyer pushed it off, afraid what human contact might cause him to do when he was this angry.

"Your father trained you to be the best. Now take that and move on with your life. Stop living like he's always over your shoulder. His training is here, it's inside you, but everything else beneath that skin and bone is you. And that's who I let stay on my team, not your father's toy soldier."

Beaumont reached for him again, but when Sawyer pulled back Beaumont grabbed him by both shoulders. "Listen to me, Kai. I get it. Your life sucks. Now suck it up and be a soldier. I've never seen a crack in that armour of yours until now. Keep it that way. Because I don't want to be anywhere near you if that happens out in the field. Do you hear me? You're a loaded gun waiting to fire. You have to find a way to deal with your personal issues …," he looked over his shoulder at the target screens, "in a less destructive way. Save the real anger for when it's needed."

"Got it. Ten-year Ranger, not an FNG."

"Sawyer, answer me this one question. What do you *really* want?"

Again, he was pressed for an answer to this strange question. "I want … I want to be the best commander out here so I can protect the timeline and save lives from being destroyed by Time Runners' selfish reasons."

"You prioritized saving lives."

"Actually, I think I prioritized command first."

"Yeah, but your first instinct is to say what your father wants to hear. Your real motivation is the second thing you said: protect the future, save lives. That's who you really are. What the soldier on my team represents. Remember that the next time you feel like firing yourself off. Now go. I'll take care of this."

10.

SAWYER felt hollow. Cold. Like a blank round fired from a Stormguard as he marched through the station's corridors without an intended destination. He'd tried to satiate his anger on the range, nearly bared his entire soul to his commander and gotten the master warrant disciplined, and he knew that if his father found out about the damage he'd caused to the target screens he'd have hell to pay. His limbs shook, though he knew it wasn't because he needed to eat. He still wanted to hit something.

When he turned left and found himself outside the station's med-bay, he stopped short. "Why the hell did I come here?"

The double doors slid open to reveal Aurora standing on the other side. "Kai … Lieutenant Sawyer …"

"It's actually lieutenant commander now."

"Oh. Congratulations." She stepped outside the med-bay into the corridor. "Were you on your way in, Lieutenant Commander?"

Sawyer looked into the med-bay, still wondering why his subconscious had brought him here, then looked back at Aurora. "No. Actually, I think I came here for you."

Aurora's cheeks flushed, highlighting her youthful complexion. "Me? I thought you wanted nothing to do with me …"

"I don't."

Aurora frowned. "Well, if you've come here to berate me some more, then you might as well leave."

She turned away and Sawyer reached out and grabbed her arm. *Am I really going to do this?* But he couldn't stop himself. "When are you off duty?"

With a deeper frown, she replied, "I'm off now. I was just leaving. Why?"

Sawyer wasn't hungry for food, but he asked anyway. "We never got a chance to finish … so, do you want to get something to eat?"

"This is not where I thought this conversation was going."

Neither did Sawyer.

She stared at him, then her smile slowly broadened as her gaze moved up and down his uniform, her stare finally coming to rest on his name plate pinned to his left chest.

Sawyer smiled back, hoping she'd understand that this could be a mutually beneficial arrangement. They both wanted something the other one had.

"I could eat," she said.

Coffee and sandwiches went down fast in the station's mess, without much chatter, until Sawyer finally asked, "So, are you staying in the medical barracks?"

Aurora's smile was coy. "I can afford my own apartment. It's not quite the level I'm used to, it's a bit small and bland, but it is private."

Sawyer knew this was wrong, but he wanted it and it seemed she did as well. "Are you sure?"

She rose from the table, glanced around the busy mess, and took his hand. "I want it, you want it. We both get what we want."

Sawyer wondered how much he really did want this to happen, or if he was just looking to feel something, anything, other than anger. But when Aurora pulled him to his feet, he didn't resist, and when they left the mess he found his arm draped across her shoulders and it didn't bother him as much as he thought it would.

THE next morning Sawyer woke in Aurora's bed, his uniform shirt loose and baggy on her very feminine form as she stood at the foot end watching him wake up. She pulled the shirt collar up to her nose and inhaled. "It smells like you. Can I keep it?"

Crumpled on the floor beside the bed was the rest of his uniform, including a Time Ranger T-shirt. He leaned over, scooped it up, and tossed it to her. "Take this instead. It's kind of against regulations to give your actual uniform away."

She caught it and changed shirts immediately, moving in a way Sawyer suspected was on purpose, slow and methodical to garner his attention.

"Fits much better anyway," she said as she sat on the edge of the bed. "Now you should go. I'm meeting my study friends in two hours."

No small talk, no aftermath cuddling nor lazing in the bed. Sawyer smiled and nodded back at her as he got dressed. Aurora understood the arrangement.

"You were pretty tense last night," she said. "How are you feeling now?"

Sawyer contemplated this a moment then replied, "I'm no longer angry, so thanks."

"You're welcome. Anytime. But just so you know, my sister is getting married soon and I'll need a date. And with a Sawyer on my arm, I'll be sure to impress. Besides, this was kind of fun."

"Just give me the date," he said and left the apartment.

11.

AS Sawyer and his team made their way through the main hub of Mediterrania Geo-Dome, one of Earth's nine main space stations located in the belt, he breathed in the fresh-scented recycled air. Since this geo-dome represented the Mediterranean climate of Earth's Old World nine climate zones prior to the asteroid war, hints of lilies, salt water, and coconut tinted the air while bright colours of shop signs, mainly in the blue-green spectrum, broke up the smooth white walls and floors of the station. Citizens ranging in dress from business attire to casual strolled through the hub, oblivious to the three disguised Time Rangers walking amongst them.

Sawyer adjusted the belt of his Acclimation acquired Space Fleet Regular uniform. "Without the overpopulation of our time, this station seems empty."

Storefronts of restaurants, shops, and businesses lined the main street of the station's hub, all open for commerce, unlike on Earth where almost every third store was out of business or illegally being kept open for black-market affairs.

"It's 2145," said Soko. "Give it some years and this place will be as crowded as a bar on World Unity Day."

"If you two are done gawking at the station," said Beaumont, "we have a mission waiting for us. We've got three days, but I want it handled in two. I plan on spending some R and R on one of the station domes when we're done. Mediterrania Station has been voted top place to live for the past five years, and I want to see what all the commotion is about."

"I hear you can actually surf on the top dome," said Sawyer. "It's mainly a beach. Like the ones in the Republic of Australia. The bottom dome of the station is designed more like the Republics of Italy and Greece. It's expensive to live here even in our time. President Crow actually has a residence on the beach when she comes up from Nunavut."

"I hear she's on her way to Mars, some mining dispute on Deimos," said Soko.

President Ahnah Crow, the current president of the Utopian government, won by a landslide during the last election. Her platform ran primarily on cleaning up Earth. Sawyer had voted for her but was still waiting to see the results of her claims for a cleaner Utopia.

Being a Time Ranger meant Sawyer got to see the world before it nearly destroyed itself with commercialism, pollution, and war. When the countries finally united and fell under one central government calling itself Utopia, technology, shared intellectualism, and progress increased exponentially. Space was no longer the final frontier; it became home to humans. But with the expansion into space, Earth almost became forgotten. With people so interested in living on stations or in the colonies, the problems on Earth became an afterthought for the government. But now that Crow was in power, she planned on changing that. She wanted to make Earth home again for humans.

Sawyer doubted he'd see that in his lifetime. At least, not in his *actual* lifetime.

"Stephanie Winters wants to meet her parents," said Beaumont, bringing Sawyer's attention back on the mission. "Her parents were mugged and killed outside this station's casino. Her dad died instantly, and her mother died several hours later in a hospital after giving birth to Miss Winters."

"Those guys on Nexus Station nearly missed this," stated Soko. "It took Overwatch hours to pinpoint the Deviation Point after the Point spit out the HCA. But it's here at the casino."

Beaumont cleared his throat. "So, we catch her outside the casino before she goes in to see them. No problem. An easy snatch and grab and then we return her to 2197 where she belongs, and where she can't contaminate the timeline further."

"Our scan-tacts won't be much use in finding her," said Sawyer. "Everyone's aura will be red on a space station. It'll be like searching for a proton in a neutron star. Impossible."

Beaumont shook his head. "But we know what she looks like. Overwatch provided pics of her, remember? For now, I'll sweep the casino, you two wait here. Maybe Miss Winters will be doing her own reconnaissance inside, and we can end this sooner than later."

After he left, Sawyer turned to Soko. "What if our Runner decides to save her parents from the mugging? How much would really change if her parents lived?"

Soko grunted, crossed his arms. "It's hard to say. Historical relevance hasn't been determined for most people born of this century. But if she does do something different from what Overwatch predicted, then things are going to get really complicated. We might have some cleaning up to do if they live. But we're the best, so that won't happen."

"You mean kill the parents ourselves?"

"It might come to that, yes. You up for it?"

Sawyer shrugged. "It's no problem for me."

Soko studied his face, his eyebrows arched. "After the *Titanic* mission I thought you might, you know, not be so okay with killing anymore?"

"It's not like these people mean anything to me. And it's not like it would be another mass execution. No, I'm good."

Soko shook his head. "Are all you Spawns this sadistic, or is it just you?"

Beaumont returned a few minutes later to report that Miss Winters wasn't in the casino. "Who knows where she is. This station is two kilometres long with over fifty-thousand people living here. Do you know anything more, Soko? Historically speaking."

"According to history, not a lot was happening here and now. Only the mugging of our Time Runner's parents and a few minor disputes. Even the Space Fleet Regulars garrisoned here weren't doing anything but training for the day. Which is why Acclimation chose this disguise. It was a pretty quiet time. I have no idea where our Miss Winters may be … Holy shit! That's Dr. Jackson going into the casino. Damn it! I forgot about this!"

Soko smacked his forehead. "How did I forget this! Fuck, how did Overwatch miss this! Dr. Jackson made an experimental trip to this day when he was testing the Nexus Point. Like I said, it was a day where nothing really happened, so he found it fitting to visit."

Beaumont stepped closer to the entrance. "Shit, it is him. This complicates things."

Like a child meeting their superhero, Sawyer stood aghast. If it weren't for Dr. Jackson, the Time Rangers wouldn't exist. In fact, time travel wouldn't have happened. "Would it be so wrong to go and meet him?"

"Probably," replied Beaumont. "Damn if I don't want to, though. But I think it's safe to say we're better off not making contact with the doctor. Like I said, I want this mission short and clean. Any contact with the man may interfere with both the time-line *and* my chances of getting a little R and R. No one is to engage him, understood?"

"Hey, look there!" Soko pointed again to the entranceway of the casino. "There's the guy from the pic Overwatch gave us. The one who killed Miss Winters parents."

Sawyer watched the mugger scan his palm at the casino's registration. "If Miss Winters found access to casino records, she'd know her parent's murderer was here tonight."

Beaumont closed his eyes and blew out a breath. "Don't say that. 'Cause if she's here to take out her parents' murderer instead of just seeing her parents, I swear I'm going to rip Overwatch a new one when this is done."

"Would she actually try and save her parents by *killing* their murderer?" asked Soko.

"If we know that …" Sawyer's voice trailed off when a strange smell triggered something in his brain. Hints of chemicals he hadn't noticed before filtered through his nares, and he tasted bitter metal on his tongue. "Do you guys smell anything?"

"Yes, lots of things. Why?" asked Beaumont.

Sawyer's brows pulled together as he gazed steadily around the promenade, looking for the source of the strange smell.

"You have something, don't you?" asked Soko. "Your Spawny senses are picking something up."

"I'm not sure." Sawyer stepped toward the casino, stopped and sniffed, then took another step. *Ozone. Bitter apple.* "Shit, it's Hellion gas. It's coming from the casino!" He launched himself forward.

Beaumont's arm across his chest stopped him cold. "Stop. There's no alarms. Are you sure you smell Hellion gas?"

"Yes! It's Hellion gas."

"Cassie, is the station's filtration system picking anything up?" Beaumont looked pensive for a moment as he listened to his AI's personal response, to which only he could hear in his head. "She reports the station's systems have been turned off," he finally reported.

Sawyer stared through the floor-to-ceiling glass windows of the casino. "More evidence she's about to do something drastic. Oh shit, she's attacking the whole damn place to kill one person."

"And Dr. Jackson is in there," said Soko.

Sawyer shoved Beaumont's arm away. "We need to get Dr. Jackson out of there! Everyone out of there! Before the first victims drop dead."

People inside the casino were coughing, some holding their throats while others wiped streams of tears from their cheeks and eyes as they crowded the narrow entrance. Sawyer's heart raced as he scanned the panicked crowd for Dr. Jackson. He saw him near the back of the casino and ran forward, but again, a strong hand pulled him back.

"Hold him, Soko."

"No! Commander!" screamed Sawyer. "I can handle the gas better than you! Just like the virus. I might be built to withstand this. Let me go in."

"Do you know that for a fact, Lieutenant Commander?"

"No ... but the chances ..."

Beaumont held up a hand. "Stop talking, Sawyer. Do as your commander orders, for once." He nodded at Soko then turned into the casino and disappeared amongst the crowd.

People piled out of the casino, squeezing themselves through the small opening. Through the glass front of the casino, Sawyer kept his eyes trained on his commander making his way through the crowd. *If you're not out here in three seconds, Commander, I swear I'm coming in after you!*

A moment later his commander was pushing back through the casino crowd toward the front entrance, shoving a sputtering and coughing Dr. Jackson in front of him. Sawyer ran to the entrance, arriving as Dr. Jackson stumbled out and the thick glass doors closed, locking Commander Beaumont in the gas-filled casino. Sawyer pried his fingers in the seams of the door but couldn't get enough leverage to open them again.

"It'll take more than your strength to get these doors open," said Beaumont, his voice muffled by the glass barrier. "They're sealed for emergencies now. The geo-dome's security has kicked in. These are security doors, my friend."

"No!" cried Sawyer. "No. We'll get you out. There's another way." He stood back to survey the outside of the casino for windows and other doors that were maybe on higher levels.

Soko put a hand on his shoulder. "This is the only way in or out that we can get to in time. Any other entrance would be too far. The commander would be ..."

"No!" Sawyer slammed his fists on the glass doors.

Beaumont coughed, doubled over, and braced his hands on his knees. "It's all right, Kai."

"No. There's nothing right about this."

"The future is secure."

Sawyer pressed his palm against the glass security door. "You are the future. We all are. We need to protect the team."

"I did."

Beaumont fell to his knees, and Sawyer could see the stagnated rise and fall of his commander's back as oxygen failed to reach his lungs. Blood dripped from his lips and pooled on the floor by his now purple-blue hands.

Sawyer slid to the floor. "It should have been me. I might have been able to survive the gas …"

"No one can survive Hellion gas," said Soko quietly. "Come on. We don't have to watch this. We'll come back to retrieve the commander when it's …"

Sawyer turned to him. "And you called me sadistic!"

"I'm burying every emotion I have right now so I can do what I have to do."

Sawyer's eyes were burning and his jaw was spasming when he looked at Beaumont. Sawyer held it all in, causing a knot to form in his throat.

Beaumont, now lying on the floor amongst the other choking patrons, pointed a finger at him. "You have a future. Go … commander you … meant to be."

"But …" Sawyer's jaw clenched harder, and he wasn't sure he could hold it back any longer.

"Go …" said Beaumont, then he took his last breath.

Sawyer squeezed his eyes shut. Each breath he took burned in his chest. *Bury it. Deal with this later. Get your ass up. Don't think about this, think about the Time Runner. She's still out there.*

He pushed away from the door in time to see Space Fleet Regulars rush the scene. Sawyer didn't look back. He couldn't look back, despite every instinct. "Finish the mission. The timeline has been compromised, we need to minimize the fallout."

"Are you ready?" asked Soko.

Sawyer swallowed his grief, pushed it as far down as he could. "Let's go catch this bitch."

12.

BEAUMONT'S funeral was held on Nexus Station three days later when the *Spectre* returned to September 16, 2197. Stephanie Winters was in custody, which left Sawyer brimming in anger. She deserved death for what she did. Yes, capturing her maintained the timeline's intergrity, and Soko and he were able to recover much of the collateral damage over the next few days stuck on the geo-dome, but that didn't matter. Not this time. Sawyer didn't care about any of that as he stood in his father's office.

"How did this simple mission turn into such a fucking disaster?" demanded his father. "What was Beaumont thinking going into that casino? He should have known better."

Sawyer looked his father in the eyes. *You asshole! Beaumont died! That's what's important! And now I'm stuck here staring at you again.*

"Tragic deaths occurred because you and your team couldn't save all the citizens in the casino," continued his father. "Fortunately, Dr. Jackson was saved, but at what cost? Beaumont got himself killed, and don't get me started on the repercussions of the other deaths that day! Mediterrania Station is a hellhole now! What used to be prime real estate is now nothing more than a hollowed-out husk drifting in space! Do you have any idea how many businesses disappeared? Gone. Just gone without a trace! It's like the damn Albatross Incident all over again!"

The rear admiral stared at Sawyer. "This was not supposed to happen! And the record will demonstrate you had involvement in this. If Commander Beaumont were still alive, I'd send his ass to the Regulars for letting this mission get so out of hand."

Sawyer forced his words through gritted teeth. "Before this happened you praised him as the most elite Ranger in the unit. He saved my life on this mission. I wanted to go in instead of him and he ordered me back! If you were any real kind of father, you might actually be grateful I'm still standing here in front of you!"

Sawyer felt about to pass out. He'd never expressed himself so freely to his father. But now that the dam had opened, he couldn't stop himself. "According to you I can't do anything right! You wanted me to die on that mission, didn't you? So you would have an excuse to go build yourself another Spawn, stronger and smarter than the one you fucked up your first time around!"

"Hold your voice! No, your genetics would have saved you from that gas attack. I don't want you to die. I'm hard on you because I need you to become the greatest damn commander the Time Rangers have ever seen. That can't happen if you're dead."

Sawyer felt his blood drop into his boots. *I can survive Hellion gas?*

"You look pale." His father passed him a bottle of cyto-juice he kept on hand in a small fridge.

Sawyer threw it at the wall. "Fuck you."

The slap came from the right, knocking Sawyer's head sideways. He ignored the sting and stared back at his father, every part of him itching to retaliate. "Fuck. You."

The rear admiral shoved Sawyer back until he hit the wall. "You're a Sawyer. Act like one. I see that jaw of yours tensing. Control it. Control that anger! I thought sending you to Commander Beaumont was a good idea, but it seems you formed some sort of emotional connection with him. And that is not acceptable. Sawyers think with their heads, not their hearts."

I could end you right now if I wanted to! But as his father stood inches from him, Sawyer saw his reflection bounce back to him from the same eyes he himself had. *I can't be who you are,* he told himself as he let his fists unclench. *I don't want to be you.* He slowly released his father's grip from his uniform and gently pushed him away. "Yes, sir. Anything you say, sir."

His father stepped back to his desk. After a long drink from his coffee, he looked back at Sawyer. "The new Ranger ship will be ready in just over a year. If I have anything to say about it, it will be your ship. Prepare for Command School. You leave in four months, and the surgery to implant your AI is in six. Until then, your new team awaits. And you should show me some respect when you talk to me. I created you, and I can do with you as I want. You have no faith. Good things will happen if you would just listen and follow my orders. I need someone out there I can trust." He paused and looked thoughtfully at him. "Kai, the future needs a hero, and it *will* be another Sawyer."

Then we're screwed. 'Cause I'm not the man you thought I'd be.

His father came around his desk and put a hand on Sawyer's shoulder. "You've been training for this your whole life. It's what you want. It's what you need. You're designed to command, and you'll do humanity proud."

Designed. What a comforting word. Sawyer turned to leave then glanced back at his father. "You can't make me take command, sir. I won't do it. Not now. I'm not willing to let people die who'd be looking to me for protection. I'm not ready yet."

"I've always told you people die. Some need to die, and it's not your responsibility to save everyone."

"But sometimes it is."

13.

P RESIDENT Kennedy must die!" Sawyer emphasized the undeniable point of the argument they'd been having for the past two hours. He sat on the bench of his new team's Earth-Lander, looking into the faces of his teammates. It was their fourth mission together.

"I repeat," he said when no one responded. "John F. Kennedy must die. That's the mission, sir. If we bag the mission, we're not just bagging our careers, but possibly the future we've sworn to protect."

Commander Awenda shook his head. "I'm sick of this bullshit. I'm sick of the Rangers ordering me to let the wrong people die. President Kennedy lives."

"We only have one chance at this, sir. Do you have any idea what this could do to the timeline?"

"Who cares about the damn timeline! It's fucked up, and Space Fleet, the Time Rangers, and all the hapless citizens of the twenty-second century can have it. That damn Nexus Point can implode, for all I care. Dr. Jackson should've been tossed out an airlock for finding that thing! It's nothing but trouble."

"I agree," said Specialist Noble, his new historian. "The Cold War of the twentieth century may have ended earlier. Humanity's launch into time travel probably would have gone a lot smoother. What if Overwatch's projections were wrong? They are far from perfect. I say we let the Time Runner we're chasing win this one. Let this Runner stop Oswald from killing Kennedy."

Sawyer couldn't believe what they were proposing. Overwatch's adjustment projections predicted that saving Kennedy would cause astronomical changes to the time continuum. Everything Noble listed would happen, but at the expense of losing their moon colony and half of the Republic of Russia. And allowing the future to change went against everything the Time Rangers … what Beaumont … stood for.

Grunting, Sawyer grabbed the Carcan rifle off the bench beside him and rested it across his knees. "This isn't right, Commander."

His commander stood, tall and official in his black 1963 Secret Service costume. "You'll do as ordered, Lieutenant Commander. We're a team and we stick together. Now stand down. You can watch our backs, that's all. Overwatch determined the Runner we are here to stop will make his move at the Depository. That's where the Deviation Point occurred. The specialist and I will proceed there and guarantee the Runner executes the job he came here to do and make sure he doesn't leave that room. Don't take the shot when Oswald misses. Let history believe Oswald *attempted* to kill Kennedy from the Depository. You just keep an eye on *us* in case the real Secret Service shows up. Stop them before they enter the building if you have to, so we have a chance to make our egress. We won't be able to return to the future after this, but you can still take the Earth-Lander and head back."

Specialist Noble stood next to the commander. "Letting the Time Runner win this one is a *moral* obligation, in my book. Besides, being stuck here wouldn't be so bad. The sixties were one of Earth's most infamous cultural decades. Civil rights, Vietnam … We can dance naked at Woodstock, *and* we'll still be alive to watch NASA's first shuttle launch. So many great historical moments we'll get to experience firsthand."

No. I need to kill Kennedy if you don't stop the Runner, thought Sawyer. *Not for me, but for the timeline. It needs to be preserved, which means John F. Kennedy needs to die. Despite the Runner's motives, he needs to be brought to justice back in 2197 for even attempting this level of historical contamination.*

But Sawyer held his tongue, as they were probably talking out of frustration. As long as Sawyer had worked with Commander Awenda, Awenda had shown he could be a level-headed man. The commander typically ran hot with emotions at first, but with time he usually cooled down when reason presented itself. On a mission to 2017, Awenda had interfered with President Trump's campaign, but after his election he'd stood down and let the forty-fifth American president live. Sawyer believed Awenda would do so again. Cool down when the time came, do the right thing and let Oswald take the historical shot.

Commander Awenda ordered Sam, his personal AI, to show them vid outside the Earth-Lander, which displayed a live feed of an empty hill on the screen beside the back hatch. "It's clear. Everyone's down on the street. No one should see us leaving."

A moment later, Sawyer and his team were standing atop a grassy knoll in the Dealey Plaza of downtown Dallas, Texas.

The Earth-Lander's mask shimmered once as it re-adjusted to the disturbance of their departure. To an outside observer, three men were standing on a small hill. Once Sawyer engaged his battle uniforms' personal mask it looked like two men standing on a hill.

Sawyer searched for his best line of sight as his commander and historian strode down the hill toward the Texas School Board Depository. Then Sawyer activated the permeable transparent computer screen on his left forearm wherein the clock in the upper corner indicated twenty-two minutes until the main event. Soon President Kennedy, the Texas Governor, and their wives would enter the plaza.

There's no way they're letting Kennedy live … Awenda will cool down.

At 1228 hours central standard time, the motorcade entered the plaza.

Sawyer pulled back the action on his rifle. "Our problems are manmade, therefore they may be solved by man. And man can be as big as he wants," he said, as he dropped a round into the chamber. "No problem of human destiny is beyond human beings."

From his position on top the grassy knoll he had a full view of Dealey Plaza, where the avenues and boulevards were peppered with twentieth-century American citizens excitedly awaiting the arrival of their thirty-fifth president. Sawyer shook his head at them. "Inspiring words, Mr. President, but unfortunately …" He dropped supine onto the warm afternoon grass. "Your words have never been truer."

Sawyer peered through the scope, breathed calm and slow, and let the afternoon breeze blow through his short black hair. It tickled his nose and brought with it the bittersweet scent of grass so sorely missed in his twenty-second century. When John F. Kennedy appeared in his crosshairs with a bright smile on his face as he waved at the crowd, Sawyer slid his finger from the guard to the trigger … just in case his team *didn't* follow orders. "You might have lived to be the best president in the history of the United States, maybe in all the world, sir, but history has already spoken. Today, I am your destiny."

Twelve-thirty hours flashed on Sawyer's screen. A single shot rang out in Dealey Plaza. But unlike the dictates of history, it was Jacqueline Kennedy who clutched her neck as her pink pillbox hat went flying.

"You fuckers." Sawyer squeezed the trigger and John F. Kennedy's brain splattered across the trunk of the black town car. Sawyer stood immediately and retreated back into the Earth-Lander, where he opened the weapon's locker and replaced his rifle with his personal-issue Stormguard. Mask still engaged, Sawyer left the Earth-Lander. Per regulations, nothing could be left in the past, especially team members. Sawyer needed to retrieve them, by force if need be.

The grassy knoll was empty, with the real Secret Service busy clearing the plaza, so there was no immediate danger as Sawyer walked down the hill, armed and masked. He hoped to catch his commander, the historian, and the Runner before they left the Depository. *Let the police catch Oswald later—seventy minutes from now, to be exact. And just like in history, he'll probably deny the assassination.* Sawyer laughed. Turns out, Oswald *was* innocent of murdering Kennedy. But since he'd had the intentions of actually doing it, Sawyer didn't care that he'd take the fall.

By the time Sawyer reached the Depository, the street was afire with emergency police lights and sirens. People were still scrambling, or on their knees sobbing at the possible loss of their beloved president. Sawyer wasn't bothered by any of it, for his anger was focussed on his teammates who were hopefully still up on the sixth floor. Kennedy was already on his way to Parkland Memorial Hospital, along with his wife, but all that was behind Sawyer now. He'd done his job. Now his concern was cleaning up the mess his new commander had created.

Two steps into the front lobby of the Depository, the elevator doors in front of Sawyer opened. Struggling between three armed Secret Service agents was Commander Awenda, cuffed and forcibly being shoved toward the front doors of the building to the awaiting squad car outside.

"Kennedy is dead, so I know you're here, Sawyer!" cried Commander Awenda. "Help me! I'm still your commander, and I'm giving you an order!"

"Who the hell are you talking to?" asked one of the officers. "You have the right to remain silent, remember?"

"I know you're here! Stop this!" screamed Awenda as he was dragged through the lobby.

Sawyer yearned to fire his Stormguard. Violence nursed his raw, splintered nerves when tension threatened to overwhelm him. Rage as savage as a spring thunderstorm coursed through his veins. He wanted to hurt someone. Anyone. *You were going to destroy the timeline!*

The front doors of the Depository closed behind Awenda and his police escort. Sawyer had missed his chance. But from what he remembered from the old history, Oswald was taken to the city jail after being arrested for killing the president. It stood to reason that in this new history, that was where the police would take his commander now.

Sawyer had four days until the Nexus Point's boomerang event, so he had plenty of time to deal with his commander. But first, he needed to secure the scene upstairs. Specialist Noble, the Time Runner, and possibly Oswald, still required his attention.

On the sixth floor he discovered their motionless bodies lying on the floor in pools of their own blood; bullet holes in the back of each of their heads as proof they were killed by the Secret Service who were still securing the scene. Sawyer was fine with Oswald's death, but he had hoped to secure Noble and the Runner.

This is not going to look good on my mission report. Fuck, this mission should have gone smoother. It's a goddamned cluster-fuck! Seriously, Beaumont, where the fuck are you when I need you the most?

Sawyer glanced up with a sigh. *Yeah … sorry.*

For security reasons, Sawyer moved the Earth-Lander from the grassy knoll to the roof of police headquarters. It was a tight fit sliding the Earth-Lander between the hydro poles and vent shafts scattered on the roof, but precise piloting wasn't difficult for someone whose father had him flying since he was five.

Sawyer sat at the helm. "Sam," he said aloud to invoke the communication's AI. "Cut communications with the commander and link in to the police radios. IDENT code, 10706. And let me know if they move the commander."

"I have already heard word, Lieutenant Commander Sawyer. Commander Awenda is being transferred for a psychiatric evaluation."

"What? Why?"

"It appears the commander has been ranting about the presence of an invisible man watching him. I presume he means you. The police will be escorting Commander Awenda through the basement."

"I'll rendezvous with them there." Sawyer went to the lock box and pulled out his Stormguard.

Masked, he headed down to the basement where he stood waiting against a concrete wall, far enough back so his mass wouldn't interfere with the gathering crowd. The smell of damp concrete and numerous efficacies of body odour wafting in the air, pungent and unavoidable in the closed space, grated on Sawyer's nerves. His anger started to rise, and his commander hadn't even showed up yet. He reminded himself of Beaumont's words: *Save it for when it's needed.*

To his right, blended into a crowd of men in drab suits, stood Jack Ruby. Sawyer smiled at him. *I guess we can throw out the conspiracy theories. It doesn't matter that it's not Oswald; you just want to kill Kennedy's assassin.* Sawyer's smile broadened. *I'm over here, dipshit. You're going after the wrong one.*

When the precinct's double doors opened and the small escort of police entered with Commander Awenda between them, Sawyer pushed off from the wall. Between two officers, his commander was being dragged, his wide eyes frantically searching for who he and Sawyer knew was there waiting. When Awenda's attention locked on Jack Ruby, he backpedalled and squirmed in the officer's grasp. "Sawyer! I know you're there! Please, stop this! He's going to kill me!"

"Shut up," cried one of the officers as he yanked the commander forward.

Sawyer didn't know why, he couldn't put reason behind his decision, perhaps maliciousness, perhaps hate, or perhaps he was simply still angry that his mentor had died and he hadn't had the excuse to release his pent up anger, but he suddenly stepped back from the crowd and unmasked.

Commander Awenda saw him and smiled like someone snatched from the clutches of death.

***

SAWYER'S commander and historian had betrayed him. Betrayed the Time Rangers. There was no loyalty with this team, and he felt no need to feel bad about what he'd done or didn't do. He'd done what he'd been expected to do, what he knew was right. He'd cleaned up the mess. Beaumont would have been proud.

"So this is how it is," he said as he sat in the Earth-Lander. He leaned his head back and closed his eyes. "Where's a good commander when ya need one, Sam?"

"I require context. Who do you believe is not a good commander?"

Sawyer opened his eyes and stared past the skyscrapers of downtown Dallas and out to the horizon. "I thought things would be like they were with Beaumont ..." His voice drifted off, and he scrubbed a hand down his face. What was he thinking trying to have a heart-to-heart conversation with an AI? "Never mind, Sam. We can't leave any tech behind, so disintegrate the commander's AI implant while I get us ready for take-off."

Sawyer didn't want to spend any more time here than he needed. He would wait for the Nexus Point's boomerang up in space where he didn't have to look at Dallas anymore. He wanted the quiet, peaceful presence of the stars surrounding him before being assigned to another new team and another new commander. One he was certain wouldn't live up to Beaumont's caliber.

14.

SAWYER stood in the doorway of his childhood room as thoughts and memories swirled in his head. Until he was assigned a new team, there was nowhere for him to stay other than his father's apartment on Nexus Station. Once a refuge from his father, and where he'd suffered alone the growing pains of being a Spawn, his old bedroom now felt like a cold tomb, reminding him of a tumultuous childhood. A faded poster still hung next to the bed, concealing a dent in the wall from a well-placed fist. It hadn't been the first argument they'd had, just the first time his father swung at him. Sawyer had been six.

He dropped his bag and barrack box at the foot of the bed, sat down and scrubbed at his face with both hands before flopping onto his back. On the ceiling were tiny glow-in-the-dark star and moon stickers that glowed a pale yellow. His father had arranged them on the ceiling when Sawyer was two years old and had purposely placed the largest sticker, representing the Nexus Point Actual, directly above the pillow.

Sawyer remembered seeking out the Nexus Point sticker every night and dreaming of his molecules disintegrating and reintegrating in another time, another land where he was no longer a tool for his father's agenda. And where and when he had friends, went on vacations, and played on an Earth where the sun always shone and the air was crisp and clean.

When the stars and moons above him blended together and his eyes were tired, he fell asleep, only to wake when his alarm blared at oh-six-hundred the next morning. After a quick shower, he ate, dressed in civvies, and sat in the apartment's living room.

Over the next few days he went out a few times to the gym and to the firing range. He drank a lot of coffee, amongst other things, argued with his father, and even called Aurora Heikkinen. She'd arrived thirty minutes later while the rear admiral was out.

Naked under a long trench coat, Aurora had held Sawyer's face in her hands and stared into his eyes. "I know why I'm here and I don't care."

"Good. 'Cause I need this right now."

She'd left the next morning with a smile on her face and a promise to return later that night.

Sawyer had needed distraction, something to keep his mind off the last mission. And like Aurora had said, it was fun.

Sawyer sat on his father's couch again, heels crossed on the table, while the vid-screen reporting the news of a worker's strike at a bio-tactical manufacturer on Earth played quietly in the background. Sawyer drank straight from the bottle of whiskey he'd procured from his father's locked cabinet. The burn no longer bothered him; he enjoyed it now.

Hanging on the wall beside the couch was a pic of him at his Academy graduation. In it, Sawyer stood tall at centre stage with all his classmates in a row behind him. He'd felt so proud that day, ready to take on the universe. He got off the couch and went to the pic. When the room stopped spinning—he drank more than he thought—he leaned in to find Hawk in the back row. Sawyer wondered if he should try and contact him.

After a long drink of his whiskey, he sat back on the couch. *Maybe if I take a command I can request him on my team?*

His gaze caught the pic hanging on the wall above the vid-screen. It was of his father at the Time Ranger's inauguration. His father stood so tall in the pic, centre stage to the highest-ranked Space Fleet officers in a row behind him. Sawyer picked up a cushion and threw it at the pic. It didn't budge. His father had secured it so strongly that it would never fall; it would always hang there where Sawyer could see what he was supposed to become.

Am I even good enough to command? Be what Beaumont thought I could be? I've lost two commanders ... but ... if I go to Command School, get my own team, I can't lose another one.

He thought back to the Dallas mission, and how both Commander Awenda and Specialist Noble had so casually betrayed the Time Rangers. Sawyer never thought it possible that Rangers could betray their unit ... their people and their timeline. He threw his head back against the couch and stared at the ceiling. *Maybe I should? What else have I got to do? It's not like I'm trained, or designed, to be anything else. And after the fiasco in Dallas, there's certainly a need for good commanders.*

Sawyer righted his head to look at his father's pic again. *I can't have you forcing me onto another team. But I don't want to be you. I want to be my own man. This has to be my decision.*

Sawyer got up from the couch, put the whiskey bottle on the kitchen counter, and turned toward his bedroom where the tiny yellow star and moon stickers still clung to the ceiling. *I wanted this once. What happened?*

He looked out the window to his right, which was displaying the lights of the station's outer ring and beyond that the stars. There really was so much out there he wanted to see, so much he wanted to do. Above all, he wanted to protect the timeline so the beauty and majesty he saw outside that window now would remain unharmed.

I handled myself well during the Kennedy mission. Fixed that clusterfuck before it got out of hand. And the Titanic? *I was the only one who could do it. Maybe I am uniquely qualified to command?*

Beaumont had given his life so Sawyer could have a future. But did Beaumont mean for Sawyer to take command so soon? Sawyer wondered if he could even be the commander Beaumont thought he could be. Or would he fall back on his father's training? Would he become a respected commander or a tyrant? Sawyer looked into the mirror beside him on the wall, past the pale-blue irises of his father's same eyes staring back at him, and into the black depths of his pupils where he saw his own reflection. Sawyer couldn't escape his destiny any more than particles or radiation could escape a black hole. A ship's name usually reflects a great battle, a great city, or the inner machismo of its captain or commander. Sawyer already knew what he'd name the new ship if he were given its command.

ON the station's OCC, Specialist Perry leaned over the railing protecting the forward window. Below and to his left, past the station's ring, he looked out into the blackness of space. With the Nexus Point Actual so close, it cut off the view of stars that lay beyond its perimeter.

Perry always enjoyed this time of night. Everything was quiet and still when the day shift had left, and all that remained in the OCC was a skeleton crew and a few hardcore brass who couldn't find it within themselves to go home after a long day's work. Perry laughed at his own expense. Here he was idling at the window, no better than the admirals and captains with no places better to go.

A door opened behind him across the OCC, startling the silence. Perry turned to see Rear Admiral Sawyer standing in his office doorway with a rare smile on his face. *It's good to see you happy*, Perry thought as he smiled back.

With the rear admiral in a good mood, Perry thought maybe it was a good time to apologize for his behaviour the last time they'd spoken. He hadn't meant to yell at the rear admiral and storm off, but sometimes that man infuriated him.

"Specialist Perry! Come into my office," called the rear admiral.

Perry pushed off the railing, crossed the OCC, and walked up and across the briefing podium at the back of the cavernous room to enter the rear admiral's office. "Sir."

"Greg, please. Call me John. Technically we're both off the clock."

"I think us wearing our uniforms denotes the opposite."

The rear admiral crossed his hands on his desk and leaned forward. "How have you been, Greg? It really has been a long time."

Perry wasn't sure where this sudden good mood was coming from, but he played along. "Yes, it has, John. How's Kai? I heard he had an incident back in 1912. Everything turn out okay?"

"He's fine. Actually, everything is exceptional. That's why I called you in here when I saw you. I figured if anyone wanted to know, it would be you. Kai has finally agreed to go to Command School. He leaves next month, which means he'll graduate at the same time the new Ranger ship is launched next year. It will be the first Intrepid class frigate, and fully run by the Time Rangers. It's a very exciting time."

Perry wasn't sure he'd heard that right. "Isn't it a little too soon for Command School? Are you sure he's up for it?" He shook his head. "What am I saying, of course he is. You probably worked him to the bone to get him this admittance at such a young age. John, are you sure he wants this, or is he just following your orders like he's always done?"

"He came and told me himself. Tonight. Not even an hour ago. It was his decision, not mine. And don't try and take this away from him, Greg. From me. You know how much we wanted this for him."

Perry frowned, only half believing what the rear admiral was saying, but completely ashamed that at one time in his life he had been eager for Kai to become a Time Ranger commander. "If you say so, John."

"There's more." The rear admiral got up and closed the door to his office then came back and sat on the corner of his desk. "There's going to be … things happening soon that are going to take a lot of patience, a lot of fortitude, and create dangerous situations that can't be avoided."

Perry noticed the rear admiral's lips thin out and his brows raise ever so slightly, a tell the rear admiral was worried. Perry sat forward on his chair. "What is it?"

"I want you to be the historian on Kai's team when he graduates. He'll need your help. Your guidance." He looked into Perry's eyes, and for the first time in nearly twenty years Perry saw the man he once knew staring back at him. "He'll need you, Greg."

"He doesn't even know who I am. When I ran into him at his graduation, he brushed me off. What if he figures it out, remembers who I am while we're on a mission? It might throw him into weird headspace. He might even think I'm there spying for you. There are plenty of other specialists ready for the job. Choose one of them."

"It needs to be you."

Perry ran a hand down his face. He would do anything for Kai, and once upon a time for his father as well, but it was different now. Perry had removed himself from the Sawyer family drama years ago, and he liked it this way. "You're asking me for a favour?"

The rear admiral nodded.

Perry stood and shook his hand, but unlike long ago there was no spark when their palm's touched, so Perry knew that by making this arrangement with the rear admiral, he was really doing it for Kai. "I'll do it. Just let me know when I'm needed. And of course I expect this favour to be returned one day."

"For this, anything you want, Greg."

15.

COMMANDER Sawyer dropped his duffle bag on the floor of his private quarters aboard his new ship. With a sigh, he reflected on the date, November 30, 2198. At twenty-four years old, too young in other commanders' opinions, Sawyer had just graduated Command School and taken control of the Time Ranger's new Intrepid class frigate: the Ranger Space Vessel RSV *BlackOut*. Kai Sawyer's new lapel pins on his dress tunic shone as bright as the new deck beneath his feet.

"Commander Sawyer," announced his personal AI over the cabin's communication system. "Lieutenant Commander Santiago is requesting your presence. She insists I tell you to meet her in the *BlackOut's* gym. It is also my duty to inform you it is protocol, as well as proper etiquette, to reply promptly. What do you wish I tell her?"

Lieutenant Commander Sara Santiago was Sawyer's second-in-command. She was several years older than Sawyer, very fit, and kept her unnaturally blonde hair short in traditional military style. They'd met a few days ago, and she'd seemed extremely competent, albeit a little short on protocol. "Do you know what she wants, Thor?"

All Time Ranger commanders were surgically implanted with AIs, which worked as communications for the ship and as wetware. After implantation of the self-learning AI, which were complete with an evolving personality, Sawyer had named his after his only pet, a grey-and-white kitten given to him by one of his father's old partners. The cat's markings resembled a Siberian wolf, prompting Sawyer to strangely think of Norse gods. He found the name appropriate for his AI since most of them developed god complexes.

"After further inquiry," replied Thor, "the lieutenant commander has stated that you are to … *bring your gloves, and bring your best.*"

Sawyer shrugged off his tunic and tossed it over the chair by his desk. As he crossed his quarters toward his personal automatic closet, his gaze landed on the universe outside the floor-to-ceiling window that stretched across the entire bulkhead behind his bed. It was a spectacular sight, made better by the fact that it was his own personal view. At the closet, he quickly changed into something more appropriate—his battle uniform, which consisted of his grey fatigues and the skinsuit underneath.

"Lieutenant Commander Santiago is persistent," stated Thor. "She continues to ask what is taking you so long."

"From what I know of her so far, she seems like the type of person used to getting what she wants. So she probably won't stop asking for me until I show up. Just bore her with the idle chatter you're programmed with until I get there."

When Sawyer approached his cabin door, it slid open—no swiping a hand or pressing a button was required when the AI in your head anticipated your approach. Now that command was upon him, Sawyer could not deny the pride welling in his chest as he walked through his ship's main corridor, the command epaulettes comfortable on his shoulders.

When he arrived at the gym located one deck down, he found Santiago standing in the middle of the sparring mats, pounding her gloves together with a sagacious smile.

"Since we have time," she said. "I thought we should get a bit more familiar with each other, and there's nothing more personal than a few rounds of me beating your ass. Sir."

Soldiers and cadets always wanted to challenge Sawyer, see if they could take down a Spawn, or just last a few rounds and survive. Typically, Sawyer found it amusing, but although Santiago danced silly around the mats in anticipation of their match, he noticed a strange look behind her eyes. He'd barely met her but had read her dossier, which only provided facts. And a person was more than facts, so he figured this would be a good opportunity to get to know her better as well.

He pulled sparring gloves from the training box and stepped onto the mat. "You sure you want to do this? You might have to pick up your self-worth after I spread it around the room. Are you okay with that?"

Santiago waved him closer. "Big words, but I've been kickboxing since I was five ..."

Sawyer's punch landed squarely in Santiago's face.

She wiped away the trickle of blood from her upper lip. "Ah, good. You're not holding back."

A moment later, Sawyer stood over her after landing her on the mats. "Actually, I am."

Santiago got to her feet and held her hands out in surrender. "You're not playing fair, sir. I didn't even say begin."

"My father always taught me there's no *fair* in fighting." Sawyer stepped back and spread his arms. "You still want to do this?" His head snapped to the left when her punch connected with his cheek. "I'll take that as a yes."

Sawyer decided to take this more seriously and jabbed forward, hitting her in the shoulder.

Santiago barely registered the hit. "I thought you weren't going to hold back, sir?"

"I have to hold back strength, or I might kill you."

"You have to do a lot of things, don't you, Commander?" She jabbed at his head and missed.

Sawyer jabbed back and hit. "What are you talking about?"

"You're a commander now. Big man on campus. You're responsible for all the lives on this ship. And you have to do as the Space Fleet admirals say. You have to do as the Rangers say ..." She kicked Sawyer on the side of his knee, but he didn't budge. "Do as your father says."

Sawyer returned with a kick that landed squarely in her chest, sending her reeling backward. "What are you getting at?"

Santiago pounded her gloves. "Your family is like royalty. Your grandfather has a statue outside the study hall back at the Academy. Your father nearly started the Time Rangers single handedly. Prior to that, he saved Queen Elizabeth on his first mission. He fought overwhelming odds at the Alamo to make sure it lost. He was the best out here. Never failed. No one questions him. Your father deserves every bit of respect he has."

One of her legs caught Sawyer behind the knees and landed him on the floor. He sprung to his feet. "Yes, he does. Everyone knows he's the best."

"Was the best. Aren't *you* supposed to take the reins now? But what have you done to deserve everything you've been given?"

Her next punch connected with his left cheek. A bruise formed instantly, but Sawyer didn't retaliate. "This command was supposed to be yours, wasn't it? That's what this is really about?"

Santiago jabbed twice, which he deflected like swatting flies. "Nope. Just wondering what kind of commander I'm being forced to work with, sir."

Sawyer sighed. "It's hard enough getting respect from an experienced team and crew being a Spawn, and being a Sawyer doesn't help. Half the crew expects miracles from me while the other half ..."

"Thinks you're just a trophy commander," said Santiago, emphasizing her point with a knee to his gut.

Sawyer stood back up, sputtering. "Which do you believe?"

"I'm still figuring it out."

Sawyer leaned hard into his next punches, releasing more strength than he'd intended.

"Fuck, that hurt."

Sawyer rushed forward and put a hand on Santiago's back. "Sorry."

"Half of Space Fleet would love to have a pic of your dad, or even your dead grandfather, shaking their hand. Including me." While bent over, Santiago grabbed his knees and threw him backward to the mats.

Sawyer stood and held his hands in the shape of a T. "My family may be responsible for a significant part in the formation of the Rangers, but the real distinction of forming them belongs to Space Fleet's Admiral Shenouda when he took away control of time travel from the ThirdEye Corporation and its vacations."

Santiago looked into his eyes, seemingly searching for something. "You actually believe that, don't you?"

Sawyer shrugged. "I have to, otherwise I have way too much to live up to. It's how I humble my wonderful self."

Santiago punched him in the arm and Sawyer punched her in the side of the head.

"Oh, it's on again, sir. Besides, I have to get this out of my system before we enter a mission."

"And what exactly do you need to get out of your system?"

Santiago tackled him to the mat and used her knees to pin his arms at his sides. "That this was supposed to be my command." She punctuated her anger with two swift punches to his head.

Sawyer shook her off and got to his feet. "I'm sorry."

Santiago punched him in the gut. "You should be." She punched him again. "You Sawyers take whatever you want while the rest of us fight for scraps. I've been short-listed for command for over a year now! And you took this from me!"

Sawyer stepped back, looked into her sweaty face, and recognized raw anger. Once again, his family name and genetic superiority was tainting his life. He wondered if he should continue this charade, let her finish taking out her anger on him so they could move past this, but instead he pulled off his gloves and dropped them on the mat. His anger was rising, and if he continued, he wasn't sure what level of irrevocable damage he would do. "We're done, Lieutenant Commander."

Santiago heaved deep breaths, sweat glistening on her forehead. "We're not done, sir!"

"We arrive at Nexus Station soon. I suggest you get cleaned up. Your lip is still bleeding."

"And you have a black eye, sir," she retorted with pride.

An internal ping pricked the back of Sawyer's head, alerting him to an important incoming message from Thor. He glanced at Santiago as he removed his personal communication card from inside the collar of his uniform shirt. Across the two-and-a-half by four-inch, paper-thin translucent card read the words:

> Code 1 transmission. Report to standing order. More information to follow.

Sawyer's throat dried like he'd swallowed a chunk of sandpaper. "We have a mission? This can't be right."

Thor pinged him again and spoke on their private channel no one else could hear. Thor's voice was only heard in Sawyer's head. *"Your crew is being dispatched to their stations, Commander."*

"I know the drill," replied Sawyer. But as for why a brand-new commander was being dispatched to a mission so soon, he was at a loss. Surely this was some sort of mistake. A drill or training exercise. Perhaps a prank played on new commanders? "The rear admiral can't be serious. He's really sending us out on a mission? I barely know my crew. There's got to be a more appropriate ship somewhere. Anywhere."

Santiago pouted mockingly at him. "Need me to hold your hand, sir?"

"Shut up."

Klaxons suddenly blared throughout the *BlackOut*. "Your orders have been downloaded into your battle uniform," stated Thor over the gym's comm system.

Sawyer pressed the small pad on the inside of his right cuff, which began the initialization of the uniform. Electrical impulses flowed through the skinsuit, creating goosebumps from his ankles to mid-way up his neck where the skinsuit ended. He now had masking capability and instant computer access, and being a commander with an AI implant, Thor could now read his every neural impulse, steroid release, and every other one of his bio-functions faster than the blink of an eye. Sawyer and Thor were nearly one and the same, minus muscle and thought control. If Sawyer's heartrate increased, Thor would know. If Sawyer was bleeding, Thor would know and alert the ship's doctor. Above all, Thor knew without a doubt who was wearing the uniform and all channels were secure.

Sawyer pressed his thumb on the control panel interwoven into his right sleeve, bringing up the small translucent computer screen over his left forearm, and read:

Code one transmission. Security access required.

Sawyer pressed his thumb on the pad again then raised his arm to blow gently across the sensor.

Security access confirmed.

"Audio please, Thor," said Sawyer. "The lieutenant commander needs to hear this as well."

Thor's generated voice relayed the message over the gym's comm system. "Report to Nexus Station. Historical Contamination Activity instigated. France, 1634. Repercussions of historical alteration: worldwide. Window to enter Nexus Point opening in seven hours forty-six minutes, twelve-seconds. Report to the *BlackOut's* secure communication room for mission briefing with Overwatch."

Sawyer's confidence dropped into his boots as he considered that maybe he should have been spending this time getting to know his ship, not just his second-in-command. He hung his head and sighed. "Not a good start to my career."

16.

FRANCE during the seventeenth century was a violent place teeming with barbarous soldiers, and war with Spain on the horizon made it all the more dangerous. Thinking about the possible excitement of the mission shooed away Sawyer's nerves and he considered maybe he could command a mission straight out of the gate. Afterall, his father had prepared him for this his whole life, and Commander Beaumont thought he could do it. "With Command School taking up my past year, it's been awhile since I've seen action," he said to Santiago. "Maybe this is what I need? A way to prove my worth right out of the gate?"

Santiago didn't answer and left the gym in a huff. Sawyer followed, and when they arrived on the *BlackOut's* bridge, Santiago with her split lip and him with a black eye, all crew turned to them.

"Commander on deck," announced Santiago, and Sawyer was relieved to see her professionalism come out.

The small crew of department chiefs and enlisted rose in formation until Sawyer put them at rest easy. He stepped onto the small platform in the convex nose of the ship, its forward curvature festooned with a handrail that mounted his personal computer, to look at his crew. All eyes were on him. "We're all Time Rangers on this vessel now," he said to the crew. "Space Fleet isn't looking over our shoulders. I know some of you are fresh out of the Academy, but remember, you wouldn't have been chosen if the Time Rangers didn't think you were capable."

The words rattled in Sawyer's brain; he was not sure if his final statement was true of himself. "As you are aware, we've been given our first mission. Lieutenant

Michaels," he said to the pilot stationed on his left, "get us to Nexus Station ahead of schedule."

"Omni-drive already firing up, sir," replied the lieutenant.

The *BlackOut* shuddered beneath Sawyer. He breathed deep as his ship came to life around him. He'd always enjoyed the omni-drive take-off. A sudden boom, felt in your chest when it kicked in, followed by stars rushing past the ship's window like ghosts in a storm. It felt like he and the *BlackOut* were one.

After enjoying the moment, Sawyer stepped off the command podium, nodded at Santiago, and gestured toward the secure communications room at the back of the bridge. They entered the small dark room that was laden with many vid-screens and stood at-ease before the Overwatch team, his father representing Overwatch-Actual.

On the largest vid-screen, Overwatch, who was transmitting from the briefing podium at the back of Nexus Station's OCC, laid out the standard protocols and parameters of the mission. It began with an overview of his landing team: Historian Specialist Greg Perry and Recce soldier Lieutenant Maxim Hawk. Sawyer hadn't had time to meet with his old friend yet, but he was looking forward to their reunion.

"Weapons will be seventeenth century, no exceptions other than the commander's Stormguard," said Lieutenant Coy from Acclimation. "Commander, since time is short, your team's attire and weaponry will be sent to the *BlackOut* once you arrive at the station. Lots of leather and layers. And keep hydrated, it's going to be hot when you arrive in France."

"Yes, ma'am," replied Sawyer.

"Your ear-pins will be initialized for both communication and translation," said Historian Specialist Anwar. "Even your Lieutenant Hawk, who I understand is fluent in both French and English since even before the Academy, will have to watch out for …"

"Actually, Specialist," interrupted Sawyer. "Lieutenant Hawk is multi-lingual. He also speaks Ojibwa."

"Which is a language that will not be needed," replied Anwar.

Sawyer shrugged. "If you're going to give the guy credit, ma'am, you should give him full credit."

Anwar dipped her head forward. "You're right, Commander. My apologies. But as I was saying, you will need to watch out for colloquialisms of the time that might trip you up. French isn't regular French in the seventeenth century. And you'll be wearing the standard uniform of the Musketeer of the Guard. It'll grant you privileges to help you investigate the Runner."

"France in 1634 was a dangerous time," said Overwatch-Actual.

Data streams and pics scrolled across the console in front of Sawyer and Santiago. Filthy living conditions, crude weapons, death tolls of the black plague, and warnings not to drink the water ran across the screens. Sawyer bit his lip. "So much to consider," he said under his breath.

Santiago raised a brow at him but didn't say anything.

"Louis the Thirteenth and Anne of Austria ruled," added the historian. "Remember what you learned about the Baroque period and you'll do fine."

The image in front of Sawyer changed to a small tavern in a village, the picture over the door indicating food and drink were available.

"Here's where the Deviation Point occurred," said Overwatch-Actual. "The Boar Tavern, located in the village of Dumont, several klicks west of Paris. Now for Nexus Point projections."

On the screens, more numbers scrolled and pics flashed in five-second intervals, showing information ascertained by the Nexus Point Actual and sorted by the Overwatch team for their needs. This is where Sawyer had told Aurora things got iffy for him.

"We presume our Time Runner's goal is to interfere with the progression of modern medicine," continued Overwatch-Actual. "As far as we can tell, this Runner was never registered on a ThirdEye vacation manifest. According to ThirdEye Vacations, all passengers of the France trip returned to our time, therefore this Runner has resources beyond any other, making him unpredictable. We know that during ThirdEye's reign, many private ships broke the Point's security barricade, so there are Runners we have no information on, so this Runner could be anyone. And cataclysmic repercussions will occur if he is not apprehended or stopped. If he succeeds in his goals, Nexus Point projections predict a twenty-five-percent chance many historical figures who created positivity in our timeline will change for the worse. The Spanish Flu of nineteen-eighteen will be eradicated before it kills its first thousand victims, but at the cost of the allies losing World War Two. Therefore, this mission is of highest priority. We cannot allow any time ripples this Time Runner creates to reach our present."

"What about the Time Runner himself?" asked Sawyer.

"As I said, no name, no face," replied Overwatch-Actual. "We know it is a man, and that if he was willing to sacrifice this much time in history to make his move, he is a determined man. Making him difficult to find, arrest, and or kill. This mission will be dangerous based on that account alone."

Sawyer looked down at the floor, and again spoke under his breath. "This isn't a typical Runner."

"Can you handle it, sir?" whispered Santiago.

"I certainly hope I'm up for the challenge." He stood straight and returned his attention to the briefing. "Coordinates for landing, sir?"

"You'll touch down here." Overwatch-Actual pointed to a field approximately forty-five klicks west of Paris at the tip of what used to be known as the Haute Vallee de Chevreuse Regional Natural Park. "The Point is giving us nine days to apprehend the Time Runner."

"Louis the Thirteenth had an integral part in shaping the ranks of doctors. He had a soft spot for barber-surgeons," said the historian. "So this deviation will not only screw up everything Overwatch-Actual mentioned, but it will also screw with what we know of medicine today."

"As for scan-tacts, you will wear the two tiered: radiation aura and historical relevance," said Overwatch-Actual.

"Historical relevance always creeps me out," Sawyer whispered in Santiago's ear. "Knowing your life was really that insignificant."

"You don't want to accidentally kill someone whose great-great-grandchild might discover the cure for cancer. Historical Relevance in scan-tacts are a technological blessing as far as I'm concerned."

"Maybe. But it's still depressing to see some people had zero impact on the future. And I'm sure there will be a lot of green auras back there. We're going to have to be particularly careful."

Santiago raised a brow, but this time she smiled, and Sawyer didn't know what to make of it.

Overwatch-Actual cleared his throat. "Overwatch-Second will be Lieutenant Commander Santiago from the *BlackOut* in orbit above Earth."

"Yes, sir," she said. "Just one thing before we continue, if that's all right, sir?"

"Go ahead."

"It seems the commander here is a bit hesitant about taking on this mission …"

Sawyer's hands shot up as if holding back a crowd. "Whoa, whoa, Lieutenant Commander." He turned to her, eyes wide, and whispered, "What the fuck are you doing?"

"Is this true, Commander?" asked Overwatch-Actual.

If Sawyer were having hesitations about taking on this mission so early into his command career, now would be his only chance to back out. He glanced at Santiago standing smugly beside him, as if ready to take this command from him at any moment. "No, sir," he said, resolutely. "I think what the lieutenant commander is referring to are my reiterations of how dangerous this mission will be, and how my team and I will have to work extra diligently. Isn't that right, Lieutenant Commander?"

Santiago kept her eyes forward, back straight as she addressed Overwatch-Actual. "If the commander doesn't feel ready for this, I am prepared to take over ..."

"That will be enough," said Overwatch-Actual. "Commander, are you confident?"

Sawyer glared at Santiago. "I am, sir. Lieutenant Commander Santiago must be confused, sir."

"Sort your shit out," replied Overwatch-Actual. "This mission is a go, and the last thing your team and crew need is conflict between the two of you."

"Sir ..." said Santiago.

"Moving on, Lieutenant Commander," stated Overwatch-Actual. "The BlackOut departs for Nexus Point Actual in five hours, forty-five minutes. Launch-through will be at thirteen hundred hours Standard Galactic Time. Time of execution thirteen hundred hours on this date of November 30, 2198. Point of entry time will be exactly oh-nine hundred hours on the date of August 4, 1634. Good luck."

A pause filled the room and Sawyer recognized the briefing was over. He'd gotten all he was going to get; it was all on him now. When the vid-screens shut down, he turned to Santiago. "What the hell was that, Lieutenant Commander?"

"Just speaking my opinion, sir. You don't seem as confident as you should be. It's a sign of your lack of experience."

Sawyer seethed, partly because he knew what she was saying was true. "I'm expecting a vid-call from Earth. I'll be in my quarters."

"Should be me receiving that vid-call," murmured Santiago.

"What was that?"

"Never mind, sir."

Sawyer had heard her perfectly well but didn't see the point in this argument. He was the commander, and there was nothing she could do about it, so he turned away and left her standing alone in the dark room.

At his desk in his quarters, Sawyer stared at the Time Ranger's emblem spinning slowly on his computer screen. The three stars inside the cobalt circle represented the first three pseudo-Time Rangers to go through the Nexus Point, his grandfather representing one of them. "I wonder if things were easier back then. My grandfather didn't have a name to live up to ... and probably didn't have a second-in-command trying to steal his job ..." He shook his head. "Thor, download everything you need for the mission and send pertinent mission data to the team ..."

"It is done, Commander Sawyer. I must also inform you the vid-call from Earth is cued. Given the esteem of the caller, I would not delay in answering."

Still angered by Santiago, Sawyer took a deep breath before answering, and rose to his feet when Utopian President Ahnah Crow appeared on his screen. "Madame President."

"At ease, Commander," said President Crow, a hint of laughter behind her soft, raspy voice. "I understand this is your first mission. It's protocol I make this call to all new commanders, which I'm sure you are aware of, but I was surprised to hear you were called into action so quickly after taking command. Unfortunately, I'm very busy today so this call will have to be shorter than protocol dictates. I almost had to reschedule, but since I know your father, I fit you into my schedule."

"Thank you, Madame President."

"Now sit, please. I just wanted ..." She looked down at the dark desk under her crossed hands, took two breaths, then levelled her gaze with Sawyer. "My sister arrived home almost three decades ago to discover none of her children were born. She ... I ... still feel the loss as if it happened yesterday. Do you understand what I'm saying, Commander?"

"I understand what you're saying, ma'am."

"I've only been in office a short time, but I'd destroy that Nexus Point if I could. Halt all time travel this instance. Unfortunately, there are ... Time Runners, as you refer to them, still in the past that must be stopped. I don't want any other families coming home to find their children, or husbands or partners gone, lost in time. If only our memories disappeared as easily as our history. Did you lose anyone?"

"It was before my time, Madame President."

"That's right. I forgot how young you are."

"I'm aware something went wrong during our early days of time travel, but I have not been read-in on the specifics of the Albatross Incident."

President Crow smiled. "Many citizens lost many family members that day. Institutions disappeared, leaving gaping holes in our cities and colonies where buildings once stood. Some replaced by other businesses, some replaced by apartments, and some just left as empty space for us to look at as a reminder that we lost more than people that day. I don't believe humanity can survive that loss again."

"This is why I do what I do, Madame President."

"And we thank you for all that you do, Commander. I must admit, I'm a bit jealous. Travelling in time, back before Earth …" she shrugged, as if indicating everything around her, "turned into the mess it has. But my place is here."

"You're doing a fine job," replied Sawyer.

"Thank you, Commander."

She stared at him, her eyes discerning as they moved up and down his body. "You are a Spawn. You've been trained by the best Ranger I know, that anyone knows, your father. You've just graduated top of your class, again, from Command School. And you look confident. I like that. This should be a cake-walk for you," she said with a smile.

Santiago's words during the briefing still bothered him, and he wondered if the president was confusing his anger for confidence.

"When you return, I'd like to meet you, Commander Sawyer. So, see to it you are successful in containing this HCA, and make that meeting possible." She stood and leaned over her desk, closer to the vid-camera. "We will have much to discuss," she said in a hushed tone. "But now I must take my leave. Good journey, Commander. And good luck. Humanity is counting on you."

Sawyer fell back into his chair, scrubbed his face, and stared at the ceiling.

"There is another request for communication coming over the Quantum Entanglement Communication Suite," stated Thor.

"Who is it?"

"Rear Admiral Sawyer."

Nothing good was going to come from answering it, and for a split second Sawyer considered pretending he didn't know his father was calling. "Open communications, Thor," he sighed. When his father's face appeared on the screen, Sawyer sat up straight. "Sir."

The rear admiral's eyes bore into him. "You're about to learn what it means to be a Sawyer. This is what you've been trained for. Did you sort out the problem with your second-in-command?"

Sawyer wanted to say no, but his father wanted to hear yes. "She won't be a problem, sir."

"Then that is all. I just wanted to wish you luck and good hunting. Oh, another thing ... don't you ever show up to a briefing with a black eye again, or I'll give you two."

His father ended the communications and the spinning Ranger logo reappeared on the computer screen. Sawyer stared at it, this time a lot less confident than he had been before the briefing. Not only was his inexperience working against him, but now he possibly had a lieutenant commander and the president of the world watching his every move.

17.

WHEN time allowed, an inspection of the landing team prior to a mission was required. With several light-years between Earth's orbital shipyard where they had been docked for their inaugural launch and Nexus Station, Sawyer knew there was plenty of time still remaining, so he ordered Santiago to set up his team in the *BlackOut's* debarkation room between the two Earth-Landers.

As he and Santiago stood outside the bay doors, Santiago turned to him with her arms crossed. "I know it's protocol, sir, but I did just perform an inspection this morning. So with all due respect, are you questioning my abilities to do my duties?"

After you questioned mine earlier, I should be, but ... "That's not what this is about..."

"Earn the team's respect, don't demand it. One inspection is enough." She swiped the panel to open the door and walked into the debarkation room. "You're gonna end up just like your dad, sir."

Sawyer bristled. It was meant as an insult, but he couldn't help feeling some pride in being compared with someone most people considered the best Time Ranger in the history of the unit. But did he want his father's command style associated with his own? *Fuck, why did you have to say that?*

With this inspection, Sawyer only meant to get better acquainted with his team, the ones travelling to Earth with him on the mission. Especially Hawk. Although Sawyer was excited to see him after all this time, he needed to make sure his old friend wasn't going to complicate things. And if he did, Sawyer wondered how he would handle himself. It was official now; he was both commander of a team and ship. His first impressions here would set the tone for his career. He counted to three in his head, relaxed his shoulders, and entered the debarkation room.

"Commander on deck," announced Lieutenant Hawk, bringing the landing team to attention.

That's a good start. "Lieutenant. Specialist. At ease. Let's get this started."

Specialist Perry cleared his throat and stood ramrod straight with his feet apart and his hands tucked resting in the small of his back. "Sir. Everything that should be in my rucksack is present and accounted for."

Sawyer frowned as he looked into the older man's face. He'd read his dossier. Specialist Greg Perry had been a Ranger for almost twenty years. Sawyer wondered if the specialist would be amenable to him in command. With that much experience under his belt, Sawyer figured underneath that professional exterior there had to lie some resentment at being commanded by someone new and young. "So ... what? You want a medal for doing as expected?"

Hawk unsuccessfully stifled a chuckle. Sawyer glared at him. *Yeah, I get it. I sound like my fucking father.* Sawyer had to stop himself from smacking his own forehead.

Perry swallowed and tilted his head. "Sorry, sir. I was just ..."

"Stop talking." Again, Sawyer mentally slapped himself for being more brusque than the situation called for. *Beaumont was hard on me when we first met. But I deserved it. Specialist Perry hasn't done anything but be professional ... 'But sometimes professionalism gets you nowhere'... Damn, I'm running in circles!* "Everyone just open your bags."

Sure enough, Perry's rucksack was in order: medkit, ration packs, and toiletries. Spare uniforms were redundant since they were to be costumed by Acclimation. When Sawyer reached Hawk, he sighed before pulling out the contents of his rucksack one item at a time. *There's contraband in here somewhere, I know it.* Sawyer eventually found it rolled into a hand towel.

Sawyer pulled the Stormguard from the bag and held it up before Hawk. "Standard issue. But not where we're going, Lieutenant. We'll be equipped with seventeenth-century weapons. Please return this to the lock box in your quarters. Now."

Hawk leaned forward as if studying the pistol for the first time. "ThirdEye Corporation," he read off the grip. "I'll never understand why Space Fleet, or the Time Rangers, entrust the production of military-grade weapons to a corporation that used to sell time-travel vacations. I mean seriously, they also manufacture cat food and diapers."

Sawyer's jaw clenched. "Your point, Lieutenant?"

"And it better be good," said Santiago. "Because that weapon wasn't in your rucksack earlier during my inspection."

Sawyer smiled smugly at her. *You just didn't find it.*

Hawk flashed a lopsided grin. "The Stormguard is capable of both incapacitating shots as well as kill shots, Commanders. Easily concealable as it's a hand-held. And it's light. It uses dissolving case-less rounds so we never leave evidence behind. And the debilitator pulse is perfect for apprehending Runners without deadly force."

"Our job is to stop contamination of the past," said Santiago.

"The Earth-Lander will be masked," said Sawyer. "Our scan-tacts can be swallowed in case of emergencies, and my AI is capable of remote disintegration from the *BlackOut* in orbit if I'm caught or compromised. That's all that goes back on this mission. Even our skinsuits weren't cleared. The only Stormguard going is mine, and it remains locked in the Earth-Lander until necessity requires its use. I know you know this protocol, Lieutenant Hawk."

"I know this, but I don't agree with it, sir."

"That's enough! You're a soldier, act like one!" yelled Sawyer.

Hawk was neither apologetic for his actions nor standing down. Just how Sawyer remembered from their Academy days. Except then, Sawyer wasn't responsible for Hawk's discipline.

"Your Stormguard will be locked in the armoury until further notice," continued Sawyer. "That way it can't find its way back into your kit without me knowing. Thor will notify me if you even attempt to retrieve it without a superior officer's clearance. As for now, Lieutenant, this inspection is over, and I expect you to re-pack yours and Specialist Perry's rucksacks. Lieutenant Commander Santiago will provide oversight. And if one thing is out of place upon re-packing, I'll have you on suspension until your whole head is grey."

Sawyer turned away before Hawk could object, and without delay, he returned to the bridge. After a short stay on Nexus Station for Acclimation to gear them up, Sawyer returned to his bridge, brought the *BlackOut* into position alongside the Nexus Point, and set bearings for launch-through.

At his command post, Sawyer gripped the railing on either side of his console with added vigour. "Prepare for launch-through of the Nexus Point," he announced venomously. Anger still controlled him; he couldn't shake it, couldn't let how he'd acted in the debarkation room slip away into the ether.

"Time to L-T ten-seconds, sir," announced Lieutenant Michaels.

"Thor, open all channels," said Sawyer.

"All channels are open," came back Thor's voice over the bridge comm.

"This is the commander." Sawyer rubbed a hand down his face to help deplete the anger tainting his voice. "Launch-through in four … three … two …"

Sawyer's world went white as the ship entered the Nexus Point Actual. When the ship lurched out the other end, Sawyer rubbed his arms to help dissipate both the chill of his molecules re-establishing themselves in a new time zone and the chill slithering up his back. Sawyer was more than a little disappointed in himself in how he'd handled the inspection. He had treated Hawk, and to a degree, Perry, like his father had treated him his whole life—like a whipping boy. Sawyer had wanted to be more like Beaumont, but all that had resonated from him was his father's upbringing.

"This is not starting well," he mumbled. "Lieutenant Commander, you have the bridge." Sawyer left and headed down to the debarkation room, hoping that by the time he got there he would be calmed down.

18.

MISSION: DAY ONE

SAWYER took his seat at Earth-Lander One's helm and did a control check as his team took their seats on the aft benches. When they were ready for take-off, confirmed by both Santiago and Lieutenant Michaels on the *BlackOut* bridge, Sawyer glanced back to the rear compartment to make sure his team was ready.

"Clear for egress," he announced when they gave him the thumbs up.

The debarkation room was empty of crew when the *BlackOut's* forward bay door lowered and was simultaneously replaced by a field of shimmering transparent webbing. Sawyer launched the Earth-Lander through the web of the *BlackOut's* door into Earth's lower atmosphere, approximately five hundred kilometres above Earth's sea level. No one of this century had technology capable of seeing this far into space, so parking the *BlackOut* closer to Earth was a luxury.

Through layers and layers of clouds composing Earth's troposphere, the Earth-Lander finally breached the last layer from where the real beauty of the planet showed itself. The snow-capped peaks of the Alps sloped into a valley rich with emerald green only to climb again as the terrain formed both the Massif Central and Jura mountains. Sawyer trailed the Soone River as it snaked north before starting his slow descent.

Everything was quiet in the Earth-Lander when Hawk stepped through the opening into the helm and sat in the jump seat behind Sawyer. "Just like old times, eh?"

Sawyer smiled at him over his shoulder. Should he apologize? He'd had every right to discipline Hawk, but so harshly? Sawyer knew he could have, should have, handled it better. With less anger and ego. "So about earlier ..."

"Say nothing more."

"I shouldn't be saying this, but I really didn't like locking your Stormguard in the armoury. And my temper ... I don't know where it came from."

Hawk shrugged. "My fault. I honestly wasn't expecting a second inspection. You turning into your dad now that you outrank me?" A moment of silence passed before Hawk spoke again, his voice soft. "You know, I always knew when the rear admiral visited you at the Academy. I could hear that angry twentieth-century music blaring from down the hall, and I knew to give you space. Or, you know, you'd punch me in the face."

"That was one time ..."

"You broke my fucking nose!"

A blue light flashed on Sawyer's control board, indicating an automated message transmission. "I didn't send anything." He reached over to investigate when the Earth-Lander suddenly pitched forward too much, too soon. Sawyer's stomach lurched into his throat.

Class 2 Emergency: software flashed on and off on Sawyer's head's up display. Out the front window he saw the ground coming up at them too fast. Suddenly, the automated maneuvering system indicator flashed. "What the hell? Strap in everyone!"

"What's happening?" asked Hawk.

"The AMS kicked in. The Earth-Lander thinks it's stalling and nose diving to gain speed so it can stay in the air."

Sawyer glanced at the other read-outs, strangely noting no other indications of a stall. "Must be a glitch." He switched to manual control, and a moment later, the Earth-Lander levelled off at 2.4 kilometres above sea level.

"That was easy," said Hawk. "Yay, Commander."

On Sawyer's HUD two new command messages appeared in red: arm and fire. Followed by the message *Class I Emergency: mechanical.* Eight distinct popping sounds came from the rear hatch. "Brace for explosive decompression! Get your masks on!"

Deafening explosions from the escape landing system reverberated in the Earth-Lander as the frangible nuts at each of the eight hold-down studs separated and the hatch flew off. Smoke from burning mechanics filled the

Earth-Lander until decompression forced the air out the gaping hole in the back. Sawyer and Hawk's oxygen masks were already in place when Perry announced he was safe. Sawyer tried to raise the hatch web, but with no joy. It too was malfunctioning.

Master alarm lights flickered everywhere, turning the Earth-Lander into a small disco. Sawyer slid his fingers up and down the servo actuators, barely capable of maintaining contact with the smooth panel. "I can't control our descent! Thor, notify the *BlackOut* we're going down."

In moments the Earth-Lander would be nothing but spare parts scattered across a French countryside. They called it a "yard-sale" at the Academy when pilots failed to land their ships safely in simulators.

Sweat dripped down Sawyer's forehead. Eject everyone and hope they landed safely, or try and salvage the Earth-Lander with everyone on board? Nothing could be left behind in 1634, and a field of technology and metal debris was definitely leaving something behind, particularly dead bodies if he didn't pull them out of this.

The Earth-Lander vibrated and rocked. Sawyer forced himself to keep his hands on the console, trying desperately to straighten out the shuttle, but with the shaking and bumping he could barely touch a button or slide a level.

"Starting to feel sick here!" called Hawk.

"Shut up!" replied Sawyer.

On Sawyer's HUD, altitude showed 1.5 kilometres and dropping at a speed of one thousand knots. The ejection would be too powerful. *Remember your time-critical procedures. At fifteen hundred metres the flare should kick in.* "Hold on! There's going to be a jolt!"

When the HUD showed the correct altitude, the flare suddenly slammed the Earth-Lander's descent to five hundred knots, giving Sawyer seconds to re-take manual control. The Earth-Lander shook violently, and Sawyer wasn't sure he could manage a controlled flight onto terrain. Again, he considered ejection.

He checked his HUD: 352 metres to ground. *Too close, some might not survive.*

The guidance system was also out. Sawyer would have to land on his own. He reached for the gimbal servo actuators, which provided force and vector control, and they were sluggish but responding.

The belly of the Earth-Lander skimmed the tops of pine trees, and screeches and booms filled the Earth-Lander before it slammed down and bounced back up as they hit the ground at over 640 kilometres per hour. It bounced again and skidded to a halt in an explosion of dirt, smoke, and tree branches.

Sawyer closed his eyes and breathed deep. It seemed only his stomach and nerves were affected by the ordeal. "Call out!"

"Lieutenant Hawk."

"Specialist Perry."

"Sir, what just happened?" asked Hawk.

Sawyer unstrapped himself from his seat and ran a shaky hand down his face. "I have no idea. Thor? Intel."

"Two malfunctions occurred," replied the AI on the private channel he and Sawyer shared. *"Your correction to place the Earth-Lander in manual control triggered the second malfunction."*

"How is that possible?"

"I do not know. I am a communications AI, not a mechanic's computer. Also, I must inform you that I have lost external communications and can now only communicate with you on our private channel. Which also means I can no longer coordinate communication through your team's ear-pins. To add insult to injury, I have also lost communication with the BlackOut."

***

DR. Arnault stood at a third-floor window of an old asylum, long since abandoned by France's medical society, scrutinizing the gardener below, who was fussing with the vegetable garden. The garden wasn't big enough to accommodate all the mouths that required feeding here, so the doctor had told the gardener to expand it twice over. Arnault sighed as he watched, then pushed his wire-rimmed glasses up the bridge of his nose. They were redundant, but he felt they made him look more wise, more acclimated to the time period.

But large gardens weren't the only thing on his mind. To understand anatomy, Arnault knew one had to dig deep within a human body to learn its secrets. Medicine would not progress without this. Hence, more bodies were needed for his school, but that was not a job for the gardener.

Arnault strolled through the upper hallway of the old asylum with his chest puffed, his hands clasped in the small of his back as he walked toward the larger window overlooking the front of the estate. The sun shone bright behind the hill in the distance, smearing yellow, orange, and white across a blue-tinged horizon. Everything was beautiful and calm out there, just like his school, which was flourishing beyond his expectations.

Behind him a calm voice called his name.

"Dr. Arnault."

"Good evening," he greeted his assistant.

"You will have to make other arrangements for tonight. I'm afraid our champion is no longer in standing order."

Arnault raised an eyebrow behind his spectacles. "Did you just give me an order?"

His assistant in the black robe bowed. "I'm sorry, sir. It just … just slipped out."

"After all I've done for you, it would be wise to remember who I am and what I can take away from you. See that this slip-up doesn't happen again." Arnault looked back out the window. "The parchments have been distributed accordingly, and I suspect the attendance will be high and we don't want to disappoint. A disappointed crowd can easily become an angry mob. And angry mobs are a contentious problem we don't want. We are flourishing, the world of modern medicine is about to make its breakthrough, and we can't afford any distractions. And an angry mob has a tendency to react … poorly. The next thing we know we have members of France's polite society clambering at our door making a fuss if we don't deliver on our promise of entertainment."

"Well, then, I guess it's time to prepare a new champion."

"I will be … elsewhere." Arnault pushed his glasses up his nose and headed toward his private office. Inside the stone-walled room, furnished with no more than a heavy oak desk and a few wardrobes, he felt his left arm vibrate. "Damn it. So soon."

He read the message on his battle uniform's computer, which he kept hidden beneath a long black robe, then rushed to one of the wardrobes, unlocked it, and threw open the doors. The black box on the middle shelf was beeping, and a red light flashed. He quickly brought up a map on his computer and found where the intrusion was coming from: an area outside Dumont. "They're already here? I've barely started. How am I supposed to work under these conditions?"

After a deep breath, he flicked a switch on the black box, throwing up an interference grid around a very large section of France's countryside. "That should hold them off for a while. In the meantime, everything continues as planned."

He went to the window and looked out where he supposed the Earth-Lander would land in the far-off distance, knowing that these Time Rangers needed to be contained. He just wasn't sure how. Killing them was the easiest option, but then he would have to deal with their Earth-Lander. How would he conceal it and keep it concealed for the next couple of hundred years? His orders were to change the timeline in one specific way, not to randomly leave technology scattered across France's countryside.

He shook his head and sighed. "This does present a rather large problem."

19.

LIGHTS flashed in the Earth-Lander, and sparks flickered from flight control, which trickled tiny plumes of acrid-smelling smoke into the cabin. Sawyer choked and waved the air to clear it for a better assessment. "Damn it."

He bypassed Thor to establish contact with the *BlackOut* through the Earth-Lander's direct comm, anticipating the tongue lashing he'd hear. The mission had just started, and he'd already broken the Earth-Lander. *What a way to boost confidence with the crew. Santiago is definitely going to chew my ass out for this.*

"Earth-Lander ... *Out* ... Hear me?"

The crackling and hissing of the vessel's comm hurt Sawyer's ears. "We're here, *BlackOut*. No injuries. No time yet to check the lander. We'll ..." A loud ping, followed by more smoke, spit out from the comm panel. Sawyer coughed. "*BlackOut*, do you read?" He switched from Earth-Lander comm to Thor. "Re-establish comms with the *BlackOut*."

"*May I remind you, Commander, I have lost communications with the* BlackOut."

Sawyer pushed out of his seat and marched out the back of the Earth-Lander, where he gathered his team outside. "We've lost contact with the *BlackOut*, including Thor's ability to communicate with them. I can still speak with the AI on my private channel, which unfortunately doesn't amount to much. We've also lost open comms through our ear-pins. More importantly, as of right now we don't have a way off the planet. In nine days, Nexus Point will boomerang the *BlackOut* back to the future without its commander and missing one Earth-Lander and its team."

"We should continue with the mission, sir," said Perry.

Sawyer passed Perry on his way to examine the trees and bushes surrounding the perimeter of their crash site. No matter if they continued with the mission or stayed and tried to fix the Earth-Lander, it would need concealment. "Start tearing down branches. The mask is in-operational. We'll have to use traditional methods to hide the Earth-Lander. Start now."

"The Earth-Lander is dead, sir. I agree we need to cover it, but perhaps we should leave that to the lieutenant while we …"

"I've given an order, Specialist."

Perry nodded. "Yes. Yes, sir. Gather branches."

Hawk came to Sawyer's side. "You do have a plan, right? I mean, really, how are we gonna get back to 2198? Historian or not, I'm not so sure Specialist Perry's delicate sensibilities can withstand living in 1634 France."

"I've got this. Now go."

Sawyer bit his lip as he considered his options: concentrate on fixing the Earth-Lander so they'd have a way off the planet or start the mission without delay. He didn't want to stay in 1634 any more than he'd wanted to stay in 1963, so fixing the Earth-Lander and getting communications back with the *BlackOut* had to take priority. For all he knew, Santiago didn't know they had crashed and wouldn't be sending help until it might be too late.

He thought back to Command School and one of its more prominent lectures concerning the hows and whys of not splitting a landing team unless absolutely necessary. And with Thor broken, the communications between his team members via their ear-pins was also out.

"Sir," said Perry. "Leave the lieutenant to guard the Earth-Lander while we get started on the mission. Dumont, where the deviation point occurred, is several kilometres away and we still need to find transportation. As in, horses, sir."

Sawyer walked away as he looked over his shoulder at the Earth-Lander, annoyed that Perry might actually be right. *I would need a historian with me … Hawk is capable of guarding the Earth-Lander. But then, so is Perry. Even specialists have to pass basics.*

Or I could leave them both here and take care of this by myself. Sawyer thought back to the Academy again. *Fundamentals of a well-oiled team require three areas be fulfilled. Technical or functional expertise, Sawyer. Interpersonal, Hawk. Problem solving based on experience, Perry. Losing one of these, like Hawk, as Perry suggests, would be breaking the whole. But it would be efficient to split up, get more done, and cover all bases.*

Sawyer paced, hoping the cadence would help govern his rampant thoughts.

Would leaving Hawk behind be wasted effort? France was sparsely populated during this time, and the Earth-Lander might not be found if we camouflage well ... Importance of completing this mission successfully is tantamount to anything else ... even our own lives.

Perry stepped within whispering distance to Sawyer. "I'm just trying to help you out, sir, let the *BlackOut* deal with the Earth-Lander. You and I should concentrate on the mission. That is our primary goal."

"Stand down, Specialist."

"But, sir, protocol states that if an Earth-Lander and or its team loses contact, in forty-eight hours, if applicable, Overwatch-Second is to send the second Earth-Lander. Communications will be secure, sir. Along with our egress."

"I know the protocols, Specialist!" Sawyer leaned close to Perry's ear. "I just crashed the Earth-Lander. Give me a second to figure things out. End of debate."

Sawyer braced his hands on his hips. *Fuck! Fuck!* He breathed deep, centred his thoughts, and finally decided to fall back on what he knew best—protocol. "We stay together, continue with the mission," he said to his team. "We can only hope the *BlackOut* saw us crash, and if they did, Specialist Perry is right. Santiago will send Earth-Lander-Two. We'll continue with our orders and leave the lieutenant commander to fix our Earth-Lander and our comms. Until then, check weapons, then Hawk, go find us some horses. We passed over an estate. You're the accomplished procurer of things here, so try there."

When Hawk left, Sawyer looked over the French countryside to ease his tension. August was harvest time for the rich, aromatic lavender, so it covered almost every field around them. Tiny purplish-blue dots swayed on the ends of long stems like a rolling wave as a soft breeze blew across the landscape. He took in a deep breath to let the relaxing aroma calm his temper. It vaguely reminded him of how his bedsheets smelled the morning Aurora woke next to him. He shook his head. *Why am I thinking of this now?*

Beside him, Specialist Perry slid his rapier into its leather sheath. "Barbaric, these things are. I'll take a clean slug ripping through me any day over the hacking corruption this thing will make."

Sawyer tightened the sash that covered his weapon belt around his waist. "I don't like the idea of any injuries. Slugs or hack marks."

Perry furrowed his brow. "Ever been hit, sir?"

"A few times. And I can't say I enjoyed any of them."

Perry's brow furrowed deeper. "Permission to speak freely?"

I really don't want you to, thought Sawyer, *but ...* "Go ahead."

"You would think your dad would have you out doing pansy runs, not getting yourself mixed up in action."

"You can't prove the Sawyer mettle without seeing action. I think he wants me out here getting myself killed, come to think about it."

"Then he wouldn't have anyone to boast about."

"Unless I die heroically."

The creases on Perry's face eased. "Your father doesn't want you to die, heroically or not."

Sawyer laughed. "You don't know my father."

"I do."

The words hit Sawyer like a cannonball to his chest. He hadn't even considered this older man, this seasoned soldier, would have ties to his father. There was a good chance they knew each other before the Time Rangers. "How so?" he asked when he found his voice.

"Save it for another time."

"I could order you to tell me. I am your commanding officer."

Perry smiled. "That you are, sir, but you can't order my personal business around."

Personal? How well do you know my father? Sawyer's brow raised as he stared at the specialist. *Why are you actually here on my team?*

Hawk arrived strolling three horses behind him, distracting Sawyer from his musings. Sawyer took one last look at the Earth-Lander, then led his team toward the historical contamination act's deviation point, The Boar Tavern, located in the nearby village of Dumont.

20.

SAWYER found it freeing riding across a clean countryside, the wind wisping through his short black hair while the hot summer sun shone high above. If only Earth retained this amount of countryside, a place for humans to escape the smog and overpopulation that predominated the cities of his century, Sawyer figured maybe there wouldn't be a need for people to charge into the past trying to change things. But Time Runners were trespassing into the past, and Sawyer knew they had to be stopped, even if it meant returning to a future not as pleasant as a seventeenth-century untouched landscape.

After a while, the sun's unyielding heat caused Sawyer to shift awkwardly in his saddle in order to ease the cloying dampness his leather pants caused between his legs. He glanced back over his shoulder and saw that Perry and Hawk looked no better than he felt, so he directed his team into the closest forest for a reprieve. A well-worn trail wound between two small hills, each hill covered in trees and bushes. Travelling at a slow pace, Sawyer breathed in the earthy moss scent of the forest floor, admired the varied green shades of the foliage, and used the saddle's pommel to hoist himself up further in his seat, hoping the movement would help rejuvenate him in this heat.

A twig snapped to his right. He raised a fisted hand, which brought Perry and Hawk to a stop behind him. A man armed with a sword launched himself onto the path from behind the trees.

"Ambush!" bellowed Sawyer as he slid off his horse. More attackers emerged with swords out and pistols drawn. Sawyer pulled out his own sword and ran straight for them.

"Green all around!" he heard Perry call out.

"Sawyer! Six o'clock!"

He heard Hawk scream the warning and heard the bang of a musket but was already engaged in battle and couldn't spare a look. But once the foe before him had been dispatched, he anxiously searched for his teammates. Hawk was still standing, still fighting, and holding his own.

Sawyer threw his knife across the field, where it landed between the shoulder blades of a goon creeping up behind Perry. The specialist would never know how close to death he had been, for when he turned around to take on another attacker, the one behind him was already on the ground and Sawyer was busy dealing with another. And with great difficulty, for his new opponent was twice his size and wielding a broadsword.

Even as a Spawn, Sawyer was barely able to deflect the larger, heavier weapon with his rapier and found himself stumbling under the force. He tried to spin away, but his foot slipped in the loose dirt underfoot and the tip of the bandit's sword caught him across his left arm, thankfully only managing to slice the thick leather of his Musketeer pauldron. His saving grace from further attack was that Hawk was there in time to dispatch the husky attacker with a clean shot through his chest.

When the battle ended, and the blood and dust settled, Sawyer let his legs give out beneath him and dropped to the ground in a relieved heap. He was thankful it was over, but even more so, he was grateful his team had survived, despite his failure to warn them of the ambush in time. He was renowned as a Spawn, and for his father's training, to sense danger. That overwhelming aura that someone was watching only gave a soldier seconds to prepare, but sometimes being ready for battle meant the difference between life and death. *I should have been faster. I should have known this was practically a kill-box before leading my team down this path.*

He stared at the distant horizon and shuddered at the thought of what could have happened, then he tilted his head back and looked to the sky. He closed his eyes and drew in a breath meant to invigorate, but instead it only managed to siphon his energy. He swayed to his left as his body yearned for rest and food, but he caught himself with a well-placed hand on the ground before completely toppling over.

"You all right, sir?"

Sawyer peered over his shoulder to see Perry leaning heavily against a tree. Sawyer got up and lumbered over to him. "Still standing. And yourself?"

Perry shifted his weight against the tree that was, without contention, holding him upright. "Too spent to know for sure, but I'll be sure to let you know if a situation presents itself."

Sawyer surveyed him nonetheless. "Don't let your pride get the better of you. I'm only content to let you lick your wounds in private so long as there is nothing serious."

"Hm."

"Hm what?"

"You look as if you've been dragged through hell and back, sir. Perhaps you should take your own advice. I'd hate to see anything happen to you."

"I'm fine," Sawyer replied. He drew in a deep breath and considered his next words carefully. "I'm sorry."

"For what?"

"I should have seen them."

Perry raised an eyebrow. "Seen them *hiding*?"

"Yes. It's my responsibility to be alert, but I was hot … exhausted, as were all of you, and my concentration paid the price."

"Then you should have said something then so you wouldn't have to apologize now, sir."

"You're right." Again, Sawyer felt like he was in over his head. First the Earth-Lander crash, and now this. "So again, I'm sorry."

"It happens to all of us, sir. You are not perfect, and no one expects you to be so. Especially me."

"My father would take offence to those words."

"Do you?"

"I'm not sure," he replied, then he looked over at Hawk. After the battle, he'd taken to the ground shortly before Sawyer had, and had given him the thumbs up in show of good health before doing so.

Sawyer patted Perry on the shoulder then approached Hawk, who was now lying supine between two dead attackers, his arms outstretched and his knees bent up to the sky. Sawyer decided to take a closer look. Medic specialist or not, he still knew what he was doing when it came to field medicine.

"Hawk?" he asked, looking down at his friend.

Hawk waved a hand lazily in the air in lieu of a verbal remark, and Sawyer grabbed it.

"What are you doing?" Hawk asked, trying to pull his appendage back.

"Hold still," ordered Sawyer as he palpated the knuckles of his friend's bruised hand. "You have a tendency to use your fists more often than not, and I want to make sure you haven't broken or dislocated any of your fingers again."

Hawk pulled his hand out of Sawyer's grasp. "I'm good, sir."

"Yes, yes, you're always good. Just like that time you broke three fingers during a bar fight at the Academy and went almost a week before telling anyone. Now get up, I want to get a better look at you. That's an order, Lieutenant."

Hawk got to his feet and turned around slowly. When Sawyer was content, Hawk returned the favour. "Now how 'bout you?" he asked, spinning Sawyer around before he could argue.

"Satisfied?" asked Sawyer when he came to a stop.

"No. Just because I can't see anything wrong with you, sir, it doesn't mean something isn't going on in that head of yours. 'Cause honestly, you look like the saddest piece of shit I've ever seen."

"Well, if my presence displeases you, I can remove myself from your view."

Hawk reached out a hand. "You know that's not what I meant. Sorry. Lieutenant and commander, not two cadets back at the Academy."

"No, I'm sorry. I'm just a little edgy right now."

"I can see that. You've got that funny look in your eyes. Like you've gotten lost in your own head. Now, what gives?"

Sawyer had no issue admitting his fault, but he didn't need Perry and Hawk's forgiveness, he needed his own. "It's my job to protect my team. I'm designed, manufactured, as my father would say, to pick up on ambushes, see what you can't, hear what you can't ..." He sighed. "Why don't we just leave it at that."

"Is there any chance I can get through that thick skull of yours? Stop you from moping around and punishing yourself for something you have no right feeling guilty about?"

"No."

"What if I punch you? It might snap you out of this."

"No." But this time, Sawyer couldn't help but smile.

Hawk looked at Sawyer with a thoughtful air. "Do you remember the first time we met? First day at the Academy. Right after you'd had that argument with your dad outside study hall in front of all of us new cadets."

Sawyer stared at the ground as he crossed his arms over his chest. He did not want to go down this road, but he also knew there was no stopping Hawk. "Yes, you'd just arrived, and we were assigned as roommates."

"Remember what you said to me? How you tried to explain away your dad's behaviour?"

Sawyer flicked his eyes away momentarily. "Jog my memory."

"A Time Ranger is only as good as his last battle. And if they couldn't continue to prove their worth, they'd end up abandoned or dismissed."

Sawyer cleared his throat as his unease escalated. "What does that have to do with anything?"

Hawk shook his head with a disheartened smile. "Right now, this mission, your first command ... you think you're failing. But this attack, the Earth-Lander's sudden descent into a grove of trees ... changes nothing. You're still good in my book, and I'll always feel safer when you're around. Your Spawny genetics saved our hides at the Academy more times than I can remember."

Sawyer was about to thank Hawk for the reassurance when movement to his left caught his attention. One of the attackers was crawling slowly toward a row of bushes lining the path's edge. Sawyer ran to him, grabbed one of his ankles, and pulled him screaming and kicking back into the middle of the path. "Going somewhere?" he asked, looking down at the bloodied man on the ground.

"Please, sir, don't kill me. I was only following orders."

Perry came up behind Sawyer. "What was that?"

"He had orders to attack us," said Hawk, standing on Sawyer's other side.

"Whose orders and why?" demanded Sawyer.

"I can't say. They'll kill me."

Sawyer cracked his knuckles, content to continue the fight if need be. "I'll kill you."

"I fear Mercier more than you," replied the trembling man.

Hawk shook his head. "Dumbass."

"Who's Mercier and why did he want us attacked?" asked Sawyer.

"Not you specifically. Any man. Men. Healthy men. That's all I'm saying."

Sawyer unsheathed his rapier and placed the tip on the man's chest. "Not green, Specialist?"

"Not green," replied Perry.

Sawyer dug the tip through the leather vest until he felt the pop of piercing skin. "Do you wish to reconsider? You do know who we are, don't you?" With his free hand he pulled back his long leather doublet to reveal the white cross on his royal blue tabard.

"Shit. Musketeers."

"That's right," said Hawk, kneeling down next to the man. "So, which do you prefer, the warm hospitality of Paris's Grand Chatelet prison or a slow death in the middle of a forest? My friend here is pretty good at killing; matter of fact, he kind of enjoys it, so if I were you I'd chose to answer his questions."

"Mercier and his associate, they hired my friends and I to kidnap men around the area," replied the man. "I don't know why. We just get paid to bring 'em to him."

"How long have you known this Mercier?" asked Perry. Sawyer looked at him, wondering where this was going. Perry smiled at him and looked back at their captive. "Have you known him years? Months?"

"I ... I ... I've known him most my life. We grew up together in the streets in Paris."

"Ah," said Sawyer. "Our Runner couldn't have been here that long. So Mercier is probably not our Runner."

"Twenty years a Ranger ... Musketeer, sir," replied Perry.

Sawyer pulled the tip of his rapier out from the man's chest and re-sheathed the sword with annoyance. Not only had this interrogation proved worthless, but Perry was grandstanding mere moments after Sawyer had confessed his self-doubts about being a commander. "Just go," he said to the man on the ground, who scrambled to his feet before tearing off into the woods.

It was time to take back his confidence, so Sawyer fetched their horses, which fortunately hadn't wandered off too far, and told his team to mount for egress. "Including today, we have nine days to catch this Runner. We can't afford complications or distractions to slow us down when we might have all of France to search. Although the kidnapping of men is serious business, it's not our business. The deviation point occurred at The Boar Tavern, so I suggest we double time it. Dumont, where it's located, is still several klicks away."

21.

IT was market day in the village of Dumont, resulting in a crowded main square when Sawyer and his team arrived. Sawyer brought his team to a stop at the perimeter of a group of stalls and wagons, and after tying off the horses, they blended in to search for a barber-surgeon. Sawyer was confident that talking to one would at least open some doors into what, or more to the point, who, they were looking for. If this Time Runner was here to make drastic changes to the timeline, he couldn't afford to be subtle; he'd have to make actual changes. Surely there had to be hard evidence for Sawyer to find.

"Thor," Sawyer said, invoking his AI. "You're my map. What are the deviation point coordinates?"

"*I am more than a map, Commander.*" There was a pause before Thor continued. "*But the deviation point is located ten paces down the alley running parallel to the main street.*"

Off to the side of the market, down a short alley, Sawyer found The Boar Tavern with what appeared to be a sleeping vagrant on a chair outside. The bearded man with rolled-up shirtsleeves was leaned back in a chair against the tavern's wall, a bottle of wine about to drop to the ground as he was falling asleep.

"Don't want to lose this," said Hawk, righting the bottle in the man's hand.

The man snapped his chair upright. "What? Ho there!" He shook himself then looked Sawyer's team over one at a time. "You men certainly don't need haircuts. Perhaps a tooth pulled? Or are you here for that new fever remedy?"

"I think I found a barber-surgeon," said Hawk, pointing at the man.

"What fever remedy?" asked Sawyer.

"Ace ... tel ... letic ... something or other."

"Acetylsalicylic acid?" tried Sawyer.

"Yeah, that's the one."

Thor spoke in Sawyer's ear. "*The compound for ASA did not come into existence until the mid-eighteen hundreds.*"

Sawyer looked sternly at the barber. "Then we need some answers, sir."

"You Musketeers got your own doctor at the Garrison, don't you? So why you bothering me? Let's hear those questions so I can get back to my nap."

"Where'd you get your medical training?" asked Sawyer.

"Medical training? Well, I apprenticed, sir. Can even unblock an intestine, if need be." He leaned over his knees and swept his gaze up and down Sawyer. "You need unblocking? You kind of look like you need unblocking."

Sawyer forced a smile at the barber. "My intestinal tract is of no concern. But out of curiosity, how would you go about doing that if someone were to, say … have an obstructed bowel?"

"Clyster, of course. I have a piston and cylinder …"

Sawyer held up a hand. "Got it."

"Does that sound appropriate?" whispered Hawk.

Sawyer turned aside to whisper to Thor. "Is a clyster and cylinder appropriate for an enema in this century?"

"*It is the appropriate procedural equipment for the time. The cylinder is inserted …*"

"Thanks, Thor." Sawyer turned back to the barber-surgeon. "I'm more interested in this fever remedy you have. Where did you acquire it?"

"A physician came through a couple of weeks ago. Nice fellow … a bit flamboyant, but he was peddling little packets of powder he claimed could cure fevers. With the plague still scratching its fingers at us, thought it'd be a good idea to snatch some up. Selling it real cheap, too. You sure you're not interested in a cleaning out? I haven't stitched anyone in a while, either. Been slow in that department. Or need a good bloodletting to ease your worries?"

"I like my blood where it is, thank you," replied Sawyer. As he looked around the busy streets, a thought occurred to him. "Why have you been slow in the stitching department?"

"Can't really say." The barber remembered the bottle of wine in his hand and nearly finished it in one gulp. "I suppose because the tavern's been less crowded with them Beauchamp boys missing. No one's been fighting. Makes for a peaceful night, but I miss the business."

Sawyer raised an eyebrow. "Missing?"

"Two or three weeks now. Think I heard about some others missing from a town nearby as well. Young men just up and disappearing. I figure they're all lying by a riverbed somewhere drunk or dead. Weren't the pleasant folk their parents tried to raise, I suppose. Or them boys have gone off to make a name for themselves fighting the Spanish."

Sawyer leaned over Hawk's shoulder. "The guy in the woods said he was hired to kidnap men."

"What was the name he said?" asked Hawk.

"Mercier."

"Mercier," repeated the barber-surgeon. "That was the doctor selling the fever remedy. So you know him? Don't suppose you could bring him back here, could ya? Could sure use more of his medicine."

"We don't know him," replied Sawyer. Now things were getting interesting. "I was hoping you knew where we could find him."

"Nope. Came through and left. Never seen him since."

"Are you the only barber here?" asked Perry.

"Yes, sir. There's an apothecary across the way, but he still believes in the humours. Waste of time, if you ask me."

"No one else practices physical medicine here? You're the only one?" asked Sawyer.

"Wasn't until a few weeks ago. Used to have a few of us here, but them young ones up and left just as fast as them Beauchamp boys. Packed up all their belongings, closed shop. Thought it would mean more business for me, but like I said, it's been slow with these young men missing."

Sawyer chewed his bottom lip. The pharmacists of this time would be interested in medical advances, but the barber mentioned the one here still focussed on the Galilean belief of the four humours. This might not help, for it could mean the apothecary simply wasn't interested in learning new advancements in medicine. There was only one way to know. Sawyer took directions from the barber-surgeon and headed for the apothecary across the road.

The establishment was busy and smelled so sickly sweet that Sawyer nearly gagged when he and his team crossed the threshold into the small shop. A mix of body odour, dried herbs, and open jars of liquids he didn't want to think about filled his nostrils. The wood floor creaked under his weight as he pushed through the gathered crowd toward the counter.

Behind the apothecary, shelf after dusty shelf stuffed with yellow bottles and black boxes caught Sawyer's attention. He read the labels quietly under his breath for his ear-pin to translate. Nothing seemed out of the ordinary. No antibiotics. Nothing labelled acetaminophen or acetylsalicylic acid, or even anything ending with 'il' typically representing modern forms of heart medication. But then, what was really in those jars?

"Aura is clear," said Hawk. "The apothecary is not our Runner."

Sawyer agreed. "But that doesn't mean he hasn't had contact with our Runner. Our man wants to change the course of medical history. He won't be able to do it alone. He'll have to teach others and have them pass the techniques or medical knowledge on in order to achieve his goal. Like he did with the barber-surgeon outside The Boar."

Sawyer pushed his way to the counter, not caring that others in the shop were cursing strange seventeenth-century French curses at him, and called the apothecary over to him. After Sawyer showed him the cross on his chest and the fleur-de-lis pauldron on his shoulder, the apothecary sighed and asked how he could be of assistance.

"I have a headache," Sawyer stated bluntly.

The apothecary reached under the counter and produced a small pouch. "I have peppermint leaves and ginger root to mix in a tea."

"Do you have anything in a pill or powder form?"

The apothecary frowned. "I don't know what this pill form is you speak of," he said, then pounded the pouch with his fist. "But now it's powder."

Sawyer held back his urge to punch this guy. "Thank you, sir." He snatched the pouch and dropped a few coins on the counter. "Have you heard of someone called Mercier?"

"No," replied the apothecary, then turned to help another customer.

Outside, Sawyer sniffed the pouch's contents, and, satisfied it was simply peppermint and ginger, he tossed it away. "I don't think our Runner's influence has reached here yet. Anyone with modern medicine would be eager to sell it."

"Where to next?" asked Perry.

Sawyer didn't know how to answer Perry's question, for everything felt like a dead end. Sawyer had hoped the apothecary would have been a lead, and glancing around the streets didn't produce any red auras. But like he thought earlier, it might not be the actual Runner they needed to find, but instead someone who'd had contact with him. And their aura wouldn't glow red. Perry mentioned there were several green auras moving about, indicating the people were somehow influential to the future. But whether it was an ancestor of someone important or someone who actually did something of historical value, Sawyer couldn't tell without the person's name and a multi-billion credit computer back on Nexus Station.

It seemed Hawk recognized his frustration. "How are we supposed to find one man in an entire country without skinsuits or computers? What did they teach you at Command School concerning these situations?"

"They taught us not to find ourselves in these situations," replied Sawyer. His blood pressure rose; he was losing confidence with himself. "It's time to hit Paris. See if anything has reached there. Or if anyone knows where to find this Mercier guy. So far he's our only lead."

22.

SAWYER and his team rode through Paris's southwest gate a few hours later, and Hawk pulled up his scarf to cover his nose. "Wow. Just wow. This stench will haunt me forever."

"Poverty and lack of sanitation, Lieutenant," said Perry. "Horse feces. Human feces. Rotten food. Putrefaction. Disease. Ah, just like Earth."

Sawyer frowned. "You aren't comparing 2198 to this, are you?"

"Perhaps a little dramatic, but yes. Most of Earth now is quite similar to Paris's Court of Miracles. Which is what we're most likely smelling right now. And, well, perhaps the underbelly of Paris itself."

"I never understood why it was called a Court of Miracles if it was a slum," said Hawk.

Perry pointed to a one-legged man wearing a long coat who was hobbling down the street with a crooked stick for a cane. "He is a prime example of one of the Court's citizens."

Perry slid off his horse, crossed his hands in the small of his back, and casually meandered toward the one-legged man. When he was in position behind the beggar, Perry kicked out the beggar's good leg and instantly the beggar's missing leg appeared from beneath his long coat to catch himself from falling. Perry resumed his Sunday stroll amongst the crowd back to his horse.

"It's a fucking miracle," sighed Perry as he retook his mount.

"Ah. Liars and thieves," said Hawk.

"Not necessarily by choice, Lieutenant." Perry pointed to a gathering of men wearing dark capes lined in a bright crimson red. "Red Guard. Cardinal Richelieu's men. In theory, they collected taxes from Paris citizens. Sometimes legally, but most times not. And let us not forget, there weren't jobs to be had in this time ..."

"Okay, enough of the history lesson," said Sawyer. He pointed at the Red Guard watching them. "If you say they are Red Guard, then we should make ourselves scarce. We're disguised as Musketeers, and they didn't exactly get along. Besides, we need to find ourselves a doctor."

The team kept riding, slow and easy, across the muck-covered cobblestone roads. Short, three- and four-storey brick and wooden buildings, squished together like overcrowded teeth, encompassed them on both sides like a rotting mouth closing around them.

Perry glanced around. "There are many different forms of physicians. The conflict of medicine during this time was between the barber-surgeons and the physicians. Particularly the long-robed physicians. We may have better luck finding our Runner out in the countryside."

"But the hospitals are here in Paris," said Hawk. "Hotel Dieu. Biggest one in Paris. Should be lots of doctors there."

"I must adamantly disagree. Medical care was reserved for those who could afford it. Hospitals were often a place where one could guarantee receiving their last rites rather than being cured by a doctor. Doctors often weren't even on staff."

"You're betting our Runner is smart enough to know that," said Hawk. "Anyone wanting to change medicine would go to where medicine was every-where. A hospital."

"You assume our Runner is an imbecile," replied Perry in a firm voice. "Anyone smart enough to find a way back to 1634 France with the intentions of altering the course of medicine must have a certain level of sensibility. Our Runner is not some run-of-the-mill bandit wanting to meet his ancestors or make himself a few credits."

"You don't know his motives," spat Hawk.

Perry stared down the street with a sigh. "You are a grunt, Lieutenant. Stick to killing things and manual labour. I'm the historian, I'll do the thinking."

"Shove it up your prison pocket, Perry!"

"That's enough!" Sawyer yanked back on his reins, stopping his horse in the middle of the street and causing a small pile-up. He turned and nodded at the grand yellow-brick building to his left. "We're here anyway."

On the Ile de la Cite, next to the Notre Dame, Sawyer had found Hotel Dieu.

Street vendors carrying bundles of wood or parcels of straw brooms on their backs, and more than a few one-legged beggars with patches covering an eye, filled the narrow street leading to the building built upon many arches, similar to ancient Greek architecture.

Sweat stuck Sawyer's clothes to his skin like glue. Sweat dripped down his forehead, between his legs, causing his leather pants to chafe again in the most unfortunate place. He wiped the sweat from his face with his scarf and looked up the myriad of stairs leading to what he presumed was the front door of the hospital. The building's looming presence looked down on him like a judgmental drill sergeant. "Looks more like a nineteenth-century prison."

"Appropriate since it was considered an asylum for the poor and prostitutes," said Perry.

Several women in drab-coloured, tainted and torn dresses of yesterday's fashions strolled up to them. "Oh, I like a man in uniform," whistled one through missing teeth.

"No thank you, ladies," said Perry. "Please move along."

Three grubby hands shot forward with broken, chipped nails poking through the torn lace of their once lovingly adorned gloves. Scratch marks marred the women's arms, and scabs and oozing pustules were quite noticeable on the soft inner part of their forearms. "Then a few sous for some bread?" one said.

Hawk doled out a few coins into each of the women's hands and the women took off toward another group of men.

"They are heading for the closest opium den, not a bakery," stated Perry.

"I know. But it was hard to say no."

Sawyer dismounted, tied off his horse, and went up the stairs, his team following behind him. After walking down a corridor lined with tall grubby windows, which looked as if they once adorned these halls with bright colourful light from the sun shining through their stained glass, but now only allowed shadows of gloom to pass through their grime, Sawyer and his team came across the first room filled with patients. The prominent room was a vast, vaulted hall filled with the sick. Rows of beds, individually curtained off in thick red fabric similar to large confession booths, lined the walls and formed rows down the centre of the great hall. The air reeked of diarrhea and wet iron.

"Physicians dressed in black robes and wide-brimmed hats," said Perry. "Watch for those."

"I don't see any," replied Hawk. "And negative contact with any red auras."

"As I suspected," grumbled Perry. "Physicians often chose academia, working in universities, or chose residence in castles where they treated the wealthy. Like I said …" He turned to Sawyer with a pleading glance. "The countryside would be …"

"We're here," said Sawyer. "We're staying."

Around Sawyer, people moved slowly from bed to bed with basins of water, some tainted red with rags soaked in blood hanging over the side. Sawyer ignored the moans and cries for help as he scanned the room for men fitting Perry's description. "So far, nothing seems out of place, but I'll do a quick reconnaissance. Stay here and don't touch anything. I'll be back," he ordered.

"I still say we are barking up the wrong proverbial tree."

"I get it, Specialist. But enough." Sawyer rubbed the back of his neck in frustration. *This is going to be a very long mission if you don't stop questioning me.*

Sawyer walked through the vast hall with his scan-tacts activated and managed to glance around enough to double check no one glowed red. On the far side of the room, he finally spotted a man fitting Perry's description.

The physician tipped his large-brimmed hat at him when Sawyer approached. "Good day, sir. Are you here to escort me back to the palace? It's about time. I'm sick of this wretched place."

"Are you a physician?" asked Sawyer.

"I am the official physician of the king's court. Are you not the Musketeer Guard here to retrieve me?"

"No. But I'm sure your escort is on their way. I'm here on other king's business."

The physician shook his head and picked up the black bag at his feet. "Disgrace leaving me here. It's only on order of the Physician's Guild I must spend time attending this hospital. I don't care what your duties are, you will return me to the palace at once."

"You mentioned the Guild. We've heard rumours of uprisings against them from the barber-surgeons. King Louis has an invested interest in this."

"Miscreants," spat the physician. "Those un-pious leeches deserve no place amongst the educated. There has been some rioting in the good streets of Paris, but that is none of my concern. I keep my mind occupied on King Louis and his court. It's blasphemy what these barbers do … they want to cut into the body, make a mess of things. And most importantly, go against the Church. The body is sacred, holy, and should not be violated by the hands of another man."

"Don't suppose you've heard of anyone speaking about medical reform or seen any large-scale advancements in medicine recently? We're looking for a man named Mercier. Have you heard of him?"

"Is this some sort of interrogation?" The physician huffed, crossed his arms, and leered at Sawyer down his nose.

"No, sir. King Louis has ordered his Guard to try and stop these riots you mentioned from gaining traction."

"Well, that sounds better. And no, I have not heard of this man. Is he a physician?"

A piercing wail from behind a drawn red curtain caused goosebumps on Sawyer's skin.

"We should speak elsewhere," said the physician. "It is too loud in here for proper conversation."

As Sawyer followed the physician through the room back toward the other end of the hall, Sawyer glanced at the curtained alcove from where the screams hailed. A small opening in the curtain gave him a view of a woman, her face pale and diaphoretic. He overheard the words, *it's stuck,* and his heart jumped into his throat. On instinct, Sawyer pulled back the curtain for a better view, where he noticed a pool of blood had accumulated around the woman's buttocks.

The woman on the bed cried out as she clutched the bedsheets and threw her head back in agony, while two nuns hovered near her foot end.

"Get out! You have no business here!" one nun yelled at Sawyer.

The other nun tried to push him back outside the curtain, but Sawyer held firm. He suddenly felt eyes on him and glanced back to the front door where the physician stared, irritated. Perry had his arms crossed and Hawk was silently begging for him to hurry up.

"The baby is stuck, you must push harder," said one of the nuns.

Sawyer turned back to the patient, his medical training from the Academy forefront in his mind. *Baby. Stuck. Possible shoulder dystocia?*

Cries and sobs wailed from the mother. Sawyer closed his eyes.

The aggressive nun wasted time trying to push Sawyer away until a loud, high-pitched scream sounded. She rushed back to the mother's foot end and stared between her legs. Sawyer's heart raced. The nuns were going to let both this baby and mother die by standing there doing nothing.

"Sawyer! Hurry up! What's going on?" came Hawk's voice from across the room.

Sawyer glanced again at the front door as his right foot slowly slid into the curtained space. When he stepped fully into the space, the mother had just finished another contraction. "How long?"

"What are you doing, sir? You need to leave."

"Don't let my baby die!" cried the mother.

Damn. How long has it been already? Sweat dripped down Sawyer's forehead when during the next contraction the baby did not progress. "It's not getting oxygen. This baby needs to come out now. Turn the mother over! On her hands and knees!"

"Please leave, sir," re-ordered one of the nuns.

Waiting through what seemed an endless ten seconds to the mother's next contractions, Sawyer breathed deep and closed his eyes. *This isn't right. I shouldn't be doing this. They are meant to die. Who knows what this kid might grow up to do? What if it overthrows France? What if it discovers flight too early?*

The woman's contractions started again, the wails even louder than before. Sawyer stepped further into the space behind the red curtain. "You need to turn the mother over, the baby won't come out any other way."

"What is this nonsense? Leave at once!"

Sawyer stopped at the side of the bed when he noticed the deadpan stare of the mother. Life had left her, and she no longer cried in agony. As it appeared, these nuns had no knowledge of modern birthing techniques. And now that it was over, Sawyer wondered if he'd done the right thing. He'd been about to break the Ranger's number-one rule: don't interfere with history. He never realized how hard that rule was to follow until now.

He turned away and quickly left the alcove. Waiting at the front door, Hawk was quick to address him. "This doc isn't giving us shit. All he cares about is getting back to the Louvre and his precious king. This is a dead end, sir. Wait … you have your angry face on."

Sawyer did, and there was nothing he could do about it. His frustration had reached its peak. Broken Earth-Lander. Dead-end leads. People dying that he could help. And a man called Mercier they couldn't find. "Forget it. Suffice it to say, it doesn't look like modern medicine has reached here yet."

And we're back at ground zero.

23.

FRUSTRATION weighed heavily on Sawyer's shoulders. As he reflected back on his earlier excitement concerning this mission, he decided that now he hated this place and time, with its stench, lack of sanitation, and oppressive heat. He wanted to leave the city, and with one last glance around the bustling streets of Paris, he decided to finally take Perry's advice and investigate the countryside.

Sawyer brought his team into the first village they came across to rest the horses, and to the local tavern in the village of Lafare, located halfway between Paris and Dumont. Sawyer also knew it was time for him to eat, which he regretted based on the smell floating from the tables and from the back room where someone seemed to be boiling a dead animal in dirty water plagued by rotten potatoes.

"Thank god for modern immunization," he said, after forcing a spoonful of stew into his mouth. It tasted as bad as it smelled.

"How could people eat this?" asked Hawk, spooning the contents of his own bowl in circles. He pulled a grey substance on his spoon up to his nose and sniffed. "This, unfortunately, was a living, breathing animal at one time."

"Probably a rat," said Perry.

Hawk turned his spoon and let the contents drop back into the grey broth. "I'm not a Spawn, so thankfully I can wait to eat." He grimaced at Sawyer and shook his head. "How can you stomach that?"

"I don't have a choice. I have to eat."

Perry had chosen wine over food and sipped from his glass before putting it back on the table. "Leave him alone, Lieutenant."

"Yeah, yeah, I know better than anyone. Get it in ya, Commander. I don't want you passing out on us. And don't worry about offending my vegetarian beliefs. I've seen you when you don't get enough cyto-greens or protein. Grr ... angry man comes out."

After a few more mouthfuls, avoiding the rat meat, Sawyer finally gave up and pushed the bowl away. "Let's just find a way to this Mercier, then get back to the Earth-Lander so I can get a hold of my cyto-juice."

With their Musketeer identities clear and visible, they approached a table of men only to be greeted with curses and threatening waves of fists in the air. Sawyer tried to temper their mood with a smile, to which one of the men spat on the floor.

"We come in peace," offered Hawk.

"Why didn't you come in peace yesterday?" said the larger man at the table.

"Were we needed yesterday?" asked Sawyer.

"Someone was." The man rose from the table, eyed Sawyer, who stood a few inches shorter than him, and huffed. "You protect the king, but what about us citizens? Who's taking care of us? What do we pay taxes for? I thought Louis the Just was a fair king ... when does that fairness see its way down to us?"

"I presume there is a problem?" asked Sawyer.

The man pointed a beefy finger at one of the others at his table. "Frederick's eldest son went missing yesterday. Sent to the market early in the morning and never came home."

"And I assume that's not something Frederick's son would do?" asked Hawk. "Just go off somewhere? Weather's been nice ... he wouldn't have just decided to have some fun or something?"

"Never," said Frederick. "It's harvest time, he knew to come home. He had a good bunch of lavender, and we were going to purchase a new horse for him when he came home. He wouldn't have gone off. Now leave us alone!"

Sawyer leaned over Hawk's shoulder. "You could be right; he could have just gone off with the money. And I'd probably leave it at that if it weren't for a certain man called Mercier kidnapping men and peddling medical advances."

"I see your point," said Hawk. "Sir," he said to Frederick. "Have you heard of a man called Mercier?"

"You ain't going to help us, so be on your way, filthy Musketeers!"

Sawyer raised his hands in supplication. "We can help ..." The standing man's hands fisted as if ready for a fight. Sawyer was okay with that. "You really want to do this?"

The man threw a punch at Sawyer's head, which Sawyer caught easily in the palm of his right hand like a baseball pitcher catching a batted ball. He squeezed the fist until the man groaned. "If you're not going to give me the information I want, I can easily take it." Sawyer squeezed the fist harder until the man was on his knees. In seconds, Sawyer knew bones would crack. "I'm offering you help, sir."

"We don't need your help!" cried the man on his knees.

"This isn't how we get them to cooperate, sir," Hawk said, as he attempted to pry Sawyer's fingers from around the man's fist.

You're right. We need to give them something they want. Sawyer glanced at the empty pitchers of ale on the table then suddenly released the man's hand. Sawyer paid for more ale for the men, and immediately Sawyer and his team were invited to sit down with them.

"As citizens of France, and therefore the king," Sawyer said, "I believe you men to be assets of the king and therefore fall under the king's guards' protection. Tell me, what else do you know about these missing men? Have you heard of someone called Mercier?"

"Sir," said the man who'd stood to address them. "You are a strange occurrence for a Musketeer, but for some reason I trust you." He smiled as he watched the barmaid arrive with the pitchers. "Perhaps it's the ale."

The other two men at the table grunted and nodded, then poured themselves generous mugs.

"It's those dirty Spanish slavers taking our citizens," said Frederick.

"Not this close to Paris," said the large man.

"Then the Protestants! They're stealing our sons, trying to convert them with their foolish beliefs. And our king isn't doing anything to stop this! It's on us to fend for our families."

Sawyer looked across the table to Frederick, then glanced at the other two men. "You might be right on either account, but it's probably safer to let us handle this. Especially if it is either of those cases. But first, do you know Mercier?"

"Can't say that I do," said the large man. The other two men shook their heads.

"You know," said Frederick. "Pellisier's sons disappeared just a few nights ago as well. Right from this tavern. Left through that door and never heard of again."

"What were the Pellisier boys doing that night?" asked Perry.

"When are they not involved in some sort of fisticuffs?" replied the man who'd remained quiet thus far. "Those boys were big and strong. Would have made good Musketeers, if ya ask me."

"Were you men here that night?" asked Hawk. Fredrick shook his head but the other two nodded. "Anything unusual stick out? More people, less people than usual here? People not typically seen hanging around these parts?"

The quiet man rubbed his chin. "Come to think of it, this establishment was rather busy. Patrons filled with a lot of pomp and circumstance, even women-folk in their gloves and fancy dresses. This isn't the type of place for them. They usually go to them parlours or opium dens in Paris."

Sawyer looked around the tavern full of dusty leather coats and grimy-handed men with unruly hair, belching and swigging back ale so fast most of it dribbled down their chins. Sawyer couldn't imagine any of Paris's burgeoning 'polite society' choosing here over somewhere more refined. "Do you know why they were here?"

"Some kept yelling and boasting about some festival or whatnot. Then they all left as fast as blood from a cut-open pig. All at once, I tell you."

"Do you know where they went?"

"I didn't bother chasing them down," replied Fredrick. "I was glad they were gone. All their money had the barmaids paying them attention and leaving us hard-working citizens fighting to be served. Good riddance, I said."

Sawyer rose from the table. "Thank you. Now just go about your business as you normally would. We'll take it from here."

"You think those rich folk had something to do with these missing men?" asked Frederick.

Sawyer shook his head. Those rich folk might have something to do with this; however, there was no connection yet, and the last thing Sawyer needed was to start the French Revolution before the eighteenth century. "No. Now let us handle it from here."

Sawyer left the table and crossed the tavern with his team in tow behind him. They followed him to the long table at the back of the tavern, where a woman poured out ale from large barrels lined up behind her. "Excuse me, ma'am ..."

The barmaid frowned. "No one's called me that before," she said and turned to walk away.

Hawk leaned over the counter and grabbed her arm. "A beauty such as your-self never been called ma'am? I'm offended." He took her hand between his own and softly stroked her knuckles. "The queen herself should shy away from your delicate features and smooth skin."

The barmaid smiled as she leaned over the counter, placing her stained teeth and most- likely horrid breath inches from Hawk's face. "So, what can I get you fine soldiers?"

"We're just looking for some answers," said Hawk. "About some people who came here a few nights ago. Perhaps overdressed? Flaunting wealth?"

"I know who you speak of. They come and go as a group when they choose. Usually leave together as well."

Perry nudged Sawyer, then nodded to something tucked under one of the barrels behind the counter.

Sawyer pointed to the parchment. "May I see that?"

The barmaid didn't take her eyes off Hawk as she reached back, grabbed the parchment, and slapped it on the counter. Sawyer took it and read it aloud under his breath for his ear-pin to translate.

"A fight club?" said Perry. "Here in seventeenth-century France? I've never heard of such a thing."

The parchment described live entertainment, free ale and wine, and money to be made. "Where did you get this?" Sawyer asked the barmaid.

"Don't know," she replied, her eyes fixated on Hawk. "Usually posted around town, one must have found its way in here. The name of the tavern is written on the bottom."

Sawyer noticed, The Wren, scrawled along the bottom of the parchment. "Thank you. Also, have you heard of a man called Mercier?"

"Mercier, you say? Yeah, I know of him. Some of his men come by now and then. They say he's a doctor. Runs what he calls a 'free clinic.' Rubbish, if ya ask me. No doctor practices for free 'round here."

"Do you know where we can find him?" asked Sawyer.

"Maybe."

Perry rolled his eyes and reached for his money pouch. "How much will it cost for that maybe to turn into an absolute?"

"Three sous."

Perry doled it out and the barmaid grinned.

"He's out at that abandoned ..." she said. "Wait, you're Musketeers. I want five sous if I'm going to tell you anything."

Perry dropped more coins on the counter. "Now tell us where we can find him or run the risk of us arresting you for extortion."

The barmaid pocketed the coin. "Don't need to get crabby. I hear he's set up out near Baron Fournier's land. This Mercier ... he works out of an abandoned asylum. Can't miss it. Big stable with white doors, lots of gardens ... mostly rotted away last time I saw, but it must've been impressive during its time."

"Anything else you want to tell us?" asked Perry.

"Nope." She winked at Hawk as she leaned back over the counter. "Unless you've got some more of that coin in your pocket? Half price for you, sweetie."

Hawk smiled and backed away from the counter. "Sorry, ma'am, but business before pleasure."

Sawyer pulled his team back from the counter and away from the leering barmaid. "Finally, some tactical information."

"Perhaps we should check on the Earth-Lander first," said Perry. "If the lieutenant commander has arrived with the second one, we would be better equipped to investigate the asylum."

"That would waste time," replied Sawyer. "We only have nine days, and our main lead is that a Doctor Mercier is running a medical clinic, sharing advanced medicine with barber-surgeons, and he's kidnapping men. But ... we don't know if he is our actual Runner or working for the real one. Maybe that bandit in the forest who said he knew him was lying to save his ass, and this Mercier showed up in this century only months ago. And he's out at this asylum."

"Don't forget the fight club," added Hawk. "We can't not talk about the fight club."

"We don't know if that's connected to anything yet." Sawyer's options were limited: check on the Earth-Landers and perhaps grab a bottle of his cyto-juice so he didn't have to rely on local food anymore, or proceed to the asylum per mission orders, which delegated completing the mission above all else. Both options had pros and cons, but in the end, neither choice out-weighed the other. It was a decision he'd have to make on his own, from his gut.

"Sir?" asked Perry, as he and Hawk awaited his final decision.

"The mission comes first. We're heading for the asylum."

24.
MISSION: DAY TWO

AFTER receiving directions from the barmaid, Sawyer and his team traversed the French countryside toward the old asylum until Sawyer called the journey off several kilometres northwest of Paris. They slept by a riverbank and were packing up at sunrise the next day when Sawyer was startlingly reminded of the AI in his head.

"*Commander.*"

Sawyer nearly dropped the bedroll he was sliding into his horse's saddle. "Yes, Thor."

"*Lieutenant Commander Santiago has landed with Earth-Lander Two and has achieved communications through me via Earth-Lander Two, where I am fully operational. She advises she saw the crash and came immediately in case rescue measures were required. She further advises you will have open communications shortly and requests a status report.*"

"Thanks, Thor." Sawyer chewed his lip. This changed things. "Tell her thanks for noticing, and we *might* have found our Runner, or at least someone who's working with him. We think it's someone named Mercier, and he's set up at an old asylum northwest of Paris near some Baron Fournier's land. No further information as of yet. And let her know ..." He paused in contemplation, not sure if he was doing the right thing. "Let her know I'm sending back Specialist Perry and Lieutenant Hawk to her. I'm going ahead to recce the situation out at the asylum myself."

"*Is that all, Commander?*"

"Yes." He waited a moment then added, "And if she questions me, tell her it's my decision. My order."

137

"You want to do what!" Perry approached Sawyer, head thrust forward and brow furrowed. "I heard what you said, and sir, with all due respect … that's ludicrous. You should not be doing this alone. At least take Lieutenant Hawk. Or send him alone, but not you, sir."

Hawk strolled over. "I heard my name?"

"I received word through Thor that Santiago has landed with Earth-Lander Two. No open comms yet, but through Earth-Lander Two she can communicate with Thor, and hence myself. I need you two to go back and help secure the site while I check out the asylum myself. We'll meet back at The Boar in Dumont tomorrow. It's central to all locations."

"It's too dangerous," spat Perry.

"I agree, sir." Hawk's eyes were large, questioning.

For a moment, Sawyer contemplated making a joke to ease his worry. But now was not the time. Sawyer was dead serious about his decision. "I'm just going to recce the old asylum. I'll take off the Musketeer uniform, talk to this Mercier guy, and see if he's our Runner. I have my scan-tacts, so I might not even need to approach him. And I promise if it's him, I'll call and wait for back-up since I have comms with the commander now. In the meantime, I want you two back at the Earth-Lander so I can communicate with you. And she might need help with everything going on back there."

"I'm with the specialist on this," said Hawk. "We can't risk you … I should go. It is what I'm trained for."

Sawyer crossed his arms. "Never send a soldier to do what you aren't willing to do yourself. Besides, I may be a commander now, but I'm still a Recce Ranger."

"That's all well and good," said Perry. "But putting yourself in harm's way … well, we have no idea what dangers may lurk at that asylum. We should find another way. Something other than throwing our commander to the proverbial wolves."

"Again," emphasized Sawyer. "This is not open for debate. Besides, you make it sound so dangerous. We just need to confirm this is our Runner and if this is his base of operations. Then I leave and we return later in full force. Easy. We don't need three men showing up on his front door spooking him. Me alone should allow for an audience with the man, if need be."

Perry's eyebrows were nearly at his hairline. "Easy? How long have you been with the Rangers, Commander? Nothing is ever easy. And your father would have drilled that into you since you were born. He would account for every little thing that could go wrong, expected everything to go wrong, and would have at least twelve different contingency plans for each path that would and could go wrong. What do you plan to do, sir, if we lose you somehow?"

As far as Sawyer saw, there was only one contingency plan needed to cover all possible mistakes or miscalculations. He'd simply fight his way out. After all, he was a Spawn. And as a commander, it was his job to take charge. Just like his father would expect him to do. "My plan stands."

Perry took a long breath before responding with a nod. "Yes, sir. But I still don't like it."

"I appreciate your concern, but my decision is final." Sawyer turned away before any more objections could be voiced that might be strong enough to make him change his mind, and he found a spot against a tree nearby to sit and gather his thoughts.

Hawk joined him a few minutes later and sat next to him. "Are you sure you want to do this? I mean, I'll stand behind you, especially in front of Perry, but … I'm not completely convinced this is the best idea. You're a commander now. You need to command, which means you need to be alive and with your team."

"I'm taking care of my team." *Like Beaumont used to say … your team is the future, and his number-one rule after completing the mission was to keep the team safe.* "I'm not putting any of you at risk." *Besides, it's just easier if I do this myself. Someone else might get it wrong.* "I'm doing this, Hawk, so stand down. Just make sure you and Perry get back to the Earth-Landers safely."

139

25.

THOR kept Sawyer company as he rode toward the old asylum. *How's the weather... tell me about your childhood ... recite the mechanics of an omni-drive FTL engine ...* It wasn't much more than forced idle chatter, which Sawyer figured was drawn from an algorithm meant to keep commanders sane during isolation situations.

Sawyer travelled in a direct line, heading northwest of Paris as instructed by the barmaid. He answered Thor's questions with bitter amusement until an ivy-draped mansion came into view. As he was crested on a hill looking down on the massive estate, Sawyer pulled out a clunky spyglass for a better view. Gardens were being tended on the right side of the mansion, and as he was told, a large stable with faded white doors was located to the mansion's left.

"This has to be the place." Sawyer tucked the spyglass back into a saddle bag and studied the area with his naked eye to gain a more rounded sense of the location. On the front steps sat several men in black robes, and at each corner of the four-storey structure, men bearing arms stood idle as they stared out into the surrounding forests.

"Why guards?"

"Guards are typically used to protect, secure and keep watch ..."

"Got it, Thor. But why would a medical clinic need guards?"

"I do not know."

"Don't you know everything, Oh Great and Powerful Thor?"

"I cannot extrapolate the motives of ..."

"I wasn't actually expecting an answer, Thor."

"Then I suggest you do not pose questions directed at me if you do not require an answer, Commander."

Sawyer shook his head and returned his attention to the asylum. The building resembled an old country mansion shaped in a giant rectangle, with its north and south wings pushed forward from the centre portion. A stone staircase led up to the main door, where someone was exiting.

"Another guard."

From the south, between the mansion and its gardens, two men on horseback came riding at full canter toward the hill where Sawyer sat, while the guard at the door pointed directly at him.

"Here goes nothing." Sawyer took his horse down the hill, where he met the guards at the end of the long drive. Dust and stones gathered at the horses' hooves as they all came to a stop.

"What business do you have here?" asked one of the guards.

Sawyer had removed his pauldrons and tabard indicating his Musketeer status, and instead wore a simple shirt and doublet. "I've come in peace," he said with a smile.

"In piece of what?" grumbled the guard.

Sawyer drew a breath, wondering which cover to use. Was he here as a patient … *No, that won't work.* "My name is Sawyer. I'm a physician from Paris. I've come to speak with Mr. Mercier. I heard of his work and had to see for myself."

The guard gestured for him to follow. Sawyer did as instructed, and as he drew closer to the asylum, he noticed more of the ivy snaking its way around the grey stone. Many windows on the first floor were covered with the invasive plant, and many windows on the second, third, and fourth floors were either broken or gone. The roof loomed above, its perimeter protected by a black wrought-iron fence, broken in many places.

"Quite the place you have here," remarked Sawyer. "Have you been here long?"

"Save your questions for Dr. Mercier," replied a guard.

At the front steps, Sawyer tied off his horse and continued to follow the guards up the stairs and through the large, heavy oak door. Inside, Sawyer passed two wide, Greek-style pillars where he was then brought to a stop in a marble-floored foyer. *Dust and vinegar. Why does history always smell like dust and vinegar?*

Many closed doors lined the walls to both Sawyer's left and right. A grand bifurcated staircase led upward from the centre of the lobby with smaller, sweeping flights of stairs leading up in opposite directions, their bannisters mostly rotted away. Sawyer stepped forward and glanced up to the roof, visible past the several open floors above, and watched as men in long black robes meandered the open hallways. Some of the men stopped and stared down at him when they noticed him watching, but some jumped back as if not wanting to be seen.

"Good day," came a voice from beside the staircase. A tall slender man wearing a black vest gilded in rich blues and magenta, and a pair of leather pants with barely a speck of dust on them, approached Sawyer with his arms open. More importantly, and to Sawyer's disappointment, he did not glow red. "A fellow physician from Paris, I hear?"

"Yes," replied Sawyer, shaking the man's rough hand. "And I assume you are Mr. Mercier? The man I've heard so much about."

"*Doctor* Mercier. Now come, let's talk. I haven't heard word from Paris in quite some time. I've been meaning to get back there. So tell me, how are things shaping up in our fair city?" Mercier led him through one of the doors on the left of the lobby into a small parlour with cracking stone walls, where several high-back chairs were situated before a cold hearth.

Sawyer placated him with a smile. Now that he'd confirmed Mercier was not their Runner, Sawyer needed to get to business and find out what was going on here. "Same as always. But I'm more interested in you, sir. I've heard rumours concerning you that might align with my interests."

"And what interests are those?"

"The advancement of medicine. A little bird told me you were involved in some rather salient work concerning our discipline. It's about time someone took up the reins. Our profession has been stagnant all too long now. There is still so much for us to learn."

Conveying a weary expression, Mercier sat and offered the chair beside him to Sawyer. "I thank you for the compliment, sir, but what exactly have you heard?"

Sawyer sat and crossed his legs as delicately as Mercier had done, knowing mimicry was in fact the best form of flattery. "Not much more than whisperings from a few barber-surgeons. You know how they love to talk ... lack of education breeds idle minds."

"Don't discredit them, my new friend," replied Mercier with a glare. "If all goes correct, they will be our future."

Sawyer remembered Mercier's rough hand at their greeting and deduced that although Mercier carried himself as a nobleman, he most likely came from much less-proper standing. Sawyer needed to change his strategy. "My pardon," he said, with a bow of his head. "Are you suggesting the advancement of their training? Bringing them further into the world of medicine? It's an interesting proposal, but how would one go about such a thing when the Church stands so firmly against it?"

Mercier rose and beckoned him to follow. "Come. I shall show you something. If you truly are interested in where medicine is going, I promise you will be impressed. And with you being from Paris, maybe what we are doing here can expand even more so."

Sawyer followed him back into the main lobby.

"Have my guards told you anything about what is happening here?" asked Mercier.

"No. I am aware of you running an impressive clinic. But now I suspect there is more."

Mercier looked back at him over his shoulder. "They must remain quiet for our operation to succeed. As must you remain quiet if we proceed. One cannot be too careful with the Church and king having eyes everywhere. But if you remain amiable, then we shall proceed. According to my patron, men like us will be needed. Your visit here is quite serendipitous."

Patron? Now things were getting interesting.

"This place is rather large," noted Mercier as they entered another hall. "But we require a lot of space. Alas, the old asylum has seen better days, but there is no need for repairs. Our stay is temporary. I ... we, my patron and I, prefer to keep this enterprise mobile, to share what we have to offer to everyone across the countryside. Many men live here at this institute ..."

"Institute?"

"This place is not just a clinic for the wretched and poor peasants the king has sorely forgotten." They entered a large portico at the back of the asylum where the cool air was a fresh reprieve from the cloying scent of dust and vinegar inside. "I'm going to show you something that in time the people of France and future generations will greatly appreciate."

Sawyer noticed a richly ornate ceiling loomed above them. A relic of time passed. The estate still held wonders for those not accustomed to grandeur. But even as a frequent patron of the Louvre back in his timeline, Sawyer still appreciated the intricately carved mouldings and faded mural of the portico ceiling. After all, it was part of what he was trying to preserve in the future.

Mercier nudged his arm. "Are you a connoisseur of art as well?"

"I am to the degree most educated men are."

A short laugh escaped Mercier. "Ah, yes, the education of man. Then you shall be pleased with what you are about to see. When you told me of your interest in modern forms of medicine, I thought ... perhaps you might understand what my patron is trying to accomplish here. I am truly excited to share this enterprise with you."

They pulled up to a large entranceway on their right, leading back into the building, where muted voices came from the other side of a time-weathered double door. A cry filled with anguish suddenly broke out, and Sawyer stepped back in surprise.

When Mercier swung the double doors wide, loud, indistinct voices resonated from the overcrowded room. Overwhelming scents of iron and diarrhea thickened the air. Sawyer blinked, long and slow, letting his senses acclimate. When he could, he looked around with discernment, his breath catching in his throat when he realized what was happening before him.

Long tables, evenly placed row upon row, filled the room, with bodies lying on top half-naked or draped with blood-stained sheets. Men in black robes hustled between the beds, some carrying bowls and rags, while some carried books with inkwells balanced on top. Sawyer's mouth hung open and he struggled to swallow down the sick sensation at the back of his mouth. "My god," he said, his voice barely a whisper. "This ... this ..."

The room resembled a form of strange purgatory where men existed on the cusp of death, their fates determined by the minions of hell moving purposely amongst them. "What ... what is this?" Sawyer stammered, as he stepped into the room.

"This is a place of higher learning," Mercier said, his voice dripping with pride as he waved an arm slowly in front of him as if displaying a grand feast.

Sobs of misery cut through the din of voices, making Sawyer aware that not all the bodies on the tables were dead. He turned away from the centre of the room to find himself looking at a man sitting on a table in front of a large, ivy-covered window. The man was bracing his shoulder with a bloodied hand while other men in robes probed his injuries without any regard to his pleas for them to stop.

145

As Sawyer turned to Mercier, he caught sight of pools of crimson blood under one of the nearby tables; thick and gelatinous and spreading out slowly as more dripped from above. These men were playing doctor, treating the bodies, both dead and alive, as cadavers on a mortician's table. It was the stuff of nightmares.

A gurgling, sucking noise to Sawyer's left forced his eyes that way. He nearly retched when he saw a man pull bloody intestines from a person's body with pointy instruments. The robed man presented the intestines to the group of men huddled around him; he was like a snake charmer dangling red, slippery snakes from a branch.

Anger rushed through Sawyer like water bursting from a broken dam, fast and furious, inciting the storm within him. *I have to save the future from this!* But he couldn't blow his cover. Nor could he allow Mercier, their only lead, to see his disgust. Sawyer had to play nice, make this man trust him enough to share more. Possibly introduce him to his patron.

"I have learned from a fellow physician," started Mercier, as he looked about the room. "That the secrets of medicine can only be discovered by the cutting open of bodies. One must get their hands dirty, study what is beneath the skin and see and learn what makes the human body tick. It is only through this that we shall further our understanding of medicine."

Sawyer managed to swallow his disgust and held his head high. "Forgive my initial reaction, it's quite a scene to get accustomed to. But what about the Church? They ..."

"They have no business in medical business. That is why we must keep our enterprise secret. France needs physicians. War with Spain is close at hand, the plague still haunts us, and our barber-surgeons can riot in the fair streets of Paris all they want, but their efforts won't accomplish anything. It is only through this form of education that I can help them rise, learn, better themselves, and become physicians and surgeons. I struggled myself to learn medicine. At one point, I even fought on behalf of the barber-surgeon's plight. I wanted more than to give enemas and pull teeth. I am fascinated in the human body. So when I met this fellow a few months back, willing to teach and show me more, I instantly fell under his spell and joined him."

"This fellow?" asked Sawyer, sweeping his gaze around the room. "Can I meet him?"

"Perhaps another day. You look pale. Perhaps we should remove ourselves from the classroom. It is rather a lot to take in all at once."

Sawyer turned back toward the door they'd entered when a red glow across the room caught his attention. Standing by the back wall, a short man in glasses was leaned over a table pointing to someone's spilled innards, his radiation aura unmistakable. "That's him," Sawyer whispered.

"Him who?" inquired Mercier.

Even though he was a Spawn, Sawyer knew he couldn't take out all the guards he'd seen protecting this place. And he'd promised his team he wouldn't do anything stupid. He also didn't know what resources this Runner had, what weapons he carried. Runners didn't follow the rules as Rangers did. Beneath this Time Runner's black robe could be a Stormguard, or other weapons of deadlier design.

"Dr. Sawyer," said Mercier. "Is there something wrong?"

Sawyer shook his head. "No. Everything is fine. You were right. I'm very pleased with what I've seen here today. Perhaps I can come back another time, when my countenance has returned and I'm better situated to handle myself. I would very much like to learn more about what is going on here."

Mercier smiled. "Arrangements can be made, good friend."

26.

DR. Arnault adjusted the glasses on his nose and stared at the now-closed door of his classroom. There was no mistaking who that guest had been, with his black hair and pale-blue eyes. *It's astonishing how much you resemble your father.* "But why the hell would you send your son when the rules say we can't kill him?"

"What was that, Doctor?" asked one of the students.

Arnault glared in response. "Get back to your studies and dissect this organ," he said, pointing to the spleen of the body cut open before him.

He moved away from the table to the front window, where he had a clear view of the asylum's main entrance, and he watched the young Time Ranger speed off on his horse. Arnault knew he would have to plan for this obstacle carefully and find a way to distract this young Sawyer from interfering with his agenda. And as a Spawn, this Ranger would require extra-special attention. Arnault wasn't sure he was equipped for this situation; surely he could not approach the man without backup or support. Was anyone of this time even capable of handling a Spawn? Arnault shook his head. "Not without an entire arsenal and small army behind them."

Arnault knew he was being dramatic, but his job here was critical to the future's very existence, and every aspect of his job required clear thinking, strong patience, and a cunning mind to avoid being caught by either the Rangers, the seventeenth-century Church, or even the real Musketeers. Arnault didn't have time for subtlety, so drama it was going to be.

"I can't have you interfere," he said, drumming his hands on his hips. "I also can't eliminate you. Why did the Time Rangers have to send you, of all people!"

"Dr. Arnault?"

Arnault spun around to see his assistant standing behind him. "What is it, Mercier?"

"Is there a problem? You seem upset. I thought bringing more physicians into the fold would please you. You were very adamant about spreading our cause, teaching as many as we could as quickly as we could."

Arnault hung his head to gather his patience. "It is not what you did that perturbs me, it is who you brought in here."

"Doctor Sawyer?"

"He is not a doctor, you fool!"

Mercier stepped back. "You know him? Why didn't you say anything when he was here?"

"That's none of your concern." Arnault turned back to the window, growled then turned back with his professional countenance returned. "But suffice to say, we need him contained. He most likely saw me, which means he will be back."

"If he is a problem, shall I send men out after him? Perhaps he'll make a fine specimen for our students to study?"

You don't know the half of it.

But although a valid suggestion, Arnault could not kill Sawyer, which made him wonder again why the rear admiral had sent his son on this mission. There was no use trying to find an answer to a question he'd never get answered while stuck in this century, so he tried to conceive a plan to detain the Ranger without actually harming him. Suddenly he remembered his assistant's earlier dilemma and smiled at him. "Mr. Mercier, I think we have found our new champion."

27.

BEFORE the first night stars appeared, and the sky still blazed an orange-pink hue on the horizon, Perry and Hawk dismounted their horses amongst the copse of trees where they'd hidden their Earth-Lander. Perry knew they were close to the spacecraft when static electricity raised the hairs on his arms. A shimmering distortion broke the clarity of the trees and he saw Lieutenant Commander Santiago, in her grey Time Ranger uniform, step through the Earth-Lander's mask.

"Thank goodness you're here. We have a lot to discuss," Perry greeted her.

Santiago wore a less than comforting smile. "Flip a coin for who goes first? Because I've got a long shit list. Commander Sawyer really did a number on Earth-Lander One."

Hawk blew out a breath. "The commander did the best he could to land us safely, and I say he did a pretty fucking good job since we're all alive. But other than that, how's everything going, sir? Do we have open comms yet?"

Santiago shook her head. "No, but we're working on it. I brought Dr. Brodeur in case there were injuries, but it seems you're both fine. I also brought an engineer and two SAR Rangers with me. They're working on your Earth-Lander's problems as we speak. We should be able to get it running and put up a new back hatch to replace the one you lost. Not sure about FTL yet, but open communications are taking priority. Especially with the commander going off on this fool-hardy mission on his own."

Hawk glared at her. "He is the commander, and his word is our order, sir."

Perry tried to temper the tension he sensed brewing between Hawk and Santiago. "Have you heard from the commander since he arrived at the asylum?"

"I did," replied Santiago. "He had to leave the area around the asylum to

151

contact me— apparently there's some sort of technology block preventing transmissions in and around the estate."

"What?" asked Hawk.

Santiago held up a hand. "We'll get to that. First, Commander Sawyer found the Runner. Or at least, who he thinks is the Runner, and it's not Mercier. Someone else at the asylum had a red aura, but he didn't want to engage without backup." She shrugged, raised her brows. "Which surprised me."

"Why?" asked Perry.

"I figured Commander Sawyer would have gone rogue ... just taken the Runner out on his own," she said flippantly. "He wants to make a name for him—"

"Watch what you say, sir," said Hawk. "You don't know anything about him."

When Perry heard the tension returning to Hawk's voice, he interrupted. "What about this red aura he saw?"

"The commander thinks Mercier is just some sort of pawn in the Runner's agenda," said Santiago. "And this clinic is also more than just a clinic. This Runner, and Mercier, have set up an illegal school to teach barber-surgeons a 'new way' of medical training. The commander didn't go into specifics, but suffice it to say, he doesn't think this mission will be an easy snatch and grab. Too many armed guards protecting the place."

Santiago stood back, hands on hips. "And I thought fixing the Earth-Lander was our biggest problem."

"But you will be able to get it flight worthy, right?" asked Perry.

Santiago turned toward where she'd appeared and disappeared back behind the mask. Perry and Hawk followed her as she spoke. "Once we got basic power up and running in Earth-Lander One, the engineer combined the two masks of the Earth-Landers. We have a five-metre circumference of invisibility. Home base for now while we get Earth-Lander One ready for flight. And yes, it will be ready for flight, eventually. Well, maybe not the FTL engine ..."

Perry was glad for the progress report, but there was something else he needed to know. He grabbed her arm as she made her way into the back of Earth-Lander Two. "Is the commander safe, sir?"

Santiago heaved a sigh. "Yes, Specialist."

Perry sensed more than a little frustration behind the lietenant commander's reply when she didn't reciprocate his looking into her eyes. "There's something you aren't telling us."

Santiago straightened. "A secure communication came to me from the rear admiral right after you guys left for the planet. I was told to deliver it to the commander after you landed groundside."

"Does the communication involve this mission?" asked Hawk.

"What's in it is above your rank and pay-grade. And apparently mine as well. It's encrypted, and for the commander's eyes only, so deal with it." She entered the Earth-Lander and sat at the helm. "Thor is still broken in Earth-Lander One, but he's fully operational and has access to the *BlackOut* from here. That's how I've been able to communicate with the commander's AI. And only his AI." She turned her head upward to invoke the Earth-Lander's comm system. "Thor."

"Yes, Lieutenant Commander Santiago."

"Any luck breaking through that comm dampening grid yet?"

"No, Lieutenant Commander."

"Tell me about this grid, Thor?" said Hawk.

"There is a block preventing me from scanning the region of France where Commander Sawyer was located. He needed to leave the grid area before I could locate him and continue passing communications between him and the lieutenant commander."

Santiago looked at both Perry and Hawk before addressing Thor again. "Can you tell yet where the grid signal is coming from?"

"I cannot."

"Does that mean a block, or could it mean his implant is broken ... or damaged? Or is it because the Earth-Lander's comms are out still?" asked Perry.

"I lack the ability to decipher if the commander's implant is either broken or damaged."

"Tech," stated Hawk. "Our Runner must have brought future tech back with him knowing Time Rangers would be coming after him eventually. But how would he know what to block? We use encrypted military frequencies."

Santiago stared at the Earth-Lander's control panel, her jaw tense, as if in deep contemplation while her fingers nervously drummed the console. Suddenly she turned to Perry. "Commander Sawyer wants you two to meet up with him tomorrow in Dumont, which is outside the grid area. I'm coming with you. Thor, you keep trying to break through that barrier. Use whatever resources you can from the *BlackOut*." She looked sternly at Perry. "It will take the commander time to reach Dumont, so we'll leave tomorrow at sunup."

Perry nodded, the pit in his stomach growing larger with each second. He thought having the lieutenant commander arrive with reinforcements would be a good thing, but with news of possible future tech working against them, things couldn't be going any worse.

"In the meantime," said Santiago, looking down at her grey fatigues. "I'm going to need something to wear."

28.

MISSION: DAY THREE

SAWYER entered the village of Dumont the next day, where he was immediately surrounded by the owners of local inns and taverns. They greeted him at the gate, soliciting their businesses without compunction. Sawyer smiled down at one of the tavern girls, obviously sent out to garner his attention by the way she filled out her dress and reminding him of Aurora coming to his father's apartment wearing only her trench coat. It seemed like ages ago.

He tied off his horse at the closest stable to the The Boar and entered. Crowded and loud, with cigarette and pipe smoke hovering like a low-lying cloud beneath the oak ceiling rafters, the tavern was everything Sawyer remembered. Except for the patrons. Most of the boisterous customers were too lavishly dressed for such a hole-in-the-wall drinking establishment. Women wore fine silk gloves, men wore long, embroidered coats, and the wigs were atrociously too high or too long down their backs.

After Sawyer had shovelled in more rancid stew and drummed his fingers on the table for a few hours, his team finally arrived along with Santiago. "Checking up on me, Lieutenant Commander?"

Along with Perry and Hawk, she sat and crossed her hands on the table. "From what you described at the asylum, I thought you could use the help. That's all, sir. Unless, of course, you prefer to do everything yourself? You shouldn't have gone ..."

"Can it, Lieutenant Commander," replied Sawyer. She'd just arrived and was already trying to undermine him. "I'm in charge, not you." He sat back to study her better and noticed her costume.

She was dressed in a gown with layers of silk embroidered skirts and pet-ticoats puffing up her dress, and a pair of thinly soled shoes peeked out the bottom. She must have seen Sawyer staring, for she raised her eyebrows and scowled. The dress and wig covering her short haircut gave her an entirely differ-ent visage. Again, Sawyer thought back to Aurora and her long blonde hair and easy smile that had initially captured his interests.

"I needed a disguise," she said, breaking him from his musings. "And without Acclimation to costume me, I didn't have much choice but to steal some clothes from a nearby estate. That's why we're late."

Perry and Hawk stifled grins.

"I am so tired of this!" she yelled, stuffing the extra dress material between her legs to sit on. Before she said anything further, she yanked the thin shawl draped over her shoulders across the high bodice, which made her breasts look like they were spilling out. "Eyes front, soldiers."

She reached for the pitcher of ale sitting on the table, blew away the strands of the elaborate wig, which had fallen in her face, then drank straight from the pitcher before slamming it back on the table.

"You look very ... refined, Lieutenant Commander," said Perry.

Santiago glared at him. "Shut it, Specialist. It's all I have."

Perry cleared his throat in an obvious attempt to steer the conversation in the proper direction. "What are our options? We found our Time Runner ..."

"I found a man with a red radiation aura," corrected Sawyer.

"He's at the old asylum working with Mercier and running a sort of illegal medical school," continued Perry.

"There's no proof they are working together yet," Sawyer corrected again.

Perry forced out a breath. "And the location is heavily guarded." Sawyer nodded. "Well, at least I got that part right."

"How many guards?" asked Hawk. Eagerness lit up his eyes. "I made sure to become fairly proficient in seventeenth-century weapons before departure."

"We can't go in there guns a blazin'," replied Santiago. "There would be too many casualties."

"I will keep my scan-tacts on historical relevance," stated Perry.

"No," said Santiago. "Well, yes. But this mission requires more finesse than a simple snatch and grab."

Sawyer sat forward, straighter, to make sure all eyes were on him. "Thank you, Lieutenant Commander, but I think I can handle this. Lieutenant Hawk and I will go in at night."

Santiago grabbed the pitcher of ale, gulped back several mouthfuls then glanced back at those staring at her. "What? You've never seen a woman before?" She turned to Hawk. "We need more ale. Now, Lieutenant. And as for your plan, Commander, you've already set yourself up for failure. But before I go into detail as to why, there's something I need to speak to you about. Privately."

Sawyer stared at her as Hawk rose from the table. For a needed reprieve before he lay into his second-in-command, Sawyer turned away and watched Hawk. After the lieutenant pushed his way through the crowd to find a barmaid, someone bumped into him at the counter. When Hawk returned to the table with a curious expression on his face, Sawyer hadn't yet calmed down from Santiago's statement and thought he might later regret what he had to say to her, so he kept his focus on the lieutenant. "Hey, Hawk, what did that man want?"

"He asked me if I wanted to join him for festivities tonight."

"Festivities?"

Hawk shrugged. "His word, not mine. He and his friends are waiting to go somewhere with free drinks and entertainment. Sound familiar?"

"The parchment," said Sawyer.

"The fight club?" asked Perry.

Santiago sat forward. "Wait, what are you talking about?"

Sawyer was about to explain when a group of men approached the table. Unlike most other patrons in the tavern, these men were large and covered in dirt and soot, with untrimmed beards.

"Musketeers," spat one man. "Your kind ain't welcome here."

"Maybe I should have a word with these gentlemen," said Hawk.

Sawyer sighed. "Stand down."

Suddenly, the people of the tavern scurried toward the front door. On further inspection, Sawyer noticed it was the lavishly dressed patrons making their way toward the exit. He turned to the man cracking his knuckles in front of him and stood up to address him. "We're leaving . . ."

The punch to Sawyer's face was unexpected.

Sawyer instinctively punched the man back, sending him to the floor unconscious. Within moments, arms flew everywhere, including Santiago's, who seemed to handle herself well in her overgrown dress and petticoats.

Hawk landed his punches and ducked and weaved as several men tried to corner him. Sawyer gave him no further thought. Hawk was a scrapper. To Sawyer's right, Perry fought much dirtier than Sawyer had expected, and as the specialist grabbed a bottle to swing at someone's head, Sawyer saw a smile on Perry's face.

Sawyer lurched sideways as a man crashed into him, breaking his watch over his team. "Don't fucking touch me!" cried Sawyer before he charged forward without considerations for the implications of this distraction. Sawyer tackled his opposer and punched and punched, letting loose the anger and disgust he'd been holding since he'd laid eyes on Mercier's victims at the school ... and since they'd landed in France.

29.

MISSION: DAY FOUR

S IR."

Specialist Perry heard a voice from deep within slumber that he could not place, so he assumed it was directed at someone else.

"Sir."

There it was again, followed by a gentle nudging of his shoulder.

"What are you doing, sir?"

"I'm sleeping," mumbled Perry.

"In the middle of the alley?"

"Apparently so. Wait. What?" Perry raised his heavy head and opened his eyes to the sight of stone and muck beneath him. "Oh."

"Oh, indeed. Are you all right?"

Perry pushed himself up to his arms full extension and blinked several times before shaking his head. "Yes."

"Perhaps you should get up, sir."

"That's a fine idea."

After a moment, the voice spoke again. "You are still on the ground."

Perry widened his eyes in an attempt to fix his vision. "What?"

"You are still on the ground, sir."

"Oh. Yes. Right." Perry pulled his legs under him and reached for the hand extended to him. Now vertical, Perry frowned at the man who had helped him up. "What? You've never seen a man hungover before?"

The man huffed and went on his way, leaving Perry to search for his team-mates. To his immediate right he found Hawk leaning up against the tavern's back wall, asleep. Perry kicked him with his boot to get him up and moving. Once standing, Hawk looked no better than Perry felt.

"What happened?" asked Hawk, wiping both wet and dry mud from his doublet.

Perry looked around the deserted alley, and seeing no sign of either his commander or the lieutenant commander, he rushed to the street.

Dishevelled and covered in mud, Santiago came striding toward him. "Where the fuck is Commander Sawyer?" she demanded.

"Where have you been?" asked Perry.

"I woke up next to you in the alley, and when I didn't see the commander, I went looking for him. I searched the tavern then tried the streets. Negative on both."

"And you left us here for beggars to pick over?" asked Hawk.

Santiago glared. "Yes. Get over it."

Perry stepped back and shook his head. "We all woke up in this alley? I don't recall drinking that much. I lost track of everyone during that fight, but that's not normal. I would never allow myself to lose control during a mission. Something is wrong."

"I certainly didn't drink that much either," said Santiago.

"I'd never lose a fight so badly I couldn't remember how I ended up in a back alley," replied Hawk. "I suspect knock-out drugs. Did they have those in these times?"

Perry needed a moment to recall that amount of detail. "Yes. Crude at best, but they did." He shook his head. "But that's not important. We need to find the commander. Lieutenant Commander, can we access Thor?"

Santiago activated her ear-pin with a tap behind her right ear. "Earth-Lander Two, this is Lieutenant Commander Santiago. Do you copy?"

"We're here, Lieutenant Commander," came back the reply over everyone's ear-pin. "We got open comms in both Earth-Landers up and working a few minutes ago. We were about to call you."

"Can we all access Thor through the ear-pins now?" asked Perry.

"Yes, Specialist," answered the AI through their ear-pins. "Do you require assistance?"

Perry glanced at both Hawk and Santiago. "Can you locate the commander?"

"I cannot establish a link with his implant. Nor is he replying to hails over the ear-pin communicator."

Not good news. "When did you lose contact?"

"Twenty-hundred hours last evening," replied Thor.

Perry's heart dropped into his boots. Sawyer could be anywhere if that much time had elapsed. Sawyer had been eager to recce the asylum on his own, but a commander, especially Sawyer after what he'd been through in his short career, would never abandon his team to take on the mission himself without telling anyone. Despite what Lieutenant Commander Santiago thought.

"Lieutenant Commander," said a voice over the ear-pin. "I've set the team on five-hour watches here at base camp. Do you have further orders?"

Santiago scrubbed her face. "Commander Sawyer is compromised. Based on our lack of ability to communicate with him, he's probably under the grid where someone with technology equal to ours is using it to block our sensors and our commander's comms."

Perry felt all his blood rush into his boots. "No, Lieutenant Commander. You can't do this."

"If a commander is captured or compromised, per protocol, their AI is to be remotely disintegrated in order to lessen the chance of future tech being discovered … and to stop any chances of the commander giving in to interrogation, " continued Santiago.

"It will kill him!" cried Hawk. "No! I won't let you."

"Santiago, please re-consider," begged Perry. "Please, re-consider your next order."

Santiago looked Perry in the eyes. "Or the implant can be dissolved," she said flatly. "Which would destroy the tech, but not the actual commander. Although, and unfortunately for all we know, my decision may be moot."

"He's not dead. Don't say that," said Hawk.

"Put me through to the *BlackOut*," stated Santiago.

She stood tall and confident, but the slight tremor in her voice did not go unheard by Perry. His heart ached. This order meant his team no longer trusted Sawyer in getting himself out of whatever situation he was in. Perry was here on the rear admiral's request, to be Sawyer's protector, advisor, but all he could think was that he was his executioner by allowing this to happen. He tried again to reason with her. "We don't know what happened to him … We can wait…"

"*BlackOut* receiving you," came back over the ear-pins.

"This is Lieutenant Commander Santiago. IDENT 18847 Alpha. Prepare for Commander Sawyer's AI dissolve on my command."

"Aye ... aye, sir."

Perry's mind's eye walked through Sawyer's childhood bedroom. Yellow stickers on the ceiling, the small grey-and-white kitten Perry had given him snuggled on Sawyer's pillow. John, standing beside him at the doorway, Perry smiling as John watched his creation read from a Time Ranger manual. *When had everything gone so wrong? How did everything lead to this?*

"Initiate the commander's AI dissolve now. Report on completion."

A moment passed. Another. Perry's heart pounded. "Everyone he's ever known has disappointed him," he whispered. "Everyone has left him ..."

"Sir," said a voice over the comms.

"Go ahead," replied Santiago.

"We do not have confirmation of dissolve. I repeat, we do not have confirmation of dissolve."

"Shit yeah!" cheered Hawk.

Perry felt his relief but kept himself reserved as the blood started to once again flow to his limbs.

Santiago's eyes went wide. "Thor?"

"Yes, Lieutenant Commander?"

"Thoughts?"

"I presume the grid blocking my communications is also interfering with other systems. The signal most likely cannot get through."

Perry breathed out as if releasing all the wind in the universe in one forceful breath. His shoulders relaxed, and after another breath his hands stopped trembling.

Santiago spoke with the *BlackOut* again. "Acknowledge receipt of message. Stand down until further notice." She turned to Perry. "We need to find whatever is disrupting comms. We need to shut down the grid. If we can't dissolve Thor, maybe we can shut down the field blocking him so we can use him to find our Time Runner. I'll return to the Earth-Landers. Your priority is to complete the mission. Get to that asylum where we presume the Runner is hiding. Keep me updated."

"Sir, what about the commander?" asked Perry.

"We can't waste time, which coincidently we don't have a lot of," replied Santiago. "Five days to boomerang and our Runner hasn't even been verified, and his whereabouts are unknown. If the commander is at the asylum where we think the Runner is located, then good, two birds with one stone. But you are not to steer off course. Capturing our Runner is our mission."

Perry's heart couldn't take the roller coaster of emotions; he needed a drink. "We can't abandon Sawyer. I won't do it, sir. At least give Lieutenant Hawk and I one day to search the area and the blackout area. We shouldn't leave any stone unturned before rushing out to the asylum. We were drugged, perhaps he was as well. Being a Spawn, maybe it affected him differently. He could be wandering around without a clue who he is or where he is. Or maybe this fight club has something to do with his disappearance. Those patrons last night have something to do with that fight club, I'm sure of this. Maybe they took our commander? We need to find him."

"Forget the fight club. You have your orders. Go to the asylum and find this Time Runner … or red aura … or both. Hopefully the commander will also be there, but if not, the Runner is your priority."

When she left, Perry turned to Hawk, who had been quiet thus far. "Lieutenant, what say you?"

"Oh, I stopped listening when she said our priority was to complete the mission."

30.

A VIOLENT shiver racked Sawyer's body, waking him in a cold sweat. When he pried open his eyes, he saw a torch flickering in the distance, its light barely reaching the corners of the small dank room in which he found himself. Beneath him, the ground was hard, packed earth. The stench of mould and stale urine permeated the air. Looking around where he could see, he noticed the only window was barred and set into a door several feet in front of him.

Sawyer pushed to his feet using the wall behind him for support, sending dirt down his neck under the collar of his doublet. Shaking out his coat, he noticed it moved too easily. Patting himself down revealed his weapons and belts were gone. Behind his ear he felt for the translation pin and with relief found it still in place. Next, he checked the status of his AI. "Thor?"

"Yes, Commander."

"Where am I?"

"I do not know."

Sawyer reached the door to his cell in four long strides and he peered through the small opening. The area was lit with torches spread sporadically along the hallway's dirt walls, and too many shadows obscured the view outside his cell for him to see anything. He pushed on the door and when nothing happened, he ran his fingers along its frame, his heart falling when he realized it was hinged on the other side, rendering his more intricate escape skills moot. He stepped back, crouched, and threw himself against the door. It banged and vibrated but did not budge.

"Throwing yourself against a solid object may inflict injury. I suggest you do

not attempt that again," stated Thor. "*I do not have contact with the* BlackOut's *medical staff.*"

Sawyer rubbed his shoulder as he backed into the middle of the cell. "How did I end up here? Why can't I remember? I remember the tavern. Fighting … Thor, where's Perry and Hawk? Where's Santiago?"

"*I am only operational as your AI while you are cognizant. I can only assume that during the fight you were rendered unconscious. At that point, to use the vernacular, I was also knocked out. My last memory of you in the tavern consists of your drinking from a rather large mug of ale. My next memory is of you waking in this room. On initial start-up, it is my protocol to establish communications with your team and your ship. I found no connection with either. We are alone.*"

Sawyer paced as the news settled in. *My father would know how to get out of here. My father … Vietnam? How did he escape? No, he had help. England … no it was a castle. Stone walls.* Sawyer glanced around his dirt room and quickly realized there was little chance at digging his way out.

His eyelids slid shut as he fell into a pool of memories in which his father had locked him in many rooms as a child in which he was forced to escape. *One filling with water… Windows… An Earth-Lander… Tools. None of these apply here.*

His eyes shot open. "What do I have that my captors don't? Strength. They have no idea what strength I possess." Sawyer smiled. "Someone will be by shortly. They captured me for a reason. Somebody will want to talk."

"*You are relying on statistical analysis for comfort?*"

"You are such a computer, Thor. But no, not comfort. A plan."

Sawyer rubbed a hand down his face, stopping to grip his chin. Where was his team? A horrifying thought occurred to him … *Were they captured as well?* He released a loud huff of breath, cognizant of the threats and torture that typically accompanied imprisonment in Earth's seventeenth century.

Movement at the window caught his attention. Sawyer listened as whispered voices on the other side of the door conversed.

"You will need to …"

"I know what I'm doing."

"Triple the dose."

"That will surely kill him."

"Trust me, it won't."

Sawyer rushed the door to see who was there, but a sharp sting in his shoulder rendered him motionless halfway across the small cell. He dropped to the ground as every muscle in his body felt as if it were disintegrating. Within moments, he was unconscious. Having no window to the outside world, when he woke later, still in his cell, he couldn't tell how long he'd been out. Only that he could barely move.

"*Commander? Are you here?*" Thor asked.

"Yes," he replied. Sawyer lay on the floor, trying to stare at the ceiling to gain focus, but his eyelids kept falling shut. He was so tired. Exhausted. His body felt like the ground itself, heavy and stagnant, unable to move properly. He remembered the sting in his shoulder and reached with a leadened hand to feel the wound. Instead, he found a small dart embedded deep into his muscle and tissue. He yanked it out, dropped it on the ground, and let his arm fall to his side along with it, too tired to hold it upright.

"They fucking drugged me, Thor. I can barely move …. Or keep my eyes open."

"*Indeed, someone has. And it appears there has not been sufficient time for it to wear off.*"

"Great."

Outside this room could be anything, anyone. A tingling in the back of Sawyer's mind, an innate sense honed by his father's training and Spawn genetics, made him turn his head. He saw, or envisioned, he could not be sure in his sedative state, two sets of disembodied eyes peep through the cell door window.

Sawyer knew he could neither escape nor protect himself; his strength, his advantage, was gone. *Was this your plan?* he asked the staring eyes. *Did you know to drain my strength? How?*

An ear-piercing screech resounded in the small cell as the door opened and a form moved toward him. It was nothing more than a black shadow floating across the ground, its fluid figure swishing gracefully as it came to a stop in the middle of the cell, its aura a mix of white and red. But was it an actual aura, compromised scan-tacts, or the firelight from the torch causing the effect?

"We meet again."

The voice was distant, an echo hailing from the depths of an enormous pit. Sawyer could barely make out what it was saying. He blinked his vision to clarity, but with little reward. The figure remained a pale, glowing, featureless head atop a shadow that flowed like vivid black silk to the ground. Sawyer was not certain if it was real or a product of his imagination.

Another figure, short and bulky in stature with eyes that twinkled like diamonds and an aura similar to the other man's, entered. Sawyer strained against the heaviness of his eyelids, battling a drowsiness and blurred vision that threatened to overwhelm him.

"Welcome to your new existence," said the short man with the diamond eyes. "Any sign of defiance shall be met with aggression. Any act in contradiction to your instructions shall be met with aggression. Any refusal to act upon given instructions will also be met with aggression."

Existence. Defiance. Aggression. These words stood out.

"I'll take your silence as acceptance of these rules," continued the man. "As I predicted, you heed instructions well. Continue to do so and your time here may be more pleasant. Don't, and Mercier will be forced to adjust your destiny toward a more painful future."

Mercier! Anger sprouted in Sawyer, fostering his instincts for self-preservation. Using his anger as fuel, Sawyer looked these two men in the eyes. "Fuck. You." It came out raspy, quiet, unlike his own strong voice.

Mercier spun away in a blur of blackness and retreated to the door, his companion following quickly on his heels. At the mantle, Mercier stopped. Metal scraped metal, followed by a deep thud of a lock engaging. Mercier looked at him through the small window. "I respect your audacity. It is, after all, *one* of the reasons we chose you for this enterprise. But your mistake was assuming the aggression would be meted out on you." Mercier smiled, quick and flat, depicting only malevolence. "I will be sure to send your regards to your fellow Musketeer who we have sequesterd elsewhere."

Two thoughts immediately struck Sawyer. First, he knew he wasn't alone in his predicament. And second, he regretted his actions, because now a teammate was going to pay for his defiance.

"Commander? Are you still here?"

"Yeah, Thor. I'm here."

"Is your plan working?"

"No, Thor. It's not." *The only way out now is an inhuman amount of self-control. Something I don't think I have.*

***

THE screeching metal of a door forced open broke through Sawyer's nightmare, snapping him across what felt like time and space and dumping him back in his cell. He opened his eyes to see two brutish, leather-clad men standing above him.

"Stand," one ordered.

Sawyer blinked.

"Stand!"

Bile rose in Sawyer's throat. There was nothing he could do, no strength to draw from.

"Stand!"

"*You should do as you are instructed, Commander,*" said Thor. "*I fear there will be reprisals.*"

Sawyer was hauled to his feet before he could answer his AI. Unable to hold himself upright, the men held him steady while another man in robes entered the room.

When something wet touched Sawyer's lips, his tongue darted out to retrieve the water, which stung as it slid down his parched throat. His body pressed forward, wanting more. And as the liquid came faster, sliding over his tongue without time to swallow, he sputtered and gagged.

"Arnault says you must eat," a guard grumbled under his breath.

Sawyer was barely able to swallow the bread forced into his mouth as he continued to choke on the water lingering near his vocal cords. When the feeding was finished, Sawyer was dropped to the ground and abandoned once again. He drew an arm up his body and draped it over his head.

"Thor?" he croaked. "Do you think whoever else they captured will be punished just once for my not getting up, or for all three times?"

"*I cannot say. But according to the rules dictated, I presume all three times.*"

Sawyer fell back into a fitful sleep and woke later feeling worse than before as wet, sharp, needle-like pain engulfed every inch of his body. Too weak to protect himself from the explosions of fire repeatedly assailing him, Sawyer cried out, with nothing more than forced air escaping dry lips.

The bones in his upper arms felt as if they were shattering as tight clamps squeezed them, pulling his body upward. Before him stood the short man with diamond eyes, and he held things Sawyer could not identify. The items simply hovered in space where one would imagine hands would be. And instead of feet, there were empty buckets. This man, and the brute squad holding him upright, all still glowed a faintish yellow-red.

Sawyer's mind was still compromised by the sedative. And his scan-tacts were dried out and useless. He couldn't tell the difference between an aura and a torchlight glow. They were damaged by lack of moisture, and he knew he would have to get rid of his scan-tacts before they stuck to his eyeballs. He dropped his head and let it hang forward. Pale and tinged blue, and dripping with water, a body stretched downward to where two white feet contrasted starkly against the dark ground.

It took Sawyer several seconds to recognize it as his own body, and when he did, a flushing heat ignited in his stomach. He was naked. The fire inside him spread to all his limbs, and he wanted nothing more than to lash out and fight. His head was yanked upright by someone pulling his hair, and while naked and trembling, the strange, diamond-eyed man scrubbed him with a brush from head to toe. Harsh bristles scratched every inch and crevasse of his body until he was raw.

"You must be cleaned," said Diamond-Eyes. "Despite what that imbecile Mercier thinks, this must be done. I can't have you falling ill. Hold still."

With Sawyer's skin burning and streaked with thin lines of fresh blood, Diamond-Eyes dried him with a coarse towel that agitated Sawyer's already sensitive skin. Each of his limbs were then forcefully thrust into either the sleeves of an oversized white shirt or into the leg holes of stiff leather pants that weren't his own.

When Diamond-Eyes was done, he held Sawyer firmly by the chin and turned his head left and right as he scrutinized him. "You are a surprise, but one that I've realized I can use to my advantage."

Sawyer's chin was roughly let go and he was deposited back on the ground.

Mercier entered carrying a large skin of water. Diamond-Eyes bid him farewell and left.

"Drink this," Mercier said, tossing the old-school canteen to Sawyer, who had neither the strength nor wherewithal to catch it. A stalemate lasted several minutes until Mercier sighed. "I will graciously ignore your lack of responsiveness if you would drink now."

"Do as he instructs," said Thor.

Sawyer wanted to rush forward and kill this man, draw his death out slowly by slicing a blade down every slow, pumping vein he could find. Instead, Sawyer pushed his violent thoughts from his mind and reluctantly stretched out his arm for the sake of his teammate. He wrapped his fingers around the canteen and pulled it back toward him and drank.

"That is enough," said Mercier. "My patron was correct; you are exactly what I need. You will give me obedience without question and without hesitation. I'm pleased he found you so easily in that tavern. Yet I am surprised he knew you were a Musketeer as opposed to the physician you pretended to be."

The anger within Sawyer rose. Every fibre of his being wanted to kill this man.

"You are most likely confused." Mercier paced before Sawyer. "In time all will become clear, but for now you need not know anything more than I wish you well in the coming days. Based on your fighting prowess, I presume you will be a proper choice. My patron seems to think so, and I have no reason not to trust him. I was at the tavern in Dumont, you know. I met your acquaintances and saw how you conducted yourself during that rather rambunctious ordeal. You showed a side of humanity I rarely see, and I think you'll do just fine with what is to come."

Mercier bent down and brushed the hair from Sawyer's forehead. "Do you know what it is that's inside you? Yes? No? I think you do. I noticed it the moment you pounded that poor man's face into a bloody pulp on the tavern floor."

Rising and turning with a swish of black fabric, Mercier moved to the centre of the cell. "And I will see it again soon enough." And with a smile that turned Sawyer cold, Mercier started toward the door. As he walked, he stumbled forward as his feet tangled with something suddenly under his feet. He turned back to Sawyer, who was smiling, his arm out at his side from throwing the canteen.

"I will forgive you for the failure to drink on my initial command," said Mercier. "But for this, your friend Hawk will suffer."

Sawyer paled. *Fuck no. Not Hawk. Control. You need to keep your cool more than ever now... until the time is right.*

31.

AFTER searching the streets for hours and discovering no leads to help in finding their commander, Hawk had steered Perry back into The Boar Tavern. No men or women in lavish attire resided inside this time, only farmers and merchant-class citizens. Perry strode toward the serving counter with Hawk at his side. "Excuse me," he said, raising an arm to attract the barmaid's attention.

She put two mugs on the counter followed by a pitcher of ale. Perry waved off the offer. "Last night this establishment was considerably more busy," he said.

"And we were here with another gentleman," added Hawk. "Don't suppose you know where he went? Or what exactly happened last night?"

The barmaid poured two mugs of ale despite Perry's insistence not to, then pushed them across the counter. When she looked at them with raised eyebrows, and with a hand resting on her hip, Perry let out a sigh and dropped a few coins on the counter.

The barmaid tucked them into her pocket with a satisfied grin. "I know what you speak of. Happens every now and then. Rich folk come, anger the regulars and then tramp off somewhere. I don't know why. They spend money, so I don't mind when they come back. As for your friend … don't know him."

Hawk hung his head. "Fucking fantastic."

"Expecting the rich folk back anytime soon?" Perry asked.

The barmaid shook her head.

"Why do they come here?" asked Hawk.

The barmaid shrugged. "Got this," she said, producing a thick, tattered paper with writing. She put the parchment on the counter, then leaned over with her chin resting in her propped-up hands. "Came in yesterday with that bunch you mentioned. A girl like me wouldn't mind an evening of festivities." She batted her eyelids at Hawk as she slid her elbows together on the counter to emphasize her bounty. "On the arm of a handsome Musketeer, no less."

Perry took the parchment then stepped out of earshot of the barmaid. Hawk leaned over his shoulder, his breath heavy on Perry's neck as he read aloud.

"Gambling and drinks. Same as the other one," said Hawk. "But no location where it takes place. It's this fight club we heard about, and it could be where Sawyer is, or where he was taken to. You know, there was that man last night who tried to get me to go with him to some party. We should have paid more attention to …"

"What was this man's name?"

"Baron something … Fournier. Baron Fournier." Hawk moved back to the counter where the barmaid stood waiting. "Do you know where we can find a Baron Fournier?"

"Comes here often," replied the barmaid. "Usually with the other rich folk. Crass individual, but what you gonna do? He can pinch me all he wants, as long as he pays up in the end. His estate is several leagues northwest of here. The one with those god-awful eyesores cluttering his front garden. That man loves his Greek statues."

Perry turned to Hawk. "Baron Fournier, haven't we heard his name before?" He snapped his fingers when it came to him. "Yes, the barmaid in Lafare mentioned him by name. His estate is near the asylum. Perhaps this fight club takes place on his grounds … or he knows something about it. If we head to the baron's estate, we'll still be on track to recce the asylum. Santiago doesn't even need to know about this detour."

Hawk agreed.

So, with the parchment under his arm, Perry left the tavern. Outside, he and Hawk gathered their horses, made for the main gate of the village, then headed deeper into France's northwest territory. They would make camp as soon as darkness prevented them from riding, but till then, Perry wanted to use his newfound eagerness to cover as much ground as they could.

***

IN the front parlour of the dilapidated asylum, Dr. Arnault met with his assistant, Mercier. They sat in tall leather chairs in front of an impressive floor-to-ceiling stone hearth, sipping brandy.

"Sawyer's behaviour was to be expected," said Dr. Arnault. "He is complying with the rules, like I expected he would. Our little ruse concerning his captured teammate will keep him from retaliating. And that, my friend, is something we do not want."

"Hopefully he will continue to follow our instructions," replied Mercier, placing his goblet on a side table, with an amused look. "Our enterprise here has proven both lucrative and helpful to the people of France. I'd hate to see it end." A soft and pensive quality adorned his face. "I don't question why you thought this man would make a fine champion. I saw it myself in the tavern. That raw, caged violence waiting to be exploited. He will definitely serve our purposes well. But if I may, how did you know he was a Musketeer and not a real physician? You saw him only briefly the other day."

Arnault knew better than to divulge the real reason, so he kept it simple. "I'm familiar with his father." Arnault sat forward, rested his goblet on the arm of the chair, and stared into the amber liquid. He needed to change the direction of the conversation. "How much longer do you think our school will go unnoticed? Sawyer had to have found out where we were from someone. I fear we may have to relocate ourselves, and we are in no shape right now to do so, as we are quite established. I can only do so much in fending off any intruders. My … capabilities are limited. But I will start scouting other locations soon enough."

"We have plenty of able bodies still to be serviced, so I am in no rush to pack up yet. Our students need more practice before they will be comfortable enough to work outside this facility, so I don't feel right graduating any of them yet. Even if it's with false credentials. And I don't think any of them would leak sensitive information regarding our school. Perhaps tomorrow I will make a visit to one of the villages nearby? Remind them why it is important they do not advertise our clinic too much."

Arnault inched further forward in his chair. "I agree. But let's not forget who is in charge here. I gave you this. I can take it all away. So please, proceed with caution. I can't afford any slip ups. There will be people coming to look for Sawyer. We must keep them at bay."

Mercier raised a hand. "Settle, Arnault. I know what I'm doing. Do you not trust me?"

Arnault glared. "Of course I do. I chose you over many other barber-surgeons for a reason."

"If we are to change the face of medicine, Dr. Arnault, we must take some risks. Until the king decides in our favour to grant education to everyman, we must remain steadfast in our operation to provide that education to the masses. France has become a much more violent place. It needs people like me. Like you. In order to progress."

Arnault smiled and took a sip of his brandy. "So you think we are doing France a favour?"

"Indeed, we are." Mercier adjusted the robe over his knees before resting his head against the back of his chair. "Mark my word, Arnault, King Louis will thank us for this one day."

The world *will thank us for this one day,* thought Arnault.

"In the meantime," continued Mercier. "I'd like to try that potion of yours on Sawyer. It worked wonders on the previous contestants, until they succumbed to its side effects, that is. Perhaps Sawyer's constitution will be formidable enough to withstand them. He is an exceptionally robust and healthy man."

"He should become addicted quite quickly. And further under our control. Just be mindful how much you give him. I don't want him destroyed by your experiments, but we do need him out of the way. That is the only reason I gave him to you."

Mercier rose from his chair. "I guarantee you, good sir, I know exactly what I'm doing. You taught me well. In the meantime, I must see to Sawyer. Prepare him for tonight. So if you'll excuse me."

Arnault watched Mercier leave, then finished his brandy in one slow drink, allowing the burn to slide down his throat. If there was any saving grace being stuck in this backward century, it was that they still stored their brandy in wooden casks, so it developed a taste no longer cherished in his twenty-second century.

32.

WHEN Sawyer woke next to find several pieces of bread and cheese next to him, he devoured every bite, enjoying not just the authentic taste or feeling of real food between his teeth so contrary to the simulated foods on space stations and ships, but that it granted him some strength. Unfortunately, not enough to overpower Mercier and his guards, but at least the sedation seemed to be out of his system.

As he chewed the last bite, he considered if Mercier telling him he had one of his teammates captured was a bluff, but he wasn't willing to take the chance. Especially if it was Hawk. The consequences were too dire. So, when the cell door creaked and Sawyer turned to face it, he kept his cool. *Behave,* he cautioned himself, and relaxed his hands, which had balled into fists. *You've been in this situation before. It's your wheelhouse. Stand and listen. Do as you're told, and everything will work out fine.*

Mercier entered and watched him carefully, as if unsure if Sawyer would react with violence. Sawyer glared and awaited instructions, not daring to move lest there be repercussions.

Mercier smiled softly. "You seem ... angry. That's good. And by the way, feel free to speak your mind. You have my permission."

Sawyer turned away, crossed his arms over his chest. "You don't want to know what's on my mind."

"Oh, but I do. I want to know everything about you. You intrigue me, Sawyer. And shortly, my curiosity will be rewarded. I will know what makes you happy, what makes you sad, what makes you hurt. And in time, I will know what makes you ... tick."

Sawyer smirked. "That's not going to happen, but at least grant me the courtesy of telling me why. Why me?"

"Violence. You have so much of it. Even now, as you look at me, I see a storm brewing behind those magnificent blue eyes of yours. You wish to kill me ..." Mercier tilted his head, his lips spread into a smile. "No. You wish to punish me! How fantastic."

By sheer force of will, Sawyer did not disprove Mercier's later statement by ripping his throat out.

"Right there! That's it," said Mercier, pointing at Sawyer. "That recalcitrant jaw. That defiant tilt of your head. That unshakable focus. It must have taken years to perfect that level of control. To keep that brutality within you from bursting out. You must have had an excellent teacher."

Sawyer held fast, believing even the smallest movement would disclose how much impact the words had on him.

Mercier searched out his eyes, locked on them with equal focus. "You have the eyes of a marksman. Is that your role as a Musketeer? I bet it is."

Sawyer neither twitched nor blinked. In fact, he barely drew breath.

"The marksman is a different breed of soldier," continued Mercier. "He is the embodiment of control amongst chaos. He turns the random act of killing in battle into something personal as he isolates his target and squeezes the trigger; the pleasure of a perfect shot outweighing any sense of remorse for taking a life. Truth be told, he really is nothing more than an assassin hiding behind honour. No one joins the military if they are not willing to kill. But you Sawyer, you have the look of someone who also enjoys it. You don't fight for money, or honour, but for the fight itself."

Sawyer's eyes reduced to slits. "You don't know me." He braced his hands on the wall behind him and dropped his head. The words stung, more than Sawyer thought possible. It was like Mercier had broken the lock to his deepest secret with a crude hatched.

"Two men will come to retrieve you," said Mercier. "You will do exactly as they instruct, or your fellow Musketeer will suffer. And yes, in case you thought I was bluffing, we are holding your man Hawk hostage. I believed that was all it would take to keep you under control. And I can see that I was right." At the door, Mercier paused on the mantle, and with a casual smile he pointed at the canteen laying on the ground. "Enjoy the water."

Sawyer drank greedily from the canteen. He hated taking anything from this man, but he was parched. When the water was drained, Mercier left, and once again Sawyer's cell door was locked.

When the men Mercier mentioned arrived to collect Sawyer, his body felt, needed, action. It took all his strength to stop himself from charging the guards. Sawyer restrained himself for the sake of Hawk and allowed himself to be blind-folded and his hands tied behind his back. Before they started moving, another canteen was brought to his lips and he was ordered to drink. The more he drank, the more he wanted.

When the canteen was empty, Sawyer was pushed forward. He filed away every detail he managed to ascertain as he was led through what he assumed were tunnels based on the dampness around him. He counted each step and marked every turn, sniffed the air, and listened for dripping water, tapping, whispered conversations. He listened for the changing sounds of his footsteps indicating a shift in terrain. The air, thick with the smell of mould and dirt, inclined him to believe these tunnels were either in a cave or basement. Eventually, he was hauled to a stop and leaned against a wall, his blindfold and restraints still secure.

"Is he ready?"

Sawyer didn't recognize the voice.

"No," another voice replied. "Still needs time."

Above Sawyer a lock disengaged, followed by the whooshing sound of a door or hatch opening. A rush of air that smelled of manure caressed his skin. A cacophony of noise assaulted him, and he staggered, his knees buckling under him. Adrenaline coursed through him in time to stop him from hitting the ground.

Sawyer's skin tingled. His bindings chaffed. His heart pounded. He found it harder to stand still with each passing second. When a hand gripped his arm he flinched, every nerve in his body reacting with a cold shiver. Every sense Sawyer possessed seemed in tune with each other. His body coiled for action. He couldn't stop the energy from engulfing him.

He was ordered to step up, which he did again and again, and his shoulders brushed against what felt like loose dirt as he climbed a narrow staircase toward the din of noise.

Suddenly his luminal space changed. Sawyer felt exposed, no longer pro-tected by walls or the presence of nearby bodies. A cool breeze tickled his skin.

A lightheadedness threatened to overwhelm him. Noise grew boisterous around him, which he quickly recognized as cheering. It filled his ears with thunderous intensity, invigorating the fervency within him.

He was spun around, and the cheering escalated. A moment later a voice cut through the noise. Sawyer recognized Mercier's voice.

"Begin."

Begin what?

Sawyer's restraints and blindfold were removed. He blinked against the harsh, unexpected light then turned around. As his vision settled, he saw people all around him, shouting and cheering, their arms waving to and fro with glasses and mugs tight in their hands.

"I said, begin!"

Sawyer turned toward Mercier's voice and was startled by the sudden presence of a sturdy, shirtless man now standing in front of Mercier's podium. The burly man's stance seemed familiar—body bent forward, arms held at chest level, fists clenched.

It took a moment for Sawyer to recognize the posture, and a moment more to realize what *begin* meant.

The sound of the crowd, indistinguishable from crashing waves, made every artery in his head want to explode, making him both dizzy and excited at once. Fire ants scurried across every surface of his body like a skinsuit initializing, motivating him to move. Fight.

His opponent swung a long, outstretched arm at his head, and Sawyer retaliated with a thrust of his own arm, which carried enough power to knock his foe back staggering. Skin and bone hit skin and bone. Human against human, testing their strength and mettle and living on nothing but instinct.

Energy and anger cascaded from each arm Sawyer thrust and jabbed forward, each hit to his mark exploding when it made contact. He'd never felt so powerful. He never knew how freeing it was to let himself go like this. He dropped his body low and swept a leg out in a semicircle, catching his opponent under the knees and landing him on his back. Sawyer rushed forward and kicked him in the ribs, not stopping when he heard bones crack.

He was so focussed. The crowd, Mercier and his school, his father, and Hawk's safety were pushed aside as his adrenaline became too much to control.

Sawyer kicked the insensate man again and again, not caring that his foe was no longer capable of protecting himself. Sawyer dropped to his knees beside him, prepared to unleash another downward blow with a clenched fist, but someone grabbed his raised arm and hauled him backward, landing him on his back.

33.

MISSION: DAY FIVE

FTER riding past farms and abandoned homes and through busy villages toward the baron's estate, Perry and Hawk entered a forest to seek shade from the oppressive sun. A shriek in the near distance brought them to a halt.

"What was that?" asked Hawk, circling his horse.

"Sounded like a child."

The shriek intensified, leading the two Rangers deeper into the forest when the direction was confirmed. They slowed when they saw a woman fall against a tree, hunched forward as she slid to the ground. Perry and Hawk tread lightly on approach, dismounting several feet behind her and walking the rest of the way to not frighten the woman.

"We are the king's Musketeers," said Perry. "Do you require assistance?"

"Please help," cried the woman.

Perry and Hawk crouched next to her, each releasing a sigh when they saw what she cradled in her arms.

"We must get to the village," said the woman. "The physician will only be there a short while. I must get Henrique there before he leaves."

Hawk reached for the child's forehead. "Fever."

There was a small village several leagues away. Perry glanced down the path over his shoulder. It wasn't far, it wasn't out of their way, and physicians were what they were looking for, aside from their commander. "Take the woman," he said to Hawk. "I'll carry the child."

Mounted once again, and with their charges secure, Perry and Hawk headed toward the village. Welcomed by a flimsy wooden gate with only one door left hanging on its hinges, they approached and quickly realized the village was more of a hamlet in desperate need of repairs. No structure stood more than a storey tall, and most of them were made of rotting wood and listing to the side. And the carts where farmers sold their wares were half empty, with fruits and vegetables drying in the sun.

Perry steered his horse next to Hawk. "These people cannot afford a physician. They were more for royalty, not peasants."

"Maybe she meant one of those barber-surgeons?"

The woman slid off Hawk's horse and fetched her child from Perry. "Thank god, he's still here," she said, and headed toward the gathering of villagers at the centre of the hamlet.

A man broke from the gathered crowd, his pant hems tattered, his grey shirt torn and roughly sewn. One arm was held in a sling, and he walked with a slight limp in his gait. His face was covered in bruises well on their way to healing based on their yellowish tinge. "Thank you for bringing 'em here. May not 'ave made it without your help."

"It was our pleasure," said Perry, his gaze searching through the crowd. "You have a physician here?"

The man smiled. "Yes. Don't come as often as we'd like, but when they ask not for payment, who are we t'argue. Especially when you have a horse as feisty as mine." He nodded at his broken arm. "Fell off just yesterday, but with this physician's medicines, I feel better already."

Hawk frowned. "A physician practicing for free?"

"Yes, come," said the man, waving them down from their horses. "Come and meet the one here today."

Perry and Hawk shared a glance before dismounting. They secured their horses to the most stable structure they could find and approached the gathering. It parted as they passed through, people stepping back when noticing the pauldrons on their shoulders, some with respect, some with discerning frowns.

Tall and slender, a man in a clean white shirt and elaborate doublet of blues and magenta turned his attention from the person in front of him at their approach. "Are you here to arrest me?"

The first thing Perry noticed was the man's green aura. Historical relevance. Which meant he couldn't be from the future. No one from their time had any historical relevance yet. "His aura is green," he whispered to Hawk, and to the man, he said, "Why would we do that?"

"We don't see many Musketeers around these parts," replied the slender man. "One must wonder, why the visit?"

"Just helping where we can," said Hawk, hitching his thumbs on his belt. "Found a woman and kid on their way here. Looking for you, I presume."

The man sought out the new arrival and her small child. "Ah yes, Henrique." He approached the pair, his arms outstretched, and took a few moments to assess the child. With a smile, he pulled a small pouch from a black bag on a table and placed it in the mother's hand. "Make sure he takes this powder twice a day. The fever should be gone before the sun reaches its apex."

After the woman thanked him, she hurried out of the crowd to find a seat in the shade where she cradled her child against her chest. The physician turned his attention back to Perry and Hawk, one arm extended. "Shall we," he said, leading them into what appeared to be a tavern, the faded picture of a wine bottle above its door the only indication.

Perry and Hawk stepped into the cool shade of the building, swiping sweat from their brows as they found seats at a table. The physician followed after them. Seating himself across from the Rangers, he ordered three plates of food and a bottle of wine from the barmaid. "It's not much, and usually I just poke around at it," he said, leaning over the table. "But these people need the commerce, and other than medical services, they are rather irreverent to charity."

When the food was placed before him, Perry decided he too would simply play with it, but the wine he drank heartily. "Have you been helping these people a long time?"

"No, just this past while. I'm new to the area, but I come from rather humble roots, and I feel that all honourable men should never forget where they come from."

Hawk raised his cup. "I'll drink to that."

"Men of your position rarely come from humble roots," said Perry. "It requires substantial wealth and title to be accepted into such universities as Montpellier or Toulouse. Which, if I'm correct, are two of the largest schools that churn out physicians."

"Come now, there must be more interesting topics than my education. You are Musketeers! I'm sure your stories are abundant. So tell me, what has two of the King's Guard out this far from the palace?"

Perry held his gaze on the doctor for several seconds. "We are searching for someone."

"You haven't heard of anyone missing from around these parts, have you?" asked Hawk.

The physician shrugged. "I've heard murmurings. That is all."

"Outside," Perry said, pointing back at the door. "I saw you give that child something that can cure his fever within the hour? That's unheard of. Care to explain?"

The physician's eyes darted away for a moment then came to rest back on Perry. A flush came over the physician's face and he spoke with a tremor in his voice. "What is it you are really doing here, Musketeers?"

Perry stared him down. "Like I said, we're looking for someone. A fellow Musketeer, as it would be. And a man called Mercier. Seen either around lately?"

The physician choked on his wine. "No. No. Don't know anyone named Mercier. As for Musketeers, I've only seen you two fine gentlemen."

Hawk leaned over the table. "My colleague asked you a question about a fever cure, and I suggest you answer it."

"The fever medication?" said the physician. "Yes, well, I don't know if it will actually work. The premise of curing a fever within hours is somewhat ludicrous. But the man … the, uh, short fellow selling the remedy said it was coming out of the schools now, and I like to give my patient's hope."

"You bought it from someone?" asked Hawk. "Who?"

The physician was quick to answer. "I believe he called himself Dr. Arnault." The physician's gaze turned down to the table, and his lips firmed as he bit his lower lip. "He … he is gone now. I do not know of his whereabouts."

Perry rose, finishing the last of his wine before reaching full height. They needed the source, not the people purchasing the medical advancements. And since this man didn't know the source's location, he didn't want to waste any more time here. But at least they had another name. "Have a pleasant day."

Hawk extended his hand across the table as he too rose from his chair. "Was a pleasure meeting you. And if you're ever near Paris, I hear there's a place called the Court of Miracles that sounds like they could use a man like you. You should visit it some time."

The physician stood. "I shall, good sir."

Perry and Hawk left the tavern, stepping back out into the hot summer heat where the crowd was dispersing. Perry didn't know where to head next, and the thought of questioning all these people seemed tedious at best. It would take all day, even with Hawk questioning them alongside him. Perry blew out a breath. There was nothing history could tell him that would help their situation. This exasperated him almost as much as having his commander missing. What could history tell him that would be useful in finding a fight club that most likely never happened in the right timeline? How could history help them find a man not meant to be here? And who was Dr. Arnault? Up till now, only Mercier's name was mentioned. *Could this be the Runner?*

Perry's resources were limited to a specialized niche, so he turned to the man who did excel in this area. "Hawk, how do you want to proceed?"

Hawk held up a finger, turned back to the tavern as if checking for the physician's whereabouts, then strolled to the centre of the hamlet where a black leather bag sat on a table. Perry watched with raised brows as the lieutenant rummaged through the bag, stuffed something inside his doublet, and returned to him.

"What were you doing?" asked Perry.

"Taking back what doesn't belong here," replied Hawk, patting his coat pocket. "He had several packets of that 'fever cure' that he shouldn't have. I'm just keeping the timeline straight, Specialist."

Perry was surprised. "Hm, I never would have thought of that. Good work."

"I'm not looking for your approval, Perry. Now let's go find us that baron so we can get Sawyer back. And then get on with this mission. We wasted enough time here."

34.

THE sound of the crowd was gone, but still a near memory just out of reach as it was forced away by the thump ... thwump ... thump of Sawyer's heartbeat keeping pace with each slow, deep breath he took. He knew he should hurt, but he didn't care that he didn't. The blackness around him created a space obtunded and muted, like being trapped in a deep fog. He floated between two worlds, no foot in either. But it was safe here. No pain. No concerns.

The ground beneath him was soft, so he burrowed himself into it and tried to fully succumb to the haven of nothingness. But muted voices invaded his sanctuary, drawing him toward wakefulness.

Sawyer opened his eyes to see colours and shapes blurring together like the portrait of a landscape still being painted. He closed them again, sweeping his tongue across his bottom lip. It stung and he tasted blood. Red splashed across his mind's eye. His body twitched as the retreating memories of last night's fight flooded back to him, each more vivid than the last. Swinging arms, clenched fists, the crunching sound his boot made when it broke human ribs.

"... that was spectacular."

Sawyer followed the voice toward alertness.

"...more than I ever imagined."

Sawyer's mind lagged. He knew he was awake, the pain now coursing through his body made it evidently clear, but he still floated amongst the fog, his mouth disconnected from his mind as words tumbled out. "Alive ..." He swallowed, blinked, tried to focus on the man looking down at him. But Sawyer was so tired and still unable to connect his mind with his mouth. "Alive," he said, again. "So alive ... Thirsty."

Someone nudged him. "Stay with me, Sawyer. This is important."

189

Sawyer smacked pasty lips together. "Release."

"I can help you feel it again," replied the voice. "You can have the world, Sawyer. With a little help, a little motivation, you can have that release whenever you want. They loved you."

Sawyer drew in a deep breath. The fight *had* exhilarated him, Sawyer hadn't wanted it to end. He'd needed that release. *Yes. Again. But not now. Too tired.*

A hand settled on his forehead, a voice whispered in his ear. "Now rest. You have sustained some injuries, and I cannot have my new champion suffering."

Champion. The fog parted, and Sawyer opened his eyes. Mercier was an inch from his face, his hot breath caressing his cheek as he spoke through smiling lips.

"There you are," said Mercier.

Sawyer recoiled and groaned when his neck spasmed. Pain shot from his occipital lobe to each shoulder rendering him unable to move. "What have I done?"

"Nothing you probably haven't dreamt of doing," said Mercier, rising to his full height. "I just helped you make your fantasies a reality."

Sawyer shook his head despite the stabbing sensation in the back of his head.

"Yes," Mercier said. "You were the prime specimen of uncontrolled rage. The feral look in your eyes, the way you continued to beat your opponent when he was no longer conscious ... It was nothing short of spectacular. It took more than several of my men to hold you back."

"No ... not me."

"Oh, but it was you, Sawyer. All that blood and anger, the crowd adored you. And we managed to fill our purses beyond expectation. The people will pay even more to see you fight again." Mercier sighed. "I just hope your body can sustain this."

"Did I ... kill him?"

"You left him in perfect condition for our purposes. Your opponent's loss was not in vain, so let your conscience rest." Mercier turned and walked out of the room.

Sawyer stared after him. He wanted to give chase in search of answers, but his body declined the action. There were also several men hovering near him, some looking at him with wonder, others shaking their heads. Their presence enraged Sawyer, but he knew he could not act on his impulses, injured or not. He looked past them to where Mercier had left. The door was only a few paces away and heavyset, with a barred window ...

Sawyer was in his cell, lying on a cot rather than the cold, hard ground, and the men surrounding him held books and bandages. *What's going on?*

He sat up, but a few of the men rushed forward and eased him back down. Sawyer had nothing in him, so he let his body be pushed back onto the cot, his spike in energy now spent by trying to sit. His eyes lids grew heavy, and he felt the draw of sleep pulling him deeper into the bed. *But the pain in my head* ... "Thor?"

"Who are you talking to, sir?" said someone.

Sawyer ignored the young voice, his instincts guiding his hand to the back of his head where the pain would not subside. His fingers parted hair to feel rough sutures. "Thor?"

No response from his AI.

Thor. What did they do to you?

Sawyer knew there were other questions to be asked, things to figure out, but his world of safety was beckoning, and he longed to be there again.

35.

LATE in the afternoon, Perry and Hawk arrived at Baron Fournier's estate. The statues previously spoken of loomed over a lush lawn, gleaming white and ostentatiously depicting naked Greek gods. Perry had no taste for such ornamentations but believed in to each his own.

As they passed through the estate gates and made their way across the expansive front lawn, they slowed their horses. Servants previously working the gardens now scrambled into the estate. Within moments, activity surrounding both the estate and the stable increased, with people running between them, stopping on occasion to look at Perry and Hawk before running off.

"Think they know we're here?" said Hawk.

"It would seem that way. And I don't think they like us."

A carriage pulled up next to a side entrance of the estate, which Perry assumed was the get-away car. "I'll make a more formal ..."

The front door of the estate slammed shut, piquing his attention. He pulled his horse to a stop, watched as more servants came around the side of the estate.

"Something is about to happen," said Hawk. "I suspect movements of a guilty man who knows he's about to be caught by Musketeers. Be ready."

Perry prayed Hawk was right, for it meant they were one step closer to finding Sawyer.

"There!" called Hawk, pointing toward the carriage stationed beside the estate.

The baron's attempt at a hasty escape encouraged Perry to believe the answers to finding Sawyer rested with this man. Perry remained blocking the carriage's only paved path of escape while Hawk charged across the lawn calling for the carriage to halt in the name of the king. A hand appeared in the carriage

193

window, frantically shooing the coachman onward, but Perry held his ground as the vessel charged toward him, while Hawk kept stride alongside it ordering it to stop.

Perry held his breath when the carriage showed no signs of halting, holding his ground through pure strength of will and perhaps a little fear. But he would not relent, no matter the consequence. If this man held answers, Perry would make him stop one way or another.

Hawk appeared on the verge of jumping onto the carriage when the coachman finally pulled on the reins, causing a sudden and chaotic stop feet from Perry and his horse. Perry breathed out in relief to have survived, then pulled up alongside the carriage. He motioned for the coachman to relinquish the reins to Hawk, then leaned over and knocked on the carriage's door. "Baron Fournier, we are the King's Musketeers, so with King Louis's authority, please get out of the carriage."

"No!"

Perry rolled his eyes then rested them on Hawk, who was busy cutting the carriage's reins. "Do not make me ask twice," Perry called politely.

"I have armed guards," shouted the baron. "They will cut you down where you stand!"

"And I have a Hawk standing beside your carriage door. And trust me, you don't want him coming in there after you. He is rather perturbed right now after having to chase you down."

The curtain moved to reveal the red, sweaty face of the baron. He eyed Hawk then quickly closed the curtain. A moment later the door opened, but the baron did not exit. Perry assumed the man felt somehow protected in his carriage, for he remained sitting on the bench as he spoke to them through the open door.

"What do you want?" asked the baron, shuffling along his seat when Hawk's frame filled the entrance of his carriage.

Fortunately for Fournier, his aura glowed green, which meant he had descendants somewhere in history that depended on his survival. Perry curtailed his anger, even though he wanted to haul the man outside simply for trying to elude them. "Amongst other things, I need you to answer a few questions."

"What sorts of questions?" The baron's voice dripped with disdain, his puckered expression distrustful. He didn't seem to know where to keep his hands other than constantly moving, indicating to Perry a level of hesitation.

"Do you recognize this man, sir?" Perry asked, pointing at Hawk.

Fournier leaned forward, squinted, then waved a dismissive hand. "No, good gentleman, I do not. Now may we proceed? I am ... on official business."

With gritted teeth, Perry held back the tirade he yearned to unleash. "I highly doubt that. Besides, we are under the king's orders to search out a fight club illegally happening across the French countryside. Do you know anything of this matter?"

"No," replied Fournier, shifting in his seat to look out the window on the other side of the carriage.

Hawk grunted then leaned on the open door, causing the carriage to tilt under his added weight.

Fournier looked aghast. "Well, maybe. But I was merely a guest at the affairs. I am not the organizer."

Perry pulled out the parchment from inside his doublet, holding it for the baron to read. "At this?"

The baron only took a quick glance before answering. "Perhaps."

Hawk raised his foot to enter the carriage. Perry moved back to grant his teammate room, gratified in seeing Fournier squirm.

"Yes! Yes, to that," replied Fournier, shooing Hawk from his personal space. "But I cannot help you further. I have no clue where the fights take place. We are blindfolded for the duration of the trip. Both ways, may I add. And the tavern where we meet changes locations frequently. Only by pure happenstance does one know if they will be lucky enough to find an invitation."

Hawk bristled. "Do you have another parchment advertising one of these fights? Do you know when the next one will take place?"

"I presume you can get us in?" asked Perry.

"Well, someone of my stature surely can," replied Fournier, then under his breath he murmured, "But I don't know if I want to."

The hairs on the back of Perry's neck stood on end. He gripped his reins until his fingers cramped. "You will take us to the next fight, or I'll have you unceremoniously paraded naked through the villages between here and Paris for treason!"

"I told you everything I know!"

"But yet, that's not enough," stated Hawk. "When is the next fight?"

Fournier slumped back in his seat and rested his hands across his rotund stomach that looked about to burst from years of over-indulgence. "Men against men," he said with a sigh. "They fight till one is no longer capable of continuing, sometimes to the death. It is not for the faint of heart. The next round I am aware of is set to pick us up at a tavern in Louens two nights from now. If there is one sooner, I am not privy to the details. I have found no other parchments."

"Did you recognize any of these men fighting?" asked Perry.

"Seen some about," replied Fournier in a cavalier tone. Then he sat up, leaned toward the door, and rubbed his bearded chin in a thoughtful manner. "Now that I think of it, a new contestant did arrive recently. Great strength ... even greater anger. Lost a good fortune betting against that one; didn't expect such savagery from such a lithe man."

"I'm sure it's him," said Hawk, looking over his shoulder at Perry.

Perry nodded, but he needed more information before he could let himself feel anything, be it grief, anticipation, or excitement. "Do you know his name?"

"No names. We make our bets based on what we see as guards parade the contestants around."

"What did he look like?" prodded Hawk.

Fournier turned pensive, pulled on his beard. "About your build," he said, nodding at Hawk. "Strange black hair like yours as well. Cut very short. I wondered if this was a new fashion coming out of Spain ... And he was very fluid. With a grace not befitting a typical fighter. Well trained, I presume ..."

"Like a Musketeer?" growled Hawk.

"Well, yes, very likely ... Oh. Oh!" Fournier clamped his mouth shut and bolted upright in his seat. Beads of sweat dotted his forehead as his face paled.

Perry tilted his head. "You now understand how important this is to us. So I beg you, please, continue."

The baron shook his head. "I know nothing more."

Perry was not deterred by the answer. "Do you know of either Mercier or Dr. Arnault?"

"No."

Perry sighed. Unfortunately, he believed him. "You will take us to the next fight. What does this place look like? What do you remember?"

"Not a thing. The place was crowded with spectators. A small orchestra took up a portion of the room ... Actually, I barely paid mind to the happenings around me. I was preoccupied with drink and entertainment. And I was blindfolded as we entered, and once again as I left."

"Don't want anyone exposing their enterprise," said Hawk.

Perry nodded in agreement.

"I guess we're staying here," said Hawk.

Fournier waved a hand. "I have business in Paris. I cannot entertain guests."

Perry pulled back from the carriage, nodding for Hawk to relinquish his stance at the door. The lieutenant followed his order with reluctance, for Perry heard a low growl escape his lips when the door slammed shut. "You have no business in Paris; you were rushing to escape our arrival. As for us staying, that is not an option. We will all attend this bout together. And if you breathe one word of our true nature, I will most definitely let Hawk kill you where you stand." Perry knew it was an idle threat due to the baron's aura, but the baron didn't.

Fournier stuck his head out the window. "Then we shall return to the estate and feast. I am famished after all this talk."

The curtain closed on the carriage and Perry turned his horse away, ready to escort the baron back to his home, when the baron called out once again. "Your man there cut my reins? Who's going to fix that? How am I supposed to travel?"

Perry sighed. "I don't know who's going to fix them, nor do I care."

"Try walking," said Hawk, patting his stomach in a dramatic fashion.

A night or two in an old French country estate would have typically made Perry's day ... month. Possibly his life. But there was a black cloud over his heart that would make the experience a dreadful one. Two days was a long time to wait for answers. In the meantime, he realized he should contact the lieutenant commander. "Hawk. Menacing is more your specialty, so why don't you escort the baron back while I confer with ... Santiago. Let her know our plans to stay here. I'll have to backtrack out of the grid to do so."

"Sounds good to me, because I don't want to hear what she has to say about our little detour. She's going to lay into you so hard," replied Hawk with a mischievous smile.

Hawk was right. Lieutenant Commander Santiago was not going to be happy, and Perry would be the one receiving the brunt of her anger. Perry prided himself on being level-headed. Mature. But they didn't have time for arguments, so he decided he would be as diplomatic as possible then end the comm quickly before she could respond. He'd hear about it later, but for now it would give him and Hawk the chance to possibly save Sawyer.

36.

IT was Sawyer's second fight.

He waited on the stairs under the stable like he had prior to his first foray into the stable. Music drifted down through the hatch above him, a string quartet by the sound of the song's lilting melody. The notes were long and sorrowful, rising and falling and filling Sawyer's head with haunting memories of Beaumont's funeral. Sawyer preferred the emotionally charged music of the twentieth-century grunge scene, music meant to feed your anger, drive your soul. Even the band names from that era illicited anger, names like Tool, Rage Against the Machine, and Alice in Chains.

Sawyer had annoyed Hawk many nights blaring that music in their dorm at the Academy, usually after a fight with his father, so Hawk never complained. The music playing now lulled him into a trance seeded in misery and guilt. A part of him longed for the feeling he had when last he fought, the feeling only his own music could elicit.

Sawyer dug his head into the rough wall behind him, pressed until he imagined the sutures splitting open and blood dripped down. The pain, the loss of his AI, distracted him, but only until he heard Mercier's voice.

"I want this clean. I need the body to remain intact. Now, it's time to begin, and you will not stop until your opponent is dead. Or your friend, Hawk, will suffer the consequences. Now, get up. Your audience awaits."

Sawyer stood once again in the middle of a stable surrounded by drunk and lavishly dressed men and women who cheered at his arrival. He refused to bait them further by looking up as he was paraded around. Behind him and perched on a raised dais, Mercier welcomed his guests with a toast. As Sawyer made a turn by the stable doors, he saw his opponent—young, slim, and wiry.

"What's your name?" Sawyer called.

His opponent sneered, but the mannerism did not fool Sawyer. Sawyer promised himself he would do this quickly and let this man keep some dignity. There was nothing worse than spectators watching you suffer. Even worse, to have them watch as your pride and strength was stripped away as another man took it from you.

The scar under Sawyer's chin began to itch.

Sawyer looked again around the stable, wishing he hadn't swallowed his scantacts. His vision was secure now; he would be able to tell the difference between a radiation and candlelight aura. But they were gone. And the faces around him were nothing more than vulgar caricatures of aristocratic gluttony.

When faced with his opponent in the middle of the stable, Sawyer again asked him his name.

"Charles," said the young man, his scowl and harsh voice betraying the fear Sawyer saw in his eyes.

Charles lunged forward, and Sawyer landed on his back with his arms wrapped around Charles's midsection. A bony fist smashed into Sawyer's left eyebrow. The skin split open. Another punch connected with his left cheek. Sawyer had been hit much harder before and felt bad for Charles.

It took only a second for Sawyer to reach up with his right arm then twist and grab the man on the side of his neck, and without much strength, shove him to the ground. After reciprocating with two swift punches of his own, mimicking the ones he'd just received, Sawyer pushed himself up to full height. Charles remained on the ground, cradling the side of his face.

Charles didn't deserve this. He was young and had no business being pit against someone as well trained as a soldier, let alone someone from the future with fighting skills not yet discovered. Sawyer didn't know how to proceed. He knew he had to kill Charles; he just didn't know if he could actually follow through. He backed up, his body unwilling to continue what his mind had earlier set to do.

Charles got up and staggered until he managed to get his feet under him. Then he charged again, a harsh war cry escaping his lips as he ran forward. Sawyer stepped aside before contact and his opponent landed on the ground. Charles rolled over and was on his feet quickly with his fists ready.

"Finish him. Finish him. Finish him." Voices fell into unison around them, chanting the same two words.

Sawyer's opponent bounced on his toes, presumably invigorated by the eager words. Charles crouched low and held something in his hand. Sawyer saw the glint of steel. Mercier had levelled the playing field by adding a weapon to the match. Sawyer shook his head. Giving Charles a blade only gave the man false hope.

Sawyer spotted Mercier to his right, perched on his dais, draped in his black robe and watching with cold eyes. They both understood the addition of a weapon was for the sake of the audience, and in the end, Charles would fall.

So, this is what you meant by keeping the body intact. As a soldier, seventeenth or twenty-second century notwithstanding, Sawyer knew exactly where to place the blade in order to make a quick kill, and Mercier knew that. There would be no slashing or hacking required to kill this man. The body would remain intact.

It took Sawyer a single breath to assess the situation. *Four-inch blade. Right-hand hold. Underhand grip. He'll slash from the left.* Sawyer moved to deflect the movements he'd predicted, swiped the blade from Charles's hand, and spun him around. Then Sawyer placed his foot in the middle of Charles's back and shoved him, but not hard enough to knock him to the ground.

Sawyer now held the knife, and the crowd was nearing ecstasy.

Tension rippled through his opponent's body, from the tremor in his hands to the stiff quivering muscles of his neck. Sawyer had to choose: kill Charles quickly or drag this out. To kill or be killed was an easy choice. It was one or the other, and in this case, save his best friend's life at the sake of another life.

Sawyer advanced and was in front of Charles with a hand wrapped around his neck and cradling the back of his head within a breath's time. Sawyer pressed his body against Charles and leaned into his ear. The tension slipped from his opponent's body like he knew the end was near.

"Please forgive me, Charles," Sawyer whispered. "For I do this to save someone I care for more than you."

Sawyer thrust the knife into the man's gut, holding it there as warm blood spilled over his hand. He stepped back, leaving the knife imbedded between the spleen and diaphragm. Charles collapsed dead before his head hit the ground.

The crowd erupted and Sawyer hated them almost as much as he hated himself.

***

KILLING people was easy, a simple process of doing something to another. It was actually a specialty of Sawyer's, but those he killed usually deserved it. He didn't know how he felt after he'd been deposited back in his cell. Charged with so many emotions, each battling for dominance over his exhaustion, his old friend anger spoke the loudest, so he let it coil around his tired muscles to give him strength.

It was night. Sawyer had caught a glance out a stable window during his fight and had seen a dark sky. But how many nights had passed? And where was he? He looked around. Cave? Basement? The stable he fought in, where was it located? Then it clicked. *I'm back at that damn asylum! This is Mercier's school! That's why he wanted the body intact. For his damn students to practice on.*

Sawyer sat up on his cot and brushed his fingers over the surgical scar behind his head. *Seventeenth-century doctors wouldn't have the means to do something this complicated. Nor would they consider an implant in the first place. Someone here knows who I am ... The Runner is here. That man I saw the other day in Mercier's school. Fuck, I wish I still had my scan-tacts. He could stand right in front of me and I'd never know it was him ... Fuck.*

He stood quickly and the room swayed. *They better not have hit anything in there. I'm gonna need every part of my brain to get out of this.* He glanced at his wrist as if a suit computer were there. *If there's still time to get out of this.* He really wished Thor were present, if only to tell him what time and day it was.

The cell door opened, and Mercier gracefully entered. "You did well. Followed my instructions without hesitation. It seems you are trained well in this regard. Now please sit so we can proceed like gentleman. When we met, you deceived me, so I'd like to get acquainted with the real you."

Sawyer gritted his teeth and sat back on his cot.

"Let us get to know each other," said Mercier.

Sawyer swallowed and looked away. "Why? Why am I so interesting to you? Why am I caged like an animal?"

"Because you are an animal. The leather and sash, the king's emblem on your shoulders ... those are clothes you wear to cover your true nature. Just like you wear that exterior of civility to hide your true beast beneath."

"You do realize the hypocrisy of your words?" After studying Mercier's slightly raised nose and delicate cant of his head, Sawyer knew this man was an imposter. "If you're calling me fake, then you should wear the title as well. I've been in the company of Admir– the King's Court far too long to be fooled by posers such as you."

"Posers?" Mercier frowned. "Interesting word."

Sawyer searched his brain. "Charlatan."

Sawyer cast his gaze downward, then raised it as he searched Mercier from the tips of his scuffed boots peeking out from under his long robe up to the dry, rough hands clasped in his lap. "There is nothing natural about the way you carry yourself. You choose your words carefully. You move deliberately. You are nothing more than a pretender. Your grace doesn't come from breeding, but more from want of breeding. You're not a physician. You just pretend to be one."

Mercier's lips twitched, and Sawyer knew he'd hit a sore spot. But he dared not push further for the sake of Hawk.

Mercier leaned forward, his head tilted to the side. "Tell me, what is it you would do if I were to grant you your freedom right here and now?"

"I would tear you apart."

"Not run away? You must like being under someone's control. Are you waiting for me to tell you to leave? Waiting for someone to give you an order to follow?"

Sawyer pressed his lips thin, his eyes piercing as he stared at his captor.

"You prove my point."

"I am no different from anyone else! Treat any human as you have me, and they'd perform accordingly."

"No, my friend. Many would have given in the moment they woke in this place. Most men give up at some point to save themselves. Most run, and perish trying. But you stay and take the punishment. And when you're gone, I'm sure others after you will fall as well."

"Gone? You're going to release me? Or kill me?"

Mercier chuckled. "There are many interpretations of the word. Only the future can reveal which applies to you."

Sawyer was both exhausted and frustrated, and he let his chin drop to his chest. "I'm tired of the riddles."

"Then ask me anything you want."

So many questions filled his head that he didn't know where to start. "Who are you?" he finally asked.

"Mercier. You know that. Now ask me something intelligent before I get bored."

Sawyer flushed with heat, and his eyes turned dark. "I didn't ask your name. I asked who you are."

"All right. I will give you an answer. I am the saviour of France."

Sawyer needed more than title and arrogance; he needed to know where this man came from, what his background was, so he could find a pattern, a reason ... something to explain why he was doing this and how he came into contact with the Time Runner. Maybe then Sawyer could find a way out of here and still complete the mission, if there was still time. "I want more."

Mercier canted his head to the side. "Well, I was born in the Court of Miracles, to a mother I've never met and a father I don't care to know. I watched the citizens of Paris walk past me every day, ignore me, treat me as no more than the dirt and sewage beneath their feet." Mercier paused, appeared to swallow his anger, and continued in a clipped voice. "I vowed to bring myself up from the gutter and better myself. Make a name for myself in history."

Sawyer had him talking, about himself, nonetheless. Eventually he'd reveal something Sawyer could use. "How?"

"I would be the one who didn't ignore the poor ... Didn't treat them as incapable of learning. I worked, pleaded, begged to be apprenticed by local barber-surgeons and became the best Paris had ever seen."

"So, you're a barber-surgeon?"

"I am a physician! A surgeon!" cried Mercier. He smoothed down his robe and spoke again in a softer tone. "I wanted more, but the Royal Court and Church would not allow it. I was poor, and therefore stupid in their eyes. When I met Dr. Arnault, a man equally malcontent with the medical advances of our time, of the plight of the barber-surgeons, the idea of the school was born. And you, Sawyer, are only granted freedom due to my needing the patronage of Dr. Arnault's experience. He insisted on your capture after seeing you the other day at our school. He figured you would be a fine specimen of a fighter due to your Musketeer background."

Dr. Arnault. A name to the possible Runner. *Seeing me at the school. The red aura I saw* ... But something else from Mercier's rant struck a chord within him. "Freedom? There's no freedom here."

Mercier coughed lightly. "That is not exactly how you saw it the other night. I believe you were on the verge of thanking me for granting you the freedom to unleash your inner animal." He paused, looked pensive for a moment. "*Alive. So alive ...* Is what you said, if I remember correctly?"

Sawyer turned away, angered by his own words thrown back at him. That feeling, the experience of discharging his rage and energy with abandon, had been euphoric. He'd let loose before, but never to this degree. He had felt free.

"I see this troubles you. Most men fear what is inside them."

Sawyer's breath caught in his throat. Coldness swept outward from his core, igniting every nerve. "Are we done now?"

"We've only just begun, my dear Sawyer. Now ask me a real question before my patience runs out. We both know what it is you feel the need to ask."

"How is my other ... Musketeer? Is Hawk still alive?"

"Yes."

"Can I see him?"

"No. Now it's my turn. To what extent would you go to save your fellow Musketeers?"

Sawyer looked away. "End of time."

"And they would do the same for you?"

Sawyer's eyes shot up. "Yes."

"You hesitated."

"No. I didn't."

"I suspect a chink in your chain of friends. Now rest. Your work here is not done. I have arranged a very special spectacle for tomorrow evening's event, and I need you in top form."

Sawyer stood and inched forward then back. His mouth opened then closed. He clenched his fists then released them. He shook as two sides waged war within him—kill this man or spare his best friend.

"This is what I came for." Mercier clasped his hands behind his back as he strolled toward Sawyer. "This anger and fury. And this is what you will give me tomorrow evening. Our school has run short on bodies. You will bring this rage and venom, and you will give me what I want. Do I make myself clear?"

Sawyer narrowed his eyes, clenched his teeth, but ultimately decided to behave. "Abundantly so, sir."

After Mercier left, Sawyer put his hands over his face. *What the hell has happened to me? Mercier ... Arnault? How do they know my weaknesses? How did they know to sedate me? I've never met Runners this competent and knowledgeable before.* He shook his head, stared at the ceiling as if it were an actual gateway to an afterlife.

I don't want to hurt these men, but what am I supposed to do when Hawk's ... a teammate's ... life hangs in the balance? What is the right thing? How many dead is too many? Beaumont...? When will I know too many have suffered for the sake of one man's life?

The ceiling didn't answer.

Right. I don't deserve your guidance. Your silence is very telling.

37.

THE old asylum, and Mercier's school, was exactly where Commander Sawyer reported it was after he'd returned from his initial recce of place. And as the sun rose, Perry and Hawk sat on their horses on the crest of a large grassy hill looking over the expansive asylum several klicks west of the baron's estate. The house governing the land was large, with a stable to its left and unkempt gardens to its right. It was situated far back from the main road and nestled up against another large hill, one dense with forest instead of grass.

There was no point in being stagnant for a whole day, and Santiago had been adamant Perry and Hawk not further their detour by staying at the baron's estate waiting for the next fight. Perry had not thought it a good idea either, so Hawk had decided the day would be well spent following Santiago's initial orders by doing their own reconnaissance of the asylum. After all, a red aura had been seen there.

"Is someone down there?" asked Hawk, pointing at the gardens.

Perry squinted before pulling out his clumsy spyglass. "There are several people down there, not just in the garden. This is definitely the place Commander Sawyer described. I see men in robes and many guards scattered all over the grounds."

"Should we introduce ourselves?"

"It would be rude of us not to."

Hawk spurred his horse down the hill and a moment later Perry was beside him. At full canter, they entered the drive of the estate. As they drew near to the school, Perry became acutely aware of the many broken and boarded windows on the third and fourth floors. The grass in front of the estate needed trimming, and some of the windows on the first floor of the east wing were broken. It definitely fit Sawyer's initial description of the asylum.

They slowed just short of the main door, stopped, and dismounted. Perry took a moment to look over the exterior of the estate once more before coming to a decision. "I see no harm in checking the grounds before we make contact. If only to satisfy my curiosity."

"And what would your curiosity be telling you?" asked Hawk.

"I'm not sure. But I'm curious to find out."

The stables seemed innocuous, albeit very spacious and in an extremely roughshod state. Lining one of the interior walls were the individual stalls that once housed horses, but on the other side, the stable dividers were knocked down, either deliberately or from lack of care, Perry could not tell.

They walked around kicking away empty bottles and peeking behind crates. "This place looks about as welcoming as the estate," said Hawk, pulling back a large canvass to reveal more empty crates.

Perry stood in the middle of the derelict stable, his hands on his hips as he looked around. "People have been here. Look at all the footprints."

Hawk spun slowly. "Yeah, I noticed those. But I don't see any hoof prints. Weird. Maybe travellers have been using it as a cheap shelter? There are lots of blankets and benches strewn about. Easy refuge from the cold in the winter or sun in the summer. Or where this Mercier guy stores his overflow patients."

Perry chewed his lip. "Perhaps."

But Perry really wanted to know where Sawyer was. "I don't see anything here," he said, his heart falling as the words slipped from his lips. He'd hoped to find something, anything, that related to the Time Runner and Sawyer, but there was nothing here but the remnants of an abandoned stable.

He took one last look around and then headed toward the large stable doors. Hawk followed and they returned to the main building.

***

ARNAULT considered Sawyer's predicament. Although Sawyer was still recuperating back in his cell, Arnault needed the Ranger for tonight's fight, and the next night's royal battle. Sawyer was to take on several men at once, which

Mercier had said would draw in a crowd, filling their pockets with enough coin to keep his school flourishing. Also, Arnault knew that bodies were needed for practicing healing techniques, and with a large-scale bout, many bodies, injured or dead, could be accumulated.

Arnault sighed, planning out in his head which contestants would fight against his champion. As he strolled through an upper hallway of his school, he looked in on the students studying in the rooms, most of them with their heads buried in books, others watching as one of the losing contestants was examined on a table, his injuries minor but still requiring needlework or joint manipulation.

With his chest puffed, Arnault clasped his hands behind the small of his back and continued down the hall toward the large window overlooking the front of the estate. Movement on the crest caught his eye, and behind him a hurried voice called.

"Arnault! Doctor Arnault! We have visitors! I believe they are the Musketeers I met in the village the other day."

Arnault spun around, his emotionless demeanour firmly in place. "I see that, Mercier," he said, his tone reflecting an ease that betrayed his actual anxiety. "Please make all the appropriate arrangements."

Mercier wiped beads of sweat from his forehead. "Stable was not yet put in order for tonight's activities. The demonstration room downstairs is all but cleaned. There should be no problem."

"Very good," replied Arnault with a nod. "I have a feeling our guests will want a tour, so see to it everything is taken care of accordingly, then meet them at the door. I do not wish to be seen."

To give his people ample time to straighten out the estate, Arnault instructed Mercier to wait for the guests outside, hoping he could detain them for as long as possible with idle chat about the gardens or perhaps a tour of the currently empty stable. Mercier bowed before rushing off, which was something Arnault admired. Although too eager to make a name for himself, Mercier was always gracious.

***

ON the front steps of the asylum, a familiar-looking man greeted Perry. "Hello, my old friends."

Perry sighed. "Ah, the physician from the village."

"We never caught your name the other day," said Hawk. "But based on what we've heard recently during our travels, I assume you are Dr. Mercier?"

"Indeed I am," replied the man. "But I'm afraid I do not have time to return to Paris with you, my friends."

Perry furrowed his brow.

"When we met in that village, you mentioned some people back in Paris needing my services?"

Hawk smirked. "We're here on other business."

Perry rested a foot on a higher step. "We are still searching for our missing man. We thought maybe if he were injured, some good citizen may have brought him here."

"We have plenty of men here," said Mercier. "But I assure you, they are all accounted for. They are students, not missing men. I give my word, none are here against their wills. And I know of no such patient as well appointed as a Musketeer."

"I would take your word," replied Perry. "But duty prevails, and we are under orders to search the grounds."

Mercier started down the stairs. "Then shall we start with the stables?"

Perry made a move to the front door. "We have seen them already. We wish to have a look inside."

Mercier's reply was a quick smile. "By all means," he said, returning to the door. Before he opened it, he looked over his shoulder. "Have you been here before?"

"Our missing Musketeer was here earlier," replied Hawk. "Told us of a school and clinic."

Mercier swallowed, then shook his head. "No. I do not remember such a visit from a Musketeer. I have been busy with administrative duties since my arrival, which has given me little time to start the much-needed repairs of the estate. But this is a place of learning that does not require posh and elegance. I prepare young men for the world of medicine where the universities fail to accept them." Mercier pushed the wide, heavy door open to allow them access to his school.

After an exhaustive tour of the estate, Perry and Hawk stood alone on the front steps of the school. Their footsteps were heavy with disappointment as they plodded down the front stairs toward their horses. Although Mercier's school was by all accounts illegal, they had found no evidence of Sawyer or the missing men, or evidence of a fight club. And no red auras, either. They'd seen nothing of the classroom Sawyer spoke of, but Perry was certain Mercier was hiding from them what would be a reason for real Musketeers to shut down his enterprise. And to push further for answers was not a situation Perry wanted to experience. Not without backup.

"It's a shame, you know," said Perry, unhitching his horse. "Mercier's intentions may be good, but unfortunately, his activities are illegal and will change the course of history significantly if he's not stopped."

As they rode up the driveway, Perry took a quick glance back at the asylum then turned back to the road ahead, spurring his horse into a gallop when they arrived at the main road. Tomorrow he and Hawk would attend the fight club, which hopefully would prove more beneficial than this recce of the asylum.

38.

SAWYER remained in his one-room prison after his last fight, healing, as men brought him food and a bucket of water with rags with which to clean himself. He was surprised, even with his Spawn genetics, how fast he'd regained his strength. But his mind was quickly growing weary. Days passed, possibly weeks … or maybe even just hours, Sawyer could not be certain. Was his team still here in 1634? Had they caught the Runner, or not? Had they already returned home to the twenty-second century without him? If this were true, he'd only have himself to worry about … *And Hawk.*

When Mercier arrived to speak with him again, he carried a chair into the room. Behind him, attendants brought in a small table, two cups, and a wooden decanter of wine then left.

Sawyer refused to imbibe. "I only drink with friends."

"I see you are looking well," said Mercier.

"As well as my friend?" asked Sawyer, sitting on the edge of his cot as he languidly played with the cuffs of his shirt.

"I'm sure you will be pleased to hear your friend Hawk has been rewarded for your obedience."

"I don't need him to be pampered. I need him to be free and safe!"

"He will always be safe as long as you cooperate."

Sawyer stood and paced the width of his cell. "Right. As long as I obey." He stopped in front of the table and rested his gaze on Mercier. "Obey what? What are we waiting for? Am I not here to fight?"

Mercier laughed then drank slowly from his cup, licking his lips afterward as if savouring every drop. "Eager, aren't we?"

"Not eager. The sooner we get on with this, the sooner it will be over."

"Then I have come at the right time." Mercier pushed the empty cup across the table. "Drink with me."

Sawyer turned away.

"It is an order ... But it doesn't have to be."

Sawyer turned back. "What are you talking about?"

Mercier pulled out a vial from an inside pocket of his robe and shook it gently in the air. "Remember how you felt that first fight? I can bring that back to you. Make it so you don't have to think, let your inhibitions run wild without the consequences of remorse."

Sawyer eyed the vial. A small voice inside him urged him to drink it and be damned with all of this, but he looked away before the thought could fully establish itself. "There is always remorse. You can't hide from your demons, no matter how many substances you put in your body."

Mercier poured the liquid into the empty cup. "Not if you keep consuming it. Dr. Arnault introduced me to this, and my students and I are still learning the effects of this rare coca substance, but so far our tests have been promising."

"Coca? Botanists have already brought it back from the Amazon?"

"You are a man of many wonders, Sawyer. A man of the world."

"And books."

"So you do know of medicine? It wasn't all a ruse."

"Yes, but what does this have to do with anything? I'm here to fight, obviously not for my mind since you seem hell bent on destroying it with that concoction of yours. So, am I to fight this evening or not?"

Mercier pointed at the wine on the table in an offering to Sawyer. "A toast to this evening's event."

With a cautious glance and steady hand, Sawyer reached for the bottle. But he did not pour the wine into the cup. He raised the wooden decanter to his lips and drank then placed it back on the table.

Mercier leaned forward, grabbed the wine, and poured a generous amount in Sawyer's cup that was ladened with coca.

"No," said Sawyer. "Now that I know what it is making me so violent, I really don't want it."

Mercier narrowed his eyes.

The small voice urging Sawyer to drink from the cup and allow his body to function without censor niggled its way back into his thoughts. It had been near rhapsodic to fight so unencumbered from morals and righteousness, to let loose what he had kept locked deep down inside for so many years. To lose control. With each passing moment of contemplation, he leaned closer to the table.

No! He squeezed his eyes shut and dropped his head, clenching his biceps as hard as he could as he crossed his arms over his chest.

"Sawyer."

Sawyer looked into Mercier's eyes and knew there was no longer a choice in the matter. It was now a legitimate order. Based on that alone, Sawyer reached forward and grabbed the cup. He poured it down his throat as fast as he could then threw the cup across his cell. "Are you satisfied?"

"Another."

Sawyer drew in a deep breath to consolidate his strength, employing Hawk's mercurial state as his bedrock, then strode across the cell to retrieve his cup. Mercier took it from his reluctant grasp and poured into it more of the coca from the vial. Then he filled the rest of the cup with wine and passed it back to him.

Sawyer drank it in one gulp then placed it on the table. Before he could retract his hand, Mercier was pouring more.

***

SAWYER was a heaving mass of coiled violence when he returned to his cell that night.

The clang of his cell door opening resounded in the underground chamber, echoing in his ears like thunder announcing a spring storm. He was pushed onto the bed roughly, but was back on his feet instantly, running at the guards who'd tossed him aside like trash. His left fist flew forward, making contact with the face of one of the guards. Sawyer stood back, crouched, and waited for retaliation. He wanted them to try and stop him. "Come on! Take me!" he yelled, begging them to unleash their fury so he could fight back.

Sawyer thought himself invincible. His blood pumped hard through every artery in his body; he heard the whooshing of air in his lungs as they expanded and contracted. He tasted liquid iron, bitter and metallic, as blood coated his throat in a thick, viscous film when he swallowed. He felt euphoric, alive, and more alert than he'd ever felt his entire life. He thought about the maxigen drug abusers of the twenty-second century, and how this was how they must feel under its spell.

No wonder it's so popular with soldiers.

Sawyer found no rest from his heightened state until several more guards entered, pounding their meaty fists into the palms of their hands as they rushed forward. It took several blows to Sawyer's head before he stayed down, and several more after that until he found respite in unconsciousness.

Hours, days, months later—Sawyer was never sure how long he was out when he slept— he heard a voice.

"Your threshold for pain astounds me, Sawyer."

The voice was distant, but somehow it penetrated the thick fog surrounding him.

"Time to wake up."

The voice pierced Sawyer's muddled thoughts with its familiar tone and condescension. Sawyer knew that voice, hated that voice, but was involuntarily drawn to it despite his abhorrence of the man to whom it belonged.

"I see you twitching," said Mercier. "Work your way through it and you'll be here with me shortly."

Unable to control more than his throat, Sawyer swallowed and groaned as he was pulled toward the palpable world. He had no control of his return to consciousness, and no ability to fight it.

"You are to be held accountable for your actions during that fight, Sawyer. I was forced to make reparations because of you. And your punishment was to be severe. It was only due to Dr. Arnault that you were spared."

What have I done? Sawyer couldn't think straight, he couldn't remember anything past the wine. He just knew he was angry, and possibly … ashamed. Cold swept through him, turned every nerve ending to ice, yet his skin burned as if he were standing next to a fire. His hands rested before his eyes, trembling and blood soaked.

"Your wounds were deep this time. Someone will be in to stitch you shortly. I trust you will behave. In the meantime, I have arrangements to make regarding your dear friend."

Sawyer reached out an arm and used what controllable strength he had to hold it up. *Hawk. No. Leave him alone! If someone is to blame, it's me!* His arm fell down, dangled off the side of the bed with his torn and shredded knuckles scraping on the dirt floor.

"You disappointed me. I expected better from you. More control and a little less … uncaged brutality! You were to fight, give a show! Give me bodies I can work with! Not leave messes of men that cannot be put back together!"

The sudden stillness in the room was jarring. Sawyer knew nothing of what Mercier spoke. Sawyer's only clues were how his body felt.

"The deaths of those eight men and guards were in vain," continued Mercier, his voice softer but not any less full of conviction. "You killed without purpose and wasted lives. Reflect on that, Sawyer, as you lay there in pain!"

Sawyer closed his eyes. *This is why my father trained me, beat me into submission … to control my temper. Mercier is right. I am an animal.*

39.
MISSION: DAY SEVEN

ON the steps of Baron Fournier's estate, Perry stared across the lawn. Having just spent nearly two days with this waste of a man, he was more than ready to leave.

Hawk approached from the north side of the building, running with a hand securing his rapier down at his side so it didn't bounce against his leg. "It's all clear," said Hawk. "All the horses are stabled, and I chained all his carriages but one for the baron to use, so his people can't take them."

"*All* his carriages?"

Hawk smirked. "The man does love his carriages. The farthest he's probably walked is to the nearest dessert table."

Perry nodded, closed his eyes. "So now we wait."

Hawk stood next to him. "I hate waiting. Especially for this. It's too bad we only knew where the school was and can't figure out where the fights take place on our own."

"True enough. I'm sure the commander's advice ..." he paused when Hawk's gaze turned downward. "Sawyer, he was your friend? At the Academy?"

"We never stopped being friends, we just lost contact with each other. But I get the feeling you knew him before all this as well. For someone so entrenched with the Rangers, you seem pretty adamant about saving Sawyer in lieu of the mission. I'm grateful, and one day I hope you'll tell me what that's about, but right now we got work to do."

The sun was setting, and Baron Fournier had sent out staff to let them know it would be time to leave shortly.

"It really is a shame," said Perry, unhitching his horse at the bottom of the stairs.

Hawk swung his leg over his mount. "What is?"

"That we are about to change the timeline. That we have already changed the timeline. I'm sure the commander's involvement in these fights has already affected people of this century. Some may have died who shouldn't have. Some men's lives may have changed because of their ordeal with the commander, and their lives set on different paths. And we cannot forget … Santiago wasn't pleased with my report. She wants us back on course, not attending this fight. There will be punishment, I'm sure."

"There isn't much she can do about it right now though."

"To further her wrath, blood will most likely be shed in our rescue, for there isn't going to be much that will stop me from saving Sawyer. Deaths of green auras may occur. Are we all right with that? Would the commander be alright with that?"

Hawk turned his horse toward the long drive. "I think he would be very conflicted. But ultimately, no. Rule One, don't contaminate the timeline. He lives by the rules. He's always been a damn Boy Scout."

"He wasn't always."

Hawk looked at him, and Perry swallowed the lump in his throat before he spoke in a hushed voice. "His father made him this way. I couldn't abide … I couldn't watch …"

Hawk's head dipped low. "You and the rear admiral, eh?"

Perry's heart stung. Closing his eyes didn't help, it only served to bring vivid memories once dulled by years of drinking and trying to forget back to life. "I was there … I had been with John for five years … the day he brought Kai home."

"Does Kai know?"

Perry shook his head. "Too young. I don't think he remembers me. I've changed. I've gotten older. I'm probably just a shadow in his mind." He cleared his throat. "Now let's go."

Perry turned to the driveway ahead, spurring his horse into a gallop when they arrived at the main road, where they followed behind Baron Fournier's carriage. The sky above was darkening, dotted sporadically with white fluffy clouds, but in the distance a darker, Prussian-blue sky crept closer. Perry and Hawk followed the carriage into the village where the pick-up was to occur, stood ready by the door while Fournier drank with the others, and then boarded the wagon when they were told. It seemed a silly ordeal to Perry, but he understood why the originators of this fight club would want to keep their enterprise a secret, so he and Hawk followed orders. They were guarded and blindfolded for the trip, and when they were released at the other end of the journey, they were ushered in a group into a large stable where the blindfolds were released.

As the baron earlier described, a string quartet played music from a corner of the stable, and drinks were being handed out like cake at a child's birthday party, but neither he nor Hawk imbibed. When someone announced the festivities were to begin, everyone moved to the sidelines and climbed up on crates, leaving the centre of the stable empty for the coming contestants.

Perry followed Hawk to a raised platform made of an old stable door held up by empty barrels. From here, they would have a good view of what was to come. Perry closed his eyes. *How bad will this be?*

"I think we're at the old asylum," said Hawk. "This is the stable we were in the other day, only now it's all set up for ... *festivities.*"

Perry glanced around the crowd, finding it hard to see past their eager, greedy faces. "Why do you say that?"

"The asylum is where Mercier is holding his illegal school. And the patients? Where do you think he's getting them from? With this fight club, he has an endless supply."

"You're right."

"At least we know where we are. Now for the interesting part." Hawk pointed to where a man in a long robe stood on a dais, calling everyone's attention to him. "There's Mercier. Not only is he running the illegal school, kidnapping men, and most likely working with the Runner, he's running the fight club as well."

Perry nearly fell off the platform when the blood rushed from his head into his boots.

Hawk put a hand on his shoulder. "We're here now. We've got this, Specialist. Don't go sentimental on me, it's time for action."

Perry pulled himself together with a deep breath, nodded at Hawk, and listened to what Mercier was announcing from his dais.

"Place your bets, good citizens of France! For tonight we bring you a spectacle like no other! We have a treat in store for you this evening. Our champion will test his mettle, his strength and prowess on several contestants tonight!"

Perry feared what he was about to witness and inched his hand toward the pistol hanging on his hip. He glanced around and saw green auras everywhere. Could he do it? Make a mess of things to save Sawyer?

"You don't think they'd pit our commander against too many men, do you?" asked Hawk, as they watched the people around them placing anxious bets and calling for the festivities to start.

"I don't know."

Hawk scanned the stable. "There are guards at all exits. A crowd of at least a hundred people. We don't have our horses, but there are those wagons outside we can use for our escape if we need to make a fast one."

"This is your area of expertise. I'll follow your lead on this."

Hawk nodded, his attention elsewhere as he seemed to be still studying their surroundings. "We can't make a move until we see him," he said, voice firm and in control.

Perry envied him, for he felt on the brink of passing out.

"The two of us won't be much of a match for all the guards here. Even with Sawyer's help, there's no way any of us will get out of here alive without backup." Hawk paused, firmed his jaw. "If we see he's in trouble, we'll act. But unless that happens, we hold ground."

40.

THERE was nothing left inside Sawyer other than anger. Every thought led to that one emotion. It consumed him as it spiralled outward to the fists clenched at the ends of his tired, aching arms.

"Just give it to me," Sawyer said, as he reached a hand toward the guard carrying the canteen. Sawyer held no doubt the water was laced with cocaine. He was already poised for violence, so he found the notion of drinking it redundant. "Give it," he said again when the guard hesitated to pass it to him.

"Let's unleash the monster, shall we?" Sawyer yanked out the cork with his teeth and spat it on the ground at the guard's feet, then guzzled the entire contents of the canteen before tossing it on the floor. He proceeded out of his cell, past the guards, with neither shackles nor blindfold, and ignored their pleas for him to wait. "No need. I'm looking forward to this."

The guards fell in step behind him as he led the way through the tunnels, and using his memory to dictate which turns to take, which halls to walk down, he reached the stairs leading to the stable faster than he'd ever done before. A guard stepped cautiously around him to climb the stairs while the other remained beside him with his hands hovering near Sawyer's arm but not touching him.

Sawyer glared, causing the man to step back.

When the hatch opened above Sawyer, he ran up the stairs, scrambling to find purchase on the dirt walls as his energy drove him upward with more force than his body could accommodate. Topside, his chest surged with heavy breathing. The crowd was loud and encouraging. Aroused by his ferocious arrival, the spectators clapped, their cheers growing in enthusiasm as Sawyer stepped further into the stable.

Might as well enjoy the road to hell while I can.

223

Sawyer's desire to destroy, and unleash his pent-up energy, increased tenfold, making his limbs shake with anticipation. He had an irrational urge to tear apart the man who stood before him over six feet tall and with biceps the size of Sawyer's thighs. There were scars on his opponent's face, crisscrossing his nose and bisecting his upper lip as evidence of success in his own fights. None of it worried Sawyer. The man was nothing. A toy. Sawyer didn't care what his name was, or why he was there; he only wanted to kill him by whatever means possible. The man who stood before Sawyer was nothing more than meat in clothes, and Sawyer was starving.

Sawyer licked his dry lips and leaned forward, straining against the hands holding him back from his prey. He'd kill those men too if need be, anything to be released and set free before his heart exploded in his chest.

***

⋀ hatch opened in the middle of the stable floor. Perry held firm, with the grip on his pistol tightening to control his trembling hand.

After several men were brought through the hatch and paraded around the stable, there was a pause before the last contestant was ushered forth. Perry's knees buckled when he saw what came up through the hatch next, and he was grateful Hawk reached out to catch him before he collapsed.

Sawyer's blue eyes were discernable under the black hair that had fallen over his face. His defined jawline was still visible under the scruffy beard that had formed. The clothes he wore were dirty, blood-stained, and not the ones he'd arrived in this century wearing. Around them the crowd cheered, so loud and boisterous it hurt Perry's ears.

"What the fuck. Look at him," whispered Hawk. "He looks like he's going to rip those men apart."

"Not Sawyer. That's not like him."

Hawk turned to him. "You knew him as a child. I knew him as a man who'd spent years of abuse under the rear admiral. Unfortunately, it's definitely like him."

Perry looked across the stable floor to several men, some tall and lanky with bandages already covering parts of their bodies, a weakness he hoped Sawyer wouldn't exploit. Several more contenders stood behind the one in front, also sporting bandages, while some brandished knives.

Sawyer took his first opponent down quick and hard while managing to sustain a lone powerful blow to his head. Now he stood ready for his next adversary. The cheers of the crowd were nothing but background noise to Perry. His heart pumped so hard, all he could hear was the whooshing sound of his pulse in his ears.

"He's going to kill someone," said Hawk. "We have to stop this."

Perry couldn't answer, his lips and mouth so dry, his mind scrambled to conceive a coherent thought.

Sawyer met his new opponent in the middle of the ring, where they collided with each other. Sawyer ducked when the man's fisted arm swung at his head. On Sawyer's way back up to standing he deposited a swift punch to the man's ribs, then grabbed the man's head and thrust it downward as he drew his own knee upward.

The sound of facial bones breaking broke Perry's heart. *What have they done to you?*

Sawyer raised his arms in jubilation, exulting himself to the spectators like a champion gladiator.

"Fuck this," said Hawk. The two men in front of him were shoved aside as he pushed his way toward the ring.

Perry, his legs like cinder blocks, wanted to move, follow after Hawk. As if in suspended animation, all he could do was watch, emotions trapped inside his frozen frame.

Hawk stood at the edge of the ring for a beat, then slowly advanced on Sawyer. "Hey, it's me."

Sawyer's face did not reflect recognition. He ran at Hawk and shoved him back. From the dais, Mercier's voice bellowed words Perry could not understand, most likely trying to contain order as the crowd cheered on the mysterious man who'd entered the ring. The crowd wanted violence, blood, and they didn't care who gave it to them.

Perry wanted to throw up.

"Sawyer! It's me." Hawk tried again to break through.

Sweat dripped down Perry's back, as he was still unable to move. He held his breath, hoping their commander would recognize the lifeline being presented to him.

"Max?" said Sawyer. "What are you doing here?"

"Yes, Kai. It's me."

Take his hand, Kai, thought Perry. *Take it.*

The crowd chanted for Sawyer to finish this newcomer to the ring, and finally Perry found the fire inside him and pushed through the spectators. When he stood beside Hawk, the crowd's cheers simmered to buzzing and murmuring. The only voice was that of Mercier calling for guards.

Through the reek of smelly bodies and stale whiskey permeating the stable, Perry sensed blood and sweat coming off Sawyer. His forehead glistened under the black shaggy hair, his eyes unfocussed, as if seeing a different world than the one around them. Scuffling sounds and shouts of anger came from behind, and Perry knew they didn't have much time before Mercier's guards stopped this intrusion. He reached out an arm ...

Sawyer knocked it away and punched Hawk in the face.

The crowd erupted as Hawk stumbled back. Perry lunged at Sawyer, but stopped the moment he saw the hatred in Sawyer's eyes.

Hawk spat blood onto the ground, his eyes glossy. "What the fuck?"

Sawyer stood over him. "My mercy comes in many forms," he said, circling Hawk like a predator. "Which do you prefer? A quick death to grant you leave from this hell, or enough pain to knock you into oblivion?"

The crowd roared, urging Sawyer to take his kill in order to satisfy their lustful needs for violence. The guards Mercier called for were now breaking through the spectators, knives and clubs visible in their hands. Perry grabbed Hawk's arm. "We have to go."

Perry pulled Hawk toward him as he shuffled back, successfully getting lost in the crowd as it pushed forward for a better taste of the action.

"We can't leave him here!" cried Hawk.

"We'll come back. Like you said, we can't do anything on our own. We need help."

With the guards encroaching from all sides, Perry moved faster as he pulled Hawk toward the stable door. *We will be back. We will be back,* repeated in Perry's head as he and Hawk ran for the wagons.

The darkness of a moonless night allowed Perry and Hawk to find a wagon, unhitch the horses, and disappear into the surrounding forest. It wasn't until the sound of chase disappeared that Perry brought them to a stop.

Hawk leaned over his horse and grabbed Perry by the lapels of his doublet. "We had him! We fucking had him! Why'd you drag me out of there!"

"We didn't have him! That wasn't our commander, it was someone else! He wasn't going to come with us, and those guards coming at us weren't going to let us take him!"

Hawk's hands released from his doublet. "I'm not leaving without him! We're going back."

Perry reached over and grabbed Hawk's reins. "If we go back there ... first, we'll most likely be caught and killed. Second, it won't help us in freeing Sawyer. We are two against a small army!"

"Fuck! All right. I get it. We come back with more force. We're returning to the Earth-Landers and getting help from Santiago, whether she likes it or not, and then we're getting this fucking mission over with."

Perry saw a venom in Hawk's eyes he hadn't seen before. Always so casual, everything rolling off his back as if it were water, Perry now saw the soldier in him. He nodded curtly at Hawk and let the lieutenant set the pace back to the Earth-Landers.

41.

SAWYER crouched and turned in a circle so the crowd could all see him. And with each face he saw watching him back, his need to inflict more violence intensified. Hawk and Perry had just ran away, never bothered to take him with them. *Why did they even come? To gloat? To see what had become of me?*

In fact, Sawyer wasn't sure if what he'd just seen was even real. He'd seen Hawk. What was that about? Did Mercier get the name of the one they'd captured wrong? Was it Santiago dressed as a man they were holding hostage instead of Hawk? Or one of the SAR Rangers Santiago had brought down with her? Sawyer couldn't think straight. But it didn't matter who it was they had actually captured, a teammate was still a teammate, and Sawyer was determined to keep them safe.

A whoosh of air and feet shuffling across loose dirt alerted Sawyer to turn around, but not quickly enough to stop the knife blade darting toward his abdomen. It pierced his skin, probably deeper, but Sawyer cared not as he grabbed the wrist of the man wielding the weapon and pushed it away to draw the blade out.

Sawyer staggered back as blood seeped from the wound.

His opponent sneered, tossed the blade between his hands as he crouched, ready for another attack. Sawyer focussed on his opponent's rage in order to fuel his own anger. With no regard for propriety, Sawyer ripped the shirt from his body, letting loose a deep, guttural growl as he tossed it away.

He felt no pain, no remorse for what he was about to do, only a yearning need for retribution. *For those dying in the school! For a lost future! For my failure as a commander!*

Sawyer ran forward, his mind clear and set as it disregarded his instincts to survive in lieu of killing everyone around him.

***

SAWYER assumed he was carried back to his cell later that night, for he didn't remember getting there under his own power. A pungent odour of wet dirt and mould filled his nostrils, enlivening his senses. With the effects of the drug Mercier was giving him having worn off, indicating to Sawyer how long he'd been asleep, his mouth went dry and an all-too-familiar agitation invaded his limbs and mind. Images of Hawk and Specialist Perry standing before him … then leaving him as they ran freely away …

He couldn't think about it. It hurt too much.

His left hand moved to the wound on his lower right side. A thick crust had formed on his skin, which Sawyer did not want to disturb. When he pulled his hand back it was dry, suggesting the bleeding had stopped, but the damage was still evident by the way his belly pinched. It felt like a sharp stone under his skin, its jagged edges unrelenting as it stabbed at his insides. For all the times he'd healed faster than he'd anticipated, this time he didn't. He suspected it was the cocaine, but at this point, he didn't much care.

With nothing to sew his wound closed, Sawyer determined his best treatment to be more of the drug-laced water. If he couldn't cure what ailed him, he figured he could at least numb the psychological and physical pain enough to forget either existed. Forget he'd seen his two teammates abandon him. But he had no water to drink.

"Hawk … how could you do this to me?" He closed his eyes and his jaw spasmed. He couldn't believe the next thought that came into his mind. "Did Santiago have anything to do with this? Is this her way of getting command?"

Sawyer squeezed his hands against his head. "No … not like this … she wouldn't. The rear admiral would never promote you after leaving his son …" He paused when he realized how awkward that word sounded. "Leaving your … commander in the past."

Nothing made sense.

He swung his legs off the bed then pushed himself into a seated position. The ground felt soft underfoot, and dampness invaded his boots. He glanced down to see a soggy ground. A deep rumble sounded in the distance. Sawyer stood. It sounded as if something heavy was rolling across the ground above, its deep, sonorous boom echoing in the small room. Small trembles came up from the ground, sending tiny vibrations up his legs. He stumbled to one of the walls and placed a hand against it, waiting to see if another sound would come.

Another boom rumbled the walls. Sawyer looked up, wondering if a hundred horses were stampeding above. Then he looked down at his damp feet. The ground was flooded. "Damn it," he said, running a hand down his face. "A storm."

He made his way back to the bed where he sat down heavily, cradling his numb right hand in his lap. With the smell of mildew and mould saturating the air, his small cell became even more suffocating. Further complications became apparent as he looked around. The air was colder than usual, and each time the thunder of the heated storm above rolled across the sky, particles of dirt tumbled down the walls, indicating to Sawyer the intensity of rain soaking the Earth.

Sawyer shivered, then looked up as a clank sounded from the door, denoting someone's arrival. Several young men dressed in robes and carrying bandages and water skins entered his cell. Sawyer breathed a sigh of relief at the sight of the water canteen. He raised a hand to accept the skin, but the robed men hesitated to relinquish it until the guards came in behind them to stand at their sides.

Sawyer rolled his eyes, beckoning with his fingers to give him the water. When they did, he leaned back and drank with greed. He found he was needing more to get the reaction he wanted, he craved, and he wondered if there'd come a time when there wasn't enough cocaine in the water to satisfy him. But he felt nothing but disappointed when he finished the canteen. It was water. Plain water.

"Let them fix you," said a guard. "And no funny business or your …"

"Yes, I know. I'm familiar with the rules," Sawyer said as he lay back on his cot.

The students poked and prodded the stab wound on his stomach. Sawyer grimaced but felt no urgent need to push the hands away. He let them work in peace for the most part, offering advice on how to hold the needle when he noticed a student using an underhand grip. *If you can't beat 'em, join 'em*, he thought bitterly. There was no point in fighting anymore.

When they moved on to his hand, Sawyer was no longer able to rest in relative comfort. Manipulating bone was not an easy task, and if done without consideration for the patient, it could be quite painful.

"Did Mercier show you how to do this?" Sawyer sat upright as he yanked his hand toward his chest. Dumbfounded by their inexperience, he pulled the joint of his right thumb back into place. It hurt, but not as much as letting the amateurs wiggle it back and forth.

The student in charge of the hand stood back, shaking his head. "I'm meant to practise."

"And I'm meant to be free. I guess we should both get used to disappointment."

The other students crossed their arms and stared at Sawyer with indignation. Sawyer's jaw hung open before he slammed it closed. He looked up at the ceiling and shook his head as if Beaumont above was looking down with just as much annoyance as he was feeling. "Why don't you go find a corpse to play with? You're obviously not trained to treat the living."

"We will be physicians and surgeons one day," said one of the young men. "You would be wise to show some respect."

If it weren't for the leaden weight of his body or the threat hanging over his now un-named teammate, Sawyer would have shown this man what respect really meant, but instead he smiled and shook his weary head. "Go play doctor somewhere else. I have no need of you. Just leave me the bandages."

The young men left the room in a flurry of billowing robes and murmured rebukes, leaving Sawyer to tend to his own wounds. He reclined back on his cot and began bandaging his hand, manipulating the dislocated and broken bones with more ease than any of them had.

Sawyer shook his head. *What have I become? I'm a damn Sawyer! My father wouldn't give up. Beaumont wouldn't give up.* Thunder continued to roll overhead. *What am I without their guidance?*

Sawyer remained on the cot, staring at the dirt ceiling. This was his life now, and he didn't know how he felt about that.

42.
MISSION: DAY EIGHT

RAIN was not a common deterrent for Rangers, but when it fell with enough intensity to flood the ground and seep in through the back hatchways of the Earth-Landers, it was enough to keep the doors closed. Perry stood in the back of Earth-Lander Two, his rain-soaked doublet dripping water onto the floor. Lieutenant Hawk sat on the bench across from him with his head back, eyes closed, and as Perry saw it, every one of his muscles tense. They were waiting for Lieutenant Commander Santiago, who was currently finishing business with the SAR team and the other Earth-Lander.

The storm was in full force when Santiago arrived in her grey battle fatigues. Perry couldn't see the top of a skinsuit peeking out above the collar, so he knew it wasn't a full battle uniform. He'd hoped she'd given up on pretence and rules due to the situation, but apparently the lieutenant commander wasn't yet ready.

"Commander Sawyer reported Dr. Mercier's clinic was also a school, and now you're telling me the old asylum is also a fight club?" Santiago read from her communications card. She held it out in the palm of her hand and swiped a finger across the screen to bring up a 3-D holo map of seventeenth-century France above it so they could all see. The large section northwest of Paris was still grey, indicating Thor's blackout area.

"The asylum, the clinic … the school … whatever the fuck Mercier is calling it, is in that area," said Hawk, pointing to the grey area of the map. "And that's where our commander is being held. As Commander Sawyer reported from his primary recce mission, there are guards. The specialist and I saw approximately twenty of them in the fighting stable. And they're armed. Antiquated weapons,

233

but then, so are ours. And from our earlier recce of the school, there are more guards inside the building. The back of the asylum meets up with forest immediately. And there's open ground around the property on the three other sides, with an approximate perimeter of five acres in each direction before they also meet forest on the north and south sides. The western perimeter is a large open hill. Not a lot of coverage for an attack ... unless you happened to bring along our skinsuits and we can engage personal masks?"

"We are not bringing in tech. We handle this by the book," said Santiago.

Hawk waved a finger around the surrounding countryside. "Several villages in the area, ones where men have gone missing, would probably be eager to join the fight. We could toss them in as cannon fodder and sneak in behind them?"

Santiago raised her brows in a look of disgust.

"What?" said Hawk. "Commander Sawyer would have no problems with that plan. As long as they don't have green auras."

Perry had been staring at the holo-map, lost in thought. His teammate's words neither relieved the despair gripping his heart nor the frenzied thoughts of doom whisking through his head. He drew in a deep breath and let it escape in a slow exhale, hoping to blow out some of his anxiety along with it. "I'm already considering my actions when I get my hands on Mercier. I have a good mind to smack all these fuckers into the twenty-second century. Regardless of their precious auras."

"Calm down, Specialist," said Santiago.

"I will not calm down!" Perry turned away, scrubbed his face, and turned back. "This mission has gone to hell! We lost our commander! We have no idea who our Time Runner is, and we are quickly running out of time! Fuck the rules and let's get the damn *BlackOut* down here and missile the shit out of this place with extreme prejudice and get Commander Sawyer back!"

Santiago and Hawk stared at him, mouths hanging open.

"What?"

Hawk cleared his throat "So, speaking of the *BlackOut* ..."

"I'm not bringing down an entire spaceship!" spat Santiago. "Are you crazy! Have you both lost your minds! You want me to introduce a space-faring ship into a time when they barely believed the world wasn't flat!"

"They knew it wasn't flat," said Perry.

"Shut up!"

"We do know where the Runner is," said Hawk. A pensive look crossed his face as he chewed his bottom lip. "Commander Sawyer said he saw a red aura at the asylum. Forget this Mercier dupe, we need to go after this other guy. Two birds, one stone. We take the asylum, rescue Sawyer, and take down the Runner in one shot." He looked at Perry and then stared at Santiago. "But even with the SAR team you brought, we can't do this alone. We need the *BlackOut*. Or at least its crew."

"No." Santiago crossed her arms. "The *BlackOut* isn't staffed like a Space Fleet ship anymore, remember? There are no marines, no Space Fleet soldiers on board. And there aren't enough Rangers to counter the number of guards our Runner has protecting him. Besides, it would take time ... too much time, to send back both Earth-Landers to shuttle them down here, find them costumes and weapons ..."

"Then I plan on going in fully cocked," said Hawk. "And loaded. And scope-locked on finding our commander. Screw anyone who gets in my way."

Santiago's mouth dropped open when she noticed Perry nodding in agreement. "Are you two serious? Do I need to remind you both of the Ranger's number-one rule? This will not be the shootout at the O.K. Corral. We do this right, by the books. We're going in with the capture of the Time Runner our top priority. The Time Rangers would never abide a cluster-fuck to happen, they would want this done with thought and precision. By the rules. Which, by the way, you two seem to want to disregard. But we'll discuss your not listening to my earlier orders later because ultimately ... you were right. I was wrong, and you found the commander. So, sorry."

Perry and Hawk nodded, but the lieutenant wasn't finished his argument. "You didn't see him in that fight, sir. Sawyer may have had a stick up his ass for rules and protocols before, but ..."

Perry ran a hand down his face. "He's ... different. And he's our commander, and I think he would be okay now with a little breaking of the rules."

"We're Time Rangers, and we do things their way," replied Santiago.

"I thought you would be more open. You're not known for being protocol driven," said Hawk, crossing his arms. "Or is this about you trying to prove yourself? You go on about Sawyer wanting to make a name for himself, but what's your agenda?"

"This isn't about me, Lieutenant!"

Perry sighed. "Perhaps it is, Lieutenant Commander. But if you do want to prove yourself, a good step in that direction would be to bring the rear admiral's son home alive."

Santiago shook her head and paced the small Earth-Lander cabin. "I've been thinking about what happened on the *BlackOut* prior to my departure. My unfortunate conversations with the rear admiral. I will … begrudgingly … admit, I may have been wrong about Commander Sawyer and his motives. But if we all want to keep our jobs when we get back, we need to do this by the Ranger handbook."

"Sir," interrupted Perry. "And if I may, I agree with the lieutenant. We should take this place down. Leave nothing but rubble."

Santiago blinked. Blinked again. "You of all people should know …"

"I say fuck 'em all."

"Stand down. Both of you. I get it. I want to go in guns a blazin' as much as you do, but remember the repercussions to the future. We know this Mercier has historical relevance. He can't be touched. And if you see any other greens out there, do not engage with anything more than reasonable force. We will stay true to the mission. What a good commander would want. If he can't be here, we should serve his name proudly."

"I'm not so sure you know what *our* commander would want," said Hawk. His jaw was tense, shoulders stiff. "I've known him a lot longer than anyone here, and trust me when I say he's a grenade waiting to explode. He's good at keeping it all in, stuffing that shit down where no one can see it, but I think this mission may have cracked his armour. And he'd want us to use whatever means possible to take this Runner and his cohorts down."

"If we find the commander, then let's remind him who he really is," said Santiago. "If Commander Sawyer is as far gone as you two think he is, let us be the beacon that brings him back by staying true to the mission and taking down the Runner. Do I make myself clear?"

Perry closed his eyes and nodded. "Yes, sir."

Hawk threw his arms in the air. "You've got to be fucking kidding me!"

"Lieutenant! Do I make myself clear!"

Hawk stood straight, saluted. "Yes, sir. Anything you say, sir."

Perry recognized the acidic tone in Hawk's voice, but Santiago had no choice but to believe in the sincerity of his words. Hawk was Sawyer's friend, but he was also a soldier.

"We need … I need, to see this place," said Santiago. "We can't use sensors, so I want eyes on this asylum and its perimeter myself. There has to be a better plan than bringing down a fucking spaceship to capture one Time Runner, and I plan to find one."

"What about Code 54?" asked Hawk.

"Hell no!" replied Santiago. "No other team has had to resort to using a Code 54, and I don't plan on being the first."

Perry raised an eyebrow. "Code 54?"

"It's a command code," replied Hawk.

"For what?"

Hawk looked at Santiago.

"Not now," she replied. "Perry, I will read you in if and when the time is appropriate, but not until then." She glared at Hawk. "A Code 54 is a last resort. And I will make that determination. No one else. It's not an order I will be forced or bullied into making. So, we are going to that asylum, together. Pack up, we leave in thirty minutes … after I put that ridiculous costume back on."

She closed down her communication card, slid it back into her collar, and left the Earth-Lander. Perry sat on a bench and leaned over his knees. From a recess in his mind, something about the *BlackOut* bothered him. There was something about it … something he couldn't put his finger on.

"You look thinky," said Hawk. "Snap out of it. I want to see that grr-angry man come back out."

Not wanting to lose his train of thought, Perry ignored Hawk. Santiago wanted this rescue clean. This takedown clean. For her own benefit? Was *she* against going in half-cocked because she wanted to save her own skin? And what was this Code 54? Did it have to do with the *BlackOut*? Perry couldn't shake the feeling all this talk about the ship was doing to him. Maybe a ride back out to the asylum, to Sawyer, would help put it all together.

43.

DR. Arnault stood with Mercier in a room appointed with lavish furniture. Arnault watched Mercier count the purse he'd collected the night before as he sipped brandy from a goblet, his body relaxed. With the two unexpected guests, whom Arnault suspected were Time Rangers attached to Sawyer, visiting their fight club last night, worrisome doubts flitted through his mind, conjuring scenarios of him being taken away in shackles or standing across from their ungoverned champion poised and willing to inflict retribution.

His plans were falling apart. His mission was failing. His boss would be very disappointed. Arnault's saving grace was that he was stuck here in the seventeenth century where the big boss man himself could not reach him.

Outside, a raging deluge fell on the old decaying roof of the asylum. The air in the room was heavy as a suffocating humidity pressed down. Arnault wiped sweat from his forehead with a handkerchief from his pocket. Across from him, Mercier flinched as a crack of lightning announced what the sky had been promising for the last hours.

Arnault sneered at Mercier's content state. This archaic wannabe doctor considered himself a hero, but Arnault thought him easily manipulated by his own greed and need to be recognized as a powerful man.

Mercier let a handful of coins fall from his open palm to the mahogany table, clinking as they landed on an already large pile.

"Mercier?"

Mercier lifted his head, which was followed a moment later by his eyes. "What is it?"

"It is time we leave. Those guests last night prove our need to relocate is imminent."

"I like it here," Mercier said, casting a languid gaze around the room. "It's large enough to substantiate our needs. And with the many outlying towns, our work is accommodated. France needs us here."

Arrogance! "Wipe that impertinent smile off your face. You are nothing but a brazen, naive upstart. I gave up my life to save the future, to save the citizens of Earth. You're riding my coattails. It would serve you well to remember that." Arnault bit his lip to control his anger and held back his further contempt. "Those two men the other night are a problem. Bigger than you can imagine. And the body count is growing; we are running out of room here."

Mercier looked around the room with a weary sigh.

"The morgue is quite full," continued Arnault. "Many men have perished from injuries ..."

Mercier raised a hand to silence him. "Unfortunately, I see your point." He rose from his chair to come out from behind his desk. He rested on the corner, his hands clasped in his lap. "It will take time to pack. So, see to the dead, kill the rest. We will move my school elsewhere. Take what wagons you can from the nearby towns. I'm sure they won't mind donating a few after all the help we've generously provided for them."

Arnault removed his glasses. "Leave Sawyer to me. And let's not forget who gives the orders around here at *my* school. You deal with the dead and wagons."

Mercier glanced at the armoire across the stone-floored room, where Sawyer's Musketeer uniform and weapons were being kept, and closed his eyes. "I remember the first time I saw him. So brave. So brash. So eager to fight. I knew what type of man he was the moment I saw him." He opened his eyes and stared at Arnault. "Why do you need him in particular?"

"I don't need him. But you can't have him. There are rules in place you can't even imagine. You are trying to save France; I am saving the world."

Mercier chuckled. "How does one man save the world?" Arnault didn't answer. "What if I don't give him to you? What if I kept him for myself? I can do wonders with him ..."

"You are nothing without me!" Arnault's face remained still as his voice rose. "I provided all of this for you! You are serving a purpose greater than France, and you will carry on serving your purpose until it is done. Mr. Sawyer must leave this place alive. I will not have sacrificed my entire life, my future, and my existence for some piss-ant little wannabe doctor like yourself to derail plans set in place a long time ago, and by people far more powerful than either you or I. You can be replaced. Many others want to see advancements in medicine. You are not a soul visionary. So, if I see fit, I will end you."

Mercier cleared his throat. "Yes. Sir."

"Now clear this place, pack everything up, and move on to the next residence. I have found another abandoned estate on the coast in Le Havre. You will like it there, it has an excellent view of the English Channel," he said with sarcasm. "I will arrange for Mr. Sawyer's departure."

Arnault left and headed for the stable. Outside, fat raindrops fell on his head like pellets of stone. He turned his face upward, letting the sting of each drop wash away the seventeenth-century grime he'd accumulated on every surface of his body.

By the time he reached the stable, he was a soaking mess. He went to the hatch in the middle of the floor, lifted it, and proceeded down the dirt staircase, his countenance now returned to the professional standard for which he'd been hired. "I was not expecting others to be so hell-bent on saving their precious commander. And I suspect this wasn't an oversight. But since I am stuck here in the wretched past, I suspect I will never get answers to this," he said to himself as he climbed downward.

When walking through the dank underground tunnels, Arnault pushed back his sleeve and activated the computer of his appropriated Time Ranger battle uniform hidden under his robe. He disengaged the grid protecting the asylum and surrounding area. "No need now, they know where we are." *And they are most likely gathering forces to attack.*

He considered for a moment what to do with the transponder box, spare skinsuit, and other tech still up in his office, and decided to leave them. If he activated the grid again, or used tech, the Rangers would know exactly where he'd set up his new school, and they could easily track the tech without the grid in place.

44.

SAWYER clutched his stomach, tucked his knees into his chest, and watched someone enter his cell, hoping they'd brought him a gift. But it wasn't Mercier.

The stout man who had entered instead remained silent. His eyes glinted a white light, which Sawyer recognized from long ago. But now he realized the glint in the man's eyes were glasses reflecting torchlight. *Diamond-Eyes? The one from the classroom who glowed red? The Time Runner. Dr. Arnault.*

When a heavy object landed beside Sawyer's head, he reached out a hand toward the bloated canteen. He didn't care that Arnault was staring, nor did he care how much he needed the drug, he only wanted to replenish his decaying body so he could function like a normal human being again. When he could drink no more, he corked the skin and put it back beside his head.

"Our situation has changed," said Dr. Arnault, standing in the ankle-deep water of the cell. "I suggest you take your fill. You must return to the future. But I suspect Mercier has other plans for you. The man is a bastard, and I suspect he will go against my orders and try to do as he pleases. This should help."

Another canteen landed on Sawyer's pillow.

"I'm sorry," said Dr. Arnault. "I wish we could have met under different circumstances, but now I must take my leave." He bent down and met Sawyer's gaze, then placed a hand on his shoulder. "I truly did not mean for it to end this way, but alas, some circumstances are beyond my control. Please take your fill of what I've provided, it will make things easier. Do as you want with the coming guards. I have no need of them anymore. In fact, I wish I could stay and watch, but I can't."

After he left, Sawyer closed his eyes. He'd barely understood what had just happened, what had been said to him, and he was too tired to figure it out. And he was freezing. Shivers racked his body as they had that day on the Earth-Lander floor when the *Titanic* sank.

His eyelids fluttered shut, and his mind's eye conjured a glowing fire burning before him. He couldn't help himself when next he imagined a body tight around him keeping him warm. He turned to look over his shoulder and saw blonde hair, short, with a lopsided cut framing a frowning face. Sawyer wanted to stay here where it was cozy and comforting, but that face wasn't right. It wasn't Aurora. The face was scowling. Judgmental. *Fucking Santiago!* He sat up, his breathing ragged and fast, his heart beat without cadence.

Sawyer swung his legs over the cot and braced his hands on the edge of the bed to help ease the congestion plaguing his lungs. His body weak, he stared at the water-logged floor, thinking of Perry and Hawk. And now, even Santiago.

Seeing Perry and Hawk on the fight floor, him hitting Hawk ... then he and Perry leaving without him. A cold hand gripped his stomach, and he nearly vomited. *They've left me here.*

A boom echoed in the small chamber, reminding Sawyer of the storm overhead. Staring at the floor beneath his boots, he noticed the water had not risen, but it hadn't receded, either. He pulled his feet out of the puddle, shook off the water, and fell back onto the cot with a deep sigh.

Sawyer's limbs trembled and an uncomfortable heat enveloped his body. Instinctively, he placed a hand on his forehead, where hot skin greeted his palm. Trapped in the cold, dank prison cell, he wasn't surprised. He rolled his head toward the door, which was large and ominous and settled into the dirt wall, hindering any chance he had of leaving his cell. His vision blurred as he continued to stare, the slats of wood blending together to form a solid wall, the small window melting away. When his vision was nothing more than swirling shades of black and browns, Sawyer closed his eyes, feeling more alone than he ever had in his entire life.

Trying to put order to his thoughts, and now feeling the effects of the cocaine in his system, Sawyer's heart nearly exploded when a loud, blood-curdling cry emerged from the other side of the door. Sawyer ran to the door and placed an ear against the heavy wood, his hands braced on either side of his head. Another agonizing screech filled his ears, followed by shouting and banging. Sawyer stepped back, then threw his body against the door. "No! No! Stop this!"

He continued to throw his body against the door then resorted to banging his fists when no one took heed of his commotion. There was no mistaking those sounds. Sawyer kicked the door hard then staggered back. He charged at the door again, his previous strength paltry compared to what he threw at it now.

"Stop!" he cried, when more voices resounded in pain.

Sawyer visualized other men, other fighters in cells such as his, being beaten to death. "No!"

When Arnault last spoke to him, Arnault sounded as if the end was near. Sawyer hadn't understood what that meant until now, and the realization wrapped around his heart like a python to its prey, squeezing until he could no longer breathe. Mercier … Arnault, were cleaning up their mess, having all the evidence destroyed. And Sawyer held no doubt they would be coming for him soon. Perhaps they had already gotten to his teammate.

"Oh, hell no. I'm not going down without a fight."

A full canteen lay on his cot and he ran to it, yanked out the cork, then leaned back to allow the water to pour down his throat without swallowing. Most of it spilled down his cheeks and chin, coating his bare shoulders before trickling down his chest. When he had finished almost half of it, he threw it across the room, where it bounced off the damp wall, falling into a puddle of stagnant water on the ground.

"Come and get me," he said, staring at the door. "I fucking dare you."

The door to Sawyer's cell banged open. He crouched, ready for the fight of his life as two guards stepped inside. Sawyer had hoped for more. And with his fever and pain having been washed away by the drug flooding his body, his mind urged him to kill. Take his revenge. It was if all the shackles holding him back were gone.

45.

PERRY sat on his horse between Hawk on his right and Santiago on his left. They sat top-down on the crest of a hill looking upon a large estate. Men and guards roamed the open fields and gardens around the estate, moving wagons to the doors and appearing to be packing up. Perry still didn't know what would be waiting for them down there. Or if he was really willing to abide by Santiago's orders to keep this clean. He and Hawk had already disobeyed her once, and it had turned out for the better. So what harm was there in disobeying her orders again?

That will depend on what's down there.

Would Sawyer still be a hostage? Would he be alive? Perry wasn't sure if he'd be able to keep a cool head through this. Although he considered it barbarous, the thought of using his rapier in battle was starting to make him smile.

He dropped the spyglass to his side before looking upward to the overcast sky. He prayed the rain would hold, then took a deep breath and glanced at Hawk. "They're leaving. It's chaos down there. We must have spooked them last night. If the Runner is amongst them, and as we suspect he knows who Sawyer is, he most likely knew who we were. Are you thinking frontal assault?"

"Front, back. I don't care where we attack from. All I plan to do is find Sawyer. And damn anyone who gets in my way."

Santiago shook her head. "Not taking my orders seriously?"

Hawk didn't respond, and Perry knew exactly what that meant. But when Perry glanced back down at the estate's compound, his scan-tacts picked up many green auras scurrying amongst the mass exodus. He wondered if he *could* do this. Was he willing to take any measures possible to save his commander?

Perry remained stoic, but inside, a feeling manifested in his stomach. He couldn't describe it, but it wasn't pleasant. He shook his head and tried to ignore it, pushing it away as thoughts of an impending rescue took over his mind. "What are you thinking, Lieutenant Commander?"

"I'm not sure yet. Lieutenant Hawk was right. It's too open. Five acres on each side, except for the forest immediately at the back perimeter. We could approach from there."

"It's still three against many," said Hawk. "And we don't even know where to look for Sawyer. The building is huge. Lots of floors to sweep. There's the stable … and from what I remember, a hatch in the middle of the floor, which means there's more to search underground. What do you think our chances are of not getting caught having to go through all that?"

"Not good." Santiago rubbed her chin and glanced around as if looking for a miracle.

"The *BlackOut* is our only option," said Hawk. "It has masking capabilities. It could swoop in, level that estate and stable with a few well-placed missiles. Quick and easy and we get the hell outta here."

"What? I said no. And I'm not dropping missiles. That's as conspicuous as a damn spaceship."

That earlier feeling of something just out of reach reiterated itself in Perry's brain. Was it about the ship? About Sawyer? Something he said … Was it history trying to tell him something? Images of the *BlackOut* hovering over a field, laying down a salvo of missiles, kept popping into his head. *That can't be right.* He shook himself, trying to make sense of why this image would not abate, until he realized it wasn't just an image. It was a memory. "We're supposed to use the *Blackout*! History has already determined this!"

Santiago scrutinized him. "Explain yourself."

"Late seventeenth century … not accurate on the year … a coin. No, not a coin. A jeton. A French coin-like object used for counting. One was made with an engraving of what they called a flying saucer over a French countryside."

"What?"

"Some thought, *think*, it's a religious depiction, but most regard it as an early rendition of a spaceship. It's already in history. It's the *BlackOut*."

"You've got to be kidding about this?"

"I'm not." Perry looked directly at Santiago. "Does this Code 54 you mentioned have anything to do with this?"

Santiago's expression was tight, and her eyes flicked back and forth as if in deep thought. "Yes. But I need to verify this jeton you're talking about before I make my decision."

"Lieutenant Commander," said Hawk. "You see what I see. There's no good tactical way into that asylum with just the three of us ... a few more if we count the SAR team, engineer, and doctor you brought." He pointed down the hill. "There's more than a hundred people down there, and that's just what we can see outside. So, unless you're okay with us breaking out the skinsuits and doing this covert, I'm not seeing any other option but Code 54. And according to our Historical Specialist, apparently it's our fucking destiny."

"I didn't bring the skinsuits," replied Santiago. Her gaze was far off as she stared down the hill.

Perry was tired of being in the dark; he wanted to know what this command code meant, because he knew deep down it was probably their answer.

Santiago turned her horse away from the crest of the hill, her back straight and voice now affirmed. "I need to confer with Thor. To do that, I need to back out of his grid area. You two remain here, keep watch. I'll be back."

After she left, Perry turned to Hawk. "We're getting our commander back at any cost. And may the Lord I don't believe in have mercy on my soul, 'cause damn if I don't feel a sin comin' on."

Hawk winked back at him. "I'm with you, Specialist."

46.

A GUARD stalked forward.

Sawyer smiled. "Oh, I'm gonna enjoy this." He swung his right arm, feeling nothing when his injured hand collided with the side of the guard's head.

Sawyer fell backward as the other guard tackled him. Air rushed out of his lungs when they landed in the cold water flooding the ground. A heavy club swung at his head. Sawyer rolled the guard over him so the club connected with his opponent's head instead of his. The guard standing growled as he threw away the club in lieu of a dagger, the change of weapon only serving to heighten Sawyer's appetite to inflict pain.

They met in the middle of the cell. Blood splattered, obscuring Sawyer's sight. But with his lust for vengeance clouding his judgement, and high on bravado and sheer savagery, Sawyer kept swinging and kicking, feeling no pain as both fist and knife assaulted his already battered body. It was like his body had taken over and he could no longer control his actions.

Sawyer didn't stop until he landed on the ground sprawled face-up, panting and delirious, with two guards lying dead beside him. As euphoria settled in, he looked down the length of his torso, where he noticed the open door of his cell.

His whole body hurt, but as he'd been trained to believe, pain was temporary. There were new scratches all over his torso, but he could handle those. Nothing else felt new, nothing felt life draining, as he scrambled to his feet and raced to his open cell door.

Wearing nothing but sodden boots over weathered leather pants, Sawyer stood at the threshold of freedom as he glanced down the long, dark hallway. Burnt-out lanterns outnumbered those that glowed, making visibility near impossible for Sawyer as he leaned further into the hall.

With freedom within his grasp, he stepped into the dim, cavernous hall. Sawyer didn't know whether to run or search for survivors in the adjoining cells. No screams or whimpers disturbed the silence, implying death had come to all the other prisoners, but a voice whispered in Sawyer's ear, suggesting he leave no man behind and confirm his suspicions.

Sawyer dashed to the closest room, and, levering himself with a door frame, he swung his body into the room, skidding to a halt when greeted with a bloody mess. Half-naked bodies covered the floor with neither respect nor dignity to sanctification. Body fluids, long since liberated from their decomposing cadavers, further polluted the stale rainwater amassed on the ground with a rancid, sweet stench that coated the back of Sawyer's throat.

"The morgue." Sawyer backed out of the room, doubled over, and heaved bile before floundering further down the hall to the next open door.

Sawyer stepped into the room, his legs weak despite the adrenaline coursing through him. The previous occupant lay dead on the ground, head caved in above his right temple, eyes open as if caught in surprise. Sawyer dropped to one knee beside the man, reached out with two fingers, and closed his eyes. Mercier said it himself—Sawyer was the reason this place flourished. Deep down, Sawyer blamed himself for these men's deaths. But there was one he still might be able to save. If Arnault meant to spare him, perhaps there was a chance he saved his teammate as well. "Maybe I still have a purpose after all."

Seeking to cover his wounds rather than to provide warmth, Sawyer pulled the shirt off the body and threw it on. His shame hidden, Sawyer now planned to rescue his teammate. But not knowing what to expect topside, let alone within the walls of the estate and who it might be being held hostage, he considered a little incentive wouldn't hurt. He also couldn't ignore the fact that with all the men dead in the underground cavern, his teammate, which ever one it might actually be, might not still be alive. Sawyer wasn't sure if he could live with that, so he grabbed one of the half-full canteens from his cell before running toward the stable's hatch door.

Topside, he raced toward the main building, the old asylum Mercier used for his demented school, possessing only a vague awareness of the chaos around him. The catalyst driving his desire was to save his teammate, so he spared no attention to anything other than the people blocking his path. When he arrived at a side door of the estate, people scrambled out of his way as he pushed through the kitchen, the men in robes seeking shelter behind tables.

"Move!" screamed Sawyer, shoving aside a man too slow to react. He turned the corner into a grand hallway where a guard stood at the bottom of the staircase. Shuffling backward, the surprised guard held a pistol within a shaky grip.

Sawyer stalked forward, and the guard dropped the weapon and ran. Sawyer dove forward, snatched the loaded pistol skittering across the floor, and fired off a shot. A loud cry echoed in the cavernous room, heralding Sawyer's perfect aim. Again, it was like he had no control over his body. It moved on instinct, faster and more accurately than he thought himself capable in his current state. Or in any state, for that matter. But he didn't have time to consider this. Sawyer scrambled up the stairs to his left with the weapon in hand and used it to smash the guard on the next floor across the back of his head.

Sawyer took in the multitude of doors lining the halls as well as the robed men cowering on the floor as they clutched books to their chests. Sawyer looked each one of them over. "Where is he!" he screamed as he arced the unloaded pistol in front of him. "Tell me!"

A weak voice sounded out. "Who?"

The word instigated a fury deep in Sawyer's gut. "The other one! The one like me! The other ... Musketeer!" He stepped toward the robed men, his elbow locked as he pressed the muzzle of his pistol into the speaker's forehead.

"There is no one else."

Sawyer glanced up the stairs then smiled down at the timorous student, pressing the muzzle of his pistol deeper into his sweat-drenched forehead. "Tell me what floor or I kill you right now."

"Third! Fourth! I don't know," cried the man at the end of Sawyer's weapon. "I don't know of anyone else except those in the stables!"

Sawyer didn't believe him and ran up the stairs, taking two at a time. When he arrived on the next floor, a scuffling to his right alerted his instincts and he spun around. A short, rotund man in a robe picking books off the floor jumped back, then dropped his items when a pistol levelled between his eyes.

"Where is he?" asked Sawyer, his voice steady as he crept forward. "Tell me or I kill you."

The short man glanced into the open room to his right then back to Sawyer. "There is no one here. Please, I beg. Don't kill me. I'm only a student."

"There is someone else here! Mercier ... Arnault ... they told me someone else was here. A Musketeer! Where is he!" Sawyer knew it wasn't Hawk, but

253

there had to be someone, or everything he'd gone through over the past few days had been in vain.

The student's hands shook at the sides of his head. "There's no one. It was … a ruse. To keep you contained."

All the blood Sawyer possessed dropped into his boots. The arm holding the pistol fell to his side as he fell against the wall. His feet slipped out underneath him, sliding his body downward until he landed on the floor. "Fuck me … I should have called his bluff. I should have listened to my instincts."

"Sir," said the student. "Can I go?"

Slow and steady, Sawyer rose to his feet. "Go? You want to go?"

"Please?"

"Go? As in leave? I should just let you walk out of here? Fuck you!" Sawyer smashed the empty pistol across the student's face, hard enough to leave him unconscious on the floor. Chest heaving, Sawyer stared down at the student, shame hitting him like a publicized backhand from his father.

Control your temper.

His father had beaten that lesson into him from a young age, and now Sawyer truly understood why. In the fight ring, Sawyer had learned what he was capable of when allowed such freedom. But this man wasn't Mercier, or Arnault. He hadn't been forced to fight or kill him. He was just a man wanting to be a doctor in a time when propriety said he couldn't.

Sawyer staggered back and almost toppled down the stairs before he caught himself on the balustrade. "But these people need to pay for what they did to me," he said, words staccato and soft. "For what they're doing to history. Fuck guilt. I'm a damn Sawyer."

He pulled himself together and trudged down the stairs as chaos continued to ensue around him. Unable to control his venomous rage, Sawyer grabbed the first man he found dressed in robes and wrapped his arms around his neck. With his anger elevated, he pulled the man's head in one direction while forcing his shoulders in the other, breaking the man's neck in one swift, calculated move. When the body hit the floor, Sawyer ran down the rest of the stairs. He turned down a hallway leading along the side of the main staircase, pausing to catch his breath in a doorway before he raced through the kitchen and back outside to where he witnessed a full-scale battle.

A perfect place to release himself of his anger.

47.

IT turned out Santiago didn't have to leave the grid area to achieve communications with either the Earth-Landers or the *BlackOut*. For some reason beyond Perry's understanding, the grid had dissolved. The first action on their part was to scan for their commander's AI, but still no joy in that regard. But Perry *was* amazed to learn that when Lieutenant Commander Santiago committed to something, she was well and truly all in. Like a good commander, she stood firm behind her decisions.

The jeton had been verified by Thor, and it most certainly depicted an etching of a spaceship hovering over a French countryside. The ship's details were off—it was round while the *BlackOut* was not—but those were details the lieutenant commander was willing to live with. A spaceship in the seventeenth century was still a spaceship in the seventeenth century.

So, on August 12, 1634, Lieutenant Commander Santiago was the first Time Ranger in history to execute a Code 54. And Perry was there to witness it.

He sat on his horse on the crest of the hill overlooking the asylum, Hawk, Santiago, and the two SAR Rangers beside him, watching as the grey clouds above parted to reveal a most wondrous scene. Most spaceships remained in space. Earth-Landers brought people planet-side. Shuttles moved people and cargo about on said planets and between stations, but spaceships, unless adapted for planet atmo, rarely made an appearance on a planet. Perry could not tear his eyes away as he watched the clouds ripple like a stone was dropped from above and the RSV *BlackOut* descended, belly first, toward the French countryside, moving much faster than it appeared to those watching below.

"So this is a Code 54," he said. "We throw out all the rules and do what has to be done."

"It was implemented after the Albatross Incident," replied Santiago.

"Motherfucker," breathed Hawk. "I never thought I'd see the day. Sawyer would love this."

"If I get fired for this, I'm killing both of you."

Below, on the asylum grounds, guards and students, gardeners and workers still ran about packing wagons and loading supplies, ignorant to the scene above them and most likely believing the sonic boom of the spacecraft's engines in the lower atmosphere to be nothing more than thunder rolling in the distance after the storm. It would be minutes, seconds, before someone looked up. It was time to make their move.

Perry gripped his reins in one hand, a loaded pistol in the other, and with one last glance up at the sky, he thought, *this better work.*

When Santiago gave the order to move forward, Perry, along with the rest of the team, charged down the hill. He found it odd that the guards and people below saw them and reacted but were still ignorant to the 'magic' happening right over their heads.

By the time Perry reached flat ground, guards were already shooting and charging toward them. It wasn't until the first missile launched from the *BlackOut* and obliterated the ground before the charging guards, spraying dirt and grass several metres into the air, that their opponents looked up.

It was as if someone had dropped an invisible force field before them as they all careened to a sudden stop, crashing into each other as their heads turned upwards, their mouths hanging open. If Perry had been a killing man, he would see this as a prime opportunity to slay his opponents. Fish in a barrel. They were frozen in time, gawking at the spectacle converging on them from above. *What must they be thinking?*

Santiago brought the team to a halt approximately a half kilometre from engagement. She had an open link to the *BlackOut* now through her ear-pin. "Keep them at bay," she said. "Nothing more. They don't have point-defences, so there's no need to get creative up there."

"Copy that," came back Lieutenant Michaels's voice over their ear-pins. "Holding them off, and having no fun, sir."

Santiago moved forward, slow and steady. "Do not engage unless fired upon," she ordered the ground team.

Perry walked his horse forward, his eyes peeled for any movement amongst the stunned guards. When they reached the outer edge of the charging line, an eerie tingle ran up his spine. It was like walking amongst ghosts, and too much movement might spook them into retaliating. He maneuvered carefully through the crowd, looking down at the gaping faces and glassy-eyed stares of those caught in a trance. When he came to a blockade of several men converged together, he backed his horse up and tried a different path.

The asylum was still far away, across the open lawn and gardens, when Lieutenant Hawk spoke, obviously also deterred by the lack of maneuverability amongst the crowd. "Dismount. Leave the horses. We make our way on foot from here."

Perry agreed it was the best option. He slid off his horse, pistol still in one hand while he pulled his rapier from its sheath and started forward again. His breathing was slow, quiet, as if any sudden sound on his part might wake these people. But as he passed slowly by a guard with a sword in his hand, head turned upward, the guard's head suddenly pivoted to face Perry.

Perry raised his pistol as his heart hammered in his chest. He stood as frozen as the guard, inwardly pleading not to have to kill this green-aura man.

"My god," whispered the guard. He didn't blink, he barely breathed as he stared at Perry. "It ... it is Armageddon."

"Not quite," replied Perry.

The guard dropped to his knees and Perry nearly fired. The guard crossed himself, bowed his head, and Perry relaxed his trigger finger. Around him, more men dropped their weapons and themselves to the ground, some raising their hands up to the ship as if it were God himself, while some wept and crossed themselves. Perry was fascinated by the scene but didn't have time to analyze or record in his mind all that was happening around him. He needed to keep moving.

He lowered his pistol and moved onward through the men, making slow progress toward the asylum. To his far left, Hawk moved forward with both his pistols raised, his head flicking right and left, on alert for an attack at any moment. Between them, Santiago in her conspicuous ball-like gown and now slightly canted blonde wig, was doing the same, while the two search- and-rescue soldiers brought up their six.

A shot rang out behind Perry.

He turned to witness a guard pointing his smoking musket up at the

BlackOut. The field before the asylum suddenly turned into a battlefield. It was discord and turmoil. Perry was lost and consumed in a raging battle. Weapons against weapons. Projectiles against projectiles. Flesh against flesh. Bodies fell at Perry's feet as he tried to manoeuvre around them. And even more bodies collided with him as they fought to keep their ground in their personal wars. It didn't take much for Perry to realize the guards were attacking each other, not just him and his team. The only reason Perry could conceive was that this had become a religious affair between those that believed God was here to save them and those that thought God was here to smite them all.

It was a situation Perry took to his advantage. But as he pressed on, he was unsure which way to run. The estate? The stable? There were green auras everywhere, and although he chose carefully who he slayed, he was not as well trained as Santiago or Hawk when it came to battle precision, and he knew he'd killed or injured more than a few of history's prominent ancestors. But it was a guilt he didn't have time to lament.

"Any sight of the Time Runner yet?" came Santiago's voice over the ear-pins. "Or ... our commander?"

"Negative," replied both Perry and Hawk. The SAR Rangers also reported no joy.

"Press forward and watch your six," said Santiago. "I'm moving to the estate. Hawk, peel off and head for the stable. Perry, you're on me. Stewart and Kamar," she addressed the two SAR soldiers, "keep it contained out here. Be ready to provide backup if any of us need it." A pause followed before she added, "Keep your heads up, be careful, and good hunting. And if anyone spots our Time Runner, I want him alive."

"Copy," replied Perry.

There was a hesitation before Hawk replied. "Yeah ... copy."

"Now let's go," ordered Santiago.

Perry maneuvered through the battlefield toward her, not just fending off attacking guards and fleeing students, but zig zagging through the spraying dirt and destruction of the occasional missile launched from the *BlackOut*. For the most part, many guards and students had the right mind to flee the scene entirely and run for their lives into the forest behind the estate. So as Perry and Santiago reached the front steps of the old asylum, there were less opponents to contend with, for which Perry was glad. He was not comfortable with the amount of blood dripping from his rapier.

On the threshold of the asylum's front door, Perry was thrust to the ground as Santiago landed on top of him. Beside them, the door frame splintered as bullets meant for them tore it apart.

Santiago rolled off him onto her stomach, firing one shot then another from her other pistol. Perry did not see what happened as he was now crouched behind a pillar covering his head. She called for his pistol, which he slid across the floor toward her and finally opened his eyes. Santiago was behind the pillar across from his, shooting at the men on the staircase shooting back at them.

"Load!" she ordered and slid a pistol across the floor toward him.

It stopped just out of Perry's reach. He reached out quickly to snatch it as more gunfire headed in his direction. Panting, Perry loaded the pistol and slid it back across the floor as another empty one came back to him.

"There are six of them," reported Santiago. "Load faster, Specialist."

"What's happening?" came Hawk's voice over the ear-pins.

"Engagement at the front door," said Santiago. "Now shut up! I'm busy!"

Perry slid a newly loaded pistol back to Santiago and retrieved the next empty one. "Any red auras, Lieutenant?"

"I'll let you know if I find *him*," replied Hawk, and Perry imagined a wink along with his words. "I've entered the stable. It's clear. I'm heading down the hatch."

"Good hunting," replied Perry, sliding another loaded pistol back at Santiago.

Santiago fired from her position behind the pillar and called out, "Four down! I don't see any reinforcements yet!"

With Perry's back pressed against the pillar, he had a clear view outside the front door. "Our six is contained. I can see the SAR guys out there at the bottom of the stairs."

"Good," replied Santiago. "Let me know if the situation … holy shit! Red aura!"

Perry peered around the pillar just as Hawk's voice came over the ear-pin. "Who is it?"

Perry saw nothing as he scanned the foyer, his heart pounding a mile a minute. "Where is it?"

"It went around the left side of the staircase!" she reported back. "Couldn't tell who it was."

"It could be the commander," said Hawk.

"It could be the Time Runner," said Santiago.

Perry blew out a breath. "Either way, a red aura is good."

48.

A SEARING pain in Perry's left upper arm made him cry out. He grabbed his arm, careful not to push the projectile deeper into his flesh, and looked at his new appendage. "Arrows?"

Blood oozed from the wound, spilling over his fingers. His left arm was throbbing in pain. "Why now?" he cursed, slowly wrapping the fingers of his right hand around the shaft of the arrow and snapping it in two. After several deep breaths, Perry pressed the palm of his hand on the ragged end of the shaft and in one forceful push, he thrust the arrow the rest of the way through his arm. He cried out as the sharp tip pierced through his muscle and skin to come out the other side of his limb. Shaking, he reached behind his arm, grabbed the arrowhead, and pulled it the rest of the way out. "That's going to leave a mark," he hissed, dropping the bloodied arrow to the ground.

Santiago pulled Perry to his feet, and he was unsteady at first until he got his bearings. The lieutenant commander pushed a Celox anti-clotting bandage into his injury with a smile. "It's a good thing I don't always listen to orders," she said. "Or I wouldn't have this on me. Now let's go. The foyer is clear. And I don't want that red aura getting too far ahead of us."

Thanks to modern medicine, the bandage did its job, not only stemming the blood flow, but providing a small dose of a strong analgesic as well. Perry followed Santiago down the corridor, which ran along the left side of the staircase. They entered a kitchen at the end of the hall where a hearth still burned, charring what smelled like chicken on its open flames and leaving the room filled with choking smoke.

Through the haze, Perry saw a man in a dirty white shirt leaning against a doorframe that led back outside the estate. "There!"

"He's red!" called Santiago. "It's the commander!"

To Perry's surprise, Santiago ran forward, seemingly forgetting her own orders to concentrate on the Runner, but Sawyer disappeared by the time she and Perry reached the door.

Perry and Santiago chased him across a field. There were guards everywhere, fighting their personal battles, and Sawyer was running through them without a weapon. Perry watched in shock as Sawyer engaged those around him without reason, punching and kicking at those he caught until eventually gathering a sword from a fallen guard and using it to hack his way through the rest of the men who dared get in his way.

It took a minute for Perry to find his voice. "Hawk! He's coming to you! He's heading for the stable!"

"What the fuck?" came back the lieutenant's voice. "You found him?"

"Yes, it's him," replied Perry. "He's running to the stable."

"I'm fucking lost down here! There are too many tunnels … too many doors … oh shit …"

"Report," said Santiago.

A coughing noise came over the ear-pin, the sounds of someone retching. "I think I found the morgue."

"Get your ass back up here!" yelled Santiago. "We need you to cut the commander off before he makes it down there."

"I'm … I'm on my way," Hawk reported back.

Perry glanced at Santiago, relieved to see her change of focus now that she'd laid eyes on their commander. "We'll get him back," he said softly.

"Yeah, yeah, Specialist." She cleared her throat. "We can't leave him here like this. Fuck the Runner. Sawyer's our priority. Let's make sure he's safe."

***

SAWYER didn't care what was happening around him, all he saw was blood, violence, and a chance to fight. With the cocaine still active in his system, anger and betrayal burning hot within him, he found his first victim and pummelled him until there was nothing left to hit. He jumped up, looking for another victim, and found one coming toward him with a sword swinging and hacking in equal rage to Sawyer's.

Sawyer ducked, jumped back, tackled the guard, and disarmed him without pause. He used the sword to embed it in the chest of the next person who came at him and left it there as a grave marker as he continued toward the stable. When he heard his name shouted, he stopped abruptly and spun around to find himself staring at two of his teammates. *What the hell?*

His jaw clenched, his eyes narrowed. Sawyer's chest heaved in unison with each short breath he drew in through his nose.

"Something is wrong," Perry said. "Hawk, we need you ground-side."

"Now!" shouted Santiago.

Sawyer heard them clearly as his attention was focussed solely on them. But he didn't want to converse with his teammates, he wanted to kill them. Rip Perry's arms off for not coming to get him. Slit Santiago's throat for trying to steal his command out from under him.

"Commander?"

Sawyer turned to see Hawk standing behind him, dishevelled and panting like he'd run a marathon.

Sawyer lunged at him with his hands poised to strangle his teammate. "You left me here to die!" he screamed, squeezing Hawk's throat.

Hawk's eyes were wide and unfocussed as he struggled to free himself from Sawyer's hands around his neck. When they fell to the ground, with Sawyer landing on top, Sawyer felt hands grab his shoulders and yank him back and upward until he landed on his butt beside Hawk. Sawyer rolled over to engage Hawk again, his anger and resentment stemming his every violent desire. "You were my friend and you left me here!"

Hawk tried to place a hand on Sawyer's chest, but Sawyer pushed it away. "I gave everything for this fucking team!"

"Commander ... Kai ... Please ... I'm sorry ..." gasped Hawk.

Suddenly Sawyer was on his butt again, now staring up at Perry and Santiago, their hands raised in supplication as they hovered over him.

"Stay back," said Hawk, but Perry and Santiago kept advancing. "Stop!"

"I should kill you both!" cried Sawyer.

"You're confused, Commander," said Santiago. "Let us help you."

Sawyer stared at her, his eyes near slits as his angered gaze took in her long blonde hair and raised eyebrows as if she were looking at him with curiosity.

Like she had on the OCC during their date … *Fucking Aurora!* "What are you doing here! How did you get here! Did you follow me!"

"What? What are you talking about?" asked Aurora, shaking her head. "Of course we followed you here. We're here to rescue you. Do you understand?"

From his periphery, Sawyer noticed movement, guards creeping in on their position. He smiled and kept his mouth shut. Perry would deserve what he'd get, and Aurora had no place here in the past, so her death would be irrelevant.

"That doesn't look like a friendly smile," said Perry.

"Get down!" shouted Hawk.

Three blasts from a Stormguard rang in the air, each fixed-mass bullet hitting centre mass on each of Hawk's targets.

Sawyer turned, scrambled to his feet. "I told you to leave that in your locker. I should have known you wouldn't follow my orders. You're just a big fucking baby … can't handle a single museum guard. Can't execute a mission without weapons from the future … Fucking pussy."

Sawyer ran at him until the thwump sound of a debilitator pulse filled Sawyer's ears and he was flat on his back.

Someone touched his shoulder, told him everything was going to be alright, but instead of the paralyzing effects of being debilitated, a shiver ran through Sawyer, seeping poisonous memories into his mind: Hawk and Perry running out of the stable … Beaumont's death … Commander Awenda ordering him to bag the Kennedy mission … His father locking him in a closet, submerging him underwater … a belt strap across his back … Aurora standing above him … here in France? He was so confused.

As he rested his head back on the ground in hopes of finding his sanity, he found himself staring up at the most unexpected thing. "Is that my ship?"

49.

"WE have him," Santiago reported to Lieutenant Michaels on the *BlackOut*. She turned to Perry and Hawk, her face flush, eyes red. Perry nearly hugged her. "Any sign of the Time Runner?" she asked.

"No," replied Perry. He blinked his scan-tacts to radiation aura and looked around. "No. Nothing."

Hawk, still sitting on the ground beside their commander with his knees up as he rested his arms across them, shook his head.

"Enemy engagement contained," came back Lieutenant Michaels's voice over the ear-pins. "A few stragglers, but Steward and Kamar are rounding them up as we speak. Should we make our ascent?"

"No," replied Santiago. "I want to recce the building before we eradicate it, to make sure no future tech remains. Hold off for now, mask, and I'll give you the word when it's all clear. We need to get the survivors out of the blast zone first."

"Maybe he's still in there?" asked Perry. His heart leapt at the thought. Now that Sawyer was back in their grasps, the Time Runner was his priority. And there wasn't much time left before boomerang. Less than forty-eight hours, to be exact. "There are many rooms in this old asylum. Our Runner could be hiding in any one of them." A thought occurred to him. "Tech. He has tech."

Hawk jumped to his feet, held his Stormguard in both hands as he turned in a slow circle. "He could have masking capabilities. He could be right here beside us!"

"Let's not get paranoid," said Santiago. "Unfortunately, he's probably gone. He probably left when the grid went down." She went to Hawk and snatched the Stormguard from his grasp. "And you have no right to be carrying this, but thanks," she added with a clipped nod.

Hawk looked at her for a moment, then raised an eyebrow as if he'd been hit by an epiphany. "You knew the Runner was gone before we came down to the asylum, didn't you, sir?"

"Of course not," Santiago replied with a wink.

"You did," said Perry. "I thought your priority was the Runner. What made you follow through if you knew he was gone?"

Santiago breathed deep, looked at the ground between her feet. "I had a change of heart."

"Care to explain?" asked Perry.

"When I backed out of the grid area to check on the jeton and realized the grid was down, I wondered why. And then I realized something else didn't make sense. Before the crash, the rear admiral broke protocol and sent me what he said was our commander's new orders. That's what's in that data card. There's something weird going on with this mission. I just can't figure out what. But I suspect the commander knows something we don't. Or he's about to know something when he sees the encrypted message the rear admiral sent him."

"So that's it? You just want answers?" asked Perry.

"Well," she said, and trailed off as she looked at Hawk. "You've known Sawyer a long time, you must have had plenty of contact with his father."

"He's our boss," replied Hawk. "But he's a dick ... no offence, sir."

"I couldn't have said it better myself, Lieutenant," said Santiago with a smile. "I was blaming Commander Sawyer for ... well, everything. But it's not him I'm mad at, it's the damn rear admiral. Commander Sawyer is just a product of his dad's controlling dickery. I get it now. The commander deserves to be his own man, to make a name for himself separate from his family's notoriety. So, I decided maybe he should be our first focus. I didn't want to finish this mission without at least giving him a chance."

Perry nodded his understanding at Santiago then crouched beside Sawyer. "Are you all right, sir?"

Sawyer swallowed. His lips moved but nothing came out. Perry assumed the debilitator's effects hadn't yet worn off. Which was a good thing, because if there was still anger in this young man, Perry wasn't so sure he wanted him awake. "We've got you. It's over."

"It's not over yet. We do still need to complete this mission," said Santiago.

She leaned over Perry's shoulder. "Commander? Do you know where the Time Runner is?"

Sawyer shook his head and mumbled, "Arnault. His name is Arnault."

Perry remembered the name. Mercier had mentioned Arnault to him and Hawk as the one selling advanced meds in the village. But Perry still didn't know what Arnault looked like or where he was hiding. "Are you sure?"

"Yes," whispered Sawyer. "He was here ..."

"Do you know where he went? Can you tell us anything?" asked Perry.

Again, Sawyer shook his head. "I thought you'd left ... abandoned me. Hawk was a hostage ... then he wasn't ... I thought it was someone else ... Then I saw you all here ... I was so confused." Sawyer closed his eyes. Perry shook him till he was looking back up at him. "How much time until ..."

"Less than two days until boomerang," said Santiago.

"Fuck ..." Sawyer's eyes closed shut again. But this time, Perry's shaking him did nothing to rouse him.

"We need to get him medical attention," said Perry.

"It was just a debilitator pulse," said Hawk. "He'll be fine in a few minutes ... maybe an hour. I had it on the highest setting." When Perry scowled at him, Hawk shrugged. "He's a fucking Spawn! What did you want me to do, hit him with the pea-shooter setting?"

Perry hung his head because he knew there was more to this than just a pulse weapon. Sawyer had attacked Hawk, the intent in his eyes nothing short of murderous. Perry shook his head again as he released a deep, guttural growl. "Okay. But what happened in that school? In that fight club? This isn't right. High setting or not, he should be awake. He was just talking to us."

"I don't know," replied Hawk.

Perry glanced at Sawyer. "If we're to help him, we need to know what happened. A few fights wouldn't have done this to him. Make him attack you, us."

Hawk ran his hands over and around Sawyer's head as if palpating for trauma, and then he carefully turned the commander's head to the side. "Here. A clean surgical scar. Did they actually remove his AI? This is so wrong. So fucking wrong."

"Oh my god," breathed Perry.

Hawk stepped back. "Oh, fuck me. What if they did something? Nicked something vital? Is he even the same person? I don't know about this shit.

They could have altered his memories, his personality. He could be a fucking zombie for all we know! Maybe that's why he attacked us. He didn't know who we were."

Perry shook his head at Hawk then looked at Santiago. "What should we do, sir?"

Santiago paced a small line, her heavy, dirt-smeared skirts swishing at her feet. "We get him back to Dr. Brodeur back at Earth-Lander One. I returned Earth-Lander Two to the *BlackOut*. I'll bring it down to take you back. It'll be quicker than horseback or carriage. Report back to me when you arrive back at home base."

"Good call," said Perry.

When Santiago finished summoning Earth-Lander Two, she approached Hawk. "I still don't know how you snuck that Stormguard into your kit before the second inspection, and you damn well shouldn't have had it now … but thanks. And just in case, here …" She relinquished the gun back into his hands.

"You're welcome, sir," replied Hawk. "Now you go find out where this Runner went, and we'll take care of the commander."

***

A masked Earth-Lander Two arrived beside the asylum a short while later. Perry and Hawk loaded the commander onto one of the benches while the engineer who'd brought the Earth-Lander down accompanied Santiago in her search of the old asylum for tech Arnault, may have left behind. And for clues as to where he might have fled.

As the masked Earth-Lander skimmed across the French countryside, Perry sat in the pilot's seat. Eyes focussed on the horizon, he felt far removed from reality. Perry wanted to get the hell out of this backwater century and return to the recycled air of spaceships and space stations.

He drew a hand down his sweat-soaked face and blew out a breath. They'd only been able to get Sawyer into the back of the Earth-Lander because he'd passed out. Perry didn't know if that was a good thing or a bad thing. He didn't know anything other than Sawyer was with Hawk in the aft section. But was he the same Sawyer?

"Kai! Calm down!" boomed Hawk's voice. "Perry! Get back here! I need help!"

At Hawk's frantic voice, Perry put the Earth-Lander in automatic control and raced into the aft cabin. Sawyer lay twitching on the bench with Hawk beside him trying to hold him steady.

Perry's eyes darted between the two men. "What's happening?"

"He's having a seizure. Help me get him on the floor before he hurts himself."

Perry helped Hawk lay Sawyer on the floor and he knelt beside the commander. "Kai. Sawyer! Kai!"

"Give him room," said Hawk, easing Perry back. "There's nothing we can do … Just make sure he doesn't hurt himself."

Perry cursed himself for letting his panic overwhelm him, but the tension running through his body over the past week needed an outlet. "So we just leave him?" he asked, his hands poised over Sawyer's body as if waiting to grab him when given the word. "This doesn't seem right."

"Trust me. There's nothing you can do with seizures until the body settles down. Unless you have anti-seizure meds? Our med-kits are in the other Earth-Lander. And I didn't think to stash any before we set out. I wasn't expecting this."

When Sawyer stopped convulsing, and his body settled into an almost coma-tose state, Perry cast his gaze up and down the length of the commander's body. Air rushed from his lungs when he saw under Sawyer's shirt. With barely a patch of skin left unbruised or smeared in blood, Sawyer's body resembled a corpse. Mud and blood-stained bandages hung from torn-open wounds like scraps of cleaved skin from his body.

"I'm gonna kill whoever did this to 'im," growled Hawk.

"My god," whispered Perry. "Is this all from fighting?" He pulled down the shirt to re-cover their commander. A small shake of Sawyer's head made Perry's heart jump in anticipation of another seizure, but the commander's body remained still, allowing Perry to breathe again.

"I think he's waking up," said Hawk. "Come on, Kai. Come and say hi to ole Hawk."

Sawyer's eyes opened, his lids fluttered, then they closed again.

"It's progress," said Perry.

"Let's get going," said Hawk. "I suggest you get us to Dr. Brodeur ASAP."

Perry didn't know much about medicine, particularly seizures, but he did know that if someone had one, they could have another. He jumped back into the pilot seat and re-took manual control.

There was only a short trip left, but Perry wondered how much longer he could hold out before passing out from exhaustion and falling out of his seat. He needed to stay awake, as there were too many unanswered questions. What did Sawyer know? Why was he running loose when they arrived? Did Mercier and Arnault do something to him? And who was this Arnault, and what were his credentials? Even if he were a neurosurgeon from the twenty-second century, there was nothing sanitary about this era—he surely wouldn't have gone so far as to remove an AI implant? But that would also explain why Santiago couldn't remotely dissolve the implant.

After a long sigh, Perry shook his head. "We won't know anything until he wakes up."

Soon afterward, Perry saw Earth-Lander One's beacon on his console and began final approach for landing. Piloting wasn't his forte, so he put the Earth-Lander in automatic for landing and stared out at the night sky. Stars twinkled above as the Earth-Lander dropped slowly beside its brother parked beside the grove of trees. But Perry found no comfort in the celestial bodies, feeling more in tune with the dark empty spaces between them. A night sky this brilliant usually brought comfort, especially when the stars shone so brightly, but tonight Perry could not find peace.

Dr. Brodeur entered the aft cabin the moment Perry lowered the back hatch, and for the first time in days, Perry felt a modicum of relief.

Brodeur went to work quickly, and to give him space, Perry and Hawk waited outside. An hour later, the doctor's initial report was confusing, stating that Sawyer's system was flooded with cocaine. Neither Perry nor Hawk could fathom why. But they sat with him in the Earth-Lander when the doctor had finished his work and watched Sawyer carefully.

A few hours later, Sawyer's head lolled to the side, and his eyes fluttered open. His words were scratchy and quiet. "I need more."

Perry's stomach hardened into a knot. "I presume he means cocaine."

Brodeur pressed a few buttons on the lifeband wrapped around Sawyer's right brachial, read the screen of his med-card, and sighed. "This is weird."

"What's weird?" asked Perry.

"I'm familiar with his genetics, his ... Spawn bio-makeup. I had to be when

I signed up to be the doctor on his ship, but this doesn't make sense. It's very … weird."

"You said that already, doc," said Hawk.

Brodeur ran a hand down his face, blew out a breath. "I gave him carbophyn-oltrate, which should flush the cocaine from his system. It's working, but way too fast for the dose I gave him. I wanted to ease him out of his body's addiction in order to lessen the stress on his system. But according to this," he held up his med-card as if Perry understood what it said, "the cocaine is already gone."

Hawk raised an eyebrow. "And … it shouldn't be?"

"No, not at all." Brodeur bent down beside Sawyer and peeled back the shirt to reveal his bandaged torso. "These wounds are healing fast as well. In his genetic portfolio it shows he's been given, amongst other things, a boost in clotting-factor IV, a calcium ion which helps clot his blood faster. But the rate at which he's healing now that the cocaine is flushed from his system is beyond anything I've seen."

"Have you dealt with many Spawns before?" asked Perry.

"Only one. An early model. She's dead now."

Hawk scratched his head. "Well, that's a happy story."

Brodeur stood up. "What I'm saying is, Commander Sawyer's medical records are not accurate. There's a lot more to him than his files suggest."

"But is this a bad thing that he's healing so fast?" asked Hawk.

"Well, no. Which is why I said this was weird, not bad."

Perry had been present when Sawyer was created, had gone with the rear admiral to the lab on several occasions to make his selections and leave his personal samples. If the rear admiral made any alterations to the mix, to the vat-produced egg, Perry was not privy to any of it. He scrubbed his face, crossed his arms. "What's his final prognosis?"

"Good. Very good. Based on these findings, and barring any changes to his accelerated healing, he should be near back to normal by sunup."

Perry nodded. "Then let's take this as a good thing and let him get some rest. I know I sure could use some sleep."

"There's just one more thing." Brodeur stepped away from Sawyer, speaking in a hushed tone as if trying not to let the commander hear him, even though he was asleep again. "I'm a medical doctor. I did rotations with psychiatry and psychology, but I'm no expert."

"Spit it out," said Perry. "There's a bench with my name on it and it's calling very loudly."

"I can cure his physical addiction, but as for a psychological one …"

Perry sighed. He didn't need to hear the end of that statement; he knew where it was going. "Great," he said, running a hand down his face. With this news now bearing down on him, he knew sleep would no longer come.

50.

MISSION: DAY NINE

THE next morning, Sawyer woke before the sun. At first groggy and stiff, after a few moments he started to feel more like himself and lifted his head to greet his teammates sitting on the bench across from him. Dr. Brodeur was with them reading from a med-card.

"How am I doing?" Sawyer asked.

Brodeur was at his side first, checking the lifeband on his arm, and removing the IV in the back of his hand. "You're going to be fine. A little stiff and sore. You should eat."

Hawk pulled a bottle of cyto-juice from the doctor's black medical knapsack and passed it to Sawyer, who sat up, flipped off the lid and started guzzling.

"Whoa, slow down," said Brodeur.

Sawyer threw up green cyto-juice and bile onto the Earth-Lander's floor, and Hawk passed him another bottle from the bag, which Sawyer sipped this time.

"That's better," said Brodeur. "Go easy."

Sawyer sipped more of the juice then stared at the mess on the floor between his feet. He noticed he was now wearing a set of grey fatigues, and the pinching in his stomach was gone. The heaviness in his head and his numb hand had all gone away, but a grumbling in his stomach made him agree that real food was in order. But first, there was business to attend. "Where's the lieutenant commander?"

"She reported in last night," said Hawk. "She cleared the asylum, sir. She's probably on her way back now."

Asylum? Right. "Sit rep."

Hawk filled him in on the events of yesterday's rescue, finishing with a

273

disturbing timestamp. There was barely a day remaining until boomerang. In return, Sawyer unloaded his past physical events over the last few days, leaving the doctor and his teammates unable to speak. "Can we get in contact with Santiago?" he asked, breaking the silence in the cabin.

"We now have open comms," replied Perry.

Sawyer tapped his ear-pin. "This is Commander Sawyer to Lieutenant Commander Santiago."

"It's good to hear your voice, sir," Santiago's tired voice came back. "How are you feeling?"

"I'm fine. Do we have any leads on our Time Runner? Dr. Arnault?"

"Only that he left the asylum a long time before we showed up. When we arrived, we had access to comms, which means the blackout grid had been turned off. I retrieved the black box along with other tech, and your Musketeer uniform and weapons. It's all secure with me. So far, Thor has not picked up anything newly activated in the region. Which is why our Runner probably left the tech behind. He knew we could track it to his new location without the grid initialized. And if he opened the grid again, then well, we'd definitely know where he relocated to, sir."

Thor. Sawyer rubbed the back of his head, surprised to find barely a scar. He sort of missed his computer-generated voice. "They removed my AI ..."

"Don't worry, sir," said Santiago. "I retrieved him as well. Inert, but intact. He was locked in another wardrobe where I also found a complete Time Ranger battle uniform."

Sawyer sat up straight. "Hold on ... battle uniform?"

"Yes, sir."

"Jesus Christ," sighed Sawyer. "How? Who is this Arnault guy?"

"Thor confirmed there is no record of any Time Ranger, missing, retired, or in active service under that name. The name is probably made up anyway."

"All right," said Sawyer. "We need to get moving." He stood and swayed on his feet until Hawk grabbed his arm to steady him. "And I guess I need to eat. Or at least get some fresh air."

"I had the *BlackOut* land to return the SAR Rangers and engineer," said Santiago. "It's back in orbit taking its position at the Point's coordinates in preparation for our arrival and boomerang capture. We need to speak privately about something, so I'm coming back to home base on horse. I'll be there shortly. Also

"... I had to stop to rest in Lafare and, well ... We'll talk when I get there. Is there anything else, sir?"

"No, that's all, Lieutenant Commander."

"Copy. See you soon, Lieutenant Commander, out."

"Why you, sir?" asked Perry. "Do you know why they wanted you?"

The question had come from left field, surprising Sawyer. The specialist had remained quiet thus far, but he did bring up an interesting question. "At first I thought it was because I was the one they saw at the school, but now I'm thinking Arnault knew who I was from the very start. I wasn't just an intruder he wanted out of the way. He knew I was a Time Ranger, and possibly a Spawn, before he even met me. He had a lot of knowledge prior to coming back here."

"Do you think this was an inside job?" asked Hawk.

"I don't know," replied Sawyer wearily. "But I'm not going to be able to think straight until I get moving. I need some fresh air and something to eat."

Brodeur tossed him a protein bar from his bag, which Sawyer caught before turning to leave the Earth-Lander.

"I'll go with you, sir," said Hawk.

Outside the air smelled fresh, with hints of lavender hidden beneath an earthy wet grass scent. It was welcoming, but not enough to ease the tension Sawyer felt building deep within him since he'd awoken.

Hawk placed a hand on his shoulder as they walked away from the Earth-Landers into the treed field behind them. "So, the doctor said you might be craving cocaine for a while."

"You don't miss a beat, do you, Hawk?"

Hawk smiled mockingly. "I'm a friend. I care for your well-being."

When they were barely within visual of the Earth-Landers, Sawyer turned to him. "I'm fine." But he wasn't. He'd been keeping it all in, buried deep in the pit of his stomach, since he'd awoken. There was still so much going wrong with the mission, time was running short, and he was at less than full capacity. And he knew that when ... if ... they returned to the future, he'd have to answer for the Code 54. Just thinking about all this made his skin crawl. He wanted to hit something. Anything. But there was nothing around him but grass, trees, and hills.

And Hawk.

"You know ..." Sawyer said. Would Hawk understand? Would he come with him or let him go? He bit his lip, stared at his friend, and remembered all the times he'd helped Hawk back at the Academy. "I need something. And I know you're always up for some fun. I need to find that release the drug gives me before I become a danger to everyone around me. I can feel my anger rising. It needs to come out or I'll fucking snap."

"You feel it that bad?"

Sawyer smiled. "We'll take an Earth-Lander. It won't take long to get to Dumont. We can go to The Boar. I don't plan on doing anything an Academy student hasn't done when they've had too much to drink." He swiped a finger across his heart and laid it to rest in the middle of his chest. "I promise to pick my battles carefully. Come on, Hawk. You know you love a good fight."

"I don't know about this. I don't think this is the way."

Sawyer clapped him on the shoulder and nudged him toward Earth-Lander One. He really was needing this; his body was starting to shake.

Hawk grabbed his arm. "Commander. As much as I love *borrowing* a good Earth-Lander, I can't let you do this. Besides, we're running short on time, remember? We can't afford delays."

Sawyer yanked his arm away, but Hawk grabbed him again with more force. Sawyer found himself being shoved against the nearest broad tree trunk. Trapped by Hawk standing firm before him, Sawyer's chest heaved.

"Whoa. Whoa, Kai." Hawk backed up, apparently sensing what Sawyer was about to do. "Just listen to me, please?"

"Get ... out ... of ... my way. Lieutenant."

"No."

"How do you plan to stop me, Lieutenant?"

"*...no matter the danger to my well-being,*" Hawk recited from the Time Ranger Creed. "I may lose life or limb challenging a Spawn, but I'm not letting you go down this road, Kai. We'll find another way."

Sawyer stepped forward, plunging his knee into Hawk's stomach.

"Commander," hissed Hawk. "What happened to ... *endeavouring to uphold the prestige, honour, and esprit de corps of the Time Rangers*? You recited those exact words at Commencement!"

Sawyer smirked.

"This is not who you are! Get a grip! This is the cocaine talking! You want more of *that*, not to beat the shit out of me!"

"Move. Now. Before I'm forced to hurt you, Lieutenant."

Hawk stood in place, stoking Sawyer's anger even more. Sawyer charged forward and they wrestled each other until Hawk got the upper hand and shoved Sawyer back against the tree.

Sawyer could break Hawk in half if he wanted to, so what was he waiting for? He ran forward, and then suddenly he was on his back staring up at the sky, his limbs unmovable. His whole body tingled.

Above him, Hawk leaned into his view waving a Stormguard. "Now that I have your attention, sir. Maybe you'll listen to reason. You're screwed up, Kai. I mean it. That place did a number on you. I get it. You're angry, you probably feel ..."

"Leave me alone, Lieutenant."

Hawk took a small step backward. "Ah, so you can speak. It's wearing off faster than I hoped." He pointed the Stormguard back at him, but Sawyer could see his hands shaking. "Stay where you are or I'll shoot you again."

"Fuck you, Max."

"Oh good, we're on first names again. So, uh ... I'm starting to get the feeling there's some missing information between us. How 'bout you fill me in on what really happened at that school, 'cause this can't all be about wanting the high of cocaine. And I'll fill you in on what the rest of us have been doing trying to find you."

"Find me? You found me and you left me there." Sawyer tried to sit up but fell back on the ground. "You all abandoned me. I swear to fucking god, there's no such thing as loyalty."

"Abandoned you?" Hawk lowered the Stormguard, shook his head. "We couldn't find you. The morning after you were taken, Perry, Santiago, and I woke up drugged in an alley. We had no idea where you were."

Lies. "Then why did you run away at the stable?"

Hawk hung his head. "I'm sorry. I'm really sorry we took off like that. But you have to understand, we were doing it for you. There was a small army of guards there that night, and it was just Perry and myself." Hawk frowned. "How much fight do you think that man has in him? I mean really, I could have taken half the room. I took you out just now, didn't I?"

"You had to use a fucking Stormguard, dipshit."

"Details. But as I was saying ... we never abandoned you. In fact, Perry and I practically gave up the mission just to save you. And by the way, you really need to talk to him. It's not my place to say anything, but you really, really need to talk to that man. And hey, let's not forget we brought the actual *BlackOut* down from orbit to save your ass. That was no easy choice on Santiago's part."

Reason finally settled in on Sawyer now that his adrenaline level had been neutralized by the debilitator pulse, so he sat up slowly, this time making it into a seated position before taking Hawk's offered hand. "I'm sorry. I don't know what just came over me. I can't think straight when ... when ..."

"Tell me."

Sawyer knew exactly what had come over him, and he considered maybe it was time to tell Hawk what really happened at the school. He looked at Hawk, knowing his expression denoted his uncomfortableness with the situation, and worked his way through it. "When that cocaine was in my system ..." His voice cracked. Would Hawk really understand?

Hawk placed his hands as if in the namaste pose, bowed his head. "It's okay. You're in a safe place ..."

"Fuck you, Hawk."

Sawyer turned away, but Hawk's hand on his shoulder spun him back. "I'm kidding. I'm sorry. Go on."

Sawyer searched his eyes and realized this time Hawk was being serious. He took a deep breath and tried again. "It was like nothing you could imagine. I was as invincible as I was deadly. I felt free." He paused, rubbed his forehead. "My first mission as a commander and I crashed the Earth-Lander, got kidnapped, basically failed at catching the Runner, got addicted ..."

"You're a good man, Kai. So you have issues. Who doesn't? Besides, how many commanders would put themselves through what you did to save a team-mate at the cost of possibly failing a mission? How were you to know they were lying about having one of us captured."

Sawyer remembered Beaumont on Mediterrania Station. *He did.* "Do you know why I became a commander?"

"Daddy made you do it?"

"Well, yeah. I was only brought into this world to serve his purposes, his name. My father gives me no other choice. But when I was younger, all I wanted to do was help people. Maybe become a medic specialist if I had no choice but to join the Time Rangers. But I learned about something at the Academy.

Violence. But not like what my father taught me. I had found my inner rage and for once I could fight back. You have no idea how good that made me feel. It was like gaining power I'd never had. But I was dangerous. And my father knew that. And when I finally graduated, joined a team ... and another team, I had to shoot John F. Kennedy ..."

"That was you?"

"Yeah. Long story short, I was the man on the grassy knoll. But what I learned that day was that it wasn't just violence I liked, it was that I could kill on order, not just in the heat of action. Just ask my commander ... Oh wait, you can't."

"What happened with him? The rumour mill said you didn't bring his body back."

"I let Jack Ruby kill him."

"Your commander was Peter Awenda? The man who went down as the one who killed Kennedy?"

"Yeah. Remember how old history used to say the assassin was someone named Oswald? It would have been, if it hadn't been for me."

"I forgot about all that. That's some crazy shit. Even for me. But I think all Rangers, soldiers, have some part of them that likes violence. They just learn to overcome it. Hide it ... Or justify it."

"An old commander, AJ Beaumont, was helping me learn to sequester my anger. But then I lost him and I ..." Sawyer stopped and sighed. "I'm scared Mercier has broken down the wall I was learning to build, and I might not be able to build it back up again. All I want to do is destroy things. Hit things."

"And the cocaine Mercier gave you allowed you to do this."

"No consequences. No remorse. All I can think about is getting more. More cocaine. To feel that free again. And of course I'll never lose the guilt of killing all those men ... And wanting to steal the Earth-Lander, find a bar where I could unleash ... was supposed to help stem the urge. And well, I really wanted to hit someone. Many someones."

"Well, it's a good thing I stopped you, then." Hawk patted him on the shoulder and pushed him toward the Earth-Landers. "Come on. I promise I won't let you go through this alone. And if they take command away from you when we get back, I'll save a spot for you on my team."

"You? Command?"

"A soldier can dream."

A moment passed where the two of them said nothing. "Oh, and by the way," Sawyer finally said. "If you ever shoot me again, you better use the fixed-mass setting because I will kill you. That's twice now."

51.

B∧CK inside Earth-Lander Two, Sawyer still felt the urge to tear people apart, but with Hawk beside him, he felt he could contain it better now. *Just breathe,* he told himself as he bit into a protein bar.

Santiago had arrived, and she seemed nervous as she paced the small cabin. "Commander Sawyer."

"What?"

"Do you have a minute? There's something I need to talk to you about. It really can't wait any longer, which is why I rushed back here even though we don't have much time till boomerang." She came to him carrying a bag. "You may want this. It's the skinsuit from the asylum. I suggest you put it on. But first ..."

Her pause drew out until Sawyer crossed his arms. "Out with it, Lieutenant Commander."

"I heard news in Lafare where I stopped to rest my horse. Musketeers were there. Real ones, and pretty impressive, if you ask me. Anyway, sir, with all the explosions and commotion out at the asylum they must have been alerted. They arrived as we were leaving. Don't worry, everything was masked. They didn't see us."

"That's good, but..."

Santiago shifted her weight and looked him straight in the eyes. "When I arrived at Lafare, like I said, there were other Musketeers, and I overheard them talking. They've caught Mercier. They found him escaping through the forest. I think some of his own guards may have turned him in. Don't know for sure, though, or if it even matters, but suffice it to say, Mercier is safe and sound behind the bars of Paris's Grand Chatelet prison. So you needn't worry about him, and we can concentrate on catching our Runner with full force."

They've caught him. If there was anyone Sawyer wanted to beat to death, it was Mercier. Possibly more so than Arnault. Was jail enough? Sawyer nearly drew blood as his fingernails dug into his palms. After what Mercier had done to him, even death seemed too peaceful an end.

But there was only so much time left, so did he want to waste it getting revenge on Mercier? Would any of his team go along with it? He watched Perry as he pulled on his doublet, his expression stoic under his salt-and-pepper hair. He was a hard man to read. And he knew his father, so what did that mean? As for the doctor, he wouldn't be much help. At the back hatch, looking out as the sun rose higher in the morning sky, Hawk would either be his easiest ally or his biggest opponent considering what just happened between them.

Let it go … Sawyer heard in his head. It was Beaumont's voice. *Save that anger for when it's needed.* Sawyer hung his head. His anger was needed elsewhere. Mercier wasn't important. Arnault was their target. The timeline would not be affected by leaving Mercier to rot in prison, but leaving Arnault to continue would make drastic changes. And Arnault was their mission.

"Sir," said Santiago. "There's more."

Sawyer wasn't sure he could handle anymore news. "What?"

"You need to put on that skinsuit."

"Why?"

She pressed the bag she was carrying into his arms. "Please. And you should do this privately." She waved the others out of the Earth-Lander, then stood in the hatchway. "When you've changed, let me know." She went down the ramp and disappeared around the corner of the Earth-Lander.

Sawyer stared at the bag, not sure whether to listen to her or not. More information would have been helpful in making this decision. *There has to be a good reason,* he concluded, and quickly undressed. When he was fully initialized, and he'd checked the computer on his left sleeve, he called Santiago back into the Earth-Lander.

She produced a red data card from the breast pocket of the battle uniform he wore and handed it to him. "It's encrypted. For your eyes only. I couldn't even open it if I wanted to. The rear admiral sent it to me after you left to come down here. He said it was new mission orders. And by the way, off the record, I don't know how you survived that man. He's an asshole, sir."

She returned to the back hatch. "I'll leave so you can watch in private. Thor's up and running now, you might want to say hi. And, yeah, sorry about the disconnect. It must have been disorienting. Also, I don't know if this has anything to do with anything, but the cause of your Earth-Lander's malfunction was due to an encrypted message that transmitted automatically when you entered Earth's atmo. I think it came from the rear admiral, but I don't know where it went. It's what I presume caused the cascade failure with your Earth-Lander."

"I remember that," replied Sawyer. "I just forgot all about it when, you know, we crashed." He clutched the data card in his hand, held it up. "Maybe this will tell us something. And yeah, he is an asshole. You have no idea how much so."

She smiled. "I got a pretty good taste of it dealing with him before I came down here. No wonder you turned out like you did," she replied with a smile, before exiting the Earth-Lander.

Seated on a bench, Sawyer slid the red data card into the suit's computer. When his father's face filled the screen, Sawyer's breath caught in his throat and he paused the vid immediately.

"Why would you send this? This isn't protocol. My orders were given …" His breathing hurt his chest, his hands shook, but this time he knew it wasn't about wanting cocaine. Although, he couldn't ignore the voice at the back of his head telling him a little cocaine would make everything better. "No."

"No what, Commander Sawyer?" came back Thor's voice over the Earth-Lander's comms.

"Thor! It's good to hear your voice."

"I am not a voice. I am generated sound with appointed intrinsic characteristics to provide tone."

"You are such a computer, Thor."

"I prefer Artificial Intelligence."

Sawyer stared at the vid-screen. "Do you know what's on this data card? What Rear Admiral Sawyer sent me?"

"If it was neither produced nor played on the *BlackOut*, or in one of the two Earth-Landers, I do not."

Sawyer blew out a breath. "I'm not sure I want to see this."

"What is its classification?"

"Highest priority. My eyes only."

"Protocol states it must be viewed. I do not understand your hesitation."

"It's not going to be good news, Thor."

"Are data cards of this priority ever good news?"

"No, not usually."

"I do not understand your hesitation."

"All right. I get it, Thor. I'll just play the damn thing." Sawyer ordered his computer to play the vid.

"You must trust me," said his father. "Forget the Time Runner and get yourself back to the twenty-second century. I'm sure you have questions. Questions I cannot answer here or in this manner. Just trust me. Your mission is over, and you are to return through the Nexus Point at your appointed time, Time Runner not apprehended. I repeat, the Time Runner is not to be apprehended. Your orders are to destroy this recording after viewing."

The vid went blank and Sawyer took a deep breath. "What the actual fuck."

He needed a moment to digest the information. It didn't make sense. Why would he receive new orders while already engaged in a mission? And why orders to do the exact opposite of what he'd been trained to do? Then he remembered Specialist Perry mentioning he knew his father, and suddenly Sawyer wanted to know what that was about. Perry was a variable. Someone Sawyer didn't know all that well. Maybe knowing more about him, his connection to his father, would help him sort this out. He bit his lip in contemplation. "Thor, is there any way I can download you, or any part of you into this skinsuit?"

"You will be restricted to general applications. Without the implant, I am simply a communication and information device for you, as I am with any other member of the *BlackOut* crew."

"You almost sound sad."

There was a pause before Thor responded. "I sense a void."

"Ah, you care."

"I am incapable of caring."

"Computer."

"Artificial Intelligence."

Sawyer stood. "Download a map of France into this suit's computer, as well as what you can of yourself." Rules about keeping the timeline contaminated from tech, be damned. Santiago had instigated a Code 54, they'd flown an Earth-Lander across most of France, so he now saw no issue with hiding a battle uniform under his clothes. He dressed back into his leather pants, boots, and white shirt. Being a little skinnier made the layers look normal.

The Utopian Space Fleet, the Time Rangers, would abandon him if he followed his father's new orders, and his father would abandon him if he didn't.

Manuals. Orders. Protocols and professionalism. Where has that gotten me? Abiding them got me here, flailing to complete a mission and barely able to control myself. And the only way to move forward is to trust what I have. Make my own decision. But I don't know if I can move forward without ... He let the thought drift away, unsure if he could actually go through with the plan forming in his head. Was it a sacrifice he was willing to make?

Sawyer decided that it was, but first he'd need help to execute an escape plan. He'd need an ally ... But who would help him?

He opened the hatch door and called for Perry, and a moment later he arrived. "Specialist Perry, we need to talk."

Perry entered and stood at-ease. The specialist typically carried himself very stiffly, very properly, but his eyes right now were contradicting his typical demeanour. They turned down at the outside edges, just enough to make them kind.

Sawyer didn't want to beat around the bush. "Hawk said I needed to talk to you. I don't know what about, but I need everything out in the open. If there's something you need to tell me about this mission, about you, spit it out now because my patience is running real thin."

Perry's gaze flicked to the ceiling then back at him. "You don't remember me, do you?"

"From when?"

"I knew you when you were very young."

Sawyer scrutinized his face. "How young?"

"I was there the day your father brought you home. You were to be our child."

Sawyer's heart skipped a beat, and he paled despite the morning summer heat. "You were my father's partner?"

"I was. I left soon after you'd learned to walk."

"Why?"

"Your father had changed." Perry moved closer to him, and Sawyer didn't back away. "He'd become a completely different person after you were created. I couldn't stay ... I couldn't watch. His determination to turn you into the greatest Ranger ever ... it ruined him. I don't know what came over him, but the first time I saw him hurt you ... I tried to stop it. I stayed as long as I could. But I couldn't. He was moving up the ranks, and I was a specialist. It became complicated."

"It's pretty *un*complicated for me," said Sawyer. "You left a child unprotected in that man's hands when you could have stopped it."

Perry looked him up and down. "He did a pretty good job raising you ..."

Sawyer leaned into Perry's face. "Good job? I'm a fucking mess!" Deep down he knew it wasn't Perry's fault for his father's child-rearing skills. Leaving his father was probably the best thing for Perry to do, especially if his career was going to be put in jeopardy. But anger was Sawyer's ally. "Were you put on this team for a reason? Did my father put you here to get in my way? Stop me from doing my job!"

"No. Why would you think that?" Perry shook his head. "I mean, yes. Your father did put me on this team, but not for any other reason than a team requires a Historical Specialist. We spoke right before you left for Command School. He asked me to join you. Look out for you."

Sawyer studied him. This could turn into a charlie-foxtrot, or he could find the truth. He steeled himself and looked into Perry's eyes. They reflected back something Sawyer wasn't used to seeing ... compassion. Like what he'd seen in Hawk's dad's eyes when he looked at his son. Sawyer couldn't stop the words coming out of his mouth. "The rear admiral wants me to end the mission and return through the Nexus Point without apprehending the Time Runner."

Perry stepped back. "That certainly does not sound like your father. Are you sure it came from him?"

"Encrypted message," replied Sawyer.

"Why?"

"I don't know. I was hoping you'd have an explanation."

"Again I ask, why?"

"You had said you knew my father. And you kept telling me what to do at first. I didn't know what to think of you. And later, when you and Hawk left me in the fight ring, I thought my whole team had betrayed me." Sawyer held up a hand when it looked like Perry was going to speak. "I know what really happened, Hawk explained. And I trust him. I'm just figuring out if I fully trust you. This was a pretty big secret you kept from me."

Perry looked deep in contemplation. Sawyer studied his face, trying to bring up any memories from his childhood where he saw this man's face. It was a blur. Everything, everyone, like a ghost moving around in his mind. There were images from his third eye of being carried, cradled, and a fluffy grey-and-white cat being put in his lap making him smile. Thor? Was this him? Sawyer couldn't be sure, but what reason would Perry have to lie?

"We both know your father doesn't do anything without a plan," said Perry. There was a long pause before he spoke again. "He probably had involvement in this HCA before the Point even recognized it. I can only assume he wanted Hawk and myself on the team because he knew we'd back-burner the mission to put you first. Furthering his agenda."

"Time Rangers always put the mission first."

"A Time Ranger puts the future first, and your team members are the future."

The words reminded Sawyer of his first mission with Commander Beaumont. "You'll know you have a team worth keeping when you first have their trust and respect," he said under his breath.

"You had mine and Hawk's trust and respect long before this mission started, sir. And your father knew that."

Sawyer nearly slid to the ground. *It can't be true. You're trying to confuse me...* "No. Stop."

"Mercier and our Time Runner, this man called Arnault, made you believe they'd taken one of your teammates prisoner to be tortured for your disobedience. Why do you think they'd do that?"

As if the answer were evident, Sawyer shrugged. "Leverage."

"That's where your mind went first?" Perry shook his head. "Your father really *did* do a number on you, sir. They probably used that tactic because they recognized they required a victim to coerce you. They recognized your loyalty and honour. After all that's happened to you ... yes, I've been following your life ... you still stay loyal to the Rangers, and to your father. Even when he doesn't deserve it. But what about now? Are you going to stay loyal to him?"

"That's the big question, isn't it?"

"Find your intuition," said Perry. "And the balance that led you through the Academy, through your first missions, and into being one of the youngest commanders in the Time Rangers. Your father could only do so much—it's you that got you this far. Time Rangers don't make weak men into commanders. Regardless of who their fathers are."

Weak. Something Sawyer knew he wasn't. In fact, he felt stronger than ever. "Screw the rear admiral's orders. We're going after the Time Runner."

"Yes, sir. I'll let the others know. When do you wish to leave?"

"Soon," Sawyer replied absently as his earlier plan took hold of him again.

Perry exited the Earth-Lander, leaving Sawyer alone with his thoughts. One thing he was sure of was he was tired of being a pawn. But for his plan to work, he'd need Hawk. He'd need backup in case anything went sideways. For the most part, Sawyer now trusted Perry, but not to the extent he trusted Hawk. And of course, Hawk had skills beyond Sawyer's capabilities. *It will be like old times at the Academy,* he thought with a smile. *And damn the horses, we've got ourselves an Earth-Lander.*

"Hawk," he called over his ear-pin. He set them to an encrypted channel when Hawk responded. "Are you with the doctor?"

"Yes."

"We're going somewhere, but first I need you to do something for me."

52.

"IT'S been awhile since I've borrowed an Earth-Lander. Feels like our Academy days," said Hawk as he lowered a masked Earth-Lander Two gently on the ground outside Paris's northwest gate.

"You were always good at procuring things," replied Sawyer. After Thor announced the area was clear, Sawyer lowered the rear hatch and stepped outside.

"Did you see Santiago's face when we took off? I don't know if she was more angry or surprised. But damn she was hilarious stomping around in that ruffled dress."

Sawyer rolled his eyes but couldn't deny Hawk was right. Seeing Santiago throw her hands in the air, screaming at them for stealing the Earth-Lander right out beside her, was something he wouldn't forget for a long time.

Hawk came up behind him and passed him a small vial. "Are you sure you're okay with this? It's not going to ..."

Sawyer snatched the vial. "I'll be fine. Now let's go. We have a long walk ahead of us still."

An hour later, they entered the Grand Chatelet in the centre of Paris. Sawyer left Hawk at the end of a long corridor to keep watch as he made his way deeper into the prison. As Sawyer neared his objective, he pulled out a bottle of wine from a satchel then carefully opened the vial Hawk had "procured" from the doctor.

Sawyer took a breath to calm his hands and keep his mind from straying in the wrong direction. *I need to do this,* he thought as he squeezed his eyes shut. *I need to do this. Don't think about what's in your hands. Just breathe. Just do this.*

When he was ready, he walked with conviction until he reached his intended cell. The prisoner lay on a cot wearing the same black robe he'd always worn, but now it was tattered and dusty. *So unlike the gentleman you claim to be.*

Sawyer watched the prisoner through the wrought-iron bars for several seconds until the man finally looked over. "Good day," said Sawyer. "You look … well."

Mercier swung his bare feet to the stone floor and smoothed down his sweat-stained robe with an upturned nose. "Have you come to watch me suffer?" he asked, sitting straighter on the side of the cot.

"No."

"Gloat then, perhaps?"

"No."

Mercier padded over to the small weathered table under the only window his cell provided. He picked up an empty bottle of wine and held it up. "Wine of such excellent vintage is not usually served in such an establishment as I find myself in. It would seem I still have friends out there." He glanced at Sawyer with raised eyebrows. "Or perhaps in here?"

"Perhaps." Sawyer held out the bottle in his own hand and slipped it through the bars. "It seems my timing is perfect. I've brought you another."

Mercier took the bottle and uncorked it immediately. "Did you send the first bottle?"

Sawyer shook his head.

"Care for a drink?"

Sawyer shook his head again.

"That's right. You only drink with friends." Mercier sipped from the bottle with a grimace, as if the act were demeaning, then took a long swig. "And we are not friends, so why don't we drop the pretense? If you're not here to gloat, then what brings you here?"

"I have something to say."

Mercier took another healthy gulp of his wine. "Then what is it? Spit it out."

"Nothing," replied Sawyer.

"You came here to say nothing? What an impossibly boring word."

Sawyer leaned in close. "No. I came here to tell you that you mean nothing. You're gonna spend the rest of your short life knowing that you mean nothing to me. And that you failed. Failed in creating new physicians. A noble goal, but not one for you to accomplish. History will leave that to better, more upstanding men than you. You may occupy my thoughts for the next weeks, possibly even months, but after that, your face, your memory, will be nothing more than a fleeting image in my mind. Perhaps there will even come a day when I ... when history won't remember you at all." He set his jaw, narrowed his eyes. "Know this, Mercier, after all you did, you won't succeed at making a name for yourself in history."

Mercier laughed. "You're wrong. My time isn't over. I have friends, students, still eager to learn, and Arnault is a very powerful man who can make things happen. And he still needs me. My escape is imminent. I'll be gone from here before you arrive back at your garrison. My days as a physician, as one of France's greatest surgeons, are not over. Le Havre awaits my expertise."

So it's Le Havre? Dumbass.

Mercier gulped down more wine as he watched Sawyer. "Why are you smiling? What do you think you know?"

"I've said all I've come to say." Sawyer turned to leave, then stopped and looked back over his shoulder. "Oh, wait, one more thing. If you'll indulge me ..."

Too fast for Mercier to react, Sawyer reached through the bars and grasped Mercier's free hand. Sawyer squeezed until he felt multiple bones snap in two, passed the point of repair, and Mercier was screaming in pain. "Good luck practicing to be a surgeon now," Sawyer gloated. "And also ... please, enjoy the wine."

Sawyer turned and strode confidently away. Behind him, he heard Mercier gasp, followed by the sound of a bottle hitting the ground.

But Sawyer's swagger was short-lived. At the end of the long hall, Hawk stood waiting for him.

"Are you finished here?" asked Hawk. "We need to bullet if we're going to make it back to home base. We still need to catch Arnault, and you've just wasted a lot of precious time. I know why you did it, why it had to be done, but we've got to move. Now, sir."

"I had to do it, Max."

Hawk held up a hand. "I know. That's why I helped."

There was such disappointment in Hawk's eyes that Sawyer could barely breathe. "I'm not dirty. I didn't take any of the drug you stole from Dr. Brodeur. I wanted to, but I didn't. I gave it all to Mercier. There's no way he won't be addicted to maxigen now."

Hawk smiled. "Good, sir. But I'm shocked the doc even had any. It's a crazy powerful stimulant. It's a derivative of cocaine."

"It's not a well-known fact. I took medical classes, so I know. But … our unit doctors keep some on hand just in case."

"In case of what?"

"In case *we* need it to get through a mission. But don't share this with anyone. If soldiers knew how easy it was to obtain, we'd have a really big problem on our hands. So keep it quiet."

They left together and walked out into the Chatelet's courtyard, which was filled with guards and prisoners moving around under a hot sun. They kept walking in silence until they arrived at the Earth-Lander.

Sawyer stopped and looked back at the city. It was time for the hard part. "Our fate, the future of humanity's fate, rests with what I, we, do here. I'm sorry."

"You set us back, Commander, but what's done is done. Let's get a move on."

"He's set up shop again near Le Havre," replied Sawyer. "Mercier told me the town is awaiting his arrival, so I assume that's where Arnault is."

"So this trip wasn't a complete waste of time. I guess it's off to Le Havre. I've always wanted to see the English Channel."

Sawyer activated his ear-pin. "Santiago, prep Earth-Lander One for launch."

"Yes, sir," she replied over the comms. "And by the way, you have some explaining…!"

Sawyer cut their comms and turned to Hawk. "We have less than a day to make the boomerang. We won't have enough time to search Le Havre for our Runner and make it to the Point in time."

Hawk's eyes went wide. "No, sir. We can do it, we just have to move quickly."

"No, Lieutenant. This is my fault, and I plan to clean up the mess I created."

"Commander … Kai, no," insisted Hawk.

Sawyer's stomach churned as it tied itself in knots. He'd finally found people he could trust, and now he was about to say good-bye to them.

53.

T̄AKE the Earth-Lander and return to the others," Sawyer ordered Hawk. "You, Perry, Santiago, and Brodeur, get back to the *BlackOut* while I complete the mission. Arnault and I will not be returning to the future. I'm staying back to stop any further contamination on his part. I'm willing to pay the price to fix this cluster-fuck of a mission."

"Hell no," replied Hawk. He climbed into the pilot seat and started the Earth-Lander's engine. "I'm not leaving you behind here. I'm coming with you."

"Hawk, please," pleaded Sawyer as he crossed the rear hatch. "You don't deserve to be stuck here. Just go."

Hawk closed the hatch and lifted the Earth-Lander off the ground. "Too late. You suck. Now shut up, we're doing this together."

Sawyer sat in the jump seat and hung his head. "You don't know what you've just done."

"I know exactly what I've done, sir. We're in this together till the end. I'm not leaving you behind. Remember rule number two? Don't contaminate the past, don't leave anything behind."

"That doesn't quite apply here, Hawk."

"It does in my book. Now shut up, we've got some ground to cover."

Sawyer wasn't sure how upset he was at losing the argument with Hawk. Sawyer would have missed him, all of his team, but knowing he wasn't going to be stuck here alone was a huge relief. He just hoped Hawk really knew what he was getting into.

Sawyer looked out over the countryside as they raced toward the coastal town of Le Havre, wondering if he'd prefer to live out here or in a city. He also wondered how much longer he'd have access to Thor when the *BlackOut* returned through the Nexus Point.

The storm now gone, the sky a periwinkle blue, endless and clear while the sun shone brightly as it descended toward the western horizon. "I could get used to this."

"Used to what?" asked Hawk.

"Fresh air. Open land."

"But is it a reasonable substitute for open space?"

Sawyer's heart fell. Would it be an acceptable replacement? He loved space. The stars, the stations, the spaceships, and the ability to flush a toilet … It was a hard question to answer. "Is it for you?"

"It'll be hard. But I'll manage."

Although Sawyer would miss those things, there was something the seventeenth century could grant him that the future could not, and that was freedom. He'd no longer be a pawn in someone else's agenda. He'd no longer be taking orders from anyone. He'd be free to do what he wanted, live how he wanted.

He'd miss Santiago, but Perry even more. Sawyer felt he had found a possible father figure in him, a real father … and he was about to throw it all away. He would even miss Aurora. But his heart didn't twinge at the thought of never seeing his father again. Although staying here meant he'd never learn why the rear admiral had ordered him to abandon the mission. Sawyer would never know why his father wanted him to fail when throughout Sawyer's whole life his father had wanted him to not only succeed, but be the best.

"I'm going to contact the others," he said, breaking the silence in the Earth-Lander. "Tell them what's going on."

He tapped his ear-pin and immediately Santiago responded. "Sir, you have some explaining to do! Where are you!"

Sawyer wrapped up the details of his and Hawk's mission to the prison as succinctly as possible before letting her know his orders. "Perry, Dr. Brodeur and yourself are to return to the *BlackOut*. Hawk and I are staying. We'll see to it Arnault is stopped and the future is saved. You have your orders, and I expect you to follow through. This is the way it's going to be."

"Sir, there has got to be a better way," she replied.

Perry's voice came back over the ear-pin next, his voice determined. "We can still work together, get this done. We just have to move quickly. We'll meet you wherever you're going. Give us the coordinates."

Sawyer reached past Hawk at the helm and switched off the Earth-Lander's tracking device. "Sorry, Specialist. I'm not putting you all at risk to get stuck here. It's better this way. It's my way. And it's the way we are doing this. Now go. Enjoy the future." He cut communications and sat back in the jump seat with a heavy heart.

Sawyer was aware he was abandoning them, but it was the only way he knew to keep them safe. His father wanted him to leave, but he couldn't. The rest of his team wanted him to stay with them, but he couldn't have that. Regulations dictated he complete the mission, and that was something he could do. *Trained as a Time Ranger… die as a Time Ranger.*

He looked at Hawk and knew that he knew that too.

When their Earth-Lander arrived at the harbour town of Le Havre, Hawk landed them in an open field and Sawyer started making preparations for its destruction. They wouldn't need it anymore. He set it on automatic pilot and entered coordinates for the deepest part of the Arctic Ocean, where it would crash and spend the rest of its days hidden under the freezing depths.

Hawk saluted the Earth-Lander as it rose into the sky. "May you rest in peace, Earth-Lander Two."

When they crossed the border into Le Havre, Sawyer could already smell the salty air and he turned his head upward as if he could see the *BlackOut* itself, but found nothing but a darkening sky. Together he and Hawk went deeper into the harbour town in search of a barber-surgeon. Then another and another, and even a few apothecaries, to find no evidence of Arnault's influence.

It's still early, Sawyer thought as they continued to walk through the streets. A short while later, they found themselves standing on a dock looking out at a night full of stars, reminiscent of the view from his cabin on the *BlackOut*. As Sawyer stared, he imagined one tiny dot, the biggest and brightest in the sky, was his ship with the rest of his team safely onboard. He'd miss it. Them. He'd miss everything, especially the views. Although, he couldn't deny what he saw now was remarkable. In the future, from any place on Earth, other than the most northern or southern continents, city lights obscured the wondrous view of the universe. *At least I'll have this.*

Sawyer nudged Hawk in the shoulder. "Life's going to be a lot different for us now."

"More so than you think," said a voice behind them.

Sawyer spun around. "Arnault."

"Doctor Arnault."

"I don't care what you call yourself. Your time here is done."

Arnault was everything Sawyer remembered from that first day he'd seen him in Mercier's school. He even wore the black robe that Sawyer was beginning to detest.

Behind Arnault the view of Le Havre's taverns, stores, and sailors scurrying about unloading their wares from the docked ships made Arnault seem as if he belonged here. Sawyer meant to quickly remedy that. "Do you want to do this the hard way or the easy way?"

"There is nothing hard that needs to be done," replied Arnault. "I knew you would go after Mercier, and I knew that imbecile would reveal our new location. Power-hungry people are so predictable. So, I've been waiting for you. My men saw you enter the town and have been following you since. And I know exactly who you are and what exactly is going to happen. It is quite simple. I will allow you to leave, and you will allow me to stay and finish my work. The young Kai Sawyer always listens to his father."

Sawyer pulled out a pistol and aimed it at Arnault's chest. "Not anymore."

"Trust me, he'll shoot," said Hawk, crossing his arms over his chest. "And he doesn't miss."

"I may be a doctor," replied Arnault. "But I'm not against taking a life when I see fit. And unfortunately for your friend here, I don't need him."

A loud bang echoed in the still night and Hawk dropped to the ground.

"Hawk!" screamed Sawyer, bending down at his friend's side.

"Stay back," ordered Arnault. "I have men with muskets everywhere around us. One move and they'll incapacitate you with another well-placed shot."

Sawyer rose slowly, anger coursing through his body as he watched a dark-red stain blossoming on Hawk's shirt. "I'm going to fucking kill you."

"There's something bigger at play here." Arnault stepped closer to Sawyer and clasped his hands in front of him. "I came to you, you didn't find me. Does that not pique your interest? You might as well put that pistol down. You will not shoot me. For both of us to get what we want, you need to put that thing down."

Sawyer tightened his grip and closed the gap between them with a step forward of his own. Days of torture, being at someone's mercy, and now Hawk dying beside him, had Sawyer really wanting to pull the trigger. But this man had answers. "Your riddles are really earning you the spectacular demise you have coming."

"I have orders, and I must obey them."

"Or you can disobey those orders," replied Sawyer, recognizing the irony in his words.

"Not if we are to save the future."

"You're killing the future! Everything about what you are doing will change history. It will change the twenty-second century. How do you not see this?"

"I see it, and I look forward to it. Now it's time I take my leave, and like I said earlier, you will allow this. You will return to your team, take your little friend with you, for all I care, and leave with them. All will be right. You will see."

Obviously, Arnault was not acquainted with all the mission details, for he didn't seem to know when boomerang was to happen. Was this information something that would make Arnault change his agenda? "My ship has left," Sawyer said calmly. "It's already in orbit at the Nexus Point. It's just you and me now."

"That's unfortunate. And I thought you could be reasoned with, but alas, you won't listen to me. But like I said that day in your cell, I can't have you following me. You are a great threat, but you are not invincible. Perhaps I should end this, let them find someone else? You can't be the only great commander. Or we can start back at the beginning? My new school will need bodies to service. You were an excellent champion."

Sweat beaded Sawyer's forehead, and his grip loosened on the pistol. "Like I'd ever volunteer ..."

"I don't need you to volunteer when I have coercion on my side. I can still save your friend. After all, I really am a doctor from the twenty-second century."

"Fuck you."

Arnault raised his hand and another bang rang out in the night. A searing pain shot through Sawyer's shoulder before he collapsed beside Hawk on the wet dock.

54.

SAWYER awoke sweat-soaked and lying on a hard, dry surface. He opened his eyes to a night sky above him, then realized the smell of salt-water and brine tickled the back of his throat. He sat up, rolled onto his hands and knees to get his feet under him, and staggered.

"Be careful. You might fall off."

With scratchy dry eyes, Sawyer looked to his right, where the dark waters of the English Channel churned almost a kilometre below. The sound of roaring and pounding waves carried up to the roof of the building where he knelt on the edge, a dilapidated railing the only fixture keeping him from falling over. He sat back down, away from the edge, and grabbed his foggy head until he remembered he wasn't alone. "Arnault." A sharp sting in Sawyer's shoulder reminded him of his last moments before losing consciousness. "What the hell did you do to me?"

"A strong sedative. A Spawn isn't the easiest thing to contain."

"Why did you bring me here?"

"I brought you to my new school because I wanted to give you one more chance to reconsider. I do not wish to actually hurt you. You are a fine specimen of future bio-medical technology. But you do need to let me finish my work here."

"Let you finish changing the timeline? You shouldn't have bothered. You might as well just kill me now, 'cause I'm not letting you get away."

"It's a lot more complicated than you think, Commander Sawyer. In fact, knowing what I know, you should be getting on with your new life here, if what you say is true and your team has already left. Or helping me save the future by remaining my champion."

Team. "Where's Lieutenant Hawk?"

"Bring him out!" called Arnault over his shoulder. A door behind him opened and several guards emerged carrying a limp body between them. They deposited Hawk on the ground and returned back through the door.

"Hawk!" screamed Sawyer, but his friend didn't move.

It felt like every organ in Sawyer's body disappeared and his bones were disintegrating. Sawyer drew from his anger, lunged forward, and fell to his knees, the sedative strong in his system. But he could see. Clearly. Blood stained the front of Hawk's shirt. Dried blood was smeared across his face. Sawyer stumbled to his feet to find himself on his knees again. *Fucking drugs!* "I'm going to kill you if anything happens to him!"

Sawyer glanced at his waist. His weapons were gone. Not surprising. His mind churned like the English Channel below as a million thoughts ran through it. *Facts. Facts. Focus on facts. I'm alive. Arnault is here. Hawk may be alive. It isn't over.*

He tried to stand again and failed. But this time, Sawyer felt something strange happening with his body. He wasn't sure what it meant.

Arnault pointed a Stormguard at Hawk. "You have nowhere to go, Commander. I have your pistols, and I have Lieutenant Hawk's Stormguard. I will use it to kill him, if he's not dead already. His life is inconsequential to our plans."

"He's not inconsequential to me."

Arnault shrugged then smiled at Sawyer. "The sedative I gave you lasts twelve hours and it's only been three. You can try and come for me, but rest assured I know my doses. Even for a Spawn. You won't get two feet without falling on your face. And it takes only a second to pull a trigger and end your friend's life."

Arnault was right. The sedative was still working. All Sawyer wanted was to lie down, let his mind sift through the intangible thoughts running through it, and find clarity. He concentrated on Hawk lying on the roof with Arnault holding a Stormguard over him, most likely set on fixed-mass. This couldn't be it, it couldn't be the actual end, for himself or Hawk. Not after all he'd sacrificed.

"There it is," said Arnault. "That Sawyer determination your father portrays so well. You're just like him."

"Problem for you is, I don't want to be my father!" Sawyer lunged forward with all the strength he could muster, and as Arnault predicted, he landed on the ground no closer to his target. Arnault hadn't even budged.

Right dose, my ass! That strange feeling in Sawyer was intensifying. His legs, his arms tingled. He trusted it was a good thing and remained still, not wanting to reveal his secret until the time was right. But maybe it wouldn't matter. With a Stormguard pointed at Hawk, Sawyer knew he'd never be able to move faster than a bullet. He gritted his teeth. The anger in him boiling through his veins more so than any time he'd taken the cocaine. "Fuck you."

"Such impropriety," replied Arnault with a mocking shake of his head. "Polite society disappeared with history, it's a shame."

Polite society. Mercier had wanted to be part of that world. Sawyer remembered Mercier sitting in his cell, asking him to behave like a gentleman, and his arms began to shake, his fingers began to curl. *Come closer, dipshit!*

"Is that why you went after Mercier?" Sawyer asked, stalling for time. "You wanted to surround yourself with gentlemen? Because I gotta tell ya, he isn't going to be any more help to you now."

"Mercier was a pawn. Someone with an agenda whose ideals I could latch onto." Arnault paced in front of Sawyer as Mercier had done many times in his cell, but he kept the Stormguard trained on Hawk, not giving Sawyer any window of opportunity.

"I did my research before I was sent here," continued Arnault. "I knew about Mercier and his interests in advancing medicine and the plight of the uneducated man. Although ..." he stopped to smile at Sawyer. "In old history ... the one that would have happened if I hadn't been sent here, he died in some random riot in the streets of Paris. His name was barely a byproduct of the old history. The ancestor of some low-level politician in the nineteenth century, which was why his aura was green. He was very hard to find amongst all the historical chronicles the Time Rangers and Nexus Point keep. But he was perfect for what I needed. Medicine needs to advance. Not just now, but in our time. We needed to jumpstart its progression so we are prepared. Our future does not exist without help from the past."

That's bullshit, thought Sawyer. *Our future will be secure if I do my job!*

Arnault continued to pace, his long black robe swishing around his feet. Sawyer looked past him to Hawk's still body. Sawyer was Hawk's commander. A Spawn, his friend. *Why didn't I make you go back with the others? I was supposed to keep you safe.*

Sawyer couldn't let anything happen to Hawk. He dug deep, concentrated on his tingling muscles. *Closer, asshole.*

"The twenty-third century needs to be prepared," said Arnault. "You have no idea what's coming. I need … we need … to do this. You had a destiny. But I guess that's moot now since you're stuck here. But if you won't help me, I need to make sure you don't interfere in our plans."

Sawyer frowned, remembered his father shoving the same word down his throat throughout his life. "What is this destiny bullshit?"

"Ah, now I have your attention. Unfortunately, the answer is very complicated, and since your destiny no longer exists, it no longer matters. So you must choose now: join me in rewriting history where we'll make an unstoppable team, or get out of my way, Commander."

"Not going to happen," said Sawyer. A gust of warm air blew up from the shore below. Static electricity crept up Sawyer's spine and pricked the hair on the back of his neck and arms.

"I will ask one more time, will you join me?"

"Never."

Arnault turned his Stormguard on Sawyer. "I don't want to do this, but I must. You are too much of a threat to leave alive."

Sawyer suddenly smelled ozone and smiled. With what he felt happening with his body, that ozone smelled like opportunity. "Go ahead."

"Last chance?"

"Go fuck yourself."

Arnault squatted in front of him. "Maybe they will find a replacement for you, maybe not."

A faint humming came from over Sawyer's shoulder and he grinned as he stared down the dangerous end of the Stormguard pointed at him.

When Arnault's finger curled around the trigger, Sawyer pounced. All his aggression, strength, and rage exploded with vengeance as he landed on Arnault. Sawyer wrenched the Stormguard free from Arnault's hand, tossed it aside, grabbed the stunned doctor by his robe, and hefted him to his feet.

"How?" stammered Arnault. "You should be impaired for hours still."

Sawyer stared into his wide, surprised eyes. "I have no idea. And I don't care. Because now I'm going to kill you."

Sawyer swung his arm back and let loose a punch that sent Arnault stumbling backward. Suddenly, the roof door crashed opened and guards armed with both swords and pistols filed out onto the roof, quickly closing in on Sawyer.

"You guys are so fucked …" said Sawyer as he smiled.

55.

THE guards storming out onto the roof suddenly stopped, mouths gaping, as Earth-Lander One unmasked behind Sawyer.

"Commander! Duck!"

Sawyer hit the ground as a spray of fixed-mass bullets came from behind him. He rolled onto his back, keeping low, and watched Santiago as she knelt in the open back hatch of the Earth-Lander, a grin on her face as she levelled the playing field.

The sound of the guard's heavy bodies hitting the roof, their grunts and groans as bullets riddled their bodies, was music to Sawyer's ears. When no one was left standing, the Earth-Lander landed and both Santiago and Brodeur rushed out and past him. Sawyer assumed they were collecting Arnault and Hawk and let out a deep, relieved breath. He was about to close his eyes, only for a moment, when Perry appeared above him.

"I thought I ordered you to leave," said Sawyer

"You really thought we'd … I'd … leave you here alone?" Perry replied. "It was pretty much a consensus between the lieutenant commander, Dr. Brodeur, and myself that we wouldn't strand you, or Lieutenant Hawk, here."

Santiago dragged an unconscious Arnault behind her by his feet. "How's Lieutenant Hawk?" she asked the doctor over her shoulder as she continued toward the open hatch of the Earth-Lander.

"GSW to the abdomen," reported Brodeur. "He needs help."

After Sawyer was helped to his feet and he ran to his friend. Sawyer slid up beside Hawk and looked into his face. Hawk's eyes were open, blinking, as he stared up at him.

"I'm sorry," said Sawyer. "I never meant for this to happen. I didn't know

Arnault and Mercier's men were following us. I should have known he was going ..."

Hawk coughed but managed a smile. "Just shut up and get this fucking bullet out of me. It stings like a motherfucker."

"Serves you right for shooting me twice. Besides, you'll survive. I know you know this, Lieutenant."

"Shut up. It fucking hurts."

Sawyer helped the doctor carry Hawk into the Earth-Lander. Sawyer took most of the weight and burden of the heavy body until they deposited Hawk on a bench. The doctor got to work as Sawyer stepped back and turned to Santiago. She had already secured Arnault with restraints and left him on the Earth-Lander floor to wake up on his own.

"Not that I'm ungrateful," said Sawyer. "But how did you know where I was ... where we were?"

"I had Thor do a search for tech. You may have turned off your Earth-Lander's tracking signal, but *he* was downloaded into your battle suit computer. Thor found it ... himself ... pretty fast."

"Thanks for thinking of that."

Santiago smiled. "We wanted to reveal ourselves earlier, but we didn't want to spook Arnault. We saw he had Hawk. But when you lunged, you gave us the opportunity to unmask and attack."

Sawyer blew out a breath. "I realized you were there. I felt the mask's static electricity. And thank god, 'cause I don't know if I could have handled all those guards. Arnault had me sedated."

"Then how did you manage ...?"

"I don't know, Lieutenant Commander." Sawyer shook his head. He really didn't know, but he wasn't about to look a gift horse in the mouth. "Maybe I'm just immune to sedation now that Hawk's shot me twice with a debilitator."

It was meant as a joke, but Santiago didn't laugh. Her expression was more curious than anything else. "Uh, what did you guys do with the other Earth-Lander?" she asked.

"It's probably at the bottom of the Arctic Ocean by now."

"Ah, good thinking." She straightened her shoulders, resting her hands in the small of her back. "So what now, Commander? I'm ready for your orders."

"You don't want to give them yourself?"

"I don't think you need any hand holding, sir," she replied with a smile.

Sawyer nodded a thank you. "Thanks for having my back. And now it's time to get out of here."

Sawyer left Brodeur to tend to Hawk and stumbled into the helm position. He ran a hand down his face, wondering if he was actually alert enough to fly this thing. He may have overcome the sedation quicker than he'd expected, but he was tired. Damn tired. He pushed a few controls, closed the back hatch, and instigated the mask as exhaustion washed over him.

"Is there enough time?" asked Santiago, coming up behind him. She pointed at the clock. "The one thing we didn't have time to fix was the FTL engine."

Two hours until boomerang. A half-hour less than they needed without the omni-drive. "We gotta try."

"Maybe I should fly?"

Sawyer considered it, but it would take expert piloting to get this Earth-Lander through Earth's atmo and landed relatively safely in the *BlackOut's* debarkation room in such a short time. He wasn't sure Santiago could do it ... he wasn't sure he could do it, but there was no way he'd let someone else take the blame for failure to get the team home safely. "I've got this. Now grab me a bottle of cyto-juice and strap in."

56.

SAWYER lifted the Earth-Lander smoothly off the roof, then it shot upward. Sawyer calculated the distance to the Nexus Point from where they were and shook his head. *Time is not on our side.*

The Earth-Lander shook, rattling its contents and occupants like a child's toy. Sawyer heard the grunts and swears coming from the back as he maintained as best control as he could. Hawk was back there, injured. The rocking and jolting could not be good for him. "How's he doing, doc?"

"He's stable. For now," replied Brodeur. "But the shaking isn't helping!"

"Do what you can." Sawyer thrust the engine harder, pulling from the engine all he could to gain as much speed as he could. "I really hope you guys fixed everything else on this Earth-Lander!" he yelled into the air.

"Shut up and fly!" came back Santiago's strained voice.

A jolt signified the Earth-Lander leaving Earth's gravitational pull, and in moments everything calmed. Sawyer took a breath, checked the clock. He'd bought them some time, but not enough. He really did not want to have to stay in the seventeenth century, not when there was a chance he could get his team home to the future. He'd been willing to give it all up for himself, but his team he wouldn't strand.

"We need a plan here people or we aren't going to make it!" he yelled over his shoulder.

Through the front window, the universe passed in a blur. Sawyer checked his trajectory, double checked the *BlackOut's* coordinates. Everything was accurate. But who knew if an Earth-Lander, or his ship, could withstand a crash landing into the debarkation room?

"Thor, tell the *BlackOut* to wait as long as it can," Sawyer said into the air.

309

"We're gonna come in hot with a tactical landing. But if they have to go, tell them to go. They are not to wait for us. I repeat, they are not to wait for us."

"Understood, Commander," replied Thor, over the comm system.

"Any ideas yet?" Sawyer called back to his team.

"Less weight? That will give us more speed," called Santiago. "Open the hatch! We can jettison the Runner! I *really* don't have a problem with that!"

Unfortunately, we can't open a hatch at this speed or altitude. "I like what you're thinking, but no. Other options?"

"Blow the hatch!" called Perry.

"I just said no to that! Wait…" *Timed properly, an explosive decompression can create extra speed when it counts! Wait. No.* "We're in microgravity, no air, and the speed would be deadly. We're not in Earth's atmo this time. We need to contain pressure in the cabin, or we'll all die. I need other options."

The galaxy rushed past the Earth-Lander's window as the ship passed spatial objects, and finally Mars. The main asteroid belt wasn't much further. Beyond that, the *BlackOut* waited within the Point's boomerang radius awaiting capture. The clock now flashed red, indicating their time was running too short. Sweat broke out on Sawyer's forehead, his arms and fingers felt like they were detached from his body. *What else? What else can we do?* "Damn. We need to get there before the *BlackOut* fires its omni-drive. We won't be able to approach with its engines fired up."

"Can the *BlackOut* meet us halfway?" asked Perry. "It'll cut our time in half."

"No," replied Sawyer. "I'm not putting the whole ship and crew in a position where they might miss boomerang capture. We need to think of something else."

"The web! Can we initiate the web when we blow the hatch?" suggested Santiago.

"That'll take some very precise timing," replied Perry.

Sawyer concentrated on the helm as the voices of his team in the back blurred together. "Thor. How much extra speed will blowing the hatch actually give us?"

"If initiated at the precise time, it should suffice."

"Set a timer, Thor," ordered Sawyer. "You tell me the instant I need to blow that hatch."

"Affirmative, Commander."

Sawyer saw Perry's reflection in the front viewing window and knew he'd entered the helm. "Can we do this?" asked Sawyer.

"It's going to take time to get the engineering right. We need the web to go up the nano-second we blow the hatch. You would think it would be an automatic safety, but I guess crew safety wasn't tantamount when they designed these things."

"Harking back to the early days of NASA and its shuttles, Perry. Redundancy systems for everything but the crew," said Sawyer.

Perry disappeared back into the cabin with a shake of his head.

In moments, Sawyer anticipated having a visual of the *BlackOut*. According to the clock he had twenty-minutes left, but his read-outs told him he needed more.

"Blowing the hatch will use extraneous power," Santiago called from the back. "Power we can't divert from engines."

"It won't matter if all goes to plan," replied Sawyer. "We'll make it up when it blows."

"Are you sure?" asked Santiago.

No. "Yes. Now let me know when we're ready!"

Sawyer skipped Thor and directed comms directly to his ship to prevent lag time. "*BlackOut*, this is Commander Sawyer."

"Go ahead, Commander," replied Lieutenant Michaels.

"Open debarkation room, hold steady. We're coming in."

"We'll leave the barn doors open and the lights on, sir. Welcome home."

Sawyer felt like he was taking a breath every second that ticked by, he needed to control himself, keep himself calm. This was their only chance at survival, and it had to work.

When Santiago called from the back that everything was ready to go, Sawyer held his breath then counted to three as he slowly released it. His heartbeat slowed, a calm came over him, and he closed his eyes, waited for Thor to give him word it was time to blow the hatch.

"Prepare for rear hatch detachment," announced Thor, over the comm speakers for everyone to hear. "Five ... Four ... Three ... Two ..."

And we just had the door fixed was the strange thought scurrying through Sawyer's mind as he forced out all the air in his lungs in one powerful breath.

The hatch blew, the mask went up, then suddenly the rear wall of the *BlackOut's* debarkation room was coming at him way too quickly. Sawyer instigated the Earth-Lander's brakes, skidded across the short landing floor of the debarkation room, slamming into crates and finally the back wall, which brought their vessel to a dead stop.

Moments later the *BlackOut* jolted, and everything turned white as a comforting shiver ran up Sawyer's spine.

57.

DR. Arnault was immediately taken into custody when they docked with Nexus Station. The team showered, changed, and were all seen by Dr. Brodeur before Sawyer stood before Admiral Shenouda in his office at the back of the OCC. His father stood behind the Space Fleet admiral's desk as well, arms crossed as he stared at Sawyer.

"Modern medicine had to start when it did," said Shenouda. "A butterfly effect in time could prove catastrophic. A hummingbird flaps its wings in London and a hurricane arrives on Haitian shores. Terrible effect. Death, starvation, destruction ensues. But when someone stomps on a microscopic species that wriggled its way onto land, the fate of all history is at stake. What if that Saccorhytus sea creature was the first to mutate? Human life on Earth may never have started."

Sawyer wondered where the admiral was going with this. "Sir, I did ..."

Shenouda cleared his throat, indicating to Sawyer he wasn't finished. "You stopped the stomping, Commander. Congratulations."

There was a lot missing in the mission reports Sawyer and his team had submitted, which had Sawyer anxiety ridden for the last few hours since they'd arrived in 2198. Should they have told Admiral Shenouda everything? Told him how the rear admiral had tried to sabotage the mission?

Sawyer had decided they leave it out of the reports so he could talk to his superior first. In this case, it meant talking with his father. As Sawyer stood listening to Shenouda, the anticipation of the conversation with his father was making his skin crawl. Punching him in the face was the first option Sawyer considered, but that would only grant him minor triumph and wouldn't erase the fact that he still had to talk to him ... but Sawyer knew he could delay the conversation for a very long time if he hit him hard enough.

Sawyer shook his head. *I can't postpone the inevitable.*

"Something you wish to say, Commander?" asked Shenouda.

Sawyer gulped. "No, sir, sorry, sir. Just reflecting on what you were saying."

Shenouda eyed him wearily. "And what was I just saying?"

Damn it. The admiral knew he'd gotten lost in thought. "Uh, sir ..." *Suck it up and take it, Sawyer.* "I'm sorry, sir. I wasn't listening."

Shenouda grumbled but formed a small smile, just enough to let Sawyer know he wasn't in too much trouble. "I understand. It was a difficult mission, but you pulled through. All unharmed. Well, mainly unharmed. But I hear Lieutenant Hawk is doing fine. I had my doubts about you being so young and new, but you proved me wrong. I'm proud to have you as one of our Time Ranger Commanders. I'm not sure many would have had the balls to institute a Code 54. It had to be a difficult decision. But who knows what would have happened if you didn't."

"That was my team, sir," replied Sawyer. "I was ... incapacitated at the time."

"But your team is a reflection of you, Commander," said Shenouda. "So take the compliment."

"Yes," stated his father. He uncrossed his arms and leaned over the admiral's desk. "Your success will go noticed. And you did it without compromising the future. You kept yourself and your team alive when the situation turned dire. Repercussions of the *BlackOut's* appearance were minimal. Thankfully, Specialist Perry remembered that French jeton. According to the consequence report, other than some minor changes to banking regulations in the eighteenth century and some advancements in astronomy, it was all that came out of it. And the jeton depiction was quickly dismissed over time as more of a religious object rather than anything else. You lead your team to a victory, Commander."

Sawyer glared at his father. *You have read my report. You know I left out the part about your actions in all this. Is this sudden praise your way of thanking me?*

"As the admiral is proud to call you a commander, I'm as proud to call you my son."

Sawyer tore his gaze away from his father to look Shenouda in the eyes. "You probably worried that me being a Spawn, or a Sawyer, wasn't enough on its own to constitute my being a commander, but do you know what is, sir? Loyalty. I can command, not because I'm genetically enhanced, or because of my father's training, but because I know an exceptional team when I see one. And the one I have now ... I trust them emphatically to help in areas where I may lack, and to have my back in any situation. Just as I assume they know I have theirs. I didn't complete this mission, my team did."

"Well said, Commander Sawyer," beamed Shenouda. He stood and leaned over the desk with his hand extended. Sawyer shook it with a firm grip. "I will want to speak to you again, go over the details of a few things I'm not sure about that happened back in France, but for now you are dismissed. You, and your team deserve a long rest. And of course, arrangements need to be made to have your AI returned. I will let the rear admiral handle that."

Sawyer nodded. "Yes, sir." He turned and left the office without addressing his father. Against protocol, maybe, but he didn't care.

Outside in the operational control centre, Sawyer's team was waiting for him behind the row of forward consoles. Hawk turned first, slowly, as he held a hand to his side where his wound was healing. "So, how did it go?"

"Not as bad as I thought," replied Sawyer. "But the worst is yet to come."

"You didn't speak with your dad in there?" asked Santiago.

"Not the place," said Sawyer.

"What are you going to say to him?" asked Perry.

Sawyer looked at the specialist and wondered what conversation *he* would be having with his father. That was a conversation he'd love to hear. But that was for later. As well as a discussion concerning his medical records. Brodeur had revealed a few interesting facts to Sawyer, but the mission came first, and that had to be discussed before anything else. "I'm going to be blunt. Give my father nowhere to maneuver. I can't imagine any way possible that he can justify his orders to bag the mission."

"Why do you think he did it?" asked Hawk.

Sawyer shook his head, crossed his arms. "He tried to make everything seem like I was the reason this mission succeeded, but rest assured, I gave you guys credit ..."

"So kind of you, sir," interrupted Perry. "But that's not important. What's important is what happens from this point on. There was a reason for the rear admiral's betrayal. And we need to find out what that is, what it means. In 1634, Arnault told you our future was over if we didn't let him finish his work."

Sawyer looked around. Everything seemed right. And Admiral Shenouda had also been right. The consequence report revealed Sawyer and his team had done their job. No truly bad repercussions had trickled through time to affect their twenty-second century.

What if Arnault meant...? Sawyer shook his head. Future time travel was impossible. "One thing's for sure, I'm not letting my father dictate my life anymore, or disband this team. He's done it to me in the past, but not anymore."

"Keep that conviction when you talk to him, sir. Don't back down," said Santiago. "Because he's coming now."

"And he doesn't look pleased," added Hawk.

Sawyer turned and saw his father coming across the OCC with a determined stride.

"I want you in my office right now, Commander!"

Sawyer felt different this time entering the office. He'd lost a lot of weight on the mission, weight he hadn't been able to put back on immediately, but the weight loss he felt was more in tune with baggage. And when his father offered him a chair, Sawyer remained standing.

"We have a lot to discuss," said Sawyer.

"Have a seat." The rear admiral indicated to the uncomfortable chair across his desk.

"We. Have. A lot to discuss."

Rear Admiral Sawyer firmed his lips. "You are not in control here, Commander. Don't come in here thinking you have some sort of upper hand because you think you hold some secret over me, because it is quite the opposite. You have no idea what you've just done!"

"Your intimidation doesn't work on me anymore, sir. Not after what I went through, what I learned, back in France."

"Are you trying to provoke anger in me, son?"

"Don't talk to me about anger!"

The rear admiral's face was red. "Do you want dishonourable discharge to be the legacy you leave? I can make it happen, so you better watch your tongue, Commander."

"You wouldn't. That would reflect on you, and that's what's most important, isn't it? Your life. Your career. And how you can benefit from me."

In an unprecedented move, Rear Admiral Sawyer sighed and hung his head. When he spoke, it was with quiet words. "Yes, I tried to sabotage your mission.

I was the cause of your Earth-Lander crash. But that was an accident. I hadn't meant for the crash to happen."

Sawyer fumed but kept his emotions from seeping into his voice. "Why did you put Specialist Perry and Lieutenant Hawk on my team?"

"I knew they'd save you, son."

Sawyer couldn't have heard that right. He grabbed the desk to stop himself from crashing to the floor.

"No matter what Dr. Arnault did to you, whatever means he used to keep you off mission ... I knew Maxim and Greg would protect you. They'd never let anything happen to you." There was a pause before he spoke again. "You know who Greg is, don't you?"

Sawyer nodded, as he couldn't yet form words. He wanted to scream. Release everything that had built up over the past nine days and scream until he couldn't anymore. "Why did you send me back there and then ask me to fail?"

"Because when I say jump, you jump. You know better than to question me. And I needed that loyalty. That discipline. That level of obedience. But you failed me."

"I almost died! I gave everything for this mission! I almost stranded the team in history! How can you do this to your only son!"

I hate you! I hate you! I fucking hate you!

Rear Admiral Sawyer came around the desk and put his hands on Sawyer.

Sawyer punched him in the face, hard enough to draw blood and have his father stagger backward until he was sitting on his desk. "Don't ever touch me again!"

His father grabbed tissue from a box on his desk to stem the flowing blood dripping onto his pristine uniform. Sawyer stared at the falling red drops, wanting to hit him again.

"I know this isn't the best time, but there is something you need to know," the rear admiral said.

"What could you possibly have to tell me?"

"Why I did what I did, and why it was the right thing to do."

"There isn't a single reason in the world that I would accept!"

"I didn't need you to fail, son. The future needed you to fail."

Sawyer's mouth fumbled for words his brain was trying to force out, but all that came out was ... "What?"

"There is more going on than you think." His father put the tissue away and stared at Sawyer with his standard grim expression. "Where you think you have succeeded, you've actually failed. The existence of our future relied on you not being successful in France. We needed Arnault to succeed. We need to make changes to history. Very specific changes that have been researched down to the most minute detail. What you've done has put us back farther than you can imagine."

"What? We? Who is this *we* you and Arnault are talking about?"

"I'm not at liberty to say. In time, perhaps, I will be able to tell you more, but for now, the less you know the better."

"That's not an explanation!" But Sawyer knew he'd never get a real answer from his father. This was just his way of exerting his power once again by holding something over him.

Sawyer decided that this time he wouldn't play his father's game. "You know what? Forget it. I don't want to know. If something, someone, has you fucking with the timeline, fucking with the future … my future, the future of all of Utopia's citizens, then I don't want to be a part of it. So, you know what, you keep doing what you're doing, and I'll be right behind you every step of the way making sure *you* don't succeed!"

Sawyer looked up at the ceiling to take in a deep breath. As his lungs filled with familiar recycled air, his neck and shoulders relaxed. When he righted his head to look his rear admiral in the face, he smiled. *It doesn't matter what lies ahead. I'll face it with my team, because now I know I have one worth keeping.*

EPILOGUE

THE office on the 134th floor of the glass and titanium building filled with the discontented cry of its sole occupant. Conrad Inwood slashed his arm across his desk, scattering data-cards and papers onto the cold tiled floor. "Unacceptable!"

Dr. Arnault had failed. Rear Admiral Sawyer had failed. "Such incompetence!"

The pollution-hazed view out his floor-to-ceiling window drew his attention. He crossed the distance in ten long strides and he flattened his palms on the glass and dropped his head to his chin. "Billions of people, and I can't find two capable enough to execute their jobs."

"Mr. Inwood, sir."

Inwood turned to see his aide standing by the door. "What is it?"

"I have the quarterly reports from our subsidiary and mirror corporations, sir." The young man, wearing a black suit and tie with immaculate tailoring, stepped forward. "There has been a significant decrease in *Spawn Conception's* numbers. Citizens are complaining the price is too high. But our weapons and technology division is seeing numbers beyond our expectations."

"And? What of our bio-tactical enhancements company?"

The aid cleared his throat. "The strike still goes strong. Everyone from line assembly to research and development are questioning the moral ethics of their division. I don't see it ending any time soon."

Inwood spun and pounded a fist on the window. Mountain peaks from the Swiss Alps jutted up through the fog and haze like white-capped teeth in a grey-gummed mouth. "It's horrible out there. Atrocious. The culmination of decades of misuse, disrespecting the Earth, and countries instigating a war consisting of

319

lobbing asteroids at each other in the name of world domination. These workers need to fall in line. It is no wonder we aren't prepared."

"May I remind you, sir, it was your innovation that ..."

"I know what I've done!" Inwood spun back to his aide, his starched shirt collar tight around his neck where his arteries throbbed. "And it is still the right choice! We just have to make sure everything else falls into place. Without these changes in the past we are doomed, but if I can stay one step ahead ... keep the program running ... we will see a different future."

"Forgive my impertinence. You are correct."

Inwood relaxed his shoulders, straightened his tie. "Is everything in order for Commander Sawyer's arrival at John Glen Memorial hospital? Will we be able to proceed with the replantation of his AI?"

"Rear Admiral Sawyer reported that although he suspects his son is becoming aware of his special abilities, there shouldn't be any reason not to continue. He believes he has the situation under control."

"Do *we* think the rear admiral has his son under control?"

"We are ninety... seventy-nine percent sure. His cruel and stringent character makes him difficult to work with, but unfortunately the rear admiral is our ace-in-the-hole. And our only link to his son."

The elder Sawyer was a bastard. Inwood despised what the man had become since their inaugural meeting. But as head of the Time Rangers, he could do what Inwood couldn't. So, the rear admiral was a necessary evil. And to some degree, Inwood understood it was his own fault for turning that man into a monster. "We proceed as planned. Are our other Runners still sitting quiet?"

"Rear Admiral Sawyer states no movement on their parts yet."

"Good. That is all."

The aide turned and left, the automatic sliding doors swooshing quietly shut behind him. Inwood took a deep breath, ran a hand through greying blonde hair, and took a seat behind his desk. He smiled at the old family portrait taken during a vacation to Chile that was displayed in a holo-pic frame on the edge of his desk. His ex-wife and twin daughters smiled back at him.

Constellation, who preferred the shorter, Consty, and the high achiever of the fair-haired twins, looked so serious. But Aurora, who'd chosen to live with her mother after the divorce, was waving her small hand as she clutched a teddy-bear in her other. Inwood was doing this for them. His ex-wife he could toss into a black hole, but for his daughters, he would give his life.

Sentimentality done for the day, Inwood cleared his throat and decided to get back to work. He sipped from a self-heating coffee mug he'd forgotten about on his desk and activated his computer.

On the translucent screen, the ThirdEye Corporation logo appeared with bright, bold fortitude.

ACKNOWLEDGEMENTS

I WOULD like to thank my developmental editor, Randall Surles (randysurles.com). Randy's expertise in editing, and his patience and creativity, helped shape this story into what it is today. I would also like to thank Catherine Beaumont and JoAnna Bigler for their tireless help, and for putting up with my endless questions, my endless need to talk about my story, and for still liking me (hopefully) after all was said and done. I also need to thank Luca Militello for his help in shaping an idea for a chapter I struggled with for quite some time, and AJ Grass for his medical expertise. And to Linda J. Groundwater for helping me become a better writer, and for working on the story during its grassroots stage. And, of course, I desperately need to thank my husband, Robert Pimpinella, for putting up with me while I sat for hours at my computer writing while he cut the lawn, did the dishes, vacuumed ... Everything I put aside in order to write. Thank you all for helping make my dream come true.

Printed in Canada